The Wrong Shoes

M K Turner

By M K Turner

Meredith & Hodge Series

The Making of Meredith

Misplaced Loyalty

Ill Conceived

The Wrong Shoes

Tin Soldiers

One Secret Too Many

Mistaken Beliefs

Quite by Chance

Family Matters

Not If You Paid Me

Bearing Witness Series

Witness for Wendy

An Unexpected Gift

Terms of Affection

The Murder Tour Series

Who Killed Charlie Birch?

Others

The Cuban Conundrum

The Recruitment of Lucy James

Murderous Mishaps

ACKNOWLEDGMENTS

Edited by Sharon Kelly

Cover Design by www.behance.net/lwpmarshala1e9

Photography by: Ferenc Almasi and Katie Harp

Clifton Suspension Bridge - Bristol

I suppose I should tell you why I became a murderer. In America they call you a serial killer if you've killed more than one person. Is it the same in England, being a serial killer I mean? It makes me shudder to think about it. If only they'd listened to me, none of it would have happened. I think I'd better start from the beginning.

I've now added kidnapping to my list of crimes. I won't kill this one.

I have killed three people, and kidnapped another. I should have been caught years ago, but for some reason they haven't even come close. I'm not sure if it's because they are stupid or simply lazy. Perhaps I watch too much television. They make it look so easy on TV, working out who did it by following the clues on those police programmes. I think it's because they're lazy. But you don't strike me as lazy, Mr Meredith. I know that you want to catch me, and I want to be caught, hence this letter. I'm writing it all out now so that you can read the letter, and then you can question me to fill in any gaps. Once you've done that, you can find out what went on back then. Get it sorted once and for all.

I haven't begun at the beginning, have I? It was the wrong shoes that started me off.

The writer paused and looked across the room, "This is what I have so far Bobby, I'll read it to you."

After a false start, the partially completed confession was read aloud. Bobby carried on eating and made no comment except to nod occasionally. His silence spoke volumes to the writer.

"You're probably right. It needs more work. I'm writing it as though I'm speaking. I can see that when I read it to you. I need to be more businesslike. Perhaps I'll have another go tomorrow. Maybe I'll do it in the form of a diary, what happened and when as the heading, and the smaller facts listed below. What do you think?"

Bobby nodded.

"Good. That's that sorted. DCI Meredith is very efficient, you know. I think he'll appreciate it more that way. Oh blimey, look at the time, I'd better go and feed her, or it will be four I've managed to bump off."

The pen was placed carefully back on the table, and the cover on the pad pulled down, hiding the words, before the writer hurried out, but then rushed back into the room, making Bobby start. "I can do it on the computer. It will be so much neater. I'll pop into the whatsit shop tomorrow. We need more ink for the printer because I've got to do the other photographs."

N ancy Bailey hurried down the stairs, smiling as the aroma of apple and sultana pie reached her nostrils, making her mouth water. She glanced at her watch. The pie still had another ten minutes. Just enough time to put a duster around the dining room. Once she'd done that, she would take out the pie and sort the sitting room. If she was lucky she'd be home by five.

Walking into the kitchen Nancy paused to look at the pie through the glass door of the oven. It was browning nicely. Opening the cupboard under the sink, she pulled out the polish and a clean duster, and, noting that the washing-up liquid was almost empty, she walked to the fridge. Unclipping the pen from the small magnetic board she wrote a note for Phillip, adding a little kiss, knowing it would make him smile. She glanced at the pie again. Perhaps she didn't have time to get the dining room finished first. She'd pop the duster in there and get the vacuum out, and see to the pie before making a start.

Wheeling the vacuum in front of her she used it to push open the dining room door. Singing softly, she parked the vacuum under the mirror, put the duster and polish on the table, and turned to leave. Her mouth dropped open, and she gasped as she caught sight of Phillip.

Patsy Hodge knelt to tie her lace, glad it had provided her with an excuse to stop running. She would later have cause to curse it. If it hadn't come loose she may not have become involved. Remaining down on one knee, she regulated her breathing, emptied the remaining water from the bottle, and wiped her mouth on the back of her hand. Standing, she stretched her legs using a nearby garden wall as apparatus. As she lunged forward for the third time she saw the curtain twitch, and lowered her foot, waving at the unseen eyes watching her.

Deciding to walk the remainder of the crescent, she set off at a sedate pace back towards Linda's modest three-bedroom semi. As she walked she pondered Linda's invitation to jump on a train and head off to London for the weekend. It would be fun; life, when Linda was around, was invariably fun, but she didn't feel like being forced to have fun. Linda hadn't seemed too put out that Patsy had turned down the offer, although she had observed that Patsy was becoming too comfortable feeling miserable at the moment.

As Patsy mentally chastised herself, she heard the moan that grew in volume. Inclining her head, she slowed her pace as she listened. It sounded like pain had taken hold of a wounded animal who howled for relief before it became a scream. It was the harrowing scream that stopped her dead in her tracks. Patsy turned to face the house, wondering if someone was watching television with the volume a little too high, but knew even as this thought entered her mind that that wasn't the case. Hurrying up the path, she banged on the shiny blue front door of the small terraced house with an inadequate brass knocker, and dropped to her knees to peer through the letter box. A woman wearing a red polka dot apron came hurrying down the hall towards her, her hand held over her mouth. Patsy stood as the woman's face disappeared from view. The door opened.

"Phillip's dead," the woman announced simply, and staggered sideways, her total collapse saved only by the door which crashed against the wall.

Stepping into the hall, Patsy took the woman's arm. "I'm Patsy. I think we need to get you a seat. Which room?" Patsy manoeuvred the woman to face back up the narrow hall. There were three doors; the nearest one to the left was closed, two more at right angles to each other stood open at the end of the hall.

"The kitchen, that pie needs to come out. Phillip loves my . . ." Nancy gave a sob and clung to Patsy, "Someone's killed Phillip."

Patsy hugged the woman to her and sighed. She had been hoping Phillip had died of natural causes, but it appeared that was not the case. As they passed the end of the stairs Patsy could see the kitchen through the open door, and steered the woman towards it. She spoke quietly and continually as they completed the journey. Establishing the woman's name, and that she was the cleaner. Patsy pulled out a chair and sat Nancy at the table.

"Right, Nancy, let's get the kettle on and the pie out." Walking to the oven Patsy pulled the mittens from the handle.

"But what about Phillip? He's dead, you know."

"I know, I'll go and see him in a moment." Lifting the pie from the oven, Patsy glanced around the immaculate kitchen looking for somewhere to put it. Crossing the kitchen, she placed it on the draining board. She picked up the kettle and filled it before turning back to Nancy. "Okay, that's that taken care of. Now, where did you find Phillip?"

"Next door, in the dining room, his desk is in there." Nancy pointed back towards the hall. "He was lying there . . . the blood was . . ." Unable to continue, Nancy leaned forward and buried her face in her hands.

Patsy walked through the open door. A dining table surrounded by six chairs led the eye to the French windows and the garden beyond. A duster and polish sat on the table. Turning to the left, Patsy found the desk and the body of Phillip Cowell. Stepping forward and, careful not to touch anything, she took in the scene.

Phillip had been stabbed with what appeared to be a large kitchen knife, the handle of which jutted out between his shoulder and his head. His body had slumped forward and fallen onto the keyboard of the computer. The large puddle of blood which had seeped from his body had dripped off the edge of the desk; his right trouser leg appeared to have absorbed most of it. Patsy wondered if there was an additional wound there. Pulling her phone from her pocket, she walked towards the French windows as she called the familiar number.

Jo Adler answered on the third ring. Patsy blew out a sigh of relief; it was a long shot, but Meredith could have answered. Walking back to the front door, Patsy explained what she had found. She opened the front door and looked for the number.

"Number seventy-three. The kettle's on."

"It'll be nice to see you, Patsy, shame it's in these circumstances though. Perhaps we can arrange to go for that drink we keep talking about. I'll update the Gov and we'll be with you soonest."

Patsy walked back to the kitchen wondering if Meredith would send someone else. She hadn't seen DCI John Meredith for almost two months, and had only spoken to him twice since she had left him. He had called several times a day the first week. She had rejected the calls after the first two. He didn't bother now, although she did receive the odd snippets of gossip from her old colleagues who still worked with him. Patsy wasn't sure whether she wanted him to attend or not. Forcing a smile, she walked into the kitchen.

Nancy Bailey had stopped crying and now stared at the pie sitting on the draining board. She glanced at Patsy as she returned.

"That'll go to waste now. I can't eat it, not allowed the sugar with my diabetes. Perhaps your lot can take it back to the station." She looked back at the pie.

"My lot?" Patsy queried, then nodded as she realised why Nancy had thought so. "No, I'm not a police officer. I was, but I left. I'm a private investigator now. But it wasn't that long ago, so I still know who to call."

"Oh, I see. When I heard you talking, I thought to myself what were the chances of a policewoman passing by? Still, stranger things have happened." Nancy looked down at her hands and sighed.

Patsy switched the kettle back on, and lifted two cups from the rack. She cursed her shoelace as she did so. If it hadn't come loose, she would be sitting in Linda's kitchen happily oblivious to the murder in the next street.

"How do you take your tea?"

"White, two sweeteners, I can't have sugar . . . I've told you that, haven't I?" Nancy pushed herself up using the table and walked to the fridge. She passed Patsy the milk. "I've been here hours you know, and he's been there. Like that." She looked towards the door and the dining room beyond.

"How long?" Patsy couldn't help herself. She knew Nancy would have to answer all these questions again, but instinct had kicked in.

"I arrived about lunchtime, around one o'clock. The postman came as I arrived." Nancy pointed to the post she had placed on the table. "I did what I always do. Top to bottom. Quick whiz around the bedrooms, I do those properly on Tuesdays. I come twice a week, so I do upstairs properly on Tuesdays and downstairs on Fridays." She turned to look at Patsy. "I won't be doing that any more, will I?"

Patsy handed Nancy the tea and sat opposite her at the table. "I'm sorry, Nancy, have you worked here long?"

"Three years or thereabouts. Such a nice man." Nancy's hand flew to her mouth. "Do you know him?"

Patsy's brow furrowed at such an odd question. "I don't think so. What's his name? Why do you think I would know him?"

"Phillip Cowell, he's a policeman. That's how I met him, he helped me." Nancy watched Patsy shake her head.

"No, I don't know him. I've only worked in Bristol for a short time. Most of my service was in Southampton."

"Phillip doesn't . . . I mean, didn't work here any more. He used to work in Bristol, but he took a job over in Cardiff. I think it was a promotion, but he liked living here. His mum used to live around the corner. This was his grandmother's house, she left it to him. He told me all about the work he had to put in to modernise it." Her face fell. "His mother died eighteen months back. I don't think he'd have gone to Cardiff otherwise."

"So when you arrived here, there was nothing strange. Nothing misplaced, or out of the ordinary?"

"Nothing." Nancy shook her head as she closed her eyes, picturing her arrival. "I put my bag in the hall and went upstairs. I dusted the bedrooms, came downstairs and made the pie. Once that was in the oven, I went back up to clean the bathroom and put the hoover over. He's so kind he even bought a second hoover so I wouldn't have to carry it up and down the . . . I mean, he *was* so kind." Lifting her apron, Nancy dabbed her eyes. "I finished upstairs and came down, I went to put the stuff in there, and that's when I found him."

Falling silent, Nancy picked up her tea and sipped it. The urgent knocking at the door made her jump and she slopped it over the table. Patsy passed her a cloth as she went to answer the door, pausing before she pulled it open. Her heart stopped as she looked up at Meredith.

"Hodge." Nodding, he stepped across the threshold.

Jo Adler followed him in, and grimaced at Patsy, her eyes revealing her amusement.

Meredith turned to face her. "An update would be nice, Hodge."

Refusing to meet his eye, Patsy turned to Jo Adler instead. "I had been for a run, and as I passed -"

"You go running now, do you?" Meredith interrupted.

"I do. Is that relevant?"

"Not to the case, no."

Patsy turned back to Jo. "I heard the scream and knocked on the door. A lady called -"

"You couldn't have been running very fast if you heard the scream. You don't use an iPod then?"

"I was walking at that stage, and no, I don't." Patsy continued to look at Jo, who was having difficulty in containing her smile. "Nancy Bailey, the cleaner, let me in. She arrived around one o'clock. The same time as the postman called."

"That was two and a half hours ago."

"Yes. Nancy went to do upstairs first. She cleaned the bedrooms, came down and made a pie, and went back to do the bathroom. When she came down and went into the dining room she found the body." Giving in, Patsy turned back to Meredith, "The body of Phillip Cowell, who, she tells me, is a police officer. She screamed, and I was outside. Walking and not running, and not listening to an iPod."

Meredith's lips twitched slightly before his brow furrowed as he tried to place the name.

"I don't know how long he's been dead, but the blood has begun to congeal. It looks as though it was a clear blow from behind. The knife is still in the wound. The body's down here." Patsy stepped forward to lead the way. Meredith didn't move, causing her to brush against him. She flinched and he smiled as he turned to follow her.

Meredith took in the scene quickly. Taking a pen from his pocket he pulled a bloodied opened cheque book from under the shoulder of the body.

"Looks like he was paying some bills. Where's this Nancy?"

Placing the pen back in his pocket Meredith followed Patsy to the kitchen.

"Nancy, this is DCI Meredith and DC Jo Adler, they'll look after you now." Patsy turned to Meredith. "You don't need me here. I'll be off if that's all right with you."

Meredith looked at her for a little too long before responding, and she looked away.

"Not here, no." He glanced at the clock on the wall above the kettle. "We'll need to take a formal statement, as you know. Can you be at the station at six-thirty?"

"I'm not sure. Linda was talking about going to London for the weekend. It may have to be Monday." Her brow furrowed as Meredith grinned.

"Trump beat you to it. He swapped weekends earlier with Rawlings to have a jolly with the loopy Linda. Unless, of course, you're going with them?" Amusement danced in his eyes.

DS Louie Trump was dating Patsy's housemate Linda, who hadn't admitted to Patsy that she had only extended the invitation to her as Louie was unable to make it. Patsy sighed; she hadn't wanted to go, but it would have been nice to put some more space between now and seeing Meredith again.

"Well, in that case I'll see you at six-thirty, Jo." Jo turn away to hide the grin.

Nancy sat at the table watching this interaction. It was clear that there was far more being unsaid than spoken aloud. Something was going on between those two, even a blind man could see that. She hoped that whatever it was wouldn't detract them from finding Phillip's killer. Meredith turned to Nancy pulling out a chair he sat next to her.

"Hello, Nancy. May I call you Nancy? You've had an awful shock, and I'm sure that you want to get home. But I need you to help me find out who did this. People will be arriving soon to sort out what went on in there," he nodded towards the dining room, "and to move the body. I don't think you want to listen to all that, so where would you rather we discussed this? I can take you home now and we'll do it there, or we can go to the station and someone will take you home later."

There was a knock at the door and Patsy used it as an excuse to leave the kitchen. She opened the door. Frankie Callaghan, the forensic pathologist, looked startled.

"Pats, what on earth are you doing here?"

"You know me, Frankie, where there's trouble. How's Sarah? Actually, Frankie, now isn't the time, you'd better get on. Give me a ring later if you can. The body is this way." Patsy led Frankie back down the hall and pointed into the dining room. "All yours."

Patsy stepped to one side as Frankie and his assistant entered the dining room. She couldn't wait to get away, but neither did she want to go. She stuck her head around the kitchen door.

"That was Frankie, I've shown him in. I'll be off now. I'll be at the station at six-thirty." Patsy smiled at Nancy. "Take care. If anyone can find who did this, they can."

Nancy mumbled her thanks as Meredith got to his feet. "I'll see you out."

Patsy called goodbye to Frankie as she passed the dining room.

He popped his head around the door. "Bye, Pats, I'll call you later. We should have a drink or something." He nodded an acknowledgement to Meredith.

"Afternoon, Sherlock, I'll be with you in a bit."

Taking Patsy's arm, Meredith steered her to the door. "He still has the hots for you." His voice was low, and his fingers felt hot against her bare arm.

"Don't be ridiculous. He's madly in love with Sarah, and you know it. I'm not going to argue with you, you know."

"Good, I'm glad to hear it. Right, the sooner I get on the sooner I'll be free. I'll see you at the station." He lowered his face towards her, and she quickly stepped over the threshold to avoid him. "Patsy," He called as she made her way down the path. Stopping, she turned to face him. "I will have you back." Nodding affirmation, he closed the door.

Patsy walked away smiling, before she cursed and broke into a run.

Several hours later Patsy shared a Danish pastry with Jo Adler in the police canteen.

"It's great to see you, Patsy. Perhaps the Gov will cheer up now. He's been a pain in the ass since you two split. He's not taking to fatherhood naturally either. May I?" Jo popped the last of the pastry into her mouth as Patsy nodded.

"I hear his daughter has been helping Jack to recuperate and catch up on his studies." Patsy brushed crumbs from her mouth.

Jack Grainger was the son of Chris Grainger, Patsy's business partner and Meredith's former boss. Jack had been badly injured in a car crash around the time Patsy had left Meredith, and at one time it was thought he would not walk again, but he was now on the slow road to recovery.

"Have you met Amanda?"

"Just the once, on the day I found out about her. She seems a nice girl, considering."

"What, considering she's Meredith's daughter you mean?"

"That as well. Oh boy, and as if on cue." Patsy looked towards the door which banged shut after Meredith. He looked around and pointed as he spotted them.

"Hodge, glad to see you're early. I'm free now. Bring the coffee. I'll meet you in Interview Four. Adler, we'll run through the interview after you've given Nancy a lift home. I'll give you a shout." Winking at Patsy he left as noisily as he had arrived.

Patsy sighed as Jo laughed.

"Nothing changes, Patsy, and you better than anyone should know that."

With her hands full Patsy kicked the door to the interview room. Meredith opened it, and watched as she placed the mugs on the table.

"Thank you." Closing the door he walked towards her. Patsy sat down before he reached her, and Meredith pinched the bridge of his nose as he considered his words. "Patsy, it doesn't need to be like this. Please give me time to explain. Is that too much to ask?"

"I don't need an explanation. Look, this is awkward for both of us. Shall we get on with it?"

To avoid having to look at him Patsy pulled her notebook from her bag. Opening it to the notes she had scribbled before coming to the station, she ran her finger down the page pretending to read them. Meredith walked to the other side of the table and pulled out the chair. Leaning back in it, crossing his legs at the ankles and, linking his fingers, he rested his hands on his midriff. He didn't speak. Patsy raised her eyes, seeing the hurt in his, she looked away.

"Do you want to record this, or will it be easier if you give me a witness statement to complete?"

Leaning forward, Meredith and hit the button on the recorder. "Patsy Hodge will now explain how she came to find the body of DS Phillip Cowell at approximately three o'clock this afternoon. Ms Hodge, in your own words please."

Glaring at him, Patsy cleared her throat and, following her notes, she explained her involvement. It was short, detailed and took less than five minutes. Meredith tapped his pencil on the pad in front of him as she spoke. He didn't take notes.

"And as you approached the house, did you notice anyone else in the area that gave cause for concern? Perhaps someone was acting in a strange manner?"

"No, I would have included that. I also don't see how that would be relevant as I understand that Phillip Cowell had been dead for some hours before his body was discovered."

"As you will know from your police training, there are some murderers who hang around to see what happens when the victim is discovered. So, you saw nothing odd outside the property?"

Meredith waited for her to shake her head. "For the purposes of the tape, Ms Hodge has shaken her head."

Patsy rolled her eyes. "Is there anything else you want to ask? I believe I've told you everything I know."

"Did you notice anything unusual in the house?"

"I only walked through the hall into the kitchen, and once I'd calmed the cleaner down I went to the dining room. No, I saw nothing unusual, murdered police officers excepted. I took the pie out of the oven, and I made a cup of tea. Other than that I went nowhere and touched nothing."

"Your thoughts on those rooms you did see?"

Patsy frowned. "Very neat and tidy, immaculate in fact. There was no sign of a struggle, and everything appeared to be in its place. From what I saw, it seemed he was attacked from behind and didn't know it was coming, so that's not surprising. The only thing I wondered was why he needed a cleaner twice a week if he was so tidy. But I suppose if he didn't have one twice a week, it may have been a different story."

"How do you think the murderer got in?"

"I have no idea. I didn't look as I didn't want to contaminate the scene. Anyway, the cleaner Nancy had been there for a while. I think that question should be directed to her."

"It was."

"And what did she say? Did she find anything unusual when she arrived?"

"No. The back door was unlocked, but that wasn't unusual when Phillip Cowell was at home. He'd been dead for approximately five hours according to Sherlock. Once the body had been removed it was confirmed he wasn't using the computer but paying his bills. He had written cheques for three of the four bills we found there."

"Cheques? How unusual in this day and age. I mean, most people do that by direct debit or online banking." Patsy shrugged. "So the murderer let himself in the back door, and killed Cowell for reasons unknown. I think that's us done. I can't add any more to that."

"How was Nancy Bailey when you got there?"

Looking down at her notes, Patsy bit back a smile. Meredith was going to drag this out as long as possible.

"She was stunned, and until I banged on the door she had been screaming hysterically. As one would expect. It's not every day that you find your boss with a knife sticking out of his neck. May I go now?"

"You took the pie out of the oven . . ."

"I did, but I don't see what that's got to —"

"Would you like a piece?" Meredith's eyes twinkled as Patsy's head jerked to look at him.

"You have the pie? Is that allowed? It is evidence, after all." Smiling, she felt her pulse increase as he leaned forward, arms folded on the table, and held her gaze.

"I've ruled the pie out. I don't think he was poisoned, and Nancy didn't want it to go to waste. She can't eat it —"

"Because she's diabetic, yes, I had heard."

Meredith's lips twitched. "You are well-informed. Would you like a slice?"

"Go on, only a sliver though."

"It's not here."

"Where, in the incident room?"

"At home."

"Ah well, another time maybe." Patsy was determined to stick to her original plan. She wasn't going to go anywhere with Meredith, especially not his home. Closing her notepad, she slid it into her bag, and stood up. "Well, that does seem to be it. I have a lot to do, so I'd better get going."

"A lot to do where? Linda will be on her way to London with Trump by now. What are you doing?"

"I don't think that's any —"

"Ha!" Standing quickly, his chair scraping the floor, Meredith pointed at her. "Don't say it, because it's not true. You will always be my business, Patsy." He stepped around the table, placing his hand on her arm as she opened the door. "Don't go yet."

"I have a dinner date, and you have a murder investigation. I am going." Patsy knew from his expression that he wasn't going to ask the one thing he wanted to know. She couldn't bear the misery they were causing each other, so she alleviated a little of his. "I'm having dinner with Sharon and Chris." Her eyes flicked to the clock behind Meredith's head. "I promised I would be there by eight-thirty, so I must go." Stepping into the corridor she added, "Good luck with this," before hurrying away.

His frown turned into a smile as he watched her leave. Amanda, his daughter, was at the Grainger's house, and he was picking her up at ten. He would try and get there a little earlier. Good old Sharon, she had probably orchestrated that. He whistled '*Que Sera, Sera*' as he walked back to the incident room, knowing Patsy would hear it echoing along the corridor. She did.

Pushing open the door to the incident room, Meredith noticed the two unknown faces speaking to Bob Travers. He assumed they were the officers expected from Cardiff. He strode in and Travers stood and introduced them.

"Gov, this is DCI Williams and DS Henshaw, they both work out of Cardiff Central."

Meredith held out his hand. "DCI Meredith. I'm sorry about your man."

There was a brief silence as they acknowledged the loss of a colleague. "I'd like to talk to you this evening if that's possible. We've no leads here as yet, and as he was a copper we can't rule out it's connected with the job. I'm on my way to look at the interview with the cleaner who found him, if you want to sit in." The two men nodded. Meredith glanced around and noted Jo Adler had returned. "Adler, come and run through the interview with Nancy Bailey. You lot try and find something, anything; they want to issue a press statement in the morning. I take it his next of kin has been told?"

"I did that," Dan Williams answered. "His girlfriend Cathy is one of our admin girls. I told her and took her home. She lives round the corner from the nick. Nice little townhouse overlooking the bay. Phil was due to move in next month, he was there most of the time anyway. He'd sold his place here in Bristol."

Meredith nodded, glad that someone she knew had broken the news to her.

"Come on, the sooner we get on, the sooner you can get back."

"We're staying the night. I thought we could be of help."

DCI Williams held Meredith's eye. Irrespective of the case, no DCI liked interference from outside his own patch, particularly when it was personal. Meredith chewed his lip before shrugging. Today wasn't the day for tantrums, and he slapped Williams on the shoulder.

"Well, the sooner we get this done, the sooner I can buy you a pint."

"That's mighty decent of you, Meredith. Appreciated."

"I'm a decent sort of bloke. Adler, lead the way."

The recording of the interview with Nancy Bailey revealed little Meredith hadn't known before watching it. It was clear Nancy had been looking forward to seeing Phillip later that day.

"I don't see him that regularly now that he works in Cardiff, but he left me a note on Tuesday saying he'd see me on Friday. I always bake him something for Fridays, he has such a sweet tooth . . . I mean had." Nancy put her tissue to her nose and composed herself, while Jo Adler patted her arm. "Anyway, I called out to him, and when he didn't answer I assumed he was out doing errands so I went upstairs. I do top to bottom, you see. I never thought to check."

Nancy went on to confirm that she hadn't noticed anything unusual or out of place. She hadn't used the back door so didn't know that it was unlocked until Meredith had tried it, and confirmed that the last time she had seen Phillip was the Tuesday before last, although they had left each other notes on the board on the fridge. Her hand had flown to her mouth.

"I think he had a girlfriend in Cardiff. Will someone tell her? I don't know her, you see, we never met. I knew she stayed sometimes of course, but Phillip said she was a nine to fiver, so she worked on my days."

Jo assured her that someone would contact her, and wound up the interview by confirming Nancy's telephone number and address. Jo switched off the tape and turned to the three men standing behind her.

"Nothing to help us. Tom is tracking down which postman saw her arrive to attempt to pinpoint the time, and Frankie promised he'd have a preliminary report," she glanced up at the clock, "anytime now."

"I'll go and give him a call. Like you say, poor old Nancy had nothing for us."

Meredith led the way back to his office. Jo and the two men sat opposite him as he called Frankie. Nancy's apple and sultana pie sat in the middle of his desk. He pointed to it.

"Do you want some . . . hang on." Holding up his hand, he answered the ringing phone. "Sherlock, mate, what have you got for us?"

DCI Williams nudged Jo. "Sherlock? I take it that's a nickname."

"Yes, it's Frankie Callaghan, forensic pathologist. He helped link a series of deaths last year. The Gov called him Sherlock and it stuck. Do you want some pie? I can make some tea to go with it."

Meredith watched her leave as Frankie explained his findings, and shortly thereafter hung up. Looking at Phillip Cowell's colleagues, he raised his hands.

"Not much, I'm afraid. Estimated time of death is anywhere between ten and twelve this morning. Nancy missed our man by an hour or so. Whoever killed him was apparently right-handed as the knife was thrust with enough force to nick the collar bone after it had sliced the artery. Sherlock can't be sure that that was intentional. He says it was either someone who knew exactly what they were doing, as a half inch either way would probably not have been fatal, or brute force and ignorance."

"And the weapon?" DS Andy Henshaw spoke for the first time.

"Left in the wound, and taken from his kitchen. It was missing from the block in the kitchen that held six knives. No prints."

"It could have been opportunist? Someone tries the door, it opens, they're in the kitchen, hear him in the next room and they take him out."

Staring at Henshaw, Meredith chose his words very carefully. "It's a possibility, yes, but unlikely unless the murderer was psycho and out looking to do some unnecessary damage. You saw the photos, I take it." Aware that the incident board was already updated with the photographs, Meredith waited for Henshaw to join up the dots. He didn't, and Williams helped him out.

"Phil was sitting with his back to the door. There was no struggle, no apparent attempt to avoid the knife. He didn't know it was coming. It's unlikely that a burglar would have done it." Williams looked at Meredith, "And your lot tell us there was nothing missing."

"Nothing obvious, no. The car was in the garage at the back of the house, and his keys on a hook in the kitchen. His wallet was in his pocket, his watch on his wrist, and everything of any value seems to be where it should." Leaning back, Meredith placed his hands behind his head. "I reckon this is personal. Someone had a reason for wanting him dead. What's the story with the girlfriend in Cardiff? I take it she has an alibi?" Meredith looked at Henshaw. "Has she been asked where she was this morning?"

Williams could see that Meredith didn't rate Henshaw. He was irritated with him himself for being slow, but he knew Henshaw was close to Cowell, and he jumped in again.

"Cathy's clean. She was working this morning. I haven't checked but she usually starts at nine, and was totally unaware of what we were going to tell her when we went to break the news. She's devastated, a real mess, and I don't think she's that good an actress." Williams stopped speaking as Jo returned with a tray of tea.

Placing the tray on Meredith's desk, Jo cut them each a slice of pie. There was silence for a short while as they all tasted it.

Meredith nodded his appreciation. "That's one cracking pie. Now, where were we? If it wasn't the girlfriend, what's he been involved in at work? Has he stepped on anyone's toes? Anyone been let out recently that could bear a grudge that you know of?" Taking another mouthful of pie as he watched Williams and Henshaw shrug in unison.

This time it was Henshaw that responded. "Nothing obvious that I can think of. I've been working with Phil for about eighteen months. I brought the current files for you to look at."

"What type of cases?"

They ate more pie and drank the tea as Williams and Henshaw ran through the three current cases Cowell had been working on. Meredith agreed that it seemed unlikely.

"We can either start digging tonight, or call it a day and get back at it first thing. Your shout, I know you're on borrowed time. Where are you staying, by the way?"

"We booked a B&B round the corner from Phil's," Henshaw replied.

"Do you know Bristol well?"

"Yes, I used to be engaged to a girl who lived in Henbury, but it didn't work out. I've been over to see Phil a few times too. Not lately though, last time must be about six months ago."

"Well, we could get you checked into the B&B, and within walking distance happens to be my local. You'll like the Dirty Duck."

It was agreed that they would take that option, and meet back at the station at seven-thirty the next morning. Meredith followed them to the B&B, and sat in the car while they dropped their bags off. As he waited his phone pinged. It was a text from Amanda:

Patsy's here!!! She's having dinner with us!!! What shall I say – oh God – nightmare!!!

Meredith responded.

Nothing just be yourself. Don't tell her I'm picking you up.

Adding a winking emoji, Meredith smiled, he had not used emojis prior to Amanda's arrival, but he was beginning to see they had their uses. He slipped the phone back into his pocket as the two men walked to his car, leaving their own on the drive at the B&B. He drove the short distance to the Dirty Duck and bought the first round. They talked in general terms about Phillip Cowell as they drank. It appeared to Meredith that Cowell had been a decent bloke and a good copper.

Henshaw stood up and drained the last of his pint. "I don't know about you two, but I'm having a chaser with this next one."

Meredith held up his hand. "Not for me, I have to drive later. I have a daughter that needs picking up." He pulled his head back as Henshaw leaned forward.

"Have you not got taxis in Bristol? My mate bought it today. He's lying dead on a slab somewhere, and tonight we are going to say goodbye. Properly. I don't know how that's done on this side of the bridge, but where I come from that's having a drink for him. A real drink. Surely she can get a taxi, or cadge a lift from someone?"

Meredith bristled as he stared at Henshaw's finger, and bit back the response which would put Henshaw in his place, since he knew he had just lost a friend. Slowly he grinned and nodded. Who better than Patsy to come to the rescue?

"She can. But don't let me forget to sort it."

Henshaw pulled away, smiling. "That's the way, boyo. Let's get this evening started."

Patsy handed Sharon the bottle of wine and the flowers she had bought, and slid her coat from her shoulders.

"Thanks for inviting me, Sharon. I could do with some company tonight. Linda's off to London with Louie and I was at a loose end. You'll never believe what happened to me today. I stumbled across a murder, and I'd only gone out for a run." Patsy held open the door of the kitchen and allowed Sharon to pass her, gifts in hand. "Of course, that meant I had to deal with bloody Meredith. Sometimes I . . ." Patsy paused as Amanda Meredith stopped dead in her tracks before her. Recovering from the surprise, she greeted Amanda warmly, "Hello. How are you?"

"Fine, thank you. You?" Amanda coloured slightly. Despite the assurances from everyone to the contrary, she was convinced Patsy had left her father because of her.

"I'm fine, thanks. I wasn't expecting to see you here."

"I've been helping Jack with his physio and stuff. I'm studying medicine at Uni."

Looking at the attractive young woman in front of her, Patsy smiled as Meredith's eyes looked back at her. She could only guess at how delighted Jack Grainger would be at having Amanda helping him.

"I bet Jack's the perfect patient. How's he doing, is his recovery going according to plan?"

"Yes, he's doing really well. He keeps having lapses but we soon get back to where we were. He's been so brave, and works so hard."

"Lapses, really? Does that mean extra hours of attention?" Patsy turned to Sharon who snorted.

"She's not worked it out, bless," Sharon laughed.

"Worked what out? What do you mean?" Amanda's eyebrows rose as the message registered, and a flush came to her cheeks. "Oh, right. I think I should have words. Excuse me."

As the two women laughed, she hurried from the room.

Patsy put her hands on her hips. "Did it simply slip your mind that Amanda would be here tonight?"

"Yes and no. Don't look at me like that. She's here so much at the moment it was a possibility. Why, what difference does it make?"

"Apart from the fact I was hoping for a good moan about her father, none. She seems to be a nice girl, it's awkward, that's all. For her too, I'm sure. I'd better get him off my chest whilst she's out of the way."

Climbing onto a barstool, Patsy updated Sharon on her latest encounter with Meredith as she helped with the final preparations for dinner.

During dinner Sharon and Patsy looked on with amusement as Jack attempted, but failed, to hide his interest in Amanda. Chris had warned them not to tease him, so they made do with exchanging knowing looks each time Jack betrayed his infatuation. The food was good and no reference was made to Meredith. As they cleared the table, Patsy decided to quit while she was ahead, and announced she would be leaving once they had had coffee. Sharon began to argue but fell silent as Amanda's phone rang.

Amanda pulled the phone from her pocket and glanced at the screen.

"It's Dad, I'll take it in here." Walking into the conservatory she pulled the door shut behind her.

She raised her voice several times during the conversation, and Sharon and Patsy finished clearing up silently, in an attempt to eavesdrop.

Amanda returned, shaking her head. "He's drunk. Well, he's been drinking anyway so he can't pick me up as arranged."

"That's okay Amanda, you can stay here. There's plenty of room, you know that," Sharon smiled.

"No, I can't. I have an early start tomorrow. There's an American lecturer in Bristol and they've convinced him to lecture on a Saturday since he has limited time. The lecture starts at eight and I don't want to miss it."

"Chris can get you back for that."

"That's kind but I have no clothes with me. I'll get a taxi, it's not a problem."

"I can give you a lift. I'm going back to Bristol. Let's have a coffee before we go." Patsy wondered if Meredith would be at home, but reasoned that there would be no need to get out of the car if he was.

"That's what he said. But I told him it was out of order."

"Well, it's not." Patsy guessed correctly that Meredith had intentionally caused the situation.

They discussed Amanda's course as they travelled back to Bristol. Patsy agreed to introduce her to Frankie, who should be able to get her some hours in the mortuary. As they neared the end of Meredith's street, Amanda rummaged in her bag for her keys.

"I think I've forgotten my keys." Amanda tipped the contents of her small bag onto her lap as Patsy pulled up outside Meredith's house. His car wasn't there. Amanda's search was unsuccessful. "Not here. If Dad's not in, I don't know where he is."

She heard Patsy sigh, and apologised, but Patsy waved her apology away.

"Go and knock, I'll wait here. If he's not in I know where he'll be. The question is, do we want to go and find him? You could stay with me, it's only ten minutes away, and I can get you back in good time in the morning."

Stuffing her things back into her bag, Amanda opened the car door. "I'll be two seconds."

As Amanda hurried down the drive. Patsy saw something fall to the floor, and climbed from the car. Stooping down to retrieve it, she called to Amanda as Meredith opened the door. They both looked at Patsy who waved Amanda's student card at them.

"You dropped this." Walking forward, and avoiding Meredith's gaze, Patsy placed the card in Amanda's hand. "I hope you enjoy the lecture tomorrow. Take care, goodnight."

She turned to go but Meredith stepped forward and grabbed her arm.

"Let me make you a coffee. It's the least I can do. You'd like Patsy to stay for coffee, wouldn't you Amanda?"

Patsy turned to face Meredith as Amanda held her hands up.

"I'm not getting involved. Yes, it would be lovely, but Patsy may not want to." She grimaced at Patsy, "Sorry."

Turning on her heel she went into the house and ran up the stairs.

His hand remaining on Patsy's arm, Meredith turned to watch her. "I think that's what's called making a hasty exit." He turned back to Patsy, "Please."

"You don't seem very drunk."

"I'm not, but I had too much to drive. I can control myself, you know."

"Well, that's new." Patsy smiled. "I really have to go. I have a full day tomorrow and I'm sure you do too." She tried to move away but he pulled her to face him.

"I didn't realise you private investigators worked on Saturdays, business must be good. If I can't convince you to come in, just do one thing for me."

"What?" Patsy was caught off guard as he pulled her against him, wrapping his arms around her.

Burying her face in his chest, she breathed in his smell. Her heart rate increased, and she closed her eyes in an attempt to resist the urge to respond as she felt Meredith plant little kisses on the top of her head, his hot breath catching the top of her ears. She opened her eyes and attempted to push him away. Keeping one arm around her back, he tipped her chin to face him with the other. Her lower lip trembled as she gazed at him.

"I can't do this."

He silenced her with a kiss. Despite everything she had promised herself, she responded.

Meredith felt the tremor in her body. He held her at arm's length. "You can," he croaked, and coughed to clear his throat. "Patsy, you know this will be, please come in." He closed his eyes as she shook her head.

"No, I can't."

"What, never, are you sure?"

"I was told you should never say never."

"No doubt by a wise man much like myself. *Que sera, sera*, Patsy." He returned her smile.

Stepping forward she planted a kiss on the end of his nose. "Indeed. But not now. Give me a call and I may let you take me on a date." Turning quickly, she pulled away from him and hurried to her car. "Goodnight, Meredith."

Standing on the doorstep, Meredith watched her drive away. Her phone was ringing before she had reached home. She chose to ignore it.

3

He was broke." Meredith eyed the two Welsh officers who looked decidedly worse for wear, glad he had left them to it the night before. "Did you know this? Did his bird, what's her name, Cathy know? Do we know what he spent his money on?" They shook their heads. Henshaw winced at the effort.

"Well, we'll need to analyse his spending. You two go and get some coffee and something to eat, and I'll see if we can get anything from the bank before Monday. All we could find was the one statement for the end of last month which showed Cowell was almost five grand overdrawn. Patsy was right, it was odd. He was probably writing cheques because they would take a while to hit his account."

"Who's this Patsy?" Williams asked. "Have we had the pleasure?"

"No, it's too long a story in your state. Mine's black with two." Standing, Meredith stretched. "You know where the canteen is. You can grab me a sandwich while you're down there."

Having watched the two men wander away, Meredith turned his attention to Tom Seaton. "Did you get anywhere with the bank?"

Seaton shrugged. "Waiting for the compliance department to come back to us, and apparently they do work at the weekend. His phone records are in, but pretty mundane stuff on the face of it. But guess who the last person he spoke to was?" Seaton didn't wait for Meredith's answer. "Henshaw. It'll be interesting to find out what it was about."

"What time?"

"Ten-thirty." Seaton nodded as Meredith raised his eyebrows. "Yep, narrows down the time of death a little more."

Meredith looked over his shoulder to make sure Cowell's colleagues hadn't returned, and called across the room to Bob Travers, "Anything naughty?"

"Nope. Pretty much what you'd expect, no complaints, no disciplinary actions, and no commendations. It's a thin file. I'm looking at the cases he was working in a little more depth, but I think you were right. Instinct tells me there's not much there."

"Okay, once you've done that I think we'll take a little trip across the bridge and speak to the girlfriend. See what she's got to say. She may tell us more than she would his workmates."

Returning towards his office as the Welsh officers returned, Meredith smiled at the bacon sandwich Henshaw held out to him.

"Just what the doctor ordered. Let's eat in my office, I need to ask you a few questions."

Meredith ate half his sandwich before questioning Henshaw.

"What did you speak to Cowell about yesterday?" Meredith watched as Henshaw placed his half-eaten sandwich carefully back onto the plate.

"Not much. The usual, you know."

"No I don't. Tell me."

"What we were doing this weekend. How his plans for moving were going. That type of thing."

"And how did he seem?"

Henshaw shrugged. "Normal."

"So despite having a non-exciting, boring type of conversation with Cowell, you didn't pick up on anything odd?"

"What do you mean odd?"

Meredith shot a glance at Williams whose frown deepened. "How long have you been a copper?"

"Ten years. Why, what's that got to do with anything?" Becoming defensive, Henshaw sat a little straighter in his chair and, leaning forward, placed his plate on Meredith's desk.

"Because when a police officer asks a witness if they noticed anything odd, it sort of has a universal meaning," Meredith shrugged. "I find it difficult to believe you didn't know what I meant." Again, Meredith glanced at Williams. "DCI Williams, had I asked you that question, would you have responded by asking me what I meant?"

Henshaw huffed and leaned back, arms folded across his chest.

Williams pursed his lips and considered Meredith. "Move on, DCI Meredith. I'm sure there's a point to this."

Meredith studied his desk for a few seconds before looking up at Henshaw. "Give us a minute please, Henshaw."

Astounded, Henshaw looked from Meredith to his boss. Williams jerked his head towards the door, and Henshaw left, banging the door shut as he did so.

Williams sighed. "Spit it out. What have you found out?"

Meredith raised his eyebrows. He'd only had one question for Williams, but it appeared he should have a list.

"What do you think I've found out? What should you have told me that I needed to find out?" Meredith picked up the remnants of his sandwich and bit into it. "I know they are both your boys, but now is not the time to make the wrong decisions on your own." Speaking with his mouth full, he watched Williams run his hands over his face.

"I didn't say because I don't think it has anything to do with Henshaw, Phil being murdered, I mean."

"What doesn't?"

"A couple of months back one of the lads picked up a promotion. We celebrated at a local club. Everyone was pissed, and Henshaw danced with Cathy. I think the drink clouded his judgement, or made him forget who she was." Williams rubbed his face again. "He kissed her. It was something and nothing. She pushed him away, but Phil had seen and we had handbags at nine paces. It was something and nothing, like I say. They shook hands and vowed not to drink again."

Meredith studied Williams as he processed this new information. "Who took the call from us at your end?"

"I did, why?"

"Who told Henshaw?"

"I did. Look, where is this going?" Williams leaned forward, his elbows on his knees, and his chin in his hands.

"What did he say?"

Williams thought for a moment and Meredith knew this was going to be messy.

"Something like, 'Fuck, you've got to be joking. How?'" Williams folded his arms across his chest. "I can't remember exactly. Why?"

"When did he tell you he'd spoken to him only hours before? In fact, possibly more to the point, where was he only hours before?"

Williams shook his head dismissively, but Meredith caught the quick frown of concern.

"He didn't mention it, no, but that means nothing. He didn't do it, you know."

"Where was he yesterday morning?" Dropping the crusts of his sandwich onto his plate, Meredith pushed it away.

"Working, he went to interview some shopkeepers. We've had a spate of gang-related hold-ups on corner shops. He got back about twenty minutes before I took the call."

"And we can verify that, can we? Because the last time I was in a hurry, I got from here to the centre of Cardiff in forty minutes, and that was stopping to pay the toll. Forty minutes here, twenty minutes to bump him off, if that, and another forty minutes back, give or take. All over and done with in less than two hours. Given that the cleaner took so long to find Cowell, he might even have chucked some interviews in for good measure."

Williams stood up and drew his shoulders back. He glared at Meredith, barely concealing his contempt. "Your theory is that Henshaw bumped Cowell off for giving him a slap in front of his mates." Williams shook his head. "I don't buy it. You're going to waste valuable time."

Meredith got to his feet. "I'm doing my job. But so you know, I'll be pulling his phone records, and the girlfriend's. I'll also want details of where he should have been. Like I say, I'm just doing my job. I'm sure you'll do yours too. Keep your boys out of my way, and encourage them to be up front if and when they are questioned." Opening the door, he pointed at Henshaw who looked up from the desk he had perched on. "Take him home, and tell him to play ball. I'll keep you informed."

He held his hand out and Williams took hold of it, pulling Meredith forward a little.

"I understand you're doing what needs to be done, and I want you to catch the bastard who did this. But don't go getting carried away and doing damage that can't be undone." Williams glanced at Henshaw as he dropped Meredith's hand. "Get your coat, we're going home."

"But, we haven't -"

Henshaw's protest was not completed as, rather than raise his voice, Williams lowered it and almost whispered, "I said, get your coat."

~ ~ ~

Patsy was awoken by the sound of her phone ringing. Opening her eyes, she blinked at the daylight flooding in through a gap in her blind. Flipping over, she looked at the clock; it was almost ten o'clock and she had slept in. She couldn't remember the last time she had done that. The phone stopped ringing. Lifting it, she squinted at it. A missed a call from Frankie. Opening the two messages she'd received, she smiled. Both were from Meredith. The first advised her he had tried to call for a date, and the second was insisting on a date. Still smiling, she returned the phone to the table and swung her legs out of bed. She needed to shower before she would be fit to speak to anyone.

Sitting at the small breakfast bar in Linda's kitchen she returned Frankie's call. It went through to his answer service.

"Hi, Frankie, sorry I missed you earlier, I overslept. Hope all is well with you. I have to run a few errands but other than that I'm free, so call me when it suits."

As she ate her breakfast she toyed with the idea of calling Meredith. She knew that if Amanda hadn't been there the night before, she would have stayed. But there again if Amanda hadn't been there, she wouldn't have either. Meredith had never actually dated her as they had been thrown together by circumstances. She wondered what that would be like, and, more to the point, if he would have the patience. Smiling, she decided to test him. Her phone rang as she reached for it, causing her to jump.

"Hi, Frankie, you gave me a fright! I was about to call out. How are you?"

"I'm fine thanks, Pats. Sarah and I are on our way to Eastwood Park, and we're going to see Sarah's grandmother after, but we'll be back tomorrow and wondered if you wanted to join us for Sunday lunch? The new hotel on the centre does a mean Sunday roast by all accounts. What do you think?"

"When you say you are going to Eastwood Park, does that mean what I think it does?"

Eastwood Park was a women's prison. Tanya Jennings, Patsy's former police colleague, was serving an eighteen-year sentence for assisting numerous suicides. Patsy had been heavily involved in the investigation, which had also revealed that, unbeknownst to Frankie Callaghan, Tanya Jennings was his half-sister. Patsy heard Frankie sigh.

"It does indeed. She's asked to see me several times, and I think I should go and see what she has to say. She has no one, you know, and if it wasn't for my mother . . . well, you know. Anyway, what harm can it do?"

"I don't know, Frankie, be careful, that's all. Is Sarah going in with you?"

"Of course. Oh, I know what you're thinking, that Sarah will protect me from myself."

Patsy laughed. "Something like that, yes. What time tomorrow? I'm really looking forward to seeing you."

"I'll call and book a table and text you later. We'll come and pick you up."

Placing the phone back on the table, Patsy pondered Frankie's news. Frankie's world had been turned upside down when it was revealed that his mother had set off a chain of assisted suicides. When she was diagnosed with a terminal illness herself, she had passed on the task to her stepdaughter, Tanya Jennings, and her long-time admirer, Jasper James. Jasper had been Frankie's mentor and boss, and had claimed to be his father once the pair had been caught, although that had later been revealed to be untrue, Frankie had found he had a half-sister. Unsurprisingly, Frankie had been devastated, and Patsy felt that his getting involved with Tanya could do more harm than good, even though she was behind bars.

As she washed her breakfast dishes and stared into the small backyard, she made the decision to agree to go on a date with Meredith. She wouldn't move back in with him, but she missed him, and there could be no harm in starting again. Walking back to the table she picked up her phone and called him. He answered on the second ring, and it was clear from the rushing sound in the background that he was driving.

"Patsy, nice to hear from you, although I should warn you before you say anything inappropriate or perhaps devastating, that I have Travers in the car with me and I'm hands-free."

Bob Travers put his hands over his ears and slid down lower into his seat.

"Hi, Bob, what a treat for you. Meredith usually likes to be driven."

"I don't know about that. I think he's going for a world record on driving from Bristol to Cardiff. I'm glad it's his licence not mine," Bob laughed

"Oh yes, poor old Phillip Cowell, how's that going?"

Meredith didn't want to talk shop, he wanted to know why she was calling. "I'm sure that's not why you called. Why did you call?"

Travers smirked, and Meredith pursed his lips, wishing he was alone in the car. Patsy was also smiling, Meredith was captive with an audience. She could have some fun if she chose to.

"Do you want to take me on a date?" Grinning, Patsy paced into the hall. She felt like a teenager.

"Always."

"Where were you thinking of taking me?"

"Where would you like to go?"

"You mean you didn't have anything planned?"

"Oh, I have a lot planned, but you probably want to eat or take in a film or something first."

Travers interrupted, "I am here, you know. Just agree a time and place, and do the sorting when I don't have to listen to it!"

Meredith laughed out loud.

Patsy pictured Meredith's face, and wished she could see him. "Sorry Bob. Right, where and when? Amaze me."

"Tonight, I should be back late afternoon. I'll pick you up at Loopy's at eight. Is that acceptable, Ms Hodge?"

"Very, DCI Meredith. I'll see you later. Bye, Bob, have a good one."

Hanging up, Patsy kissed her phone. Every promise she'd made to herself had been broken, and she was glad. Picking up her bag, she collected her car keys and hummed softly as she climbed into her car.

As she walked into the office and greeted Chris, her phone rang. "Hi, Jo, how are you? Up to your eyes I'm sure after yesterday."

"That's why I was calling. We must get together and I was going suggest tonight, but now I'm working tomorrow as weekend leave has been cancelled. We've pulled a schedule together and I'm free on Tuesday and off on Wednesday. Patsy, I have to go, I've promised to do a favour for someone, and need to get a move on. I'm absent without permission. What do you think?"

"Sounds good to me, let me check my diary here, and I'll call you back in five. Should be fine though." Sliding her phone back into her pocket, she smiled at Chris. "I wasn't expecting to see you today. I thought you were bound for a meeting in Swindon."

"Cancelled until Monday. Sharon is shopping, again, and I thought I'd check the paperwork was up to date. Not much to do though, Linda has it all buttoned down."

"Yes I know, she has my updates filed away before I blink. I think she's getting bored now she's cracked the system and updated it to her standards. I take it no news from Penny?"

Penny was Chris's secretary whom Linda had replaced while Penny spent time with her sick mother.

"Not really. To be honest, I don't think she'll be back. Her mum needs round-the-clock care for a while. Having Linda step in has been great, but she was hinting to me that she wanted to do something more rewarding the other day."

"Anything likely to come up? It's not only about exercising her grey cells either. She turned down a good job via the agency the other day, so her finances could do with a boost too."

"There may be something from the Swindon thing for her, but until I get the details I can't be sure. I'd like to keep her on if we could manage it. Make some coffee and pull up a chair. I didn't want to talk shop last night, so you can update me on the Reynolds case now."

"Will do, but I just want to check nothing's been put into my diary that I haven't picked up. Hopefully, I can have a late start on Wednesday."

Chris sighed. He had caught the gist of the conversation, and had worked out that Patsy had made a date with someone called Joe. He wouldn't want to be near Meredith when he found out, and decided the less he knew the better, so he didn't pry.

"Get on with it. There's international rugby on this afternoon I'd like to catch."

Patsy put the kettle on and went to her office. Having checked her diary, which had not changed, she blocked out the first two hours of Wednesday morning, made the coffee, taking it back to Chris's desk, where she pulled out a chair.

"Okay, here's the latest on the Reynolds job for you. I'm about done there now. Alex Walters is involved in New Beginnings. I followed him on Wednesday and he met with the MD of New Beginnings in town. I set up three bogus leads with email addresses and numbers that come back here, and Linda took two calls on Thursday and all three have been emailed. I've set up a meeting at the Hilton on Monday afternoon. I'll record the conversation and present it to Reynolds on Tuesday. After that, I'm pretty much free unless he wants me to do more."

"He's stealing customers?"

"No, that's where he's being clever. He's stealing leads. All of them have made contact with Reynolds Relocation but none of them have signed up. What I really need to clinch it is to get hold of New Beginnings' database."

"Okay, so you prove that Walters is siphoning off potential new business, then what?"

"That's up to Reynolds and how much money he wants to throw at it. There is a clause in their contract of employment to the effect that any contacts made as a result of working for Reynolds must not be approached in any way, other than on Reynolds' business. That lasts for a year after any employment has terminated. It makes it quite clear that the company will take legal action to recover perceived losses. It gives monetary examples too." Patsy shrugged. "It will be messy and expensive, and we know how the courts work. Even if proven, the results of these civil actions are more unpredictable than the law courts."

Chris finished his coffee and, standing, he stretched his bulky frame. "Well, keep me posted. I'm off now. I have to take Jack swimming this afternoon, good for his muscles, and good for my weight loss regime." He laughed and patted his expanding waistline, "And his mother hates getting her hair wet." Chris inclined his head, "Did Amanda get home okay?"

"What, did I lose her along the way, or was she carsick, you mean?" Patsy smiled at him and shook her head. "For a private investigator, you're not very subtle, you know. I'm seeing Meredith tonight, which I believe is the answer to the question you didn't ask."

Pulling on his coat, Chris raised his eyebrows. "Good. Busy girl, Meredith tonight and Joe on Tuesday. I'll be off, enjoy your weekend."

Patsy opened her mouth to explain, but Chris was already closing the door behind him. His comment reminded her she had yet to call Jo back to confirm. She listened to the ringing before the answer machine cut it.

"Jo, it's Patsy. We're on. I've cleared a few hours on Wednesday morning in case I am in need of them. Give me a call back and let me know where and when." Patsy hesitated, "And I should confess, you were right, I'm seeing Meredith tonight. Okay, confession over, give me a shout."

~ ~ ~

Meredith followed his satnav's instructions and pulled into Cathy Davies' street. He continued to complain as he did so.

28

"I thought they made all these road changes to ease traffic flow. All that did was put another two miles on our journey, polluting the clean Welsh air as we go. Bloody one-way systems, I . . ."

Interrupted by his phone, Meredith hit the answer button as he pulled up outside number fifteen, Bayside Avenue. He took in the modern three-storey townhouse as the caller started speaking.

"Gov, it's Rawlings. I've found out something very interesting you need to know about before you see Cowell's missus. You're not there yet, are you?"

"Just arrived, Dave. What've you got?" He nodded and Travers pulled his notebook from his pocket.

"In the last fortnight there have been no fewer than twenty calls exchanged between Henshaw and Cathy Davies, one being ten minutes after Henshaw spoke to Cowell yesterday, and another at one-thirty this morning. Not looking promising, is it?"

Meredith pinched the bridge of his nose and sighed. "No, not at all. Keep this to yourself. We'll see her and then go and visit Henshaw. Anything else turned up?"

"Nothing. They've released a brief statement. Alison in PR was a tad miffed when you weren't here. I did explain you were trying to solve the case. I think she's taken me off her Christmas card list."

"I'll talk to her later. Keep me informed." Meredith climbed out of the car as Cathy Davies opened the front door, and hurried towards them.

"Have you got anything? Do you have any idea who did it?" Her eyes were swollen and dark rings beneath them revealed she hadn't had much sleep the night before.

Travers slipped his arm around her shoulders and turned her back towards the house. "We're that obvious, are we? Come on, Cathy, love, let's talk inside." Leading her into the hall, he asked, "Which way is the kettle?"

Cathy opened the door to her left, and they walked into the open plan living space. A large red L-shaped settee had a duvet folded on one end. Cathy looked at it as she walked into the dining area. "I couldn't sleep," she sighed as she opened the door to the right of the dining table.

Meredith looked at the black glossy kitchen units. The shiny steel handles were catching the mid-day spring sunshine.

"Smart kitchen, how long have you lived here?"

"Six months. Well, we bought it six months ago. I moved in about four months ago and Phil was due to move in properly in about three weeks." Her hand shook as she filled the kettle. "He had advertised most of his stuff on the internet. We bought new for here. New house, new furniture, new start." She stepped to one side as Travers took the coffee jar which she was struggling to open.

"Go and sit down with DCI Meredith, I'll see to this."

Meredith walked back into the other room and stopped at the table. He lifted three coasters from a small box and arranged them on the table. Cathy stood motionless, watching him. Pulling out a chair, he took her by the shoulders and sat her down.

"I know this is tough, Cathy, but the sooner we can get as much information as is possible, the sooner we'll catch whoever killed Phil." He took the seat at the head of the table and pulled a notebook from his pocket. "I'm going to ask you lots of questions. Some will seem random, but bear with me." He smiled at her, "I might even repeat myself, I'm told it's to do with my age."

Cathy looked up at him and took in his appearance. He was patronising her; he looked no older than forty, if that. Her face hardened. She didn't need patronising, but she didn't have the energy to tell him that. Instead she looked back down at her hands.

Meredith had noticed her shoulders stiffen, and studied her closely as he waited for Travers to place the coffee on the coasters.

"How long have you been in a relationship with Phil?"

Meredith continued to look at her, as Travers clicked out the nib of his pen ready to take notes.

Cathy glanced at Travers. "Twelve months almost."

"Wow. Love at first sight."

Her brow furrowed. "Sort of, but why did you say that?"

"You told us you bought this house six months ago. It takes a couple of months for a purchase to go through, if you're lucky, and that's after finding the right property. That tells me you both knew very quickly you wanted to live together. A big step if you're not in love."

Sipping his coffee, Meredith allowed the silence to drag on.

"What do you want me to say? Just keep asking the questions." Cathy looked at Travers out of the corner of her eye as she saw him make a note.

"When did you last see Phil?"

"Thursday lunchtime. We had lunch in town before he went back to Bristol to continue sorting the house out there"

"How often did he stay in Bristol?"

"Once a week or so, to make sure everything was okay."

Meredith thought back to Patsy's comments about Nancy Bailey attending twice a week. "How often did you go with him?"

"Not often. Our home is here."

"Did you not want to help him sort out the house in Bristol?"

Cathy's head jerked up. "What does that mean?"

Meredith returned her frown. "Exactly what it said, I wasn't implying anything." He held his hands up in surrender to her frown. "Tell me about his job. How was that going, was anything worrying him?"

"I don't think so. We didn't really talk about it."

"What did you talk about?"

Again, her head jerked up.

Meredith explained the question. "If we know what he was interested in, it's possible we could have a few more leads."

"Not much really. He wasn't sports mad like most blokes."

"So what did he do, when he wasn't working and organising the house in Bristol?"

"Nothing, you know, just living. Going to work, coming home, eating and watching TV, then going to bed and starting all over again."

Meredith sighed; it sounded much like his own life. "So no outside interests, and a boring sedate life when not working? Why was that?" Meredith caught Travers' movement from the corner of his eye, but pressed on. "Didn't you want to go out? A meal, the cinema, or perhaps the odd concert? I hear they have all the big names come to the Millennium Stadium."

Travers scratched his head with his free hand. Meredith was getting this all wrong. Instead of relaxing Cathy, and bringing her on side, he appeared to be trying to wind her up. This was a new tactic, because with women Meredith usually used a charm offensive. He looked at Cathy who had yet to answer. She was staring at Meredith, who held her gaze.

"We did those things, but not daily."

"Once a week?"

"Sometimes. Why is this relevant?"

"Why did he need a cleaner twice a week if he only went home once a week or so?"

"This was his home!" Cathy rapped the table.

Meredith bowed his head a little. "Of course, so why did he need a cleaner twice a week in Bristol?"

"He didn't. He felt sorry for the woman. I told him many times to get rid of her, but he said when he sold up would be soon enough. It's not like he could afford it."

"Paying her stopped him taking you out, did it?"

"Did I say that? How is any of this going to help you catch whoever did this?"

"So what do you reckon happened?"

He watched Cathy shake her head. "Andy said it looked like a burglar came in through the back door and did it."

Meredith pursed his lips. "Andy being DS Andy Henshaw, I take it."

Cathy nodded.

"Why did he feel sorry for the cleaner?"

Cathy held her hands up indicating her frustration. "What?"

"You said Phil kept the cleaner on because he felt sorry for her. Or was it because he wasn't actually going to move in here?"

Cathy stood abruptly and her chair fell back against the wall. She pointed at Meredith. "No, it bloody doesn't. Whoever told you that is lying. We had a few problems but they were sorted. Come upstairs and I'll show you his things. Of course he was coming. He met the cleaner years ago. She found her sister after she'd hanged herself. Phil was the first on the scene and sort of adopted her."

Meredith stood and placed a hand on her shoulder, applying a gentle pressure. "Sit down, love. I'm not trying to offend you, but I have to deal with all the information I've been given."

Nodding, Cathy pulled the chair forward.

"Why do you think Henshaw would suggest it was a burglar when all the evidence points to the contrary?"

Travers sighed. Meredith was like a bull in a china shop.

Cathy gave a little gasp. "What do you mean? What evidence?"

"You will be pleased to know that Phil didn't see it coming. He let someone into his house, and when his back was turned and he went about his business, they attacked him. Luckily, the first blow did it, so he would have known little if anything about it. There was no struggle, and nothing missing. I'm surprised Henshaw suggested it was a burglar. Right, show me round."

Before Cathy had time to process what Meredith had said, he stood and walked to the door. Holding it open, he swept his hand forward, indicating she should lead the way. Cathy glanced at Travers, who gave an uncertain smile and stood up. They followed Cathy up the stairs.

She pointed to a door as they approached the top. "That's the family bathroom."

Meredith opened the door. The room glistened much like the kitchen, and unless she had just cleaned it, it wasn't being used. Cathy turned left and opened the door opposite her.

"This is the study, or will be, or was going to be." Her voice cracked and she stood a while to compose herself. "We haven't really used it yet. You can just about see the water in the Bay."

Meredith walked in and slid open the top drawer of the desk. "May I?"

Cathy nodded and he moved around a few pens and looked at a couple of receipts there. When he slid the bottom drawer open, it was empty. He turned and scanned the bookcase. It contained more ornaments than books.

"Not readers, I take it?" He smiled warmly at her.

Travers raised his eyebrows. Meredith was returning to form.

"Phil was, but most of his books are still in boxes in Bristol. He put a couple in the loft but decided he would give some to the charity shop. We haven't got enough room for all of them."

Meredith nodded at the door. "Let's keep going."

He followed Cathy to the spare bedroom. She stayed on the landing as he and Travers stepped inside. The room was immaculate, the curtains held back by cord ties, and the matching bedspread hung perfectly over the mattress on the brass bedstead. He nodded at it and Travers followed his gaze and made a note. "It's like Bedknobs and Broomsticks. Nice room."

Meredith rubbed Cathy's shoulder as he returned to the landing. "Nearly done."

They followed her to the top floor.

"Wow," Meredith exclaimed as they stepped into the room. "What a fantastic room." He pointed to a door to the left of the huge bed, "En suite?"

Cathy nodded as Meredith walked into the room and pushed the door open.

"I thought so, that bathroom downstairs was far too perfect. Mind you, this house is perfect. You keep a lovely home, Cathy." He held her gaze as she gave a little smile. "Would you mind, I do need to spend a penny." He pulled the cord and light flooded the little room; the extractor fan hummed as it sucked out air. "Won't be a tick."

Meredith relieved himself, and having washed his hands, he opened the bathroom cabinet. Finding what one would expect to find there. Lifting down a toiletry bag, he peered inside before zipping it up and replacing it.

When he returned to the bedroom Cathy was staring out the window at Cardiff Bay, and she turned to face him.

"Which side of the bed is yours?"

Walking to the opposite side, he slid open the drawer in the bedside cabinet. He lifted out the book and read the enthusiastic reviews on the back. Placing it on the table he gave the remaining few items a cursory glance before replacing it.

"That's his," Cathy pointed to the chest of drawers to the left of the smaller wardrobe, "and the small wardrobe is his too."

Meredith nodded to Travers who opened the wardrobe and looked through the clothes hanging there. Meredith made a quick inspection of the contents of the drawers.

"Nothing here that would give us much of a clue; shall we?" He held his hand towards the door and Cathy followed Travers out. As they turned onto the final flight of stairs, he sighed, "You do have a beautiful home, Cathy. You must both have been very proud. I'm so sorry."

Cathy gave a little groan and her head fell forward. She stifled her tears as they returned to the ground floor. Travers led the way back to the kitchen and refilled the kettle. Cathy stood watching him, but spun to face Meredith as he asked the next question.

"Why would Andy Henshaw think that it was acceptable to call you at one-thirty in the morning? Especially given what you were going through?"

"He was drunk. He wanted to say sorry and make sure I was all right. How did you know he called me?"

Meredith shot a glance at Travers and stepped closer to her, indicating they should take a seat. He followed her back towards the table.

"Because that's my job. If I took the glass from the bedside cabinet in the spare room, whose prints would be on it?"

Cathy stopped dead in her tracks and Meredith bumped into her. She turned to face him, her bottom lip trembling.

"I don't know." She looked down and Meredith tilted her chin up towards him. She blinked as he gazed at her.

"Tell me, Cathy. It's better it comes out here and now."

Cathy blinked again and Meredith gently brushed the tears aside with his thumbs.

"They would be Phil's."

It wasn't the answer Meredith was expecting. He tilted his head slightly. "Why?"

"Because he thought I was having an affair with Andy. We had been mucking about on the dance floor, that's all. He read too much into it."

"If there is nothing to it, why have there been more than twenty calls between you over the last couple of weeks?"

Cathy's body swayed and Meredith put his hands on her shoulders to steady her.

"Sit down." He walked her to the table, sat her in the nearest chair, and crouched down in front of her, his face level with hers.

Travers leaned against the door jamb, watching, knowing Meredith was about to find out what he wanted to know.

"Tell me," Meredith said so quietly that Travers only just heard.

Cathy shook her head, which Meredith countered by nodding.

"Tell me."

"Nothing happened. It could have, it might have. But not now."

"You were going to though, so what stopped you?"

"No, I wouldn't have. It was exciting. Our life was boring; when we weren't knackered from work, we didn't have any money. Andy was like a breath of fresh air. I think he's in love with me, it was flattering. I wouldn't have done anything about it. I loved Phil."

"Apart from in the middle of the night, after Phil had been murdered, when did you last speak to Henshaw?"

"Yesterday morning, early . . . he called me," she added, as if that would help.

"What did he want?"

Screwing up her eyes so that Meredith couldn't see in, more tears fell. This time Meredith let them complete their journey.

"Nothing really."

Her eyes still screwed shut, Meredith watched the frown deepen on her forehead as she replayed the conversation in her mind.

"Just to check . . . just to say hello."

"Just to check what? Check if Phil was coming home that night, check to see if you got home all right, check if he could see you? What did he want to check?"

"Check that Phil was still in Bristol."

"Why? Was he coming round to see you?"

Shaking her head, Cathy opened her eyes.

"Or going there to see Phil?"

"No! He wouldn't." Wrapping her hands around her body as though she were cold, Cathy leaned forward, avoiding Meredith's eyes.

"Was it to find out if you were pregnant?"

Cathy knocked Meredith off balance and he fell onto the floor as she rushed to the kitchen and vomited into the sink.

Sinking to the floor, she pulled her knees to her chest. "How did you know?"

"Phil uses condoms; they were in his bedside cabinet and yet in your toiletry bag, you have a packet of contraceptive pills that were only dispensed eight days ago. Why would you need both, and isn't that shutting the gate after the horse has bolted?" Meredith's tone was harsh.

Choking back a sob, Cathy looked up at him. "It was once, spur of the moment madness. I'm not pregnant, my period arrived last night."

"But Phil knew about it?" Meredith's nose wrinkled.

"No. He thought he did, but he was guessing."

"Only for the right day, not the occurrence though. How did you feel about that?"

Cathy pushed herself to her feet. Her tears fell untroubled, and she wiped her nose with the back of her hand.

"I want you to go now. Who are you to judge? Leave my house now."

Jerking his head, Meredith walked to the door, Travers followed him. As he opened the door, he half turned to face Cathy.

"I'm not judging you. You have to live with it." He stepped out onto the doorstep before turning back. "Who benefits from Phil's death? Did he make a will?"

Cathy opened and shut her mouth but nothing came out. Meredith simply nodded and walked briskly to the car.

"Cardiff Central I take it, Gov?" Travers fastened his seatbelt.

"I think so. I hope she doesn't warn him before we get there."

"Can I say something?" Travers twisted in the passenger seat to look at Meredith.

"Nope, but you will anyway. Spit it out."

"Why did you treat her differently? You usually turn on the charm when interviewing ladies." Travers cleared his throat. "And if you don't mind me mentioning it, it was bit pot and kettle in there at one stage." He watched Meredith purse his lips before glancing over at him.

"That's why I was qualified. Cowell's broken his back and his bank account to make her happy. You don't accidently snog someone new in full view of everyone else. You do it because it's natural, and you've had too much drink to remember it's not supposed to be. She slept on the couch because she was feeling guilty. I knew it as soon as I saw her," Meredith shrugged. "Been there, and done that too. The old 'it takes one to know one' thing is spot on, you know."

Travers turned away and thought about Meredith's date with Patsy. "But now you've changed?" It was a question not a statement.

"I have." Meredith smiled out at the road ahead.

"We'll see," Travers muttered.

Meredith chose to ignore him.

Twenty minutes later, Meredith ran up the steps to the main entrance of the central police station in Cardiff, Travers hurrying along behind. Meredith showed his badge to the duty sergeant and they were shown up to the first floor. They sat in a tatty reception area, and watched as various police officers went about their business. A few paused to glance at them. Meredith looked at his watch. He would give it ten more minutes before he got angry.

DCI Williams had five minutes left, when Meredith stood and drew his shoulders back, but he relaxed as Williams came through the double doors at the end of the corridor and waved them towards him.

Opening a door off the corridor and sliding the sign to 'Engaged', Williams switched on the light and showed them into a cramped interview room. They were sitting before the light finally flickered to life.

"Sorry to keep you. I've had one of my chaps doing a bit of background checking to save you the time."

Meredith frowned at Williams who shrugged, and wagged his finger.

"Don't bullshit me, and don't tell me you would have done it any differently if it had been one of your lads involved."

"Judging by the look on your face, the news wasn't good," Meredith observed drily.

Williams rested his elbows on the table and rubbed his face as he shook his head.

"No." Williams pulled his hands away from his face. "He didn't do the first interview until half eleven. Shopkeeper said it lasted five minutes at best. After that he turned up at one other, but the owner was out, so he said he'd call back. I still can't believe it was him. Why would he? Why risk everything?"

"Because he was banging Phillip Cowell's missus, and she gets everything if Cowell pops his clogs. Enough to take a risk, don't you think? Where is he?"

Williams shrugged, and tired eyes stared at Meredith.

"I sent him home yesterday. He didn't turn up this morning, and he hasn't called in. I went to his flat and he wasn't there. He shares with one of the other lads, and he gave me a key."

"Is he in, the lad he shares with? If so, I'd like to speak to him."

Williams pushed himself up wearily. "I'll send him down."

Thirty minutes later, Henshaw's flatmate had confirmed that he knew Henshaw had been having an affair, and guessed it was someone already spoken for as he hadn't boasted about it. Henshaw was never usually backward in coming forward when it came to his conquests. The flatmate never for a minute thought it was Cathy Davies. Henshaw had been very quiet over the last couple of weeks, which he'd assumed was due to the embarrassment at the party. He'd heard Henshaw come in very late the night before, but he'd gone out again early that morning. It didn't appear that any clothes had gone. DCI Williams had his passport.

Williams showed Meredith and Travers out.

"Twenty-four hours to bring him to me, or I go public," Meredith reminded Williams as he pulled open the heavy glazed door.

"I'll do my best." Williams held out his hand, "Don't stop looking, Meredith, you may have this wrong."

"I won't. You have my number, call me when you find him."

Meredith tossed the cars keys to Travers. "You can drive." He climbed into the passenger seat, and adjusted it so he was almost flat. "It took me forty-five minutes to get here. See how fast you can get us home. I have a date tonight." He closed his eyes and a smile twitched as he relaxed.

"You think we have our man, Gov?"

"I don't know. I know it takes all sorts, but unless she's dynamite in bed, I can't see anyone doing that for our Cathy. I don't suppose she's a bad looking girl, but shallow."

He turned his head to look at Travers.

"No, if you knew she was with someone, and your judgement was clouded, you'd shag her and have it on your toes if you had any sense. I'll bet you a pound to a penny that Cowell was in debt because of her. Now put your foot down."

4

Running her finger along the lip gloss on her bottom lip, Patsy checked her appearance for the third time in twenty minutes as she waited for Meredith. She had no idea where he was taking her, and was glad that Linda wasn't at home to witness this unusual bout of nervousness. Perhaps expecting Meredith to date her was going to be more difficult for her than it was Meredith. Smoothing down her dress, she turned away from the mirror. Meredith still had ten minutes, and that was if he was on time, which was unlikely.

Picking up her phone she dialled Jo's number. A chat with Jo would distract her. The call went straight through to the answer service. Leaving a brief message, Patsy walked into the sitting room and gazed out of the window into the half-light of sunset.

The minutes ticked by slowly. When Meredith was five minutes late, she pulled out her phone and tried Jo again, as much as anything to have a moan about Meredith. This time it didn't ring, and was picked up by an electronic voice. It told her the phone was switched off and to try again later. Sighing, she dropped the phone back into her bag. As she looked up she saw Meredith jump out of a taxi and hurry down the path. He was carrying a huge bouquet.

"Hello, thank you for these, they are lovely." Taking the flowers, she pecked him on the cheek.

"You're welcome, now chuck them in some water, and let's get going. The taxi's waiting."

Patsy filled the sink with water and placed the bouquet in it. Lifting her coat from the stand in the hall she followed Meredith to the taxi. He held the door open for her, and she bit back a smile.

"Where are we going?"

"It's a surprise. You look good, Patsy."

"Thank you, and so do you. How was your day?"

"Don't ask, we are going to have a work-free . . . date."

He smiled and her heart skipped a beat. Reaching out, Patsy took hold of his hand. "Good." A thought occurred to her and she grinned.

"What tickled you?"

"I was wondering what topics will come up if we don't talk about work. I'm looking forward to this."

When the taxi driver left Bristol, and headed towards Bath, Patsy turned to Meredith. "You've clearly put some thought into this. Where are we going?"

"We'll be there in a minute."

The taxi had turned off the main road, and Patsy could see nothing but hedgerow on either side. A few minutes later it turned left, and drove through some imposing wrought iron gates. Patsy looked at the sign: Hawthorn Lodge.

"Never heard of this before . . . wow, that's picturesque." She smiled as the Lodge came into view.

Meredith opened the door and took her hand as she climbed out. He paid the taxi driver and led her through the oak panelled reception and into the bar. A huge fire burned in the inglenook fireplace.

Meredith nodded to an overstuffed couch in one corner. "Take a seat, I'll order some drinks. What would you like?"

"I'll stick to wine I think. I don't want to embarrass you and get tipsy by mixing my drinks."

Meredith grinned and walked away to the bar. He came back empty-handed.

"They're getting a bottle of Chateau something or other from the cellar." He raised his eyebrows. "I asked the barman what their best red was and he reeled off three different names, I think. I'd never heard of them so told him I'd go on his recommendation. I'll probably have to take out a second mortgage."

Patsy laughed and, taking his hand, pulled him to sit next to her. "Well, I'm sure it will be fabulous. How did you find this place?"

Her brow creased as Meredith shook his head.

"Can't say."

"Well, that speaks volumes."

Patsy's smile fell away, and realising that she thought he'd brought another woman here, Meredith added quickly, "I arrested the manager here about three years back, and he's now doing five years for fraud. Sorry, I was trying not to talk about work." He winked as her smile returned.

"Ah, I see. Well that was a necessary breach. Have you read any good books lately?"

Meredith shook his head.

"Been to the cinema?" She laughed as he shook his head again. "I'll tell you what, you keep shaking your head until I mention something you can nod at."

Grinning, Meredith moved his head from side to side slowly. His eyes twinkled as they locked onto Patsy's. Patsy felt the familiar flutter deep inside.

"So, from the beginning; books, cinema, theatre, concerts, holidays, day trips . . ." she giggled as he continued the slow movement. "I know something that you must have done."

Meredith stilled his head and raised his eyebrows expectantly.

"Shopping!"

Meredith's shoulders drooped dramatically and he recommenced the negative movement. Patsy laughed out loud, and the barman looked over and smiled at her.

"Oh, I can see you've had a ball of fun while I've been away. I'll try a different tack now; have you given up smoking . . ." she paused but the movement continued, "drinking, eating fried food, eating six meals a day? Blimey, Johnny, I'm running out of ideas here. You've done nothing new, and stopped nothing old. Something must have happened or changed," she slapped her forehead, "except, of course, Amanda. How's that going? She's a lovely girl."

"Go back to the previous bit. We can talk about Amanda later."

"What, you have done something new?" She smiled as he shook his head. "Aha, so you have stopped doing something."

Meredith nodded and a smile twitched at the corner of his mouth. His eyes left hers briefly as the waiter arrived with the wine, which Meredith tasted and approved. The waiter departed and Meredith held up his glass and tapped it lightly on Patsy's.

"Cheers, Hodge. Carry on, you haven't finished."

Patsy placed her glass on the table, and placed her index fingers on each temple, and feigned concentration, before shaking her head. "No, you're going to have to tell me."

Meredith pursed his lips to hide the smile, but the dimple on his right cheek gave him away.

"What? Tell me."

Patsy looked up as the waiter approached them. He advised them that their dinner table was ready, and placed the wine and glasses on a tray. Meredith stood, took Patsy's hand, and as they followed the waiter he leaned down.

"I haven't had sex. Not for seven weeks, four days and . . ." he looked at his watch, "approximately seven hours." He hadn't lowered his voice and Patsy flushed as she noticed the slight hesitation in the waiter's step. She nodded towards him, but Meredith carried on anyway. "I've thought about it, mind you. Lots. What about you?"

"Meredith, please!" She avoided the waiter's eye as he stopped at their table and pulled her chair out.

Meredith shrugged as she took her seat. "You asked, I'm telling. I'm sure Paolo is a man of the world."

Paolo lifted the wine and glasses from the tray and placed them on the table. He nodded at Meredith. "I am, sir. Your starter will be with you shortly." He turned to face Patsy. "Miss," he nodded formally, "I hope you enjoy your stay." He turned and walked away.

Patsy knew he was smirking, and, her face stern, she looked at Meredith. "Stay? What does that mean? Have you been presumptuous, Johnny?"

"Nope. Prepared, and stop calling me Johnny."

"Really, I would have thought presumptuous was more apt."

"No. Prepared. If you want to go home, we will go home. It's why I didn't drive and we arrived by taxi. If nothing else, I wanted to have a drink with you." He smiled. "On the other hand, if you did want to stay, I have booked their deluxe suite, complete with four-poster bed. So I say again, prepared." He looked up, "Ah, here comes the starter."

The waiter placed the plates and made a hasty retreat.

"So prepared, in fact, that you also ordered for me."

Patsy looked down at the bowl of mussels, sniffed in the aroma, and her mouth watered.

Meredith nodded solemnly.

"Indeed. I didn't want to spend hours trawling over the extensive menu they have here. That would have wasted unnecessary time."

"Are we in a rush?"

"I hope so." Unable to maintain his serious manner, Meredith threw his head back and laughed, and Patsy wished he would do it more often.

She smiled at him. "At least you've chosen well. Now, tell me about Amanda."

Meredith's smile faded, and he pinched the bridge of his nose, not wanting to discuss his past. "Can I do this quickly with only the necessary detail? We can talk about Amanda herself another time."

Patsy nodded and picked up her first mussel.

"I was the grand old age of nineteen when I met her mother, Karen. She was my sister's best friend."

"Julia?"

"Yes. Look, you're going to have to listen and not interrupt or we'll be here all night, and I'll die of starvation." He waited for her to nod, and quickly ate several mussels. He waved his fork at her. "These are good."

"Get on with it."

"We started knocking about, and she fell pregnant. We didn't have an

42

exclusive relationship."

"When you say *we*, I'm assuming you mean *you*."

"No, I mean *we*. We were mates, we also happened to like each other too." He shrugged as though that were explanation enough. "I knew she'd been out with a couple of other lads, so when she told me she was pregnant, I asked her what she was going to do. She told me it was mine. I asked how she could know that and she announced she just knew. She admitted that she had slept with another bloke, but the dates told her that the baby was mine, and she was going to have it."

Meredith paused to eat, and refreshed his wine glass.

"I didn't love her, I liked her, and I wasn't ready to settle down, certainly not with her and a baby. I promised that I would help her through the pregnancy, pretend to be her partner for ante-natal stuff and the like. But that it wasn't going to be more than that, even if the baby was mine. She agreed, so we stayed mates and I helped her where I could. She was sharing a flat with Julia at that time."

"And this helping out, did it include sleeping with her?"

"It did. We sort of grew into a couple, and when Amanda was born, I thought why not, since she's mine? My chance to be a decent family man, and we moved into our own pokey little one-bed flat." He looked up at Patsy, "I loved being a father. I mean *really* loved it. So I saw less and less of my shady mates, and when two of them went to prison, I thought sod that for a game of soldiers, I have my baby to think of, and I joined the police."

"I remember that story, but it didn't include a partner and a baby the first time." Patsy pointed at the bowl in front of him, "Eat something before you go on."

She watched him finish his mussels and half the bread basket. When he smiled at her the rest of his face didn't relax, and she felt guilty. He pushed the bowl away.

"She didn't like me being a copper. She didn't like the hours, she didn't like the salary. My previous involvements had paid better. It was my twenty-first birthday when I realised we were only together because of Amanda. Her mother was looking after Amanda, and I had a do in the upstairs room of our local. Karen was dancing with one of my old mates, who had forgiven me for the night for becoming a copper, and when the dance finished she kissed him. She kissed him in a way that told me she was used to kissing him. It wasn't mad passion or anything like that, it was a comfortable kiss." Meredith shook his head, "I can't explain what I mean, but I knew she had kissed him many times before. Does that make sense?"

Patsy nodded and refreshed their glasses. "It does." She smiled at the waiter who cleared the dishes, and when he walked away, she added, "So what did you do?"

Meredith shook his head again. "Nothing, absolutely nothing, because I didn't care. It was like a weight had been lifted, so I simply got plastered. The next day, once the hangover had subsided, I pulled her up about it, and she was as relieved as I was. We agreed to go our separate ways. I promised I would see Amanda whenever I could, and make sure she wanted for nothing. I opened a post office account for her too," he smiled. "Still have it. Still put fifty pounds a month into it." He picked up his wine and sipped it. "I'm going to cut this short because I want to eat my steak while it's still warm, if that's all right."

He watched her nod and winked at her.

"To the finale. Tony, that was my mate, moved in, and for three years I had Amanda every weekend that I was off, and babysat in the week when needed. Amanda called me Daddy, and Tony, Tony. Not long after, Tony got in a bit of bother, which I steered well clear of, and they wanted to move to Devon. I refused and there was a massive row. Karen told me Amanda wasn't mine, and added that she wasn't Tony's either. She told us who the father was. At the time she fell pregnant he was a good friend, or so I thought. Although everyone knew that we weren't a couple in the traditional sense, you still didn't step on toes. It hurt because it was him," Meredith shrugged, "but he'd disappeared a few years before, and what was done was done. Karen told me that she'd wanted a dad for Amanda and the security of a partner, of course. Apparently I was the best bet. I was devastated I wasn't her father. They moved away and I lost contact. Tony ended up in prison, but they stayed put in Totness. Then about eight years ago, Karen got breast cancer. Julia went to see her and brought me some photographs of Amanda. One look told me she was my daughter; I didn't need DNA tests. So I went down to visit them, and Karen, glad of the respite, allowed me to see her. We even went on a couple of holidays, me and my girl. Karen survived, by which time I had met Nicola and we married. Karen was evil about it, she had been expecting another pay cheque . . . Oh bugger, here come the steaks."

"Tell me when we've finished eating." Patsy stretched across the table and took his hand. "In fact, don't say any more. I can see how upsetting this is for you."

She pulled her hand away to allow the waiter to place her meal.

Meredith shook his head. "No, let's get it all out there, too far in to stop now." He thanked the waiter and ordered more wine. "Amanda was twelve by that time, and Karen filled her head with some crap about Nicola being a wicked stepmother, and how I didn't love my daughter any more. Amanda refused to come and stay with us, and my visits were once a month or so, if that. When they moved again, and I didn't know where, by this time I was struggling to deal with Nicola and I left it too long to trace them. When I did find them, Amanda refused to see me at all." Meredith smiled at Patsy. "Shall we eat?"

They ate their meal quickly, and in silence, both cursing the fact that they were having this conversation, but both glad it was almost over. The waiter cleared their plates and offered the sweet menu. They declined and ordered coffee.

"Would you like that in the lounge or at the table, sir?"

"The lounge, I think."

Meredith took Patsy by the hand and they went to reclaim the overstuffed couch. Once they were settled, he lifted her hand and kissed it. "Nearly there."

He emptied his wine glass and cleared his throat. "Karen contacted Julia again about a year ago. The cancer was back but in her liver this time, and she wanted me to go and see her. I had recently split from Nicola and refused; I still had hopes that something could be salvaged. I tried to contact Amanda but she wouldn't speak to me, and then I met you." He smiled at her. "And you filled my world, every inch of it."

He placed his hand on her thigh and drew circles with his middle finger. His gaze locked hers, and she blinked for him to continue. He sighed. "And, selfish though it may seem, I didn't tell you because I didn't want you to believe the crap Karen spouted about me. You already knew enough of my true shortcomings, and I wasn't going to risk that you would believe her stories too. I wasn't going to risk losing you." He snorted, "Which is exactly what I did do, of course."

"If it was the end, why didn't you tell me?"

"You remember the day Julia turned up at the house?"

Patsy nodded, "Of course."

"She had been to see Karen, and Karen was apparently begging me to go and see her. I refused. I'd been there and done that too many times before, but I agreed to go and see Amanda. Amanda refused to see me unless I saw her mother too. She thought I was callous not going to see her mother on her deathbed. She told Julia she hated me." He shrugged. "I can't tell you how much that hurt, but it didn't matter because I still had you."

Patsy felt her lip tremble, and her eyes glistened. To break the spell she leaned forward and poured the coffee. She held the plate containing petits fours out to him, but he shook his head.

"Maybe later. So Karen died, and Amanda texted me to tell me. She told me she didn't want me at the funeral, and given what she thought I had done, I understood that. Then, out of the blue, she texted to say she wanted to see me and would meet me in Broadmead. I was surprised that she was prepared to come to Bristol, but as it turns out, she goes to university here. She's in her second year." He pulled his shoulders back and smiled, "She's studying medicine, you know. I've moved her out of the crappy flat she was in too, but it's a bit of a struggle sometimes. You want to see some of the blokes she knows, and they're supposed to be sensible enough to become doctors. It's scary, Patsy. On my life, I worry for the future."

Patsy laughed and picked up his hand to kiss it. "I wonder how many fathers have thought that about you. I'm glad she's forgiven you, even if there wasn't really anything to forgive."

"As it happens, her mother told her the truth. She obviously wanted to make some sort of peace before she went. A deathbed confession, and of course now, Amanda thinks she did it all for her, which makes her feel guilty, but we're getting there. It doesn't help that she also feels guilty about you. It doesn't matter what I say." He shrugged and tutted.

"Me, why?"

"She thinks you left because of her. I've told her it was me, but she says it's too big a coincidence et cetera. Anyway, there you have it. For all the wrong reasons, as always, I did my best and cocked up." He leaned forward and pushed a stray hair from her forehead. "Am I forgiven?"

"Of course. You may now court me, Johnny Meredith, on the understanding that you tell the truth at all times. The whole truth, not just the bits you want me to know, and you won't leave whopping great gaps like grown-up daughters. Do you think you can do that?"

"By court, you mean 'date' I assume? You're not coming home?"

His shoulders hunched and he pinched his nose as she shook her head.

"Not yet anyway. Amanda has had you for only two months. Spend a little more time with her on your own first. She deserves that, and so do you!" She slapped his hand. "Move your legs, I need to powder my nose."

When she returned Meredith watched her every step. He looked so happy, relaxed and hot, that Patsy knew she would have to be strong to avoid moving straight back in with him. At that precise moment the thought of choosing not to share a bed with him every night seemed totally ridiculous.

"You were wrong, you know, she's had me for seven weeks and four days, give or take a few hours, as I do have to work. Shall I get our room key?"

"Are you being presumptuous again?" Patsy laughed.

"No, prepared. As you came back with your knickers poking out of your handbag, I think it's best we have somewhere to go. This is a decent establishment, and I don't think they'll let us do it in the bar."

Patsy's hand flew to her mouth and she pulled her bag onto her lap. It was zipped shut. She looked up at Meredith.

"What . . ."

She joined in his laughter as he threw his head back. Several of the other guests turned to look.

"I was testing you, and I'm glad to say you've passed! Come on." Standing, he pulled her to her feet, Patsy picked up the petits fours. "What do you want those for?"

She raised her eyebrows. "Because you will need to replenish your energy sometime during the night, and I don't want to wait for room service."

The phone rang first at three-thirty in the morning. Patsy ignored it and snuggled closer to Meredith who didn't stir. She smiled and opened her eyes. Meredith usually woke on the first ring, but he was dead to the world. The room was dark, and as her eyes became accustomed to the lack of light, she could make out the awning on the huge four-poster bed in which they lay. She sighed contentedly and Meredith shifted position, his hand finding her breast.

"Mmmm. Is it time for the chocolates yet?" he murmured into her neck.

"Why, do you need more energy?" she whispered.

"I hope so . . . bugger, is that your phone?"

He groaned as Patsy pulled away from him and sat up.

"Yes, and yours rang ten minutes ago too. We'd better check."

Meredith's eyes opened. Patsy was right; everyone knew they were apart, and the fact that they'd both received a call would not be a coincidence. He swung his legs over the side of the bed and fumbled for the light switch. They both squinted. Meredith located his trousers from where he had let them fall, and retrieved his phone. Patsy went to the dressing table and pulled hers from her handbag.

She held it up. "Tom," she announced, and walked to Meredith, who had dialled out.

"It was the station, must be serious if they . . . Meredith here, did you call, George? . . . Okay, put me through. Seaton, it's Meredith, what's the panic?"

Patsy saw his shoulders stiffen as he listened. He bent and picked up his boxer shorts. Hopping first on one leg and then the other, he managed to get both feet in. Patsy assisted and pulled them up.

"Hang on a minute." Meredith turned to Patsy, "Call a cab and get dressed, Adler's missing."

"Jo Adler?" Patsy asked unnecessarily.

Meredith tutted and went back to his call as Patsy dialled the taxi firm recommended in the hotel guide.

"When was this? When did he realise?" Meredith rubbed a hand over his eyes. "How long since he last had any contact? Shit! Right we're on our way. Get on to the telephone company and find out when the phone was last used and where."

By the time he had finished the call, Patsy had dressed and was holding out his shirt in one hand and his trousers in another.

Six hours earlier, Jo Adler had looked up as the door opened at the top of the stairs. She smelt fish, and walked to the wrought iron grill at the bottom of the staircase. She watched the feet coming down.

"Oh good, you're awake. Sorry I've been so long. Stand back now, or I won't be able to slide this to you. You must be starving. I'm sorry I had to leave you for so long but I had a few things to take care of."

Jo stepped back and allowed enough space for the tray to be pushed under the grill. She looked up at her captor.

"Why are you doing this? You promised you'd explain why. I'm not cross any more, but I am worried in case anything happens to you. What would happen to me then?"

"Don't be daft. As soon as they know it's me, I'll tell them you're here."

"But what if you get run over by a bus or something? What if you have a heart attack? What then? Look, I know you don't intend to hurt me, but I'm not convinced you've thought this through."

"Eat."

Jo picked up the tray and took it to the small table. She forked a piece of fish and nibbled on it. Once more she marvelled at her surroundings. The basement of the house had no windows that she was aware of, as all the walls had been lined with thick sound-proofing boards. Surrounded by the silver walls she felt as though she were in some futuristic pod. The only furnishing was a small table and chair, a fridge on top of which sat a kettle and a two-ring plug-in hob, and a single bed. There was an alcove in one corner which contained a toilet, a washbasin and a small shower cubicle hiding behind a blue floral curtain. The only other item was a deep-shelved bookcase. One shelf held a small DVD player with a handful of DVDs and CDs, together with a few paperbacks. On another were some basic toiletries and a folded towel, and on the last some plates, a stack of bowls, a saucepan and a frying pan.

"How long have you been planning this?"

"I wasn't planning this, dear. It was a spur of the moment thing. Well almost, about an hour before we met actually."

"But you were clearly planning on holding someone prisoner down here." Jo held her hands out to the room.

"Oh no, this was for quite a different purpose, but that's a long story which I don't feel like telling at the moment."

There was silence for a moment, and Jo watched the shoulders slump before rising with a long sigh. Jo didn't want to irritate, so she took a huge mouthful of the potato.

"Mmm, that potato is great. I can't do mash without leaving lumps in. Is this a cod or haddock?"

"Cod. I have to go for a couple of hours, I must check the news. I'll bring you back a newspaper. I'm sorry, but the television doesn't work down here. You can watch a DVD though."

~ ~ ~

As Meredith and Patsy hurried into the incident room, Tom Seaton went to meet them.

"We've put Aaron in your office, Gov. He wouldn't go home, and it seemed too cruel to put him in the waiting room."

"Well, he needs to go home, Jo could call there . . . or they could." He pursed his lips. "Anything new? Have we got anything on her phone yet?"

"Not yet. It'll be here in a minute. Had to speak to India, because of the time. Why they have to put call centres over there I'll never know, had to cut through some of the red tape. I reckon I made one of them cry."

"Give me a shout as soon as it arrives. I'll go and speak to Aaron. Patsy, you make some coffee and come join us." Leaving Patsy with Seaton, Meredith strode away to his office.

Patsy picked up a sheet of paper from the nearest desk and pulled a pen from her handbag.

"Right, who wants what?" she asked.

She took the orders, knowing that on any other occasion she would have taken some serious stick for arriving in the middle of the night with Meredith. But this was for Jo Adler. Their Jo. There would be little mirth in the incident room until she was found. Patsy made the coffee and tapped Meredith's door with her foot. Aaron jumped up and went to open it.

Patsy placed the mugs on Meredith's desk and hugged him. "Hello, Aaron, how are you doing?" He clung onto her but didn't answer. "It'll be all right you know. There's probably some rational explanation for it."

Aaron Adler pulled away from her and shook his head. "We all know that's not true. She was due to work tomorrow, or today as it now is. We'd planned a meal and an early night. I know you lot get caught up in your work, so I wasn't worried when she was late. I put a film on and fell asleep, but when I woke she wasn't home. No missed calls, no texts, nothing. Even

if she'd run away with the milkman she would have at least texted me."
He turned to Meredith, "I shouldn't have fallen asleep. I should've known
hours ago. You have to find her for me."

"And I will. I promise you that. You should go home. She may call the
house. Would you like me to send someone with you?"

"No. I'm not going, I need to do something. Give me something to do."

Meredith sighed and stood up. He walked to Aaron and faced him.
"You need to go home. You need to be there if she phones or turns up.
Waiting here will drive you up the wall. As soon as we have anything I
will call you." He placed a hand on Aaron's shoulder. "I'm not going home
until we've found her, but she won't be contacting me."

Meredith gave a negligible jerk of his head and Patsy stepped forward.
"Come on, Aaron, I'll find someone to give us a lift."

While Aaron was collecting his coat, Meredith followed Patsy to the
corridor outside the incident room, and pinned her against the wall.

"Thank you, Hodge, for a splendid date. We must do it again tomorrow,
or today, I should say. Have you got your key to my place?" He kissed as
she nodded. "Good, whip in there and pick me up a clean shirt, razor, and
some deodorant. I'll be here for the duration, and although I have no
problem smelling of you, it has the ability to send the others a little crazy."

Pressing his body even closer he kissed her again, stopping only when
someone coughed behind him. He jumped away guiltily and spun round
ready to apologise to Aaron Adler. To his total surprise, Dan Williams and
Andy Henshaw stood watching them.

He groaned. "Shit! I need you two like I need a hole in the head."

"Yes, I can see you're busy." Williams looked from Patsy to Meredith.
"Henshaw came to me. I thought I'd give him a lift."

"It's five-thirty in the morning, couldn't you sleep?"

"Something like that. I called to get your mobile number and they said
you were in. I thought a personal visit would be better. A word, if I may."

Aaron Adler entered the corridor and looked hopefully at the new faces.
"Is there news, has something happened?"

Meredith shook his head and patted him on the shoulder. "Sorry mate,
a different case I'm afraid. You get off with Patsy, try and get some sleep,"
Meredith shrugged, knowing that was unlikely, "and I'll be in touch as
soon as anything happens." He looked at Patsy and winked. "I'll give you
a shout later." He turned to Williams and Henshaw. "Come on, I'll stick
you in an interview room down here."

The two men followed Meredith down the corridor. He pushed open
the door and switched on the light. "There you go. I'll try and rustle up
some coffee."

"Show me where, and I'll do it."

Williams gave a slight nod and Meredith knew he wanted to speak privately. He looked at Henshaw. "Make yourself at home. I take it I don't need to lock this?"

Henshaw shook his head and sat down. Meredith closed the door and he and Williams walked slowly back to the incident room.

"What's his story? Why did he go AWOL?"

"Look, Meredith, you need to go easy on him. I think he's near breaking point. He's been on the piss for the best part of twenty-four hours, and he's convinced that in some way he's responsible for Phil Cowell's death."

Meredith stopped and looked Williams. "Perhaps that's because he is."

"He no more stabbed Phil than I did, I'm convinced of that."

"Hmm, we'll see. But if it wasn't for him shagging his mate's missus, his mate wouldn't have been in the house." Meredith held the door to the incident room open. "Got a kitchen up at the top there, canteen won't be open for an hour or so."

"What's happened to get you lot in at this time?" Williams nodded at the four officers huddled around one of the desks.

"One of my girls has gone missing. Almost twelve hours now, so not looking good. You sort the coffee, I need to see what's got them excited."

Williams walked towards the kitchen and Meredith called to his team as he walked across the room. "What have you got?"

Tom Seaton looked up and shrugged. "Nothing, I hope. We had a call from Frenchay Hospital, they've had a woman brought in that fits Jo's description. Found on Kingswood High Street, definitely beaten up and almost certainly raped. Still unconscious. One of the nurses is going to get a photo and send it to Dave's phone."

Meredith joined the group looking down at Dave Rawlings' phone, which sat in the middle of his desk.

"Anything else?"

"Last time she used her phone was yesterday at The Mall, Cribbs Causeway, around six o'clock. She had a call from this number and then the phone went dead." Seaton handed Meredith a printout on which several numbers had been highlighted. "She had a couple of exchanges with that one. I'm waiting for detail on the registration. Bloody Indians don't do quick."

Rawlings' phone gave a hoot like a steam train coming into a station, and they fell silent as he snatched it up. He opened the photograph and grinned as he turned it to face Meredith.

"It's not her."

Meredith pursed his lips and nodded. "Good. I've got to see the Welsh boys. When I get back I'll expect the details of what she did, where she went, and who she saw yesterday, hour by hour, on my desk." He looked at Williams who was perched on the edge of a desk listening, and jerked his head towards the door. "Come on, let's get this done. As you can see, I'm up to my ears."

"Two police officers in two days. Bloody nightmare for you. I hope you find your girl safe and sound. But Henshaw can't tell you who killed Phil. This will be a waste of time for you."

"We'll see, shall we?" Meredith led the way back to the interview room.

Williams put the coffee on the table, and Henshaw picked one up, wrapping his hands around it and hunching his shoulders as though he were sitting in a chill wind.

Meredith hit the record button. "Interview with DS Andrew Henshaw, also present DCI Dan Williams, and DCI John Meredith. We'll commence with reading DS Henshaw his rights."

As Meredith ran through the familiar words, Henshaw shot a puzzled glance at Williams, who simply shook his head.

"Would you confirm for the recording that you have come here voluntarily, and that you have chosen not to have legal representation?"

"I confirm both." Henshaw drank his coffee and looked down. Williams pushed his own towards him and he nodded his thanks.

"When Cathy Davies told you she was pregnant and it was yours, what were your first thoughts?" Meredith raised his eyebrows at the sharp intake of breath from Williams. It was clear that Henshaw had been less than open with him.

"I shit myself. I think I'm in love with Cathy, otherwise I wouldn't have bothered, what with her being with Phil. But I knew that if he found out, it would crucify him. I thought . . ."

"What did you think?" Meredith caught Henshaw's eye, and Henshaw looked down

"My initial thought was, shit, he's going to kill me."

"How did he react when he found out?"

Henshaw's head snapped back up. "Did he find out? Did she tell him? She didn't tell me she told him."

Meredith ignored the question. "So what was the call to him about yesterday morning?"

Henshaw scratched his forehead and shrugged. "Nothing, just chatting."

"Quick chat. Two minutes, hardly worth the effort. If you'd said we arranged to meet in the pub, or he wanted to know if I had tickets for the match, I'd go for it. As it was two minutes to *chat* I don't buy it. Why are you lying?"

Meredith could feel the tension in Williams. He had done what any good Governor would do; given the facts he knew, and stood by his man. Now he was questioning his own judgement. Meredith let the silence drag on a little. Without warning, he banged the table with his fists as hard as he could. Both Williams and Henshaw jumped.

"Right, stop fucking about. Now! I've got a copper with a ten-inch knife sticking out of his neck on a slab, and one of my female officers has disappeared." As Meredith shouted, he thought Henshaw was going to cry, and he wanted to punch him. He detested everything he knew about him, and now, to top it all, he was shitless.

Leaning forward he pointed into Henshaw's face, his finger perilously close to the man's eye. "Now you start telling the truth, or I'll bang you up for as long as I can, then apply for an extension, because quite frankly, pissing about with you is stopping me finding my officer. Which would you rather?"

Meredith wiped away the spittle at the corners of his mouth with the back of his hand. Henshaw cleared his throat and held his hands up.

"All right, all right. He thought he knew. He didn't but he put two and two together, he had no proof. He'd given Cathy a hard time on the phone the night before and she was scared of him. She asked me to have a word. But he wouldn't listen."

From the corner of his eye Meredith saw Williams lean back and cross his hands across his chest. The negative gesture wasn't lost on Henshaw.

"Gov, you have to believe me, I didn't kill him."

"So what was the two-minute conversation?" Meredith didn't allow Williams to respond to Henshaw.

"He answered the phone and told me to fuck off. I asked him to listen, told him he had it all wrong and that he shouldn't read something that wasn't there into something that meant nothing."

"So you simply spouted bullshit?"

"Pretty much, yes."

"He didn't believe you, though, so how was it left?"

"He told me he saw, he knew, and I would pay dearly for crossing him."

"So you thought, sod this for a game of soldiers, jumped in your car, sorted him out, and went back to your interviews. Is that what happened, Henshaw?"

"NO! No, he hung up and switched his phone off. I didn't do the interviews because I wasn't in any fit state. I had two problems now, him telling me he was going to sort me, and Cathy being pregnant."

"What if he had believed you? What then? How were you going to deal with the pregnant Cathy?"

Henshaw lowered his head. "She was going to get rid of it. It wasn't going to be a problem."

Meredith snorted. "Let's see if I've got this right. You're shagging your mate's missus, and knock her up. You tell us you *think* you love her, but you're quite content to sit back and let her destroy your child and carry on letting him break his back to keep her in the manner to which she would like to become accustomed. Nice."

Meredith stared at Henshaw with contempt. "And once the baby's dispatched, and they snuggle down again, what then? Because at no stage have you even suggested that what you had going with that whore, Cathy, was over."

It was Henshaw's turn to bang the desk. "She's not a whore!"

Meredith watched the veins bulge in Henshaw's neck and smirked. He'd got there. "Oh right, because in my book men that shag around are bastards," he nodded knowingly, "and women who do, and continue to empty the bank account, are whores. So it was true love, was it?"

"I think so, yes."

"Ah, there it is again, that word. Think." Meredith looked at Williams and shook his head before turning back to Henshaw. "So, you do know it's wrong, but you can't stop because you *think* you're in love. You get rid of the baby so everything seems normal, but I ask again, what then?"

Meredith stood abruptly and started pacing. "You see, Henshaw, you've told me nothing to convince me that you didn't want him out of the way. You wanted him dead. You were scared of him, and you wanted what was his. The whore inherits everything and you settle down to a nice little life, all paid for by his insurance, and the bonus? You get to keep the baby."

Henshaw flew up out of the chair and marched towards Meredith. "If you call her a whore one more time . . ."

Williams jumped up and stood between them. "You'll what?" taunted Meredith. "You'll kill me?"

Henshaw's arms fell limp at his side, Williams pushed him back to his chair.

As he sat and covered his face, Meredith arrested him. "Andrew Henshaw, I'm arresting you on suspicion of the murder of Phillip Cowell, you do not have -"

"I didn't do it," Henshaw said quietly.

Meredith finished what he had to say and opened the door. "This way. I can't waste any more time on you at the moment, I've got an officer who deserves my attention."

Williams grabbed Henshaw by the elbow and yanked him up. He didn't resist, and they followed Meredith to the cells. Meredith nodded at the custody sergeant.

"Morning, George." He jerked his thumb at Henshaw, "Andrew Henshaw, arrested on suspicion of the murder of Phillip Cowell. Book him in, bang him up, and check if he wants a solicitor in a couple of hours. I've got to get back to the team." He turned to Williams, "I'll leave you to observe, I need to get on."

Williams nodded as Henshaw was asked to empty his pockets.

Having established that the team had nothing new, Meredith went to his office to think. He wasn't at all sure that Henshaw had done it, but it would be cleansing for his soul if he hadn't, and if he had, he could wait. There was no hurry.

Linda and Louie Trump burst through the front door giggling like teenagers. Patsy, who had fallen asleep on the couch, woke with a start.

She yawned and stretched as they came into the room.

"Late night, PHPI?" Linda chirped. PHPI was short for 'Patsy Hodge Private Investigator', Linda's pet name for her. "Patsy, we had such a good time. We went to see *The Lion King*, it was absolutely brilliant. I'll put the kettle on and tell you all about it." She unbuttoned her coat and revealed a bright orange tee shirt, emblazoned with the words, 'Hakuna Matata'.

"Right, kettle." She turned to leave.

Patsy smiled at her before turning to Louie. "I think you need to get to work. Once you've had a cup of tea, of course."

"Oh boy, what's happened? I heard about the stabbing of the police officer but was told I wasn't needed until tomorrow. Has there been a development? In fact, how do you know?" He looked puzzled for a moment, and grinned at her as the penny dropped. "Patsy Hodge, have you been keeping company with DCI Meredith? You have, haven't you?"

Patsy raised her eyebrows and gave a wink, as Linda came scuttling back down the hall. Patsy held her hand up, "That's a story for another time. No, it's not the murder, it's Jo Adler. She's gone missing. Not been seen or heard of since about six o'clock yesterday evening. What time is it?" Patsy looked at her watch; it was twelve-fifteen. "Blimey, I really did have a nap."

Louie leaned across and pulled Linda's face forward and kissed her. "I have to go, Linda. You do understand, don't you? I'll give you a call later."

As Linda nodded her agreement, he disappeared back the way he had come. Linda smiled at Patsy. "I know she's a mate, and you are naturally very worried and what have you, but if you have been with Meredith I want to know about it now. I'll make coffee first because I want details!"

Linda placed the coffee on the table in front on Patsy. Sitting in the opposite chair, she leaned forward, her face serious. "Before I grill you about you know who, I am aware that Jo going missing is serious and you must be very worried. Do you want to talk about that first? Exactly what happened?"

"I'm not sure. Jo was working because I happened across a police officer who had been murdered. Her weekend leave was cancelled and we should have been -"

"Whoa! What do mean, you happened across a dead copper? Where? How?"

Patsy told Linda the story, and Linda sat open-mouthed, looking at her.

"We decided going out last night was not a good idea, and I was trying to reach her yesterday while I waited for Meredith and couldn't get her."

"Bloody hell, a murder just around the corner, and what with Jo . . ." Linda paused, leaving what they were both thinking unsaid. "I'm sure she'll be fine. But it must be very worrying – two police officers in two days. Do they think they're connected in any way?" Linda sighed. "Well I have to say that's taken the wind out of my sail. I almost don't want to know what's been going on with Meredith." She allowed a small smile. "But only almost."

"I don't think they are connected. It seems as though the poor chap I found yesterday was a domestic thing. Whatever has happened to Jo isn't going to be a part of that."

Patsy fell silent.

Linda could only contain herself for a few minutes. "And . . . you were going to tell me what happened with you and Meredith. Come on, spit it out, you're smiling just thinking about it."

"I've been avoiding any contact with him, as you know, but finding a dead body sort of put me in his line of fire." Patsy raised her eyebrows, and Linda grinned. "Anyway, I told him he had to date me, and last night he . . . I must get that, it could be news on Jo."

Patsy jumped out of the chair and rushed to pick up her phone. She groaned as she picked it up.

"Hi, Frankie." Patsy listened as Frankie told her he would collect her in half an hour. She shook her head as she responded, "Sorry, Frankie, please don't take this the wrong way, but can we do this another time? Jo Adler has gone missing and I'm not in the mood for socialising."

For the second time in the last thirty minutes, Patsy repeated what she knew about the disappearance of Jo Adler.

"I'm sure she'll turn up safe and well," Frankie didn't sound confident. "But, Patsy, I really would like to see you. We won't do anything flamboyant, a pie and a pint will do, but I have something to ask and I would prefer to do it face to face."

He sounded concerned and would not be drawn. Patsy agreed to be ready for collection.

She turned to Linda. "Sorry, Linda, I have to go and get ready. I forgot I had a lunch date with Frankie today, so I need to shower. We'll catch up later, if that's okay?"

"No, not at all okay. You make yourself look respectable and I'll listen."

Linda sat on the toilet as Patsy showered and told her about the night before.

"So you gave in and stayed the night? Ha! How could you resist, what a stupid question."

Standing, she retrieved a towel from the back of the door, which she held out to Patsy. Patsy wrapped it around her body and stepped out of the shower.

"So come on, tell all. Was it worth it?"

Pulling the shower cap from her head, Patsy's hair tumbled around her shoulders as she turned to Linda, her expression serious. Linda was momentarily concerned that something had gone wrong.

"I don't know how to explain it, I really don't. The best I can do is that even when what he's doing is nothing special, if you know what I mean, it's so special it scares me. Now go away and let me finish getting ready."

Linda looked at her friend with a mixture of envy and awe before she shrugged and sniffed. "Patsy, you should see your face when you speak about him. Really, get a grip. Stop messing about and get it sorted. Now, I'm going to make myself some lunch and ponder on how to get Louie to scare me."

While waiting for Frankie to arrive, Patsy had texted Meredith to find that Jo's car had been found parked in The Mall car park, and CCTV had shown it had been there all night. The team were now working through a myriad of recordings trying to spot Jo. So far they had been unsuccessful, and her car was being brought in for forensic examination. Things weren't looking good. Patsy told Meredith that she would get Frankie to take her to the Dirty Duck, and pop over and see him once they'd had lunch. Meredith hadn't responded, and she assumed something had happened. She crossed her fingers, hoping it was positive.

The Wrong Shoes

5

Frankie took the orders and went to the bar. Other than to state how horrified he'd been to hear about Jo, he'd been quiet on the ten-minute journey to the pub.

"What does he need to see me about?" Patsy was concerned at Frankie's insistence on seeing her, and thought forearmed was forewarned.

"Let's wait for Frankie. He's been so concerned about it, I'm convinced he didn't sleep last night," Sarah smiled apologetically. "Here he comes."

Frankie walked back to the table carefully, clasping the three drinks between his hands. The pint glass slowly dribbled beer over one hand. Patsy stood and took the two wine glasses from him. He shook the beer from his hand before wiping it on his jeans.

"Thanks, Pats. It was touch and go for a moment. I ordered extra chips, by the way, I know you two will eat them if they arrive." Taking a seat, he sipped at his pint. The two women watched him. His eyes narrowed. "Why are you watching me? What have I done?"

"Spit it out, Frankie. Tell me why I'm here. Other than to enjoy your charming company, of course." Patsy screwed her face up and tutted. "I forgot, you've been to see Tanya, haven't you? How did that go?"

Frankie smiled and shook his head. "Shouldn't that be, 'You've been to see Tanya, how is she?'?"

Shrugging, Patsy drew her fingers around the ring marks on the table. "Probably, but to be honest I'm not sure if I care. I'm more worried about how it will affect you." She caught the silent exchange between Frankie and Sarah and took a large sip of her wine. Placing her glass on the centre of the coaster she turned to face him. "Okay, that was worrying. I say again, Frankie, spit it out."

Frankie raised his eyebrows, and shrugged at Sarah. Deciding to take the bull by the horns, he said simply, "Tanya wants to see you."

Patsy had been taking a sip of her drink and coughed violently as the shock of that statement caused her to choke. Frankie was patting her on the back as Meredith walked in.

"Sherlock, unhand that woman."

Frankie rolled his eyes and Patsy gulped in air as her coughing fit subsided. Meredith called to the barman for a beer and eyed the group. To his mind they all looked a little guilty. Taking his drink from the barman, he sat between Patsy and Sarah.

"Who's going to tell me what's going on?" He looked first to Sarah, who shook her head, and he smiled. "Right, that tells me something is going on, so what?"

"Tanya wants me to go and visit her."

"Jennings does? No wonder you were choking. Why?"

They both looked at Frankie.

"I don't know. She wouldn't tell me. I promise you I asked, didn't I, Sarah?" Looking to Sarah for confirmation, Frankie put his hand into the back pocket of his jeans and pulled out an envelope. "She even had the visiting order ready for you." He held it out to Patsy.

Patsy opened the envelope and pulled out the contents. It was a letter informing her of prison protocol and a visiting order. Patsy looked at the date.

"But this is for Wednesday. That's only three days away. How could she possibly know I would go?"

"She didn't. She's allowed visitors twice a month. Visits are Wednesdays and Saturdays. I assume if you couldn't make it, she would send one for a different date."

"But why did she give it to you? Why not write to me?"

Frankie looked at Meredith who had pursed his lips. "I'm not sure. But it's probably something to do with Meredith. You know how she was."

Tanya Jennings had loved Meredith from a distance for years. Biding her time, believing that one day he would notice her. She had encouraged his wife to leave him and watched as he had one affair after the other. On one occasion she had even ejected a spurned lover from the police station. When Meredith had taken an interest in Patsy, Tanya had been devastated.

"Do you really have no idea? Because I'm not going all the way there to be insulted. She hates me, Frankie, you know that."

"She said she needed your help."

They all turned to look at Sarah.

"When Frankie expressed his doubt, she said 'Tell her I need her help, that will make her come'. She looked so sad when she said it, like she was giving in, or showing weakness. She clearly thought that you would like to feel needed by her."

Patsy shook her head. "Still as weird as ever then. I'm sorry, but even if by some miracle I can be of help to her, I don't know that I want to go. She probably has some twisted plan up her sleeve to mess me about, or attempt to belittle me." Patsy looked at Meredith. "What do you think?"

Meredith looked from Patsy to Frankie. The lines at the corners of his eyes betrayed his bemusement. He wished he was alone with Patsy.

Pushing his glass to the centre of the table, he leaned forward. "I wasn't sure I was allowed an opinion. But as you've asked, I can see nothing in it for you."

"What's that supposed to mean?" demanded Frankie.

"What it says. Even if Jennings does need Patsy for some reason, although I'm buggered if I can guess what, what's in it for Patsy? Jennings did her no favours, and she's not about to start now. It will be a one-sided arrangement, if, of course, there is anything to arrange. Why should Patsy bother?"

"Do you know, Meredith, you never cease to amaze me. Just because there's nothing in it for you, doesn't mean that you can't do some good for others." Frankie shook his head, a look of distaste on his face.

Meredith stared at him a while and chose his words carefully, and tried to deliver them without sarcasm. "Sherlock, I know you're related, and that you feel in some way responsible for what she did, given your mother's involvement. But look at it from Patsy's point of view. Is trying to be a Good Samaritan only going to bring her more grief?" He looked at Patsy. "End of the day, Patsy, it's down to you. Can you spare the time? Are you willing to risk a wild goose chase, or do you want to get on with your life?" He sipped his pint and shrugged. "It's your shout."

Patsy was saved answering by the arrival of the food.

Meredith finished his drink. "I'll leave you to it. I only popped in to say 'hello, enjoy your lunch'. Are you still coming in later?" He tried to keep his tone casual, but it sounded like an order. Patsy bit back a smile and nodded. "Good. Bye, Sarah, as always it's been a pleasure." He looked at Frankie, "Sherlock." Leaning across the table he grabbed a handful of chips and walked away.

~ ~ ~

Taking a bite of his pasty, Meredith pushed the play button again. He watched Jo Adler enter the Mall via the south entrance. She walked through the Mall, paused at the fountain and something appeared to catch her eye as she turned and walked briskly to the staircase. She took the first two steps and her image was lost; the camera at the top of the stairs wasn't working. Fifteen minutes later, Jo was picked up as she entered the top floor entrance of the John Lewis department store. Pausing at the perfume counter, she sprayed a tester on her wrists before she walked away to the back of the store. Despite watching hours of coverage of the various exits, she was not seen leaving the Mall. He already knew that she had arrived alone, and only the security guard had given her car a second glance at ten-thirty the night before.

He turned to Trump. "So, she went in and apparently didn't come out. Is that because she's still there, or because someone managed to take her out without being noticed." He scratched his head. "You and Rawlings get up there with a couple of uniforms, and search every storeroom, cupboard and toilet in the building. Starting with John Lewis. I'll get someone to watch this lot again, this time concentrating on large packages coming out and tracking back where they came from."

Meredith's phone rang, and he rummaged in his pocket. He listened for a few minutes, said only two words, his name and "right", then shook his head and hung up.

"They've bailed Henshaw pending further inquiry. He has to report to Cardiff Central. I need to draft a few more bodies in." He looked at Trump and shook his head. "Go on, get going."

Standing, Meredith tossed the remainder of his pasty into the bin. Hands in his pockets and shoulders hunched, he walked slowly back to the incident room. It was four o'clock and Jo had been missing for almost twenty-four hours. The door to door enquiries in Phillip Cowell's street had been fruitless. Henshaw had claimed to have spent the morning in the McDonald's on Castle Street, prior to making the two calls. If that checked out, Henshaw would be released from bail, and Meredith had nothing to go on with either case. He looked at the pale, tired faces of his team as he pushed open the door to the incident room, knowing he would have to send most of them home in the next couple of hours or they would be of no use to him.

Trump was standing next to Rawlings, who was pulling on his jacket. Seaton was sitting on the corner of Rawlings' desk. Meredith hoped something, anything, had turned up. He looked across expectantly.

"Anything I should know?" He held his hand up as his phone rang. It was Patsy. He told her to give him five minutes.

Seaton walked towards him, several papers rolled into a cylinder in his hand. He waved them at Meredith. "Good shout sending them up to John Lewis. Jo made a call there on Friday night. The last two people she spoke to on Friday were Patsy and Nancy Bailey, the woman that found Cowell."

Meredith picked up the receiver and called Nancy Bailey. As he replaced it, Patsy knocked on his open door and stepped into his office.

"Any news?" She didn't feel hopeful; there were only a couple of officers manning the phones, and Meredith.

"Not as yet. Her car has revealed nothing obvious. They're analysing some crumbs of something from the footwell, but it's unlikely to be anything useful. A gang of lads are up at the Mall searching anywhere she could be hidden, et cetera, et cetera. And Jo spoke to Nancy Bailey yesterday, so I'm popping in to see her. I need to be sure she didn't say something to her that would help us. How was your lunch?" His eyes locked hers, and she grinned at him.

"Once you'd left, for some reason the mood was much lighter. Although I haven't decided what I'm going to do, if that's what you're asking. Is there anything I can do now?"

"You can come and see Nancy with me. She likes you, she told me so. Where is your car?"

"At Linda's, Frankie picked me up." She watched his eyebrows rise.

"And is he taking you home too?"

"No! He's gone. I told him you would take me home, but if you can't I can grab a taxi."

"Sounds like a deal. Let's go and see what Nancy knows, if anything."

~ ~ ~

The door opened as Meredith reached forward for the bell.

"Come in, come in." Nancy ushered them through to the kitchen.

Patsy smiled at the faint smell of furniture polish as she walked through the hall to a spotless kitchen, and her thoughts drifted back to Phillip Cowell's home. Nancy clearly kept her own home in the same condition as she afforded her clients.

"Do you know? Have you found out?" Nancy looked up expectantly from the tea cups she was arranging in their saucers. She shook her head, looking more than a little irritated, as Meredith told her he didn't. "I got quite hopeful when you said you needed to see me urgently. If you don't know who killed him, what is it I can do for you?"

Patsy raised her eyebrows at Meredith who had also caught the irritation. Nancy opened the cupboard and took out a brightly coloured tin from the lower shelf. Patsy noted the regimented organisation in the cupboard. In order of height on the upper shelf sat several cereal boxes, a large bag of pasta, flour, sugar and birdseed. Two further highly coloured cake tins were stored on the shallower bottom shelf.

"We have some thoughts on that, Nancy, which I will speak to you about, but first I need to speak to you about DC Adler."

"Jo, you mean. Why?" Nancy put the cups down on the kitchen table, and slid the biscuit tin to Meredith. "Help yourself. Chocolate chip cookies, I made them yesterday." Nancy looked at Patsy with a faint smile, "I thought you told me you weren't with the police. Did you lie for some reason?"

"No, no, of course not," Patsy assured her. "It so happens that I am friends with both DCI Meredith and Jo Adler. I was with Meredith when we heard Jo was missing."

Nancy spun back to Patsy. "She's missing? I only saw her yesterday."

"Saw her? I thought you only spoke to her." Meredith re-joined the conversation. Having Patsy with him, despite her connections, was unorthodox. He inclined his head and looked at Nancy. "Would you rather Patsy waited in the car?"

"No, of course not. After all, two heads are better than one." Nancy flipped her hand dismissing the question. "Tell me what you think has happened to Jo, and how you think I can help."

Ignoring her question, Meredith asked one of his own. "When did you see Jo, Nancy?"

"Yesterday, she helped me with a flat pack I had bought for my nephew."

Meredith stared at her as though she were speaking a foreign language. "Flat pack?"

"When she took me home on Friday, you know, after I found Phillip and came to the station, she offered to help. I'm getting my nephew's room ready, you see, and needed help getting this flat pack stuff out of my car."

"But that was the day before yesterday," Patsy commented, frowning.

"I know that, I'm explaining." Nancy gave Meredith a glance and smiled patiently at Patsy as though she were a little slow. "Jo gave me her card and said I should shout if I thought of anything else, or if she could help. So she came round yesterday to help me bring it in and put it in his room." Nancy tutted and put her hands on her hips, "You look tired the pair of you, shall I show you? Will that help?"

Meredith shook his head and smiled. "We are tired. Jo has been missing since around teatime yesterday. What time did you say she was here?"

"Mid-afternoon, I don't know exactly, but she did say she was going shopping. I didn't ask where, I should have, shouldn't I? Poor Jo. You will find her, won't you DCI Meredith?" Nancy lifted her apron and dabbed her eyes, "She'll be safe, I know it. Not like poor Phillip."

Meredith stood up and took hold of her hand. "I promise you two things, Nancy. The first is that I will find Jo, and she will be well, and the second is that I will catch whoever killed Phillip. I need you to believe that."

Nancy squeezed his hand before lifting it and kissing it. "I believe you." She nodded. "You will, I know. You didn't have a biscuit. Look, take them with you for the boys at the station. You can drop the tin back round when you're passing." Nancy handed Meredith the tin and showed them out. "As soon as you know something, you will let me know, won't you? Just pop in, if I'm here there will always be a cup of tea on the go."

"I'll hold you to that, Nancy. I must go now, but we'll be in touch." He paused before asking, "One other thing to do with Phillip, did you know he had sold his house and was planning on moving to Cardiff?"

"I did. Not long ago, mind you." Nancy grimaced briefly as she thought back. "I'm not sure why he left it so long to tell me. He must have known months ago. But I think he could have been having second thoughts, and only told me once his mind had finally been made up."

"Second thoughts? What did he say?"

"Not a lot, and that's what hurt." Nancy ran her hands down her apron and looked at the floor momentarily before looking up at Meredith. "He said that he had meant to tell me, and something had happened that made him question whether he was doing the right thing, but now he had made his mind up." She shrugged, "That's all he said, something had happened. He looked sad, but I didn't like to pry. He was going to help with Gary's room. Did I mention Gary? He's my nephew, more like a son really, now that his mother's gone."

Meredith nodded and thanked her for her time. Nancy watched them walk back to the car. She saw the little pat Meredith delivered to Patsy's backside before he opened the door and smiled. They made a lovely-looking couple, and Meredith seemed such a genuine man. Much like Phillip had been. She dabbed her eyes again as the car pulled away.

"I thought you were going to get drawn into redecorating or something for a moment," Patsy laughed as they pulled away. "She's a sweetie, but she clearly knows how to encourage assistance."

They had reached the end of the street and Meredith turned left.

"Hang on a minute, I'm in the other direction."

"But my need is greater than yours. I haven't showered for nearly twenty-four hours, and I stink. You, on the other hand, smell fabulous. I think I can grab a couple of hours. You haven't got to be anywhere, have you?"

"I haven't, but I'm not sure about this. What happened to taking it slow and courting me?" Patsy shook her head as though disappointed.

Meredith grinned at her and raised his eyebrows. He knew from her demeanour that she had no intention of going home just yet.

"I was simply asking you to wait while I got cleaned up. A nap would have been nice, but I'll take you home when you want."

As he pulled onto the drive, his heart sank. A young girl hugging a bag to her chest was knocking at the door. Amanda opened it, and waved to Meredith who was climbing out of the car.

"You timed that well. Kelly has come round to do some course work with me, and I've made chilli con carne." Amanda smiled as Patsy opened the passenger door. "There's enough for four, I always make extra chilli."

"Bugger," Meredith muttered, before calling back. "Lovely, can't think of anything nicer." He ignored Patsy's snigger as she followed him along the path.

An hour and a half later, showered, fed and more than a little frustrated, Meredith dozed on the settee in the living room as Patsy helped the girls clear up. He was jolted awake by a message arriving on his mobile. Sighing, he rubbed his tired eyes and picked up the phone. He was fully awake in a split second, and swinging his legs to the floor he called to Patsy. The message was from Jo.

Help me. Please be quick, don't let it happen again.

He passed the phone to Patsy as she hurried into the room.

"What the hell does that mean? Don't let what happen again?" he asked as she read the message.

An hour later he was sitting in the incident room with Louie Trump.

"Jo disappears on Cribbs Causeway, doesn't use her phone for over twenty-four hours and then we get this from the centre of town. Now the phone is off again so we are no further forward."

"We have officers down there, and those that don't know her have been issued with her photograph. The problem we have is the response time. Twenty minutes from when you received the message to the call being placed is simply too long. If she was in a car she could be anywhere by now. It's not looking good, is it?" Louie stood and stretched, and covering a loud yawn, he added, "At least there's a live alert on the phone now. If she tries to make contact again, even if we can't get there, we'll be able to build a pattern of where she's been. At least she made contact."

"Did she? How do we know it was her?"

"What, you think it's her abductor? To what end?"

"Taunting us, or perhaps me. The message said: 'don't let it happen again'. That would imply that they've done something to her, God knows what, and if I don't find her sharpish, they'll do it again." Meredith rubbed his hands over his face and gave a roar. "Bollocks, I feel so fucking impotent! Let's do something useful while we wait and see if she tries again. Bring the files on Cowell's cases over. Too late to save him, but we can get the bastard that did it."

"You've changed your mind about Henshaw?" Trump asked as he walked towards the pile of files on Rawlings' desk.

"Never say never, Trump, but I think it's unlikely."

Trump dropped the files onto the table and sat down with a sigh. He picked up the top one.

"Hit and run. A blue Mondeo apparently lost control, mounted the kerb and hit two suspected drug dealers in Bute Town, Cardiff. It was found burned out the next day on an industrial estate about five miles away. They found evidence of drug paraphernalia in the car, and think it was a rival gang. Cowell had pulled several in for questioning and -"

"Nope. Don't think they'd come to Bristol and sneak up on him. Next."

Trump placed the file to one side and took the next. "This one's waiting to go to court. Scorned woman case. Mistress of a married chap set fire to his family home. House was gutted, dog died, but the family escaped."

"I don't think so, do you? Next."

For the next two hours Trump took Meredith through the cases Phillip Cowell had dealt with during the last year. As he closed the last file, Meredith looked up at the clock.

"Come on, Louie, let's get out of here for a couple of hours. I'll call Cardiff in the morning and get a list of the cases he was involved with prior to this lot. But for now I need to sleep."

The house was in darkness when he arrived home and he closed the door quietly. As he climbed the stairs, he hoped he would find Patsy waiting for him. He was disappointed. Dropping his clothes where they fell, he climbed on the bed, and without even lifting the duvet he fell into a deep sleep.

~ ~ ~

"I know I said I would do this properly, Bobby, you know, using the computer and a diary, and I will. But I've been so busy time seems to run away with me."

Bobby didn't respond, but he watched as his companion flipped open the notepad to a new page and picked up the pen.

"I've decided to write bits down and later I'll type it all up when I have more time. I've got to prepare dinner in a moment so I'll jot down some notes on Wendy. That shouldn't take too long, should it?"

Bobby stretched his neck and rolled his head around before looking back at the pad.

"You're right. I should get on with it, and then I'll see to you first. I think you deserve a treat."

The chair was pulled closer to the table, and the notepad forward. The pen moved hesitantly at first before seeming to find a momentum of its own as words filled line after line in the pad.

I had no intention of harming Wendy. We'd become friends. Despite her important job, she was lonely too. Her husband running off with that young girl really knocked her hard. She started avoiding going out, unless it was something she couldn't avoid. Her so-called friends stopped calling after a couple of months, so she was glad of my company. I needed her too. We were very different, of course, but it worked, and we settled into a pattern of discussing things that we could both relate to.

One night, just after the six o'clock news, she called and asked if I had a couple of hours as she'd decided to clear all traces of him, her husband that is, out of the house. I could tell she'd been drinking again. I went straight away. I even got a taxi so I could have a drink with her. Things went well until she suggested that I move in. I was flattered, I mean, who'd have thought that Wendy Turnball would want more of my company. But it wasn't what I wanted. I still had so much to do to sort myself out, I couldn't see that it would work. I knew that she only needed someone there, you know, that I was better than nothing. That didn't matter to me, but it wasn't right for me. I tried to explain as best I could. She was quite drunk by this time and didn't take it very well.

"Are you doing this for the right reasons?" Wendy demanded. She put on that voice she uses at work and it rankled a little, but I poured her another drink, sat her at the kitchen table, and I tried to explain.

"Of course I am. You must understand that I have to see this through. I will sort it in the end, and then we'll see." I reached to pat her hand but she pulled it away.

"See what through? Please don't tell me you still think you know better!" She laughed at me. "I'm telling you now, as I've told you before, you're simply barking up the wrong tree. Keeping on about this will simply cause you more grief. Get me another drink. If you're going to start on this road again, I'll need more alcohol."

"Wendy, I know what you think, and I understand why you think that, but I know." The cork came out of the bottle with a pop and I pointed it at her, still attached to the cork screw. "It was the shoes, even you can't explain that."

She lifted her chin and pointed back at me. I saw her hand was trembling again; I think it was the drink, and I wondered whether I should give her another one. I think she was becoming an alcoholic and I shouldn't really encourage her. But then she said it and I froze.

"You stupid, stupid, little person. Do you think that you were so special that they wouldn't leave you? You knew how unhappy they had become, how confused." She shook her head and looked down her nose at me, "But still you think you were worth it. Well, take it from me, you weren't. None of us are in the end. Selfishness is a human condition, as is a sense of self-importance. In the end none of us are important. Not me, not you." She pointed at me again and rolled her eyes at me.

I carried the wine across the kitchen and I knew with certainty she hadn't even tried. That she hadn't ever believed me, and she had lied about trying to help. For a moment I thought I would kill her right then and there with the bottle. I thought about it as I walked towards her, and then it came to me. Let's see how clever you lot really are. I poured the wine into her glass and purposely missed. I poured it into her lap instead, all over her favourite white trousers. When she screeched and jumped up, I slopped some over her top for good measure.

"I'm so sorry. How clumsy. You need to get those in the wash. Come on, strip off and I'll put them in the machine."

Cursing, Wendy stormed off to the bedroom. I followed her up the stairs.

"I'll run you a bath," I called. "Then I'll get those clothes sorted."

The bath was deep and the scent from the bath salts will always remind me of Wendy. She had her towelling robe on when she came out of the bedroom and dropped her clothes at the top of the stairs. She smiled at me.

"Don't worry, accidents happen." She paused before she went into the bathroom. "I'm sorry if I was harsh. I didn't mean to be, but you do have to let it go."

I returned her smile, knowing that that was impossible, and as I smiled, I knew that it was too late for her to be sorry. I picked up her clothes and heard the bath water sloshing against the side of the bath as I hurried downstairs. I threw the clothes into the washing machine with an extra scoop of powder, switched it on, and prepared her another drink. I took five of her sleeping tablets, she'd been on those for about six months, and I crushed them up. I mixed them into her wine, went back upstairs, and tapped on the bathroom door. She smiled as I held out the glass.

"Thank you. I don't think I'll manage it though. I think I've had too much again. I feel quite sleepy."

"Well, you need to relax. Have a sip of this. I have to go and clean the floor too. I'm so clumsy. I'll call a taxi while I'm at it."

The taxi came, and I was home in ten minutes. I waited for an hour or so, and I drove back to Wendy's and let myself in. I knew she would have drunk the wine and would be sleeping. My plan was to suffocate her. It wouldn't have taken much, not in the state she was in. You can't imagine my surprise when I found her asleep in the bath. The water was stone cold and lapping around her chin. I sat on the toilet watching her as I wondered what to do. Suddenly it seemed so simple.

I took a rubber glove from the cupboard under the basin and put it on. I walked to the end of the bath, put my hand on her head, and pushed it down. Simple! Her eyes opened and I could see her staring up at me through the bluish water. She opened her mouth to speak and water rushed in. She coughed, causing more to follow. Her foot shot out of the water

69

and hit the tap and her hands splashed about a little, and then she was still. I dried the glove and put it away. I dried the edge of the bath and the floor tiles with a towel, which I hung over the radiator. I locked up and went back to my car which I had parked at the other end of the street, and drove home to Bobby.

It was almost two days before anyone contacted me. Her brother, it was. He told me Wendy had had an accident. That she had taken a mixture of sleeping pills and alcohol, fallen asleep in the bath and drowned. They had an inquest of course. The verdict? Accidental death. The idiots! Just too lazy to bother, and she was important too. What hope was there for the rest of us mere mortals?

"Well, Bobby, that's that one done. Let's get dinner sorted."

~ ~ ~

Jo Adler didn't bother to get up when she heard the door open. She watched the metal grill until the now familiar feet appeared.

"It's only me. I've brought you some dinner. I thought that as we had fish yesterday, we'd have Italian today, and if I do say so myself I make a good lasagne. Garlic bread too."

Jo closed her eyes and sighed. Who else would it be? Her breath caught in her throat. Maybe there were two of them, or perhaps more. After all, despite the assurances to the contrary, this had obviously been planned for some time. The tray was placed on the floor and she watched it slide beneath the grill. She had left her plate and mug from lunchtime on the other side, and as they were picked up, she wondered why it was she who had been taken. Was it chance, an opportunist thing, or perhaps because she was a police officer? A lump welled in her throat and she swallowed. She forced a smile, and swinging her legs off the bed she stood to face her abductor.

"It smells great. My husband loves lasagne, but I doubt he'll be eating though. Please let me at least call him to let him know I'm safe. He'll be out of his mind with worry, you must understand that. You've been so kind to me, I need to let him know that. At least that will help him."

Jo saw the hesitation. She pressed the point.

"I know you don't want to hurt me, that's obvious, but I don't know why I'm here. Perhaps if you tell me, I can help in some way. Are you holding me hostage for something in particular? If so I have to tell you we don't have any money. We have a mortgage and very little equity in the house, and we blew what savings we had on a holiday to Mauritius at the end of last year."

"I don't want money, you silly girl. I want help."

Despite thinking that was the understatement of the year, Jo bit her tongue. "Is that why you took me?"

She watched the puzzled frown. "That's what I just said, isn't it?"

"No, not really, you said it was because you needed help. Is it because I'm a police officer, or because it's me the person?"

"Oh, I see. It's because of DCI Meredith," came the explanation, which explained nothing. "How do you rate him, your DCI Meredith?"

"What? How would holding me here help you? What's Meredith done?" Jo walked towards the grill, her dinner still sitting on the tray before it as they turned to go. "Please don't go, I'm going crazy down here. Please at least stay and talk to me."

"I'll try and come down later. I have to go now. I promised Bobby. Eat your dinner, and if Bobby nods off I'll come back down. You didn't say what you thought of Mr Meredith."

"He's the best copper I've ever worked with, why? Tell me what you want from him."

"Good, that's what I thought. Now, I must dash."

As Jo bent to pick up the tray, she saw her hands were shaking. The mention of Bobby had confirmed it, there were at least two of them. Placing the tray on the table she looked at her watch. She had been here for over twenty-four hours. Pulling out the chair, she slumped down, and wondered what Meredith had done to cause this situation.

6

Meredith slammed the phone down and called to Trump. "Bring that list of cases in here. Let's go through them again. The top brass are getting jumpy, and rightly so. We've got one dead, one missing, and bugger all to go on."

Trump picked up the list of cases that Phillip Cowell had been working on. Phillip had been dead for four days and they were no further forward. They were now going through the painstaking task of burrowing into the detail of each and every case he had worked on. Henshaw's alibi had held up, and he was currently on leave. Trump placed the sheets in front of Meredith. Each case had been summarised on one page of A4.

"Are you sure I have to be the one to liaise with the *Crimebusters'* team, sir? I rather think it must be Tom Seaton's turn."

"I'm sure. You speak proper so they like you." Meredith looked up and gave Trump a brief smile. "Seaton has been assigned to inputting the detail of this lot together with the two new chaps they've given us. By the way, did you speak to Aaron?"

Trump dropped into the chair opposite Meredith, his face grim.

"I did. He's in a bad way. What can one say? It's all right for us, I mean at least we're doing something about it. However useless that is. His mother's moved in too, and she's driving him mad. I feel so bloody useless."

"Well, we are useless, aren't we? Other than that text yesterday, asking me to help her again, we've got sod all to work with? We have to hope someone on *Crimebusters* saw something at the Mall before she disappeared." Meredith pinched the bridge of his nose. "In the absence of anything happening with Jo, let's crack on with the Cowell case, not that that's much better. I don't suppose we've heard from the postman?

"He gets back to Bristol sometime this afternoon."

"In which case we'll go and see him sometime this afternoon." Meredith tapped the pile of papers in front of him. "Tell me about this lot, anything jump out at you?"

Taking back the sheets, Trump leafed through them, allowing several he had marked to drop onto the desk. He replaced the pile and picked up those he had separated, and skimmed the first sheet before handing it to Meredith.

"This one may provide a reason for revenge. Cowell arrested Brian Catchpole's son, Simon, when he got into a fight in town. He had a lot of cash on him, and several bags of coke. He was drunk and trying to get into his car at the time. Anyway, long story short, he was done for possession with intent and is currently serving five years. Catchpole senior made all sorts of noise about it being a set-up, and vowed to get Cowell. This was two and a half years ago. Simon is due out in the next few months, so the thinking is, if Cowell is going to be sorted it should be done before anyone can link it to Simon."

Meredith shrugged and turned his nose up. "Catchpole is a bad boy, but doesn't go in for this level of violence. The odd slap when someone steps out of line, but not this. He hasn't got the balls. Catchpole is all mouth and no trousers."

"Then there is this. Cowell worked vice for a while and was key in bringing down Vladimir Kolstoy. Now he is a bad boy, and the French are working on a warrant once he's finished his sentence here. Apparently, he killed two of his girls in Paris, both native, and both kids. Two of his men tried to frighten off Cowell and another chap pre-trial. It all got very messy."

"Yep, that's more promising, but not violent enough. These Ruskies like to make their punishments public. I think he'd go for more of an execution, and somewhere public. You remember that lad that tried to take one of his girls?"

Trump frowned and shook his head.

"Probably before your time. Some young lad, all ginger and freckles, fell for one of the girls he used regularly. He convinced her that they could get her away and set up home together, and the girl got high and boasted to one of the others. She disappeared and he lost his left kneecap; it would have been both but for an inexperienced lorry driver that backed into the wall of the lock-up. Couldn't pin it on them though, the lad would only speak off the record. Last I heard he was going to live with his grandmother in Cyprus. Everyone knew who did it and why, but we couldn't get him for it. But keep it out, you never know."

Trump put the sheet to one side and the pair discussed the merit of the other six he had marked. Meredith picked up the rest and read through them, passing comment as he did so. The only one so far Meredith thought was a real possibility was Kolstoy. With only three to go, he waved the third from last at Trump.

"So that's how he met Nancy Bailey. She doesn't have much luck, does she? Finding your sister has hanged herself, and finding your boss stabbed,

I bet she worries about crossing the road. Poor woman." He paused and squinted at the text. "How old do you reckon she is?"

"I have no idea. Sixtyish? Why?"

"That's what I would have said, but she's only fifty-two. Clearly had a hard life." Meredith shook his head and looked at the remaining two sheets, which he also rejected. He patted the small pile to his left. "Right, we have five cases here, so take Rawlings and start looking into the main characters. What are they up to now, has anything happened recently that would have caused them to go for Cowell?" He picked up the sheets and handed them to Trump. "And don't forget to call *Crimebusters*."

~ ~ ~

Patsy strode confidently into the foyer of the Hilton. She had spent the morning working with Linda, running through the evidence they would have to provide when in court the following week. A previous client had called in the police when it was proven by Linda that both his accountant and IT consultant had been siphoning off income. Patsy was glad to be out of the office. She glanced around and found her target sitting in front of the window, studying his phone screen. As she was not supposed to know him, she pulled her own phone from her pocket and dialled his number, turning to look in the opposite direction as his phone rang.

Alex Walters smiled at the screen as he pushed the answer button, and raised the phone to his ear.

"Patsy, I take it you're here. I'll stand and wave, I'm by the window." Standing, he waved his arm, Patsy turned slowly, and raised her hand in greeting. His smile grew as she made her way towards him. Slipping her hand into her pocket, she activated the recorder.

Walters held out his hand. "Glad you could make it, please take a seat. Can I order you something to drink?"

Patsy assured him she didn't want anything and sat in the opposite chair. She crossed her legs, causing her skirt to rise and reveal a little more thigh. Smiling, she glanced at her watch. "Nice to meet you too, Alex. As I mentioned I only have thirty minutes, so I think we need to get straight down to business."

"Absolutely. Let me recap on what I believe you require." Walters listed from memory the information Patsy had given in her email. "Nice that it's all in the South West to start with, that's my home patch so I can be hands-on." He smiled broadly as his eyes flickered to her exposed thigh.

"If you get the contract, of course. I have to say I think your fees are a little top-heavy. Reynolds Relocation was a recommendation on the basis that they didn't rip you off. Run through the breakdown again." Alex did so and Patsy wrinkled her nose. "And that's your best price?" She shook her head. "I have almost one hundred staff to relocate. Only ten here but I was expecting discount for volume."

"I'd have to refer that to Mr Reynolds, I've already given fifteen per cent." Walters shrugged apologetically. "He will require full details. I've yet to discover what company you represent. I admit to trying to find out, but when I googled Patsy Meredith I didn't find you. There were obviously more than a couple of options, but none of them were you. I would have remembered."

Once again his eyes flickered to her thigh and he leaned forward to receive her response. Patsy was momentarily thrown. She had chosen an alternative surname to ensure she wasn't traced, but now she wasn't convinced she should have chosen Meredith. She also leaned forward.

"That's because that isn't my name." She watched his eyebrows twitch. "As I have mentioned, this move is top secret at the moment. When announced it will cause quite a stir. It makes no difference to you who we are, or why we're relocating. Perhaps I should have used a London agent." Sighing, Patsy leaned back in her chair. She shook her head as she continued, "If Mr Reynolds has a problem with that, and we can't even get near an acceptable fee, perhaps we are wasting each other's time." She placed her hands on the arms of the chair to push herself up. "Still, at least I will be -"

Walters waved his hands. "I'm sure I will be able to sort you out. Although I do need to know if I can depend on your discretion."

"Why? With what?" Patsy's brow furrowed, despite knowing what was coming next.

"I will be leaving Reynolds Relocation shortly, and I know the new company will be able to offer a better price. The thing is, it's not quite the done thing to pass you over. But if you are saying you won't use Reynolds anyway, well what's the harm?" He smiled at her encouragingly.

"Ah, I see. So I should make contact with -"

"New Beginnings. But I can do that for you. After all, I already have the information."

"But you're not working for them yet. How soon will you be starting with them?"

Walters smirked and winked at her. "I'm sort of there already. I assure you I can get you the deal you want. New Beginnings is a new venture, therefore they are discounting standard fees at the moment to build their client base."

Patsy shook her head and Walters frowned. "Do you have a problem with that?"

"If they are a new venture, I'm concerned that they won't have the necessary contacts or perhaps the professionalism that my company is used to."

Walters gave a snort. "I can assure you that you will have no issue in that respect. The MD, Mr Edwards, worked for Reynolds many years ago, and his staff, including me, will all be coming from within the industry."

Patsy raised her eyebrows. "Are you saying from within Reynolds? If that's the case, my concerns would be alleviated a little."

She watched Walter's features change as he wrestled with how much he should reveal.

"Well, I'm not sure I should have that conversation."

Patsy stood, and by chance her phone sounded in her pocket.

"Look, Mr Walters, I'm not convinced about this. You get me a list of employees and the credentials, and if I'm satisfied you, or New Beginnings, will have a deal. At present I'm not happy to proceed." She held out her hand to terminate the meeting.

Walters jumped to his feet. "Alex, please call me Alex. Look, Patsy, I'll have a word and give you a call. Let me show you out."

Patsy nodded and they fell into step as they made their way to the exit. Patsy recovered her phone from her handbag and opened the message she had received.

Patsy, help me please. Speak to Meredith – he can sort this out – it's in his hands.

The message was from Jo and Patsy stumbled as she read it.

Walters grabbed her elbow. "Are you all right? Not bad news I hope." He made to slip his arm around her back but Patsy stopped him with her stare.

"I'm fine, thank you. Get the information and call me. I must dash."

Patsy rushed from the hotel, and once in her car she called Meredith, and he asked her to go to the station. He held out his hand as she walked into the incident room.

"Let me see." Meredith took the phone from Patsy and pinched his nose as he read the message. The room fell silent. He turned to Travers. "Have we got the location yet?" He watched as Bob Travers shook his head. "Well, tell them to get their fingers . . ."

He stopped as Bob waved his hand.

"Downend. It was sent from Downend." Travers stood and walked to the map to the left of the incident board. He picked up a red pin with his left hand and with his right he traced the streets in Downend until he found the location. He pushed the pin into the map and shook his head. "This doesn't help us at the moment, Gov. We haven't had enough contact to build any sort of pattern."

"But why does the bastard think I know what's going on? Who is he? Come on you lot, what are your thoughts? Can this be related to something that both Jo and I were involved with? Or do you reckon it's just me, and that Jo is caught up in this simply because she works for me and was an easy target." Meredith frowned and looked at the floor. The others remained silent. He lifted his head and looked around the room. "If you have any thoughts, however wild, tell me." He chewed his lip. "I have an idea."

Still holding Patsy's phone, he turned and strode to his office. Patsy and Travers followed him. Placing Patsy's phone on his desk, he picked up his own.

"It's obvious it's not Jo sending these messages. So, let's start communicating with him." Frowning he tapped his message into his phone.

Patsy stepped forward and placed a hand on his arm. "Be careful. Choose your words carefully. You don't want to wind him up."

Meredith was about to hand her the phone when there was a shout from the incident room.

"Gov. The phone's been used again. Frenchay this time, they are going to get the detail now."

They left Meredith's office and Travers walked to the board.

"What street?"

"The hospital."

Travers put another pin into the board. Meredith's phone rang and Patsy watched him take a deep breath before he answered it.

"Hi, Aaron." He listened for a while, nodding his head. "Yes, Patsy had one too. Forward what you received to me, would you? I'm sorry, we have no other news." Having assured Aaron that they were still doing everything they could, he hung up. He held the phone towards Patsy. "That soft enough for you?"

I would really like to help you, but you're going to have to give me more to go on. I'm sure you are looking after Jo Adler but I would like proof that she is safe and well. Please contact me urgently.
John Meredith

Patsy nodded her head, and handed the phone back to Meredith who pushed the send button.

"That's good. I wonder how long before they'll pick it up." Walking forward she patted his arm. "I'd better get going, please keep me informed."

Waving to Travers, she turned to leave. Meredith walked back to his office and called to her as she opened the door. "You'll need this." He held up her phone. Patsy hurried to his office and took it from him. "I can update you tonight if you like." His smile disarmed her and she agreed to meet him that evening.

His phone alerted him to an incoming message.

Hi, Aaron, I need you to know that I am safe and well. They have no intention of hurting me.
Love you Jo x

Meredith read the message to Patsy. "Let's hope it gives Aaron some peace. He knows that it's not Jo, but still." Stepping forward he hugged her. "I'll call you later to arrange where and what have you. I need you Patsy." He kissed the top of her head. "Now get going, I've got work to do."

Watching her leave Meredith smiled. He felt at peace when she was close by, and whilst he hated his need of her, he relished the comfort that she provided, and that he had not previously known existed.

~ ~ ~

Jo raised her heavy head from the pillow and looked towards the noise. Her vision was blurred and she screwed her eyes shut before looking again. The iron grill was open. Her heart beat increased, but she remained perfectly still as her eyes scanned the rest of the room. Someone was putting something on the shelving unit. She could make a run for it. Regulating her breathing, she counted silently. One . . . two . . . three. Grunting, she threw herself forward ready to run, but nothing happened, except her right arm now dangled off the side of the bed.

They turned to look at her.

"Oh good, you're awake. I've just about finished, so give me two minutes and I'll make you a nice cup of tea."

Jo opened her mouth to respond, but her tongue was heavy and she barely managed a grunt. Saliva trickled from the corner of her mouth onto the pillow.

"Don't worry, you'll be back to normal shortly."

Jo watched blurry hands make several quick movements towards the shelves. Her eyes followed the walk back to the grill. As she listened to the locks being secured and a tear ran down to join the saliva.

She couldn't move, she couldn't speak, and the warm sensation growing around thighs told her she had emptied her bladder. If she had the ability, she would have sobbed.

~ ~ ~

"Oh, Bobby, you'll be pleased. I got almost all of it done before she woke up. I'll put the rest under the grill later when I take her dinner. Shush now, I need to tell DCI Meredith about Gary." The second name was spat out, as though causing a bad taste in the mouth. The pen flew across the paper, the writer giving the occasional tut as mistakes were made and corrected. Having finished, the pad was waved at Bobby triumphantly. "Right listen carefully, we're almost done."

Gary was always a nightmare, what you would call wild, I suppose. But this had brought us together, as at one stage he was virtually living with me. We even went to New York together. After a while though, his visits became less and less, and he was spending a lot of time (and money) trying to get his career off the ground. I tried to help, but I didn't know enough about it. Then I had that little windfall and knew what I could do. I took advice, and I hired the right people. I knew there was only so far I could go without showing him, so when it was ready for the final touches I arranged to meet him there.

He whistled when he saw it.

"Wow, you have been busy, this is fabulous. You should have said, I would have helped. This is fabulous." He said that a lot as I showed him round.

"We can move in properly now, if you like." I saw the hesitation, and didn't want to scare him away, "If you want to. Otherwise you can just work here and I'll keep the supplies coming." At least that way I would still have contact, and he would be able to help me. He rushed over and hugged me.

"Thank you so much. You've done so much more for me than anyone else."

I was so happy. I can't begin to tell you.

So, I told him what I was doing, and how Phillip was helping. He got so mad. I'd seen him angry, but this time it was different. I won't tell you what he said to me, it still makes me cry now. Perhaps I'll tell you when we speak, but suffice to say, I saw red. I picked up the shovel that was leaning against the wall and I swung it at him, to stop him saying all those foul things. He dropped like a stone, and just lay there staring at me. I told him to stop messing about and waited for him to jump up and scare me. He didn't, he simply stared. It was probably twenty minutes before I closed his eyes. I'd killed him. I didn't mean to, I promise you that. He was all I had, except Phillip.

Without thinking I started to move the rubble; the builders had yet to finish the floor. That was one of the reasons Gary had come to see the progress. I needed him to tell me what he wanted for the floor. Apparently it makes a difference. Over three hours it took me to make a hole big enough, and of course deep enough to put him in. Once I'd managed to get him in there, I covered him with some polythene that the wall panels had been wrapped in, and I put the rubble back on top. I didn't remember doing it until the next day when I was talking to Bobby.

It's been like that with all of them. It's like my mind closes but my body does what's necessary. The builders never noticed a thing, and within two days a smooth layer of concrete covered him. They put down the special flooring that he had wanted once it was dry. A total waste of money now, but what could I do? They finished the room as agreed, I paid them, and they were off. That was a year ago now. I haven't told Jo, I'm sure she'd hate it there if she knew.

"There it's done." They turned to face Bobby. "Calm down, of course I know I have to finish the other bits before I send it. Actually, I think I'll give him another clue first. Oh be quiet! I'll not forget about you."

~ ~ ~

Meredith was pulling his jacket on, ready to leave, when his phone hooted the arrival of a message.

Thank you for your text. I understand completely, I'll sort it out. This should help.

Standing perfectly still, Meredith stared at the phone, wondering what would help. There was no attachment. Perhaps that was to follow. He called to Travers who was calling goodbye to the others.

"Get on to the phone company. I've had a message, and I think another one will arrive shortly."

He watched Travers walk back to his desk and pick up the phone. A little while later he called to Meredith as he went to place a new pin in the board.

"Henleaze. It was sent from Northumbria Drive." He pushed the pin into place and traced his finger from one pin to the next. "Looking at this, there is no pattern. Nothing else yet?"

"Nope. The message said this should help. What should? I thought they were sending a clue, that's what I asked for." He glanced up at the clock; it was seven-fifteen. "That was twenty minutes ago. You get off. I'll wait a while just in case. One of these two can make me a coffee. I take it Seaton got away all right?"

He turned to face the two officers who had been drafted in. Seaton had instructed them on what information they should pull from Phillip Cowell's records and where to log it. They were working their way through the stack of paperwork. The younger of the two officers nodded.

"Yes, sir, he said he'd be back at six-thirty in the morning, and we could go once we'd finished what we're working on here, but I'm happy to stay on if it will help." PC Patrick Dalton rolled his chair back and got to his feet. "I'll make coffee, shall I?"

Meredith smiled at him. He'd caught Dalton's colleague's grimace as he offered to stay. They'd barely worked nine hours, and yet he was keen to go.

"Thank you, Dalton, black with two sugars. I'll let you know about staying on. I take it you do get overtime for this?" Meredith already knew the answer.

"Yes, sir, but that's not why I offered. If it's a problem I'll not log it."

Meredith turned to the other officer who was attempting to look as though he were absorbed in his work.

"What about you, Hutchins? What are you going to do?"

Meredith pursed his lips as Hutchins froze before looking up. Meredith knew they hadn't asked for this shout. He also knew that he was taking his frustration out on an innocent, but he didn't care.

"I don't hear you offering to work unpaid overtime to locate a missing colleague. The rest of this team have been working fourteen to sixteen hour days on this, and even then I have to send them home. What do you think is reasonable to help find a copper being held for some unknown purpose? What would you expect us to do if it were you that had been taken?"

Hutchins coloured and as he opened his mouth to answer, Meredith batted his words away with a flip of his hand.

"No, don't tell me, go on, get going. You too, Dalton, once you've made the coffee. I doubt anything else will happen this evening. I'll call you in if it does."

He turned to find Travers had pulled on his jacket, and was shaking his head at him. He narrowed his eyes at Travers as he walked towards him. "Don't say a word. They need to get it into perspective, and I'm helping. Now go home, I'll see you back here in the morning."

As he sat at his desk, Hutchins switched off his computer and tidied the papers on his desk. Walking to Meredith's door, he tapped on it.

Meredith looked up. "What?"

"I'm straight off to the hospital. My wife went into labour this afternoon so I'll have to switch my phone off. But I'll call you when it's all over, if that's all right. If we don't speak, I'll see you in the morning. Goodnight, sir."

Meredith sighed. "Sorry, Hutchins. That's me told."

Hutchins forced a smile. "I have perspective, don't worry." He turned and left Meredith rubbing his hands over his face.

Meredith called Patsy and explained the situation. They agreed that she would go to his house and cook dinner. Meredith hung up and stared at his phone, willing it to communicate with him. It remained silent.

~ ~ ~

Jo was splashing water on her face when she heard the door at the top of the stairs open. She walked to the grill and watched the now familiar feet approach.

"Now, you tell me what this lot is about?" She pointed at the now full shelving unit. "It looks like we are preparing for a siege. Pasta, baked beans, peas, fruit, sugar, coffee, tea bags, cereal, and I saw that the fridge is full too. What the hell is going on? This is not what you promised." The feet had reached the bottom of the stairs. Jo took hold of the bars and forced her face into the gap between two of them. "And what did you drug me with? There was no need of that. I'll cooperate with you, you know that. I keep my word."

She watched the shrug become a sigh.

"I'm sorry, Jo, but Meredith does need to get a move on. I've decided I need to write to him to tell all, and once he's helped me, I'll tell him where you are."

"Tell him what? You haven't explained. Are you telling me you're simply going to leave me here? For how long?" Jo heard the fear in her voice, and she bit her lip to stop it quivering as she looked at the food piled on the shelves. "What if he can't help? What if Meredith fails in whatever it is you want of him?"

"He won't, I know it. He doesn't know me so why should he help? Although I know won't patronise me like the others did. But he knows you, Jo. He'll do it for you."

Jo let out a scream of frustration, and banged her clenched fists against the grill. "Do what? At least tell me that."

"Okay but it's getting late, I still have some things to do. Go and sit down and I'll tell you a short version." A finger wagged at Jo. "But I'll not answer questions, so don't bother asking."

Nodding agreement, Jo went to sit at the table. As the story was told, various items were slid under the grill. Her eyes grew wide as the story reached its conclusion.

"So you want Meredith to catch you? You want to be punished for what you have done, but you won't tell him where I am until he solves a crime that he thinks may not have happened." Jo buried her face in her hands. "Even you must realise that he may not be able to. Not this long after the event."

Giving a sob, Jo looked back at her captor, waving her hand towards the supplies. "How long do you think this lot will last me?"

"Well, working on a basic meal three times a day, I reckon two and a half to three months. I do realise -"

With a roar Jo jumped to her feet. She stumbled over some of the new supplies as she rushed to the grill.

"Please no. I'll go mad down here on my own for that length of time. Even when they catch you, they won't lock you up on your own. I've done nothing to deserve this, please, I beg you."

Sinking to her knees, and sitting back on her feet, Jo attempted to control her temper.

"I've left plenty of long life milk, I hate it on cereals but it's the best I can do, although there are eight fresh pints in the fridge that will last two weeks. Let's pray that DCI Meredith can sort this quickly. If there was any other way of doing this, I would have taken it. I also remembered that you would need other things too, so in that bag by your ankle is some ibuprofen and doodahs. Now I need you to hold this whilst I take a photo of you."

Reaching out, Jo pulled the bag towards her, and peered inside. Grabbing a box she waved it at the grill.

"Tampons. They're called tampons, not doodahs." She rummaged in the bag and pulled out the blister pack of pain killers. "Eight tablets? Do you think that's enough?"

"I didn't want you to be able to hurt yourself. I don't want you hurt. Only take them if it's necessary. Now scoot back, I've got a stack of books from the charity shop for you. I got a selection as I didn't know what you liked to read."

Jo watched as her captor retreated back up the stairs to return with two more carrier bags a few minutes later. She didn't move. The bags were placed next to the grill.

"There are also a few more DVDs, a writing pad and some pens. I'll leave them here if you don't want to move. You can reach through the grill for them. I have to go now." The sigh was deep and heartfelt. "The next time we see each other will probably be in court. Bye, Jo, I hope this doesn't take too long."

Jo didn't bother responding and she allowed the first tear to fall, wiping it away as they hurried back down the stairs.

"I meant to say, although I'm sure you will work it out for yourself. If you have any food waste, flush it away as you go. Wash all the tins and stuff out in the sink and it should all remain nice and fresh in here. Right that really is it. I'm off."

Jo threw the tampon box across the room and allowed sobs to control her body.

~ ~ ~

When Meredith arrived home a little after ten, Patsy welcomed him with a hug. She took his jacket from his shoulders, hung it on the newel post, and told him to have a shower while she dished up dinner.

"Come to bed with me. I need you."

He screwed his face up as Amanda gave a cough behind him.

"Sorry. It's been a long day." He stepped to one side to allow Amanda past. "I'm off to bed. Patsy has knackered me out. Give me five minutes and the bathroom will be all yours." She kissed her father on the cheek. "And keep the noise down, I have a lecture in the morning." She raised her eyebrows and grinned at him. "'Night, Dad." She turned to Patsy, "Goodnight, Patsy. Have fun."

She dashed up the stairs before either of them could respond.

Meredith turned back to Patsy shaking his head. "I keep forgetting she's here. I'm glad you are, though. I need a drink. Am I allowed a drink before I prepare myself for you?"

Smiling, Patsy led him into the living room. Meredith looked around. "Ah, so that's what she meant. You've had a clean-up."

"Yes, and I expect it to stay this way too, so be warned. I almost gave Nancy Bailey a call on your behalf. Whisky or wine?"

"Wine, that way you'll drink with me." Meredith's stomach rumbled and he sniffed. "What's that gorgeous smell? I think I'm hungry now."

"Moussaka, and all the trimmings. Sit down, I'll bring it all to you."

Patsy watched Meredith clear his plate, and take second helpings which were almost as large as the first. He told her about the latest message, and how he felt increasingly helpless. He asked her to stay the night and she agreed. His smile was broad.

"Good. In which case I'm off to have a shower, and I'll meet you in the bedroom."

"I'll be up in a while. I'll get this lot cleared up first." Standing, she pulled him to his feet. He kissed her gently and hugged her to him.

"This is where you belong. I need you here. It doesn't feel so bad when you're here. I hate needing you, you know. It's the only bad thing about loving you. I've never needed anyone before."

"Good. Now go and shower and you can show me how much you need me."

Patsy didn't rush with the clearing up. Pottering about, she considering their situation, and how best to deal with it. By the time she had finished and was climbing the stairs, she could hear Meredith was already snoring. She silently stripped out of her clothes, allowing them to drop to the floor, before climbing carefully into bed. She lay still for a while listening to his snoring and, needing to sleep herself, she gave him a nudge.

"Turn over, you're snoring," she whispered.

He rolled towards her and pulled her into his embrace. "That better?"

"Much." She pressed her back against his warm body.

"This takes me back, except you don't have those crappy PJ's on."

"Hmmm."

"Night, Hodge."

"Night, Gov."

They both smiled into the darkness.

"Welcome home."

"Thank you."

7

Waking with a start, Jo stared into the darkness. She lay there listening to the sound of her heart pounding in her chest. It sank as she remembered where she was, and why. Groaning, she turned over. It mattered little what time it was, there was no point in keeping office hours. Closing her eyes she hoped sleep would return. A frown creased her brow as she heard again the sound which had woken her. She turned to face the grill. The room was pitch black, and although she had five light bulbs she didn't want to waste them. The door opened at the top of the stairs and a little light filtered down from the outside world. Jo leapt out of bed and fumbled for the light switch as she called out.

"Hello. I'm down here, please help me," she yelled, anticipation causing a fleeting smile as she found the light switch. The smile fell away and her shoulders drooped as the familiar feet appeared.

"Don't be silly. It's only me."

"I thought you were going to Meredith?"

"I was, but by the time I got home last night it was so late, and I remembered I had to do a few more things first. Stand back now."

Jo did as she was bid, and the tray was slid under the grill.

"What's that?" She poked the tray with her foot.

"That's Irish stew. I'm famed for my Irish stew, or I was. It's the last meal of that type you'll get for a while so make the most of it, don't let it go to waste. This is another cake." A brightly coloured tin pushed the tray further into the room and away from the grill. "Carrot cake, my favourite. And these," a carrier bag from a chemist joined the other items at Jo's feet, "are various vitamins and minerals, and some other bits. I don't want you getting poorly while you wait. Finally, these are for the rubbish you can't flush away. Lemon scented which should help."

A roll of yellow plastic bags was held out through the bars towards Jo. She reached forward and took it.

"Thank you for your consideration." Jo caught the flinch as her sarcasm registered. "Are you going to see Meredith today? What's the time?"

"It's eleven. Early for lunch I know, but needs must. Now there's one more thing we need to do, but I have to pop out first. You eat your lunch, and I'll be back shortly."

"Where are you going? Why can't you go straight to Meredith and put this nightmare plan of yours into action?"

"Oh I will, but he will want to know you're alive and well. We need to take some photographs. I need a newspaper for that. It won't take me a couple of minutes."

Jo gave a little nod as she watched the feet disappear. She could see the relevance. As the door closed at the top of the stairs she bent and lifted the tray. The stew smelt good. Turning, she walked the few steps to place it on the table, where she eyed it suspiciously. Perhaps this had been drugged too. She considered this for a few moments. If it was drugged and she passed out like last time, the planned photograph would not show her alive and well. If it was drugged, what difference did it make to her? It would simply mean a few hours that she didn't need to be conscious of her circumstance. Lifting the lid, she found several homemade bread rolls surrounding the large dish of stew. As she dipped the bread in and took the first mouthful, she wondered whether she was already losing the ability to reason.

~ ~ ~

"Oh, Bobby, I don't know how I forgot. I'm too stupid for words. Still, it's only one more day, and I've sent DCI Meredith another message. I know he won't work it out quickly, but I hope she doesn't take too long to come round." They looked at Jo, still unconscious at the table. "It wasn't that big a dose, perhaps I'll call her. Brace yourself."

The grill was closed and locked. A fork was used to bang against the grill.

"Come on, Jo, wake up. We need to take that photograph."

Clang, clang, clang. Jo winced and raised her head a little; it thumped furiously at the temples. She squinted towards the noise. It stopped as her head turned.

"Thank goodness for that. Drink the water I've put in front of you, that medication can cause headaches but a couple of pints of water will clear it."

Jo laid her head back on her arms and groaned. "You did it again. What time is it?"

"Twelve-thirty, and I've texted DCI Meredith so hurry and wake up or we won't get this photo done. I can't hang about."

Sitting upright, Jo stared at the water before picking it up and drinking it down.

"Do you want to check yourself in the mirror, you know, to make sure you're happy with how you look?"

Jo winced as she spun around her arms held wide in wonderment. "Are you mad? Why on earth would I give a shit what I look like?"

"Because they may show your husband, and I didn't think you would want to worry him. Well, not any more than he will be already."

Jo pulled at her hair and groaned again. "For someone who didn't plan this, you do think of everything. Give me five minutes."

She walked unsteadily to the basin, splashed cold water on her face, and peered at her reflection in the mirror. Walking back to the chair, she lifted her handbag and pulled out a hairbrush and lipstick and went back to the mirror. Running wet hands through her hair, she brushed it back off her face. She attempted to flatten down any hair still sticking up, deciding she would wash it later. Taking the lipstick, which was the only makeup she had with her, she made two dots on her cheeks before applying it to her lips. Placing a middle finger on each of the dots she rubbed it out along her cheekbones. Stepping back, she eyed herself critically. She still looked like shit, but at least it was a little better. Turning back into the main room, she stopped dead in her tracks and pointed at the cage in the corner of the room.

"What the hell is that for?" she demanded as she walked back to the grill.

"Oh, that's Bobby. I didn't know what to do with him, so I thought I'd leave him for you. He's good company and he gives you someone to talk to other than yourself."

"There sounds the voice of experience."

"Quite. He's been the only one I could tell up to now. He's a sweet little thing. You can let him out, he'll always come back to his cage to do his business. Don't know how he knows to do that, I didn't train him. I haven't been able to get him to talk though."

Jo shook her head in disbelief. A bloody budgie! What if she was allergic to him? She wasn't, but Bobby's owner clearly hadn't thought about that. "What if I'm allergic to feathers?"

"You're not, are you?"

"No, but I could be."

"Well, you're not, so pick up that paper and stand over there."

Jo bent to pick up the early addition of the *Bristol Evening Post*. She scanned the headlines as she positioned herself in front of the grill. Turning the paper around, she held it across her chest, ensuring that the headline was clearly in view.

"Now I think I can do this. Stand still" The hand reached through the grill and held the phone towards Jo. It flashed twice. The hand withdrew and they squinted at the phone. "It's gone. How do I get it back to send it?"

Jo sighed and held out her hand. "Give it to me."

"Do you think I'm stupid?"

"No, do you think I am? What could I do? Call someone? Text them? Without you on the other side of that door, they may still never find me. I have no idea where I am."

Jo saw the hesitation. That wasn't quite true. She knew what street she had last entered, although not the number of the house, but knew they would be monitoring her phone. She hoped it was her phone; it looked like it was, but without getting hold of it she couldn't be sure. Jo's shoulders drooped as her captor's head shook from side to side slowly.

"I'm sure you're right, but I'll work it out."

"Take a seat, I'll talk you though it."

Sitting cross-legged on the floor, Jo spent another ten minutes explaining how to send the photographs to Meredith.

"Right this time, I really am off. I'll not call DCI Meredith until tomorrow. I've set him a test, you know, given him a clue. It'll be interesting to see how long he takes to find me."

"What if he doesn't? He may not work out your clue."

"I'm sure he will, but if not I'll send the letter tomorrow."

"Send it?"

"Of course, I have to know he can work things out. If not, we're all doomed."

Jo was speechless, and she watched helplessly as the feet retreated up the stairs.

"Look after Bobby for me. None of this is his fault."

~ ~ ~

Meredith yelled at Seaton as he strode back to his office, "But there must be something. They missed it. Get the car, we'll go and look. It's true, if you want a job done properly . . . Trump, you too." He paused and turned to Dalton, "And you, about time you did some proper police work."

"But, Gov, they turned the place upside down. Everything is on the list."

Meredith swung towards Seaton and the rest of the room fell silent. He waved his phone. "It says to check Phillip's papers. That's a clue. It tells us whoever killed Phillip Cowell also has Jo. Now that's where he lived, and that's where we'll check. I don't care what the . . . " Meredith fell silent for a moment, and looked up at the ceiling, releasing a breath which caused his lips to reverberate. He looked back at Seaton. "We'll need to split into two groups. You and Trump take Bristol, Dalton and I will be going to Cardiff." He eyed Dalton, "I take it you know how to drive?"

Dalton was pulling on his jacket. "Yes, sir. I passed the advanced course last month."

As Meredith held the door open, he called to Hutchins, "Get down to the hospital and give your son a cuddle. This will take a couple of hours and then it could be a long night."

"Thanks, Gov. Good luck." Hutchins smiled and nodded his thanks.

~ ~ ~

At the same time as Meredith was beginning his journey to Cardiff, Patsy had reached a conclusion. Locking her car she looked up at the prison. She gave a shudder and tucked her hair behind her ears before making her way to the visitor's entrance. Now that she was actually here her resolve to remain cool and reserved had abandoned her, and she found that she was nervous about seeing Tanya Jenkins, whatever the reason for the invitation. Pushing the bell she was allowed into the reception area.

Once the formalities were over Patsy was taken to the visiting area where she joined the queue outside the visiting room. She tried not to look too closely at the other visitors, or wonder what their loved ones had done to be locked up, and was surprised that most of those waiting appeared cheerful, chatting casually with those they had recognised from previous visits. She jangled the coins in her pocket as she waited. The advice note attached to the visiting order, had explained that refreshments could be purchased from vending machines within the visiting room, and she guessed she would need coffee.

She swallowed as the door opened, and she followed the line into the visiting room. Scanning the room, she walked towards a table a little off-center, and not too close to the vending machines. The table had four chairs, three of them red for visitors. Pulling one out she sat down. A few minutes later the door at the back of the room opened and a line of prisoners walked in. Tanya was at the back of the line and Patsy listened to the squeals of delight as prisoners spied their visitors and vice versa. She spotted Tanya and almost didn't recognise her. Patsy looked away quickly to process the image she had seen.

Tanya's hair had been cut short, and the muddy brown colouring was flecked with grey, particularly at the temples. The extra weight Tanya had carried had been lost, and an oversized tee shirt hung from her shoulders. But the most shocking difference was the angle of Tanya's nose, which had clearly been broken. She looked up as the chair on the opposite side of the table was pulled out.

For a moment, she actually felt sorry for her, but the glint of hatred was still there, and Patsy blinked to dispel any sympathy.

"You wanted to see me."

"I did, and I'm shocked you came." Tanya drew her fingers along her shoulders, "As you can see I didn't dress to receive guests." She coughed out a false laugh. "You look well, Hodge, unlike myself."

Patsy sighed and pinched the bridge of her nose, causing Tanya to snort.

"I see you've picked up his mannerisms as well. I was sorry to hear you two had split up. I did warn you he wasn't a keeper. Do you remember, way back, that first week we met?"

Dropping her hand into her lap, Patsy studied Tanya for a moment. "Tanya, can we get on with this please? We don't like each other, I have no sympathy for you, so let's not waste time discussing how either of us are."

"Fair enough. I have a job for you."

Patsy's eyes widened in mock amazement. "Really, and why would you ask for my help?"

"I'm not asking for help, I'm giving you a job. I understand that you get paid by the hour to investigate these days." Tanya looked Patsy in the eye. "Unless you're not up to it."

"You are well informed. But if you didn't think I was, I wouldn't be sitting here, would I? Spit it out, Tanya. I'm already bored and, as you rightly say, I'm paid by the hour, which means I'm not earning while I'm sitting here." She gave an almost unperceivable shake of her head to indicate her lack of interest.

Folding her arms on the table, Tanya leaned forward. "If you're that strapped for cash you can bill me for this meeting. I -"

Throwing her head back, Patsy laughed. "Really? Because your allowance will cover that, will it?" Patsy moved her chair back and made to stand.

Tanya's arm flew out and her hand rested on the table in front of her, indicating Patsy should stay. Her eyes darted left to the other side of the room and back to Patsy. "Just hear me out . . . please."

A look of desperation had replaced the hatred, and Patsy casually glanced across the room. There were three tables in line of sight. At two of them the occupants were engrossed in conversation, at the third the prisoner looked at Patsy and nodded, ignoring the teenage girl sat in front of her. She was, Patsy thought, in her mid-forties, and her attractiveness was marred by the cold stare and look of distaste. Patsy returned the nod and looked back at Tanya.

"Who's that?"

"You need to listen carefully because I can't write any of this down. It can't come back to her."

"She being . . ." Patsy shrugged, "Should I have recognised her?"

"Possibly, though probably not. Her name is Kathryn Wilkinson, Kate. She's doing five years for arson. Look it up, we haven't time for those details. Her husband disappeared about three years ago. She says she was glad to be rid of him, but I don't think that's true. To cut a long story short, police now think she may have bumped him off. She burned down her own house, and half of her neighbour's, to claim the insurance. When her husband disappeared, she didn't report him missing, and as she started the fire to make an insurance claim, the police are now starting to ask questions about what happened to him."

"Why the interest now, what happened to start this off?"

Tanya shrugged and sighed. "I only know what I'm told. They started looking for him after the fire, to make sure he wasn't involved. Wilkinson says that they seemed satisfied at first. He'd had a string of affairs and she had assumed he'd run off with one of them. But something happened before I came here, someone asked the question, or reported him missing. I don't know. All I do know is she's running scared and wants him found." Tanya paused and glanced at the vending machine against the wall. "Are you buying me a coffee?"

Patsy nodded, glad of the distraction. She hadn't known what to expect but it wasn't that. Walking to the machine, she purchased two coffees. The hot liquid burned her fingers through the flimsy plastic as she made her way back, glancing at her perspective client as she did so. She received another nod which she ignored.

"A bar of chocolate wouldn't go amiss either," Tanya announced as she returned.

Patsy placed the coffee on the table and looked around. The vending machine containing snacks was situated behind Kate Wilkinson. As she approached the machine, the young girl visiting Wilkinson jumped up and got to the machine in front of Patsy. She made a pretence of feeding the coins incorrectly. Patsy stood behind her and resisted the urge to look around to see who was watching.

"You the copper?" the young girl asked.

"I am." Patsy stepped forward, "Can I help with that." Opening her palm, she held out some coins.

"Thanks." The girl chose two of the coins. "I'll be at the bus stop up the road. Turn left when you leave the car park." Turning back to the machine, she pushed a button and the Mars bar gave a thud as it hit the dispensing tray. The girl pocketed the two pound coins she had taken from Patsy.

Returning to Tanya, Patsy placed two bars of chocolate next to the coffee. "They think I'm still a police officer." Sitting, she picked up her coffee and blew on it before sipping it. "I didn't correct her. Do you want to tell me why she couldn't see me herself?"

Tanya ran her hand over her face before she reached for one of the bars of chocolate. She fiddled with it as she spoke to Patsy, unable to meet her eye.

"As you will no doubt find out, Kate Wilkinson comes from a known family. She married Darren Wilkinson against her brother's wishes. When he started messing her about, her brother wanted to sort him out, but she wouldn't let him." Tanya gave a bitter laugh, "Mind you, she probably did quite a good job herself, this nose job wasn't requested, you know." She raised her eyebrows as Patsy glanced at her misshapen nose. "One day Wilkinson goes off to see one of his lady friends, Kate knew because of the aftershave he had on, and he never comes back."

Tanya finally opened the chocolate. She removed it and placed it on top of the flattened wrapper.

"She thinks her brother had him sorted. Money had gone missing from her elderly mother the day after their last visit. Money that belonged to her brother, Brian Catchpole."

Running her fingers through her hair, Patsy placed it back behind her ears. "So let me recap. She wants me to find her cheating husband to get the police off her back, but she thinks he's probably been killed by her brother. If he hasn't been killed, he could be anywhere because he took the brother's money." She waited until Tanya nodded. "Sounds like a wild goose chase to me. I don't think -"

"He didn't take the money."

"What?"

"He didn't take the money, she did. When he disappeared, she didn't want to admit it to her brother in case he had done something stupid. And wait for it . . . she didn't want to make him feel bad. So if you're worried about your fee, she can afford it. If you discover that her brother bumped him off, she's off the hook. If you find him, she's off the hook. I don't think she cares much what the outcome is, provided she doesn't have to do more time."

Patsy raised her hands in wonderment, but despite herself she was beginning to take an interest. "Okay, but that doesn't explain why she thinks I am still on the force."

"In her book, once a copper always a copper. She thinks it will help you. Thinks you'll have someone on the inside able to provide information if it's needed. Shame that's not true any more."

Tanya smirked, and was miffed when Patsy simply smiled at her.

94

"And what do you get out of this? What's in it for you?"

"I get to go about my business quietly and without bother. Strangely enough, they don't like ex-coppers in here. If you sort this, I will have no more doors to walk into, or showers to slip over in." Tanya lifted the bottom of her tee shirt to reveal a large, ugly bruise that covered most of the visible flesh. "I thought it would make you feel superior helping me out." Again, the smirk appeared.

Patsy closed her eyes and shook her head. Her patience was at an end. "I've been told that you were a good copper, if a little misguided. How on earth can you know so little about what makes people tick. I don't need to be made to feel superior to you, I already am. Now, I really have got to rush. I'd like to say it's been nice, but it hasn't." She stood up and picked up her now empty coffee cup. "Enjoy the chocolate."

As she turned to leave, Tanya stood and touched her arm.

"You'll do it?"

"I doubt it, but apparently I have to pick someone up from a bus stop, so who knows. Bye, Tanya."

Tanya didn't bother responding but simply turned and walked towards the door at the rear of the room.

~ ~ ~

Meredith closed his eyes several times as Dalton showed off his driving skills on the journey to Cardiff. Normally he would have commented, but bit his tongue, knowing that time was of the essence. He breathed a sigh of relief when they pulled up outside Cathy Davies' house. He caught the movement of the blind in the top floor bedroom window as he slammed the car door. Striding up the path he rang the doorbell several times. After a few moments, Cathy opened the door. Meredith noted she was looking a lot better.

"Have you caught him? I heard you had to let Andy go, I told you he didn't do it."

Meredith stared at her for a moment, causing her to look away.

"Not yet, but we have a lead. Can we come in?" He pushed the door, making Cathy step back. Walking straight through to the kitchen he picked up the kettle. "May I?"

Cathy pulled back her shoulders. "Doesn't seem like I have a choice. What lead? Why are you here?"

"Cathy, it's a long story, which I haven't got time to tell. Last time I was here you said Phillip had papers in the loft. I take it they're still there?"

"Books, I said books."

Meredith was already walking away. "Well, they'll do for starters. We need to have a look at them, you get the kettle on, and we'll get the books."

Cathy didn't have the energy to argue, and Andy Henshaw was coming around later so the sooner they were out of her hair the better. Lifting the mugs out of the cupboard, she listened to Meredith telling his sidekick to hurry up.

Twenty minutes later the coffee mugs were empty, and Meredith was sitting in the back of the car next to one of the three boxes Cathy had allowed them to take. He'd bitten his tongue when she'd told him she didn't want any of it back.

"Right, we're not in a race now Dalton, so nice and steady back to Bristol. I don't travel well in the back and I want to see what's in this box, not throw up in it."

~ ~ ~

Patsy climbed into her car and opened the glove compartment. Removing her emergency packet of cigarettes, she fumbled for the lighter. As she did so the young girl who had spoken to her in the prison hurried past without looking at her. Having found the lighter, Patsy opened the window and lit the cigarette. Blowing the smoke out of the window, she checked her messages. She crossed the fingers on her free hand as she read the message from Meredith.

First lead – long story. On my way to Cardiff but am free later
tonight – would you like to cook me dinner again?

Dropping her phone back into her bag she decided not to answer until she got back to Bristol. After all, he was supposed to be dating her, and the way it was going all he was doing was sleeping with her. She smiled at the thought as she started the engine.

Turning left as directed, she followed the road. About half a mile along she spotted the bus stop. Three people stood there, and one of them was the girl. She pulled in and opened the window. "Can I give you a lift?"

"Yep." The girl climbed into the car and closed the window. "Drive. Head back to Bristol. I'll direct you once you hit the interchange."

"Who are you?"

"Why?"

Patsy glanced towards the girl and shook her head. "Can we establish something straight off? I have been asked to take on a job I'm not sure about. I need to ask questions, firstly, to help me decide whether to do it, and secondly, if I do decide to take it on, to help me do the job. Now, I'm assuming you are the mouthpiece for Kate Wilkinson, so I need to know who you are, and how much you know. If you don't want to talk, that's fine by me. I'll give you a lift home and you can let Kate know I've turned her down."

The girl sighed deeply. "Okay. What do you want to know?"

"Everything. Who you are, what you know, where I'm supposed to start? Let's start with your name."

"Angel Wilkinson. Kate's my mum. My dad's a bastard and always has been, and I don't want my mum doing more time for him. Especially as she didn't do it."

"You think he's dead?" Patsy watched Angel's response from the corner of her eye.

Angel shrugged, and twisted her hands together in her lap as though she was washing them. "Don't know. I've not seen or heard from him for three years." She snorted, "Maybe longer than that. I avoided him."

"How old are you?"

"Eighteen, two weeks ago. Why?"

"Because if I take this on, your memories of what your father did, who he spoke to, where he went, will all help me."

"I've got it all written down, I'll give you it when we get home."

"Where's home? Where do you live?"

"Just off Gloucester Road now, in the new-build development. Do you know it?"

"I know Gloucester Road, but I don't know where the new development is." Patsy turned to look at the girl. "Do you live alone?"

"Yep. My uncle owns this house. He lets me live there almost rent free, but I pay the bills. I've been there since they arrested Mum."

"What, on your own, at your age? That must be lonely."

The girl tutted and turned to look at Patsy as though she were dense. "I can look after myself, and Uncle Brian and Aunt B have me round a lot. I also have friends believe it or not."

"Do you work?"

"Of course, what do you think I live on? Uncle Brian is great and all that, but he's not a saint."

Patsy chewed her lip, deciding not to say anything about the money Tanya had mentioned. "I was trying to ascertain how I get paid if I take this on. I still haven't decided."

"Don't worry about that. I have access to Mum's money. She told me I could use it, but I haven't. She'll need it when she gets out."

"What do you do for a living?" Patsy negotiated the roundabout under the motorway. "I'll head towards Gloucester Road, and you can direct me from there."

Patsy took the A38 towards the city.

"Head towards Horfield Prison, it's around the corner from there." The girl settled lower in her seat. "I'm an insurance clerk for Red Eagle. I've been there since I left school, just been promoted. I started as a junior, filing and doing the post, that bottom-of-the-ladder stuff. Now I'm allowed to open claims and allocate them numbers. It's heady stuff."

Patsy laughed at the irony. Angel was obviously a lot brighter than she had given her credit for. "I take it they don't know about your mum?"

Frowning, Angel considered this, then smiled. "Do you know, that's never occurred to me. It wasn't her insurance company anyway. But ironic, huh?"

Angel directed Patsy to a small cul-de-sac. Twelve identical houses looped around a small parking area. Angel jumped out of the car and led her to one of the houses at the top of the close. She held the door open for Patsy.

"Come on in. Do you want a cup of tea, or shall we get on with it?"

"It depends. Am I allowed to take any of it away?" Before Angel could answer she added, "Go on, I'll have tea anyway."

The house was a compact two-up, two-down, each of the bedrooms having a small en suite bathroom. Tea made, Angel led Patsy back to the sitting room. She scooped up the magazines and an empty pizza box from the coffee table and deposited them on the table in the kitchen. Patsy sat on the sofa. Returning to the sitting room, Angel opened the small cupboard built into the void underneath the stairs. Patsy was surprised when Angel emptied the cupboard of its contents, and was soon surrounded by a mop and bucket, vacuum cleaner, and various boxes containing bric-a-brac. Rolling back the carpet on the floor of the cupboard, Angel took a butter knife from the back pocket of her jeans and used it to prise up a panel. Lifting out a large box that had once contained a pair of very expensive boots, she placed it on the coffee table. Sitting next to Patsy, she lifted the lid.

Patsy leaned forward and peered into the box. Underneath a large spiral notepad, the box housed various sheets of paper, a couple of newspaper clippings and a passport.

Angel flipped open the notepad. "I'll leave you to read this at your leisure, but I'll quickly run through how it's made up. I've split the information into three sections. The first is identity stuff, national insurance number, date of birth, where he's worked – when he was working, of course." She raised her eyebrows at Patsy, and turned to a page marked by a strip of coloured card, "The second, is what we definitely know about where he was, who he was with et cetera. You know, for the last couple of weeks before he went missing. Finally," she turned to the last marker halfway through the pad, "these are Mum's thoughts and suggestions. I've added my own at the back."

Patsy nodded approval. "That's great, very thorough. What's all this?" She pointed at the documents in the box, and lifted out the passport.

Opening it, she turned to face Angel. "So he's probably not out of the country?"

"Who knows? Mum thinks there's a chance he had a false one so he couldn't be traced. He knows people apparently. The rest is stuff you may find useful. Photographs and . . . well, take it with you and have a look."

Patsy picked up the newspaper clippings. It was the lonely-hearts column from the local paper. Both had entries that had been circled and underlined. Patsy read the first one.

Attractive brunette (35) seeks discreet male company for dinner and fun. Must be tall with a good sense of humour.
Replies PO Box 7856.

"Your mum thinks he was having an affair. What did you think?"

"Thinks! She knows, she caught him more than once. He wasn't as bright as he thought he was. I saw him with one of them too. He crossed the road when he saw me, pretended he hadn't been arm in arm with her. She didn't like it, not one bit. I watched from a shop doorway while they rowed about it."

"Do you know who she was?" Patsy watched Angel shake her head. "Did your mum?"

"I don't know. If Mum did, she's not told me."

Patsy read the second clipping.

Merry Widow (42) Bristol Area, seeks companion for dinner, outings and maybe more. 40 – 50 age group.
Replies PO Box 2334.

"This lot will certainly give me something to get my teeth into."

Angel startled Patsy as she leaned across and hugged her.

"So you'll do it? Thanks so much." Releasing Patsy, she clapped her hands together. "Mum will be so pleased. Can you start straight away?"

Patsy was flummoxed for a moment. She hadn't intended agreeing to anything before she'd discussed it with Chris, but she was intrigued, and she felt sorry for Angel.

"I have to discuss it with my partner, but there is still the cost to sort out. I can see how much this means to you, Angel, but if I take this on, I will need to charge."

Placing her hands on her hips, Angel rolled her eyes. "I know that. I told you I could sort that. I've done my homework and know you charge two hundred to five hundred a day, depending on what it is you're investigating. I know there may be expenses on top." She leaned forward and pulled open a drawer on the coffee table and withdrew a white envelope. She waved it at Patsy. "There's a thousand quid here, I reckon that will buy your services for a week. The initial stuff should all be local, but if it's not, give me a shout and I'll get more. When can you start?"

Smiling, Patsy tutted. "You are a cheeky whatsit! I have a couple of other things on at the moment, but I promise I'll read through this lot by tomorrow, and start things rolling." She waved her finger at Angel, "*But,* these things take time. I doubt I'll have a full day's work to do straight off, so I don't want you on the phone every five minutes. I'll let you know how it's going every three days or so, unless of course I need anything. How often do you speak to your mum?"

"Thanks . . . what's your name? I only know you as Hodge. I speak to her a couple of times a week. She calls between six and seven if she can."

"Patsy." Patsy inclined her head and leaned towards Angel. "Now I'm going to ask you a few questions, and I want the truth. I know it's your parents we'll be discussing, but if you're less than honest it will hinder me. If I find you've intentionally lied to me, I'll stop. I'll walk away. Do you understand?"

Angel looked concerned. "What do you want to know?"

Patsy took a notepad from her bag and pulled the pencil from the spiral. "Why did your mum burn the house down? And did you know about it?"

"For the money, she says. I knew something was going on, but I didn't know it was that."

"Why do you say 'she says'? Don't you believe her? Why do you think she did it?"

Angel held her hands up and shrugged. "I have no idea why any of this is relevant, but if we're going to be long do you want another cup of tea, or I have some white wine in the fridge?"

Thirty minutes and one cup of coffee later, Patsy had established that Kate and Darren Wilkinson had had a turbulent marriage. Their regular bust-ups were always followed by extravagant reunions. They had an expensive lifestyle, but Darren was in and out of regular work. Kate hated that, but could do little about it, given her family history. She also resented the financial implications when he was seeing someone else, as she considered that he was spending her money on the other women. On the day he disappeared they'd had a massive row. Angel knew it was about another woman as her mother was screaming about a whore. Her father left in a hurry. Angel couldn't provide any details as she had turned her television up to drown out the noise.

Bitter, and fed up with her lot, Kate Wilkinson had wanted a new start, and one day she decided how she would achieve that. She removed anything of value from the house – jewellery, expensive clothes, and other valuables – and booked a weekend in Torquay. On the second night, when she believed Angel was sleeping, Kate had left their room. Angel knew she hadn't been gone long enough to set the fire, but certainly long enough to arrange it. The front of the house had been totally destroyed, and the fire had taken half their neighbour's house with it, but the rear was not too bad. Kate's bedroom had extensive smoke damage but other than that remained unscathed. It was noted by the investigators that there was little of value in there, and the fixings from a plasma TV remained on the wall. The insurance company was also suspicious when no jewellery was found in the wreckage, as Kate had a considerable number of pieces insured.

Patsy asked if her mother had known Tanya Jennings prior to her prison sentence.

Angel shrugged. "I don't think so. She's just some copper that got banged up so she's useful. What did you do, by the way?"

Patsy frowned. "What do you mean?"

"Why did you have to leave the police? Mum gave me the impression that you'd been up to something too."

She grinned as Patsy laughed out loud.

"It was a man, as simple as that, Angel. No naughtiness, simply a man I thought was special."

Angel looked at Patsy as though she must be mad. "You won't catch me leading my life for a bloke. No way."

"I should hope not," Patsy smiled. "Back to it. Would you consider your mother to be dangerous or violent?"

"She's got a temper. My dad was a big bloke, but she did him some damage on a few occasions. She's also had a -"

"You said 'was'," Patsy interrupted.

"Was what?"

"My dad *was* a big bloke. Do you think he's dead?" Patsy watched as Angel shrugged.

"I don't know, but I honestly don't think that my mum did it. She wouldn't be wasting her money on you if she did."

"Other than beat your dad up occasionally, was she violent? Has she ever hit you?"

Angel closed her eyes and blew out a breath. "Let's just say it was a bit of a relief when she was sent to prison. I deserved it sometimes, I can be a cow. But she was unpredictable." She looked down at her lap. "I won't be living with her when she gets out. I'm saving to make sure of that." Looking directly at Patsy, she added. "But, she's my mum. She was always there, unlike him. I know she never meant to hurt me, and I'm pretty much all she has, so I need you to help her."

Patsy nodded and asked more questions about their home life and her parents' relationship.

Angel was incredulous when Patsy suggested that her father may have been involved in the fire. "You must be joking. She hated him in the end. It's why she wanted to move on. In case he came back, she said. I didn't even want to go, but what could I do?" Angel sighed deeply. "I didn't know you would want this much information, not on personal stuff anyway."

Smiling, Patsy patted Angel's knee. She put the newspaper clippings back in the box, and replaced the lid. "I'll take this with me and read through it. I'll do it by tomorrow lunchtime and let you know. Is that okay?"

Agreeing, Angel showed her out. As Patsy crossed the threshold, Angel held out the envelope containing the money.

"I haven't said I'll do it yet."

"But I know you will..." Angel placed the envelope on top of the box and quickly shut the door. "Bye, give me a shout if you need anything," she called through the closed door.

Patsy thought Angel was probably right as she walked towards her car.

It was early evening by the time she got home. Placing the box on the stairs, and sitting next to it, she called Meredith. The call went through to his answer service.

"Hi, only me calling for an update on Jo. Sorry, I know you have enough on your plate. I visited Tanya and . . . well, that's a story for another day. I'll speak to you tomorrow, but please let me know if there's any news on Jo. Bye."

She got up, placed the phone on top of the box, and took it to her bedroom. She dropped it on her bed and went to the bathroom to run herself a hot bath.

~ ~ ~

Meredith looked up as Trump waved a notepad in the air.

"I think I have something." The team fell quiet and stopped what they were doing. Trump stood and walked towards Meredith. "There's a list of initials and or names and numbers, and then it says: 'Debbie C check underwear and jewellery'. There's a bit that doesn't make sense, but it says: 'spoke to coroner fifteenth November 2010'. If I'm right, Debbie C was a suicide he attended in 2010." Trump looked across to Seaton. "Bob, have you still got that list?"

The team looked from Trump to Seaton, who was leafing through pages in a file.

"You're right. Debbie Charles found hanging from her banister in April

102

2010. Inquest in May, open verdict recorded."

Meredith reached for the notebook. "So why is he speaking to the coroner in August? Did something else come up? Bob, get the full file soonest. Let's go through this notebook page by page. It seems like our Phillip may have been on to something. You lot speed up. There must be something."

They spent another two hours going through the boxes containing Cowell's papers. All printed books were leafed through and any loose papers taken out; those with notes were examined and either repacked or left out, depending on whether the note was related to the book. They ended up with all the boxes repacked and the equivalent of a box load of loose papers and pads and ten files. Both Meredith and Trump scrutinised the notebook in which Trump had found the first lead, back to front, and both came to the same conclusion.

Meredith banged the desk and walked to a blank white board.

"Listen up. Debbie Charles was found hanged in April 2010 and an open verdict recorded at the end of May. But for some reason Cowell thought there could be more to it. According to this, he was investigating it in his own time. He was keeping a log of what he did and when, not very neatly, but that's what it looks like."

Meredith wrote on the board as he spoke. He detailed relevant dates, names, and places Cowell had listed as having visited. He turned back to the team.

"We can check those names we do have easily enough. But there is no detail, or not yet anyway, on these initials so we need to see if we can find anything that tells us who or what these stand for: RS, FM, NB, DW, and PT. I reckon they're all names but they could be places, or even streets." He looked across at Seaton, "Is it there?"

Seaton nodded. "Yep. I'm reading it now, but it's short. Found by sister, investigated, no signs of foul play. Son said she was a fruit cake, but coroner did record an open verdict. So there may be something in it . . . . Oh, the coroner's report isn't here. In fact, there are no witness statements either." He raised his eyebrows and grinned. "And now we're on to something. Right, let's hit the files first. Witness statements, reports, anything that looks like it should belong on a police file. I'll give his Governor at the time a ring."

They spent a further fruitless twenty minutes looking. Meredith was becoming increasingly irritated.

"There must be something. The bastard said to check his papers. I reckon we know this has to do with Debbie Charles, but where's the good stuff? Seaton, you got hold of Cowell's Gov yet?"

Seaton held up a finger to silence him, and thanked the person he was speaking to and hung up.

"He's gone to the cinema. His daughter reckons he'll be home at ten-thirty, IF he doesn't go for a drink. I've got his mobile number so I'll leave a message." Seaton picked up the phone and dialled out again.

Meredith looked up at the clock. It was almost eight. Most of them had been there since six-thirty in the morning. He rubbed his hands over his face and called for their attention.

"Right, it's been a long day, no point in all of us staying here all night. I'll stay on with . . ." he looked round the room for a volunteer. Hutchins beat Trump and Seaton by a whisker. "Not you, Hutchins, you've got nappies to change. Trump, you haven't got anyone waiting, you stop on."

"But, sir, they're letting them home tomorrow, and I start paternity leave the day after, so I'd like to do my bit." Hutchins stood and stretched, "And I'll make the coffee." He walked briskly to the kitchen, not allowing Meredith to respond.

Meredith watched him leave. He had no idea whether he would be a hindrance or a help, but he couldn't risk the former so he shrugged at Trump. "You can stay too. Before I release you, confirm again that you checked every cupboard in every room at Cowell's place."

Trump nodded. "We did, as I'm sure you did too."

Meredith eyed him, wondering if that was some form of challenge. "We did. But it was easy. New house, minimalistic furnishings, all Cowell's stuff in the loft. You did do the loft, didn't you?"

Trump resisted the urge to roll his eyes. "We did."

"Well, you missed something. I'm sorry, we're going back there. HUTCHINS." Trump winced as Meredith yelled. "Forget the coffee, we're going out. You lot go home. Now. Be back here early in the morning, bright-eyed and bushy-tailed. If anything gives and you're needed, you'll get a call."

~ ~ ~

The final words of the letter were read aloud.

So I carried on as normal. Phillip and I got on so well. I didn't even mind that he stopped working on it quite so hard, what with working in Cardiff and finding himself a young lady. I always assumed he'd stay in Bristol when he married or settled down. Can you imagine my shock when he told me he was leaving? I stood there, my mouth opening and shutting, I couldn't speak. He hugged me and told me he would come and see me, and that I could visit. I pushed him away. I'm ashamed to say I was crying.

He told me all about his girlfriend. She didn't deserve him. She'd had an affair, do you know that? I told him so too. I won't go into the detail of what he said, he said it very nicely of course, but in a nutshell, he told me that if he hadn't been looking after me and running two houses, he would have been able to spend more on her, do more with her! I froze, and it happened again. I hugged him and told him I understood. Afterwards I went into the kitchen and got the biggest knife. He was talking on the phone as I went back towards him. He was swearing at someone, and I almost didn't do it. I stood there listening to him shout as he ended the conversation.

"I don't need your help. Case closed, she killed herself, I've wasted enough time here already, I'm coming back and you had better keep out of my way."

Wasted time here? I stepped forward, and sort of hit him with the knife. He slumped forward. There was a lot of blood.

As always, I forgot what happened. I must have left him there like he was working.

"There you go, Bobby. Finished, just the last bit. Oh, you're not here any more." The writer gave a deep sigh, signed the letter with a flourish, and folded it. Talking constantly, the person moved around the house. Plugs were pulled from sockets, house plants taken and stood in the bath, and bins were emptied. "Jo's right. Anything could happen. I'd better deliver this by hand, can't afford for it to get lost in the post. I'll take it in the morning. I'd like to think that he'll come for me before I need to."

The letter was placed next to the photographs on the table and, sitting in the armchair, eyes closed, the waiting began.

~ ~ ~

Patsy was awoken by her phone ringing. It stopped before she was fully conscious. Sitting up, she blinked into the darkness before reaching for the bedside lamp. She frowned as she looked around. The papers that had been spread over her bed were back in the box on the floor, and the notebook on her bedside cabinet. Realising she was fully dressed she pulled back the blanket and stretched. She had obviously fallen asleep whilst working, and Linda had been playing mother. She stripped off her clothes and, grabbing her robe, she went to the bathroom. By the time she had showered she was fully awake, and she considered the case of Darren Wilkinson. She knew she would take it on. If nothing else, it was messy enough to take her mind off Jo. She banged her toothbrush on the side of the basin. She hadn't checked her phone. That was what had woken her. She pulled the towel tighter around her body and rushed back to the bedroom.

One missed call from Meredith, and a text. She opened the text.

Assume you are in bed. Mmmm. I think we're on to something, looking into it now. Call you in the morning. Sleep tight.

Patsy looked at her watch. It was almost midnight. She called Meredith. He answered on the first ring.

"Not now. I'll call you as soon as I can."

Patsy replaced the phone and smiled. Meredith was definitely on to something.

~ ~ ~

The door opened and Meredith smiled. "Hello, I need to have a word, if I may. I've found some papers that Phillip Cowell seemed to be working on, and I think you can help me."

"Yes, come on in. Oh, there are two of you."

Trump flipped open his identification. "DS Louie Trump, nice to meet you." He replaced his ID as he followed Meredith into the hall.

They went into the sitting room and each took a seat in an armchair.

Meredith waited until they were all settled. "It appears that Phillip Cowell had, on his own time, been investigating the suicide of Debbie Charles -"

"Yes, she was my sister. And it wasn't suicide. Here, read this, it will be quicker."

Meredith opened the envelope and withdrew the folded letter. As he read it his eyes grew wide in amazement, and he kept glancing at the two people watching him. He read the final paragraph and his face hardened.

"Fuck. You can't be serious," he waved the letter.

"Now, I know it's a shock, but there's no need for language like that. We're here to help each other. You must know that now."

Meredith held the letter out to Trump. "Read the last paragraph."

Trump's eyes scanned the final page.

So, with Phillip dead, my last hope for justice was gone. But now I have Jo, and she's perfectly safe, I assure you of that. I needed to ensure that someone would find out what happened. So you see, DCI Meredith, it's all up to you. You sort out what happened and you can have Jo back. I know you can do it.

My kindest regards
Nancy Bailey

Trump glanced up at Nancy and back to the letter. He shook his head, and, temporarily at a loss for words, he looked at Meredith.

Meredith jumped to his feet.

"You stay right there." He pointed at Nancy, who had no intention of moving, and he left the room.

Nancy and Trump listened to his feet as they pounded up the stairs. Doors were banged and their ears followed his feet as he searched upstairs for Jo. Nancy walked towards the door and Trump jumped up and put his hand on her arm.

"She's not here. I'm not stupid, you know." Nancy pulled the door open and called to Meredith. "She's not up there. Come down, you're wasting time."

Upstairs Meredith froze. What had she meant, he was wasting time? The letter said that Jo was safe. He ran back down the stairs and almost bumped into Nancy as he stormed into the room. His face was like thunder. He jabbed his finger at her as he shouted, "Where is she? The letter said she was safe. Why have I now got a time limit? COME ON!"

Flinching, Nancy cowered before him. Taking a step back, Meredith collected himself and Trump led Nancy to the sofa and sat her down.

"I need you to help me here, Nancy," Meredith said in a quieter voice. "She's been gone for four days now, she'll be frightened."

Nancy waited until her bottom lip was under control. "She's not too bad actually. Fuming with me, obviously, but she's a tough cookie, that one. You need to start work on finding out what happened to Debbie. I have all the stuff to get you started." Nancy pointed to the table in front of the window. "You read that lot, and you'll see that she didn't kill herself."

Meredith returned to his armchair and buried his face in his hands for a while before looking at Nancy. He forced a small smile.

"I can see from what I have already read that you believe your sister was murdered. Phillip obviously believed that in the beginning, and I hear he was a good copper. But this is three years old now, Nancy. It was an open verdict and I'm sure, that given the circumstances, I'll be allowed to reopen the case. But three years is a long time. I haven't got a magic wand or a crystal ball, it will take time. What will happen to Jo while I'm sorting it out for you? Who will be looking after her?"

He exchanged glances with Trump as Nancy relaxed and leaned back against the cushions on the sofa.

She smiled at him. "I knew you'd do it. I knew I'd picked the right man. Both Patsy and Jo have told me you're the best."

Nancy shook her head. "No, don't worry about Jo, she'll be fine."

"Is someone else with her? I mean, is someone looking after her, because seriously, Nancy, this could take months, years even. You don't want another death on your hands. There's been enough of that already, don't you think?"

"Yes I do. Why do you think I did this?" She shook her head. "Bobby is with Jo, so she has company. You have three months is my best guess."

Trump leaned forward and smiled at her. "Who's Bobby, and what do you mean by 'guess'? You see, Nancy, we need to be sure if we are to concentrate our efforts on finding out who murdered your sister. We don't want to be distracted by worrying about Jo. You do understand, don't you?"

Nancy smiled and looked across at Meredith.

"I'm glad you brought Louie. Now I have two of you that will get this sorted once and for all."

"Bobby?" Trump prompted as he returned her smile.

"Bobby is my budgie. Well, he's Jo's now, I realise I probably won't see him again."

Nancy pulled a tissue from her sleeve and dabbed her eyes.

Meredith bit his tongue as Trump continued, "That was thoughtful, I'm glad Jo will have some company. What colour is he?"

Trump ignored Meredith's sigh, and Nancy seemed not to hear it.

"Blue, absolutely beautiful he is. I think she was pleased."

"Oh, I know she will have been delighted. When you say three months, what do you mean by 'best guess'?"

Nancy explained about the provisions she had left Jo. She told them that Jo had all she needed to keep her alive and well.

"That's fabulous, Nancy, don't you think, sir?"

Trump turned to Meredith for confirmation.

Meredith released his nose and smiled his smile at Nancy.

"I do, Trump, yes. Nancy, I'm sorry I lost my temper. I have, as you can imagine, been very worried. I blame myself, because if it wasn't for your meeting with me, she would be tucked up in her own bed now. But I can see you have done everything you could to make her comfortable. You have been very kind. I suppose the only thing I'm concerned about now is what if something happens to her supply of water. Food is all well and good, but what if the water supply goes off?"

"That's not likely, is it? We're past the risk of frost now, so the pipes won't freeze, and even if they dig the road up and damage the water supply, they'll repair it." Nancy shrugged. "You can keep me informed of what is going on, out there," Nancy nodded towards the window, "and I'll let you know if there's cause for concern."

Placing both hands over her mouth, she yawned. "I'm so tired now, I think it must be because I've relaxed. I could do with a nap, but I doubt . . ." She lifted up her shoulders as she smiled, looking from one to the other. "I don't suppose there is any chance I can stay here, is there? Just until you've found Jo? I know I'm going to prison for a long time, but until you find Jo, I'm sort of in charge, aren't I? I could say I won't help you unless you let me stay here."

Trump looked at the floor as Meredith jumped to his feet. "Oh no, Nancy, that would never do. They, you know the top brass, will think that you're not helping us on purpose if we allowed that. They'll think you're stringing us along to get to stay here." He leaned down and gently took her arm. "In fact, I think the sooner we get you back to the station the better. Come on, let me help you."

Meredith pulled Nancy to her feet and jerked his head at Trump. "You take Nancy back to the station. I'll call Hutchins for a lift."

An hour later Nancy was dozing in a cell, and Meredith, Trump and Hutchins were poring over the papers that had been collected from Nancy's home. Meredith linked his fingers and stretched his hands above his head. He sighed.

"Right, let's call it a day. We should let her sleep, and at least we've made progress. We've solved three murders, have a confession from the murderer, and we know Jo is being kept somewhere in the city. So, there's no need to go searching barns and the like. It shouldn't take long." He pulled his jacket from the back of the chair. "Hutchins, enjoy your maternity leave. Come on, let's go home."

"Paternity, sir." Hutchins pulled a hoody over his head. "Pa. Not Ma."

"Well, Pa, enjoy it. Hopefully this will all be wrapped up by the time you get back, and you'll be back in uniform." Meredith switched off the lights in the incident room and closed the door.

"About that sir, now's not the time I know, but if I put in a request to join CID would you consider it?"

"Like you say, Pa, now's not the time. Put in your request though."

Meredith held the door open and Hutchins called his thanks as he hurried away.

Trump patted Meredith on the shoulder. "He's a good lad, you know. It was him who found the clue that led us to Nancy after all."

"Yes, it was. But solving one should've-hit-us-in-the-face clue does not a detective make. Goodnight, Trump."

Sitting in the car, Meredith tapped his phone lightly on the steering wheel. It was two o'clock, technically morning, and he had promised to call Patsy, but it wasn't a conversation he wanted. Smiling, he pulled out of the car park.

Patsy fumbled for her phone. It was Meredith. He began speaking as she answered it. She listened frowning.

"Yes, where are you? I'll come now." Patsy replied and switched on the bedside lamp. "Oh right."

She pulled on her robe and went to open the door.

"I didn't ring the bell, I didn't want to wake Loopy." Meredith grinned and pointed into the hall. "Are you going to invite me in?"

Patsy stepped back and Meredith crossed the threshold. The flowers he had bought earlier in the week stood resplendent on the small hall table.

"I doubt she's asleep, I think I heard Louie arrive a little while ago."

"Bugger. I need some rest. I don't want to be up all night."

Patsy looked at his weary face. Additional lines creased the corners of his eyes, and he needed a shave. She took hold of his lapel and pulled him towards her.

"Come on, and I mean sleep. This is a one-night-only offer." Leading him upstairs she closed the bedroom door quietly behind them. Meredith stood facing her, and with one quick movement, he released the tie of her robe, and smiled appreciatively.

"Good. I wanted to check that I wasn't going to get the fluffy PJ treatment." He winked as he pulled off his tie and threw it onto the dressing table, before beginning to unbutton his shirt. "You know, Hodge, there was a time when you needed to sleep in my bed. I know this is not what you want, but I need to sleep in yours tonight."

Meredith's grin fell away and his expression told her he wasn't fully with her. Sliding his shirt and his jacket from his shoulders, she laid them over the stool in front of the dressing table. Allowing her gown slip to the floor she climbed into bed, throwing back the duvet on the other side by way of invitation.

"I know. Come on."

Meredith climbed in and hugged her to him. His eyes closed and his breathing was ragged. Patsy switched off the lamp, and turned her back to him. He pulled her into his embrace.

"Do you want to talk?" she whispered. "I'd like to know about Jo if nothing else."

Meredith gave her his version of Nancy's letter. He knew her hand was over her mouth and her eyes wide in disbelief. He completed his story and his body relaxed against her.

"I have a million questions, but tomorrow will do. Get some rest, Meredith."

"I . . . thank you."

Patsy lay silently, enjoying the closeness of his naked body, as she replayed the story he had told her. His breathing slowed, and regular puffs of breath heated the back of her neck. After ten minutes, she drifted off too.

8

B ut should we let them sleep?" Linda whispered and gave an exaggerated shrug.

"It's only seven, and it was gone two o'clock when they got here, so another half an hour won't hurt." Patsy took two more mugs from the rack and threw teabags into them. "But we've probably woken them anyway so I'll make them tea too."

"Good, because I need to get going. I've promised Chris I'd get in early today. There's some stuff he needs sorted and printed before he goes. I think his train is at eleven. I'll get in the shower first." Linda was already leaving the kitchen. "Leave ours there, I'll pick them up when I'm done."

Patsy pushed open the door to her bedroom by bumping it with her hip. The movement was a little too harsh and it banged against the bedside cabinet. Meredith mumbled and turned over. Patsy froze, hoping she hadn't woken him. He adjusted his position but didn't open his eyes. Placing the mugs on the cabinet she closed the door quietly. Hanging her robe on the back of the door she tiptoed to the bed, and climbed in as carefully as she could. Screaming as Meredith grabbed her.

"Come here."

"I nearly had heart failure! Why didn't you let me know you were awake . . . Oh no." Patsy fell silent and they listened to the sound of running water and Linda belting out 'It's Raining Men' at the top of her voice.

Meredith laughed. "I said come here." He pulled her closer and wrapped her in the duvet. "I should be in work, but as I can't get in that shower, I have some time . . ."

Patsy was sitting at the table and smiled at Louie as he came into the kitchen. He looked crisp and clean, and raised his eyebrows as he placed the cold mug of tea on the table.

"I take it that's DCI Meredith enjoying a cold shower."

"Did you hear him scream too?" Patsy laughed. "You and Linda used all the hot water."

Louie filled the kettle and sat with Patsy. "I assume he updated you on Nancy Bailey?"

Patsy asked Louie all the questions she had stored up for Meredith. They were so engrossed in their conversation that they didn't hear Meredith come down.

"You ready, Trump? I thought you would have been there by now, given that you sneaked into the shower first."

Trump stood and looked Meredith in the eye. "Sorry about that sir, I had the impression you were busy," he said, straight-faced.

Patsy flushed and hid a grin as she looked at Meredith. His trousers were crumpled, his shirt looked as though he had slept in it, and he had a square of toilet tissue sticking to a cut on his chin. He did, however, have a twinkle in his eye, and the tension of the day before had left him. Patsy knew that would last until he got into the car. Meredith watched her assessing him and touched his chin gingerly.

"I don't know how women use those crap disposable razors." He looked Trump up and down. "You came prepared, I see."

"Always, I was a Boy Scout."

"Well, that was a given. Now get your arse in gear, we have to get going."

"I'll pop up and say goodbye to Linda, she's doing her hair, and it takes hours."

Meredith frowned as Trump left them. He walked to Patsy and pulled her up from the chair. "Hours? Her hair always looks windswept to me."

"That's how it's supposed to look. She cultivates it. Do you want me to pick you up a clean shirt? I've got to go in and see Chris before he leaves for a meeting, but I could get it there by lunchtime. You could update me on Jo then."

"So, you're attempting to bribe me. You want me to divulge details of an ongoing case, you know the rules." He shook his head. "It'll cost you more than a clean shirt. You leave a clean pair of knickers at mine, and we're in business." He cocked his head listening to Louie coming back down the stairs, before he pulled her to him and kissed her. "I have to go, keep in touch. Hopefully, I'll be free when you bring that shirt in."

"Will do, and be gentle with Nancy. She trusts you, don't give her reason not to. You have to be the good cop."

"Aren't I always?"

~ ~ ~

Meredith held his coffee in one hand, and pinched the bridge of his nose with the other. He stared over his fingers at his team.

"I want her house taken apart, properly this time, not some half-assed job like Cowell's place got. She has Jo somewhere in this city. Jo should be safe for now, but let's not miss anything. I want floorboards up, the lot. Speak to the neighbours too. I'll talk to Nancy and try and get more information from her. Volunteers to hold the fort?"

There were no volunteers. They all wanted to be out doing something more practical in search of Jo. Meredith let his hand fall to his side and eyed them.

"Okay I'll choose. Bob, you're in charge of the search, don't cock up. Trump, you stay here with young Dalton. Get the board up-to-date, and start listing who we need to speak to. Dalton can find their whereabouts. When you've done that start listing the Debbie Charles case over there." He nodded to an empty white board. "I want a call the minute anything useful turns up. What are you hanging about for? Get on with it!"

He swigged down his coffee, placed the mug on the desk in front of him, and headed for the door.

~ ~ ~

Patsy waved the envelope at Chris Grainger.

"She gave me this. I haven't said yes but . . ."

"But you want to take the case." Chris sighed and jutted out his bottom lip as he considered his words. "I can see you are all fired up on this, Patsy, and if she wasn't doing time I'd say go for it without a second thought. But it's so messy, I'm not convinced."

"Look at this information." Patsy flipped open the notebook to the list of contacts. "Not just names, but numbers, email addresses, and even how to find them on Facebook and Twitter. Where things have been noted in brackets means there is a diary entry here." She turned to the appropriate section. "I use the word 'diary' loosely but it's so much more than you would usually get with a missing person."

"How much is in that?" Chris nodded at the envelope.

"One thousand pounds – used twenties," Patsy winked at him.

Chris shook his head. "Give the money to Linda to bank. Then I want you to draw up a schedule of how you're going to attack this over the next week. That buys her a week. Do what you can and we'll see where we are. But you have to finalise the Reynolds Relocation case this week."

"Draw up a schedule, what like homework?" Patsy grinned, "Can't remember the last time I had to do that. I'll set a meeting up for Thursday with Reynolds."

"No, not like homework, like we may have to dump this back with the girl, so let's make sure we show her what you've done and when. But before you start, sign her up."

"She won't see me, won't even admit she's doing this. I don't know why, it would look more positive."

"Not the mother, the daughter. We're not working directly for the mother."

Patsy shrugged. "Okay. What time are you off?"

"In an hour, as long as Linda has that stuff ready for me."

"I'll have you a schedule ready by then."

"You've already worked out how you're going to attack this, haven't you?" Chris smiled for the first time during the conversation. "Go on, get on with it."

~ ~ ~

Nancy Bailey thanked Meredith for the tea and looked up at him expectantly.

"What have you found out?"

"What, when I was sleeping, you mean?"

Nancy looked him up and down. "You don't look like you've slept."

"It wasn't for long." Meredith switched on the recorder, announced those present in the room, and dragged out a smile. "Let's make a start. Nancy Bailey, you have been arrested for the murder of Wendy Turnball, Gary Charles and Phillip Cowell and for the abduction of Jo Adler. You have been read your rights and you have refused legal representation. Is that correct?"

"Yes."

"You understand your rights?"

"Yes, can we get on?"

"Why don't you want a solicitor?"

"Because they would stop me saying things that need saying, you know, to protect me from myself. That's not why I'm here. I've seen it on telly. They sit there saying no comment, no comment, until the policeman loses his temper. I don't want you to lose your temper, Mr Meredith. I want you to find out who killed my sister."

Meredith bit back a grin. He studied Nancy for a while. Leaning forward on his crossed forearms he gave a sigh. "A couple of things we need to establish, Nancy. The first is that police work is not always, actually is rarely, like it is on the telly. I think you should have a solicitor. You can always get rid of her if you don't like her, or if she doesn't help you, and I promise to try and keep my temper."

"Her? What do you mean, 'her'?" Nancy's eyes narrowed a little, and Meredith realised she was sharp. But she had to be, he reasoned silently, to have achieved all that she had.

"I only said her, because today's duty solicitor is female. I've worked with her a couple of times before and I think you'll like her. Like I say, you can always get rid of her."

Nancy smiled knowingly. "Do you like her? Is that why you're suggesting this? I thought you were after Patsy. I heard everything you didn't say, you know. Do you know you speak with your eyes?"

Meredith laughed out loud. "It has been mentioned, yes. I do like Ms Roscoe, very much, but she doesn't like me. The last time we met she called me a bully." That wasn't quite true; she had called him a bully after their first meeting, but a lot had happened since, and Meredith knew Jane Roscoe would help him.

Nancy raised her eyebrows. "And Patsy?"

"We have a history, you are very observant. Shall we crack on?"

"Please."

"I have briefly read through the file on your sister's case. I understand that you found her, and I understand that you have caused quite a fuss over having the case treated as though she had been murdered. I've seen the basic post-mortem report, and read, actually skimmed, all the witness reports from the inquest. I know you have this thing about her shoes, and _"

"My shoes. She was wearing my shoes. At first I believed that there was a possibility she had done it, no evidence of a struggle, no apparent motive for anyone to kill her, and she had been down." Nancy waved her finger at him. "I mean fed up. Not depressed, not suicidal, just down. All that . . . that . . ." Nancy struggled not to swear, "I'm going to have to say it." She shrugged an apology. "All that bloody twaddle they gave at the inquest. Total crap! There I've said it. If you ask me they were just trying to close another case, or get home for their tea." She looked at Meredith and turned up her nose. "They didn't want to earn their money and do what they were paid for."

Looking down at her lap, she smoothed out some of the creases, which sprang back into place as her hand reached her knee. She looked back up at Meredith. "That's why Phillip was helping me, he believed me. You know, if I'm going to be staying here, I'll have to get some clothes. The stuff I had last night is all creased."

She looked at Meredith's appearance but didn't say anything. Meredith looked down and ran his hands over his shirt.

"We'll get you sorted. Back to the shoes."

"What you have to understand about Debbie is that when Bill, that's her husband, left her, she thought it was her fault. She thought she hadn't been good enough, didn't matter what anyone said, especially me," Nancy tutted. "She wasn't good enough, so she set about making herself perfect. Well, as perfect as anyone can be. She changed her hair, went on a diet, joined the gym, went to dancing lessons, and did cookery at night school. You name it, she did it or tried it. Some of it fell by the wayside, of course, but the one thing that stuck was her appearance." Nancy gazed somewhere behind Meredith's head, lost in her thoughts. Meredith coughed and she looked at him. "Can I have my handbag back? I want to show you something."

Meredith nodded at the duty officer sat behind them.

"Go and grab it for me. PC Blakey is leaving the room to collect a handbag." He smiled at Nancy as Blakey left. "Would you like a drink?"

"Only water please. I need to drink a lot of water with my diabetes."

Meredith smiled as Patsy flew into his mind; she would have remembered the diabetes.

"You wait here, I'll be two ticks." He announced that the interview was suspended, and hurried to the custody desk where Blakey was releasing the tie of a large clear plastic bag containing Nancy's handbag. "Anything yet from Jane Roscoe, Sam?"

"She said she can give you twenty minutes at lunchtime. She sounded

116

very suspicious. Louie asked for a word when you had a moment. Shall I buzz him?" Sam placed his hand on the receiver, and picked it up as Meredith nodded. "DCI Meredith for you, Louie." He handed Meredith the phone.

"Yes, Trump?" Meredith listened as Trump told him that the autopsy report on Wendy Turnball was extremely detailed, and under questioning, the pathologist had ruled out any possibility of foul play. "Get Sherlock to look at it. See what he thinks." Meredith replaced the receiver. "If I'm still in there interrupt me when Roscoe gets here." He turned to Blakey who stood holding Nancy's handbag. "Give me that, get Nancy a glass of water and me a coffee."

Meredith placed the bag on the table, and announced the interview had resumed. Nancy thanked him as she lifted it into her lap. She pulled out a large leather wallet and fished around in the bottom of it. Pulling out a bunch of keys and handed them to Meredith.

"You'll need these. They're the keys."

"The keys to the house where Jo is, you mean?" Meredith took the keys and held them in his palm as though weighing them. Nancy nodded as she flipped open the wallet, and withdrew two photographs.

"That's Debbie a week before, and that's her about a month before. We'd had a day out at Weston, we had such a laugh." She waved her hand in the air. "But, let's stick to the subject. What do you notice?"

Lifting one of the photographs, Meredith peered at it. Two women smiled back at him. He squinted closer.

"Is this you with her, Nancy? You were a fine-looking woman." He glanced up and smiled, before returning his attention to the photograph.

"Thank you. That was three and a half years ago, give or take."

Meredith's head shot up, and Nancy looked down at her hands, embarrassed by his scrutiny.

"I know. Grief and injustice do this to you."

Her bottom lip quivered and Meredith looked back at the photograph. He studied Debbie Charles. She was an attractive woman, probably in her mid-forties. She was wearing a navy skirt with matching jacket. The jacket had a red trim on the cuffs and lapels. Beneath the jacket she wore a white, round-necked blouse, and on her feet a pair of navy court shoes with a red trim. Over her shoulder she carried a red and navy handbag. In her pose she was holding her chin with one hand, and Meredith noted that her nail varnish was the same shade of red as on her outfit. He glanced briefly at Nancy who was watching him closely before picking up the second photograph. In the second shot, Debbie was wearing a pair of wide cream linen trousers, and Meredith quickly noted that her shirt, shoes and scarf complemented the outfit. He placed the photographs side by side on the table.

"Like you, your sister was an attractive woman. She certainly knew how to dress and make the most of herself. Now, tell me about the shoes."

"You will have seen the photographs taken by your lot. I couldn't look at them, but Phillip described what she was wearing. Blue skirt, blue floral shirt, and my brown shoes. I knew she was wearing my shoes, I saw her legs dangling . . ." Nancy looked down and swallowed. "I saw my shoes, one of them was hanging off. I'd left that pair there a couple of weeks earlier as they were rubbing my corn. I wore her flip-flops home."

"And you are suggesting that she didn't take her own life, because her shoes didn't match her outfit?"

"Initially I was, yes. They're what started it. I looked at the shoes, and before I called the police or threw up, which I did all over her pot on the porch, I wondered why on earth she would have put on my shoes. They were two sizes too big, and as you saw they didn't match her outfit. Not only that, but they didn't fit her, do you see?" Nancy shook her head as she spoke. "I called the police, of course, but you see it was so very odd that it was my first thought."

Nancy shook her head as Meredith gazed at her impassively. The message clearly wasn't registering. She gave a little huff before continuing and Meredith pinched the bridge of his nose.

"Those first few days we're a blur, as you can imagine. I had to find Gary and tell him, I had to call the rest of the family, and I liaised with the police, Phillip, about everything they needed. Phillip came round and told me the pathologist had completed a report to say the injuries were consistent with someone who had taken their own life by hanging themselves. There was no sign of a struggle, and as there was no obvious reason for someone to murder her, the coroner would probably record a verdict of suicide and release the body for burial." Nancy threw her hands into the air. "I went mad. I explained about him and the other men."

Meredith raised his eyebrows to question what she had said.

"Yes, I know, I'll get to them, and about the shoes. Phillip, bless him, said he'd have a word. Well, I couldn't sleep that night. Just couldn't sleep, it all kept going around and around in my head, and then I remembered."

"Remembered what?" Meredith was keen to find out how the search was going and wanted her to get to the point.

"I had gone round to see her, and I made the tea while she folded the washing. She had finished her housework and had brought the washing in off the line. She looked fabulous. I sat there watching her fold bras in half before storing the matching panties in the cup. When she finished she didn't have one odd pair of knickers. I laughed at her and told her every woman had odd knickers, it was like men with odd socks." Nancy looked at Meredith, her face serious. "Do you know what she said?"

She watched Meredith as he shook his head and took a breath.

"'When I was with him' – she was talking about her husband – 'I went without so that everything was perfect. I'll never go without again. I don't want expensive stuff, or to be flash, but I want to feel good. It takes very little to make sure you look good and feel good, and if I live to be one hundred, my undies will always match. Even if they are Marks and Spencer's thermals,' and we laughed." Nancy smiled at the memory. "When she came back down from putting the washing upstairs, she said, 'At least I'll never have to worry about getting knocked over by a bus.'" Nancy tapped the desk with her fingertips. "There, you see."

Meredith resisted the urge to sigh. He forced a smile. "Not really, no."

"I asked Phillip to check what underwear she was wearing, and it didn't match."

"But if, and I am saying *if,* Nancy, she had been so distraught, upset, unbalanced that she chose to take her own life, the last thing she would have worried about was what she was wearing. I can't see it would have been top of her agenda."

"That's what Phillip said. So we went round and I checked her undies drawer. I showed him what I meant. When I opened that drawer it was perfect, all the little pairs lined up. Except two. The white bra didn't have the panties with it, *and,*" Nancy emphasised the 'and' by nodding her head, "the blue panties had to be moved for her to get the bra. If she was so distraught or upset, why would she bother to do that? Why would she change her normal daily habit? I'll tell you why." Nancy was becoming animated, and she shook her finger at Meredith. "Because she was scared and she wanted me to know that something was wrong. She topped it off

119

with the shoes. Why would anyone put on the wrong shoes to hang themselves?" Nancy tapped her finger on the desk. "Because, Mr Meredith, she didn't do it. She must have been forced in some way. I know it was not a voluntary action. Now you find out who, or even why, and I'll tell you where Jo is."

Nancy drew in a deep breath, blew it out, and leaned against the back of the chair, her hands folded across her chest.

Meredith pursed his lips.

"Yes, I can see the logic, but if there was something to find, why did Phillip fail? Why couldn't he get anywhere with it?"

"I don't know. Perhaps he didn't try hard enough." She smiled but her eyes were cold. "He didn't have an incentive."

Meredith picked up the keys Nancy had given him. He needed to keep her on side, so he nodded in agreement.

"Perhaps, but I can tell from the notes he'd made that he did try. But I'll try harder." He smiled. "Now these two blokes you referred to, will the notes on them be in the papers, or do you need to tell me?"

He watched Nancy's shoulders relax.

"The basic details should be there. Bill Charles, that's her ex, is still in Bristol somewhere. Now he thought he would get the house. They never divorced but he signed the house over to her to avoid paying maintenance for Gary. He never thought she'd have the wherewithal to leave a will, and technically he was still her next of kin. I actually smiled when I read her will." Nancy grinned at Meredith. "She left him the lawnmower." Laughing, she dabbed at her eyes. "I have no idea why or what the relevance was. But it did make me smile, and still does. He felt short-changed, you know. The house only had a small mortgage, and the area was becoming popular; it went up in value. He'd the cheek to go and see her and suggest she sell it and give him a share. He used such language when she refused. It made me blush when she told me. When that plan failed, he wanted her to sign over an endowment that he'd put in her name for tax purposes. He had paid the majority of the money that went into it, but she gave him a similar response. He said he'd lost his job and was desperate, but she told him she was glad. I'm not convinced she meant it, but she knew he was having trouble with his lady friend. The one that caused them to split up, so she wouldn't help him. Principle, you see."

Nancy sipped at her water and leaned towards Meredith.

He mirrored her action.

"I don't want you to judge her on what I'm going to say now. She was lonely, and she needed to be needed. She met some men – there were several – but two of them she got quite close to, if you know what I mean. She wasn't loose or wayward, simply in need of some affection. It's the only thing we fell out about, because I never got to meet them. I told her it was wrong that she was seeing two men at the same time if they didn't know. I tried to be open-minded about the 'you know what' element." Nancy glanced away from Meredith. "She implied that it didn't matter because one of them was temporary. I guessed that she meant he was married, but I didn't push it. I'd said my piece and I didn't want to fall out with her. Other than Bill, none of them turned up afterwards. None of them came to the funeral, none of them made contact, and there was no trace of who they were amongst any of her things. I checked." She looked back at Meredith. "Now that's odd in my book, unless you have something to hide."

"You're absolutely right there, Nancy." Meredith rubbed his hands together. "Now I have something to get my teeth into. Well done."

Nancy beamed at him. "Thank you," she said quietly.

He held her gaze. "Don't thank me yet, Nancy, thank me when I've caught him. I understand now. I'm going to have to leave you for a bit so I can get on with this. That means you have to go back to the cells. Not enough manpower to keep you here, I'm afraid. You understand that, don't you?"

Nancy nodded and Meredith scooped the keys off the desk.

"I'd better put these somewhere safe." He picked out the long, cast iron key. "This looks ancient. Where are you holding her, a castle?" He attempted a light-hearted laugh.

"That's for the grill." She held her hand out, and he placed the keys in her upturned palm. She moved the keys around the ring in turn. "Front door top lock and front door bottom lock. This is the cellar door," she waved the long key at him, "the grill, and these others are for the windows and shutters, but you won't need them." She gave him back the keys. "Now, you go and do what you've got to do. I'm sure you'll be using those in no time."

Meredith put the keys in his jacket pocket as he hurried along the corridor. He didn't think he had a chance in hell of finding out who, if anyone, killed her sister. If the ex had been involved, he'd have been arrested the first time round. He hadn't been, so he must have had a watertight alibi. The men to whom she had referred were probably just after the sex. He wasn't surprised they hadn't surfaced. But at least now he'd narrowed down the search for Jo a little. He now knew that she was being held in a house that had a cellar, and that had some form of shuttering on the window. That would save some time.

He called to Trump as he entered the incident room, and made his way to the white board. "What news, Trump? I've got a little more out of her."

Trump walked across and watched as Meredith put the basic house description on one part of the board, then added 'Bill Charles' and 'Lovers' to the list of names to be interviewed.

"Not much, Gov. The immediate neighbours say she keeps herself to herself, she's only lived there two years. Haven't noticed any visitors, haven't heard anything out of the ordinary, et cetera, et cetera. They've almost finished the search and found nothing."

Trump held his hand up as Meredith turned to face him, "And before you say it, not because they're not being thorough, but because there is nothing there. Literally, nothing. No paperwork except a gas bill that's been paid. There is evidence of a printer as they found used cartridges in the dustbin, so that indicates a computer, but no sign of one. She knew we were coming and she's cleaned up."

Meredith nodded. "Get her purse. She must have bank cards. Find out who she banks with and what she's been spending her money on. What?" Meredith frowned as Trump shook his head.

"I have the purse, got it this morning when I saw the inventory of her handbag. No cards, fifty-five pounds and sixty-two pence in cash. It also had her driving licence, a store loyalty card and some receipts. We're onto the banks now, but that'll take a while, as you know."

"Right, I'll have another bash at her in . . ." He paused to look at his phone which was vibrating in his top pocket. "Hello, yep come on up." He looked across at Dalton. "Get the desk to let Hodge up, would you?" He turned back to Trump. "This," he tapped the white board with the pen, "indicates an older property. Pre-war at least. Find out where both Nancy's and Jo's phone have been used. Start with the last week, and find out what type of property is close by. It's a long shot but it's a start. Hallelujah for

Google Earth, that'll save some shoe leather. Anything else?"

"Aaron called again. I didn't tell him too much but I've told him we have a photograph showing Jo alive and well yesterday. Oh, and Frankie has the autopsy report on Wendy Turnball, said he'll get back to you later. He's got one of his own to finish first."

Patsy opened the door and smiled. Meredith noticed that she was reading the boards as she approached rather than looking at them, and, in particular, him. He took her by the shoulder and turned her around.

"If you want to know anything, you ask me." His eyes twinkled, and he pushed her in the direction of his office.

Trump looked at Dalton. "Don't ask, and don't get involved. This case is far simpler than they are."

Meredith closed the door to his office and Patsy held out a bag.

"How's it going?"

Meredith shook his head. "Slowly." He narrowed his eyes. "That's because I'm being nice." He winked at her smile. "We know the property is in town, and it has shutters and a cellar." He peered into the bag. "And deodorant," he lifted his arms and sniffed. "Fair point, well made. Did you bring clean knickers?"

"That's for me to know and you to find out." She stood on tiptoe and kissed him on the chin, leaving a lipstick imprint. "Now I must dash. Your face needs washing now too."

~ ~ ~

Patsy hurried up the stairs and into the serviced reception area. As she waited for the receptionist to finish a call, she stared out of the window at the traffic on the M5 and wondered if the roadworks would ever be completed. She ignored a call from Linda as the receptionist hung up.

"Patsy Hodge to see Ted Reynolds."

She watched as the receptionist ran her finger down the screen in front of her.

"Ah yes, Mr Reynolds is running ten minutes late, would you like a drink whilst you wait?" The receptionist waved to a seating area to the left of her desk.

Patsy shook her head. "No thank you. I'll take a seat."

Taking a seat on one end of the curved sofa, she returned Linda's call. Linda had been tasked with making appointments for Patsy to meet the contacts listed as friends of Darren Wilkinson. Linda explained what she had achieved and that she would send the list of appointments via email.

"One of them sounded a bit suspicious. He wanted to meet you at home, but he agreed to a pub when I said it was urgent. I thought that would be preferable, you know, meeting in public. Oh and I'll be out for a few hours this afternoon. I'm meeting Trevor, he's going -"

"Why are you meeting him, and where? I don't want you disappearing again."

Linda had caused Patsy, Louie and Meredith a lot of worry once before when she and Trevor, a computer geek, had met up and lost track of time discussing computers. Linda had seemingly vanished off the face of the earth for a while.

"Starbucks in town, and he's training me on this new software. I'll be no more than two hours as we've done loads of it remotely."

"Hmm, well I don't like the bloke, he's creepy. Keep in touch, okay. I don't know why he can't come to the office. That would be so much easier."

"He's harmless and he has a soft spot for me. He's only creepy because he has this conspiracy theory about people hunting him down. He won't come to the office, in case he's followed. Too difficult to escape. Right, email sent, it'll be there when you hang up. Bye."

Patsy hung up as Ted Reynolds came out to meet her.

He gave a tight-lipped smile as he shook her hand. "I take it it's not good news?"

"I'm afraid not, it's now a question of how far you want to take this."

Reynolds led the way to a side office and they sat opposite each other at a round table. Patsy slid her report across the desk, and placed the recorder on the table and switched it on. Reynolds' frown deepened as he listened to her conversation with Alex Walters. The recording ended and he drummed his fingers on the table.

"Thank you. I take it I can have that." He nodded to the recorder. "I can deal with him, but I have no way of knowing how many clients he has taken, or if I can retrieve them. It's not all about the money; I'm hoping the solicitors can get their hands on that. I just hate losing custom to that bastard." He held his hands up. "Excuse the language, but . . . well."

"I do. The report and recording will be emailed with our account. We don't know how he was getting the information out. That would be a start.

I think it's safe to say he wasn't writing it down on paper, so my guess is personal email. I doubt he would have been stupid enough to use his company account."

Reynolds stood as he nodded agreement. "You're right. I'll get our IT chaps on to it." He opened the door and looked out into the reception area, his expression thoughtful. "That's if they're up to it. Anyway, thank you, Patsy. At least we can stop the flow now." He stepped back to allow Patsy to pass.

"If you need any help on the IT side, give us a call. We have a whiz kid who may be able to help. It won't take her long to know if she can do anything."

As Patsy shook Reynolds' hand, his eyebrows rose.

"And here comes the man himself. Early for a change, I had hoped you'd be gone."

Patsy followed his gaze, and through the smoked glass, which shielded the reception area from the stairwell, she saw Alex Walters approach the glass door. He was smiling as he entered. His smile became more hesitant as he spotted Patsy and Reynolds.

He walked forwards, his eyes darting from one to the other, and held out his hand. "Patsy Meredith, a pleasure to meet you once more. Is there anything I can help you with?"

Patsy ignored his hand as Reynolds answered.

"I think you've been helping yourself a little too long, don't you? Now, shall we go to my office and have a chat?"

"I'm not sure what you mean, Ted. Is there something wrong?"

Walters' words were mild but his features had hardened, and his lip curled a little as he looked to Reynolds for an answer. Reynolds waved the report at him.

"It's all in here, Walters, and there's taped evidence. The game is over. I think we need to talk about compensation while you empty your desk, don't you?"

"Taped what?" Walters turned to Patsy. "You bitch, you stupid fucking bitch, you'll regret this. Mark my words." The finger which had been pointing at Patsy, poked her shoulder in time with the last three words. Patsy stepped back a little. Walters stepped even closer. "Too late to move away darling, the damage is done."

"Don't shoot the messenger, Walters. You're in enough trouble."

Reynolds, older than Walters by a good twenty years, weighed up his chances if Walters got violent. He didn't fancy them.

Patsy waved her hand at him.

"Leave it, Mr Reynolds, Mr Walters was just about to step away, weren't you? I'm sure those threats were in the heat of the moment." She looked up into Walters' face and gave a slight nod.

Walters snorted, and pointing his finger into her face, he said through gritted teeth, "What? You don't know who you're messing with, you stupid bitch." His finger was touching the end of her nose. "I don't know who you are," he applied a little pressure to his finger. Patsy leaned back a little, and held his gaze her face impassive. "But you will regret this."

"So you've said. Now step away please." Her lips twitched into a brief smile.

"Or else -"

In one swift movement, Patsy grabbed his wrist with one hand, and with the palm of the other, she flattened his hand at right angles whilst twisting his arm. The momentum caused him to fall to his knees. Patsy held his arm behind him. The pain increased as he tried to move. She leaned closer and said quietly, "Or else someone may get hurt. As I see it, Mr Walters, you have two choices. You can stop throwing your weight around and leave. Mr Reynolds can deal with you via his solicitor, or we can call the police. Which would you prefer?"

"I'll go, get off."

Patsy released his hand and he cradled his arm, rubbing his shoulder. Getting to his feet he made towards the door. As he pulled it open he turned.

"Let this drop, the pair of you. You don't want to get involved."

He hurried away down the stairs as the door slowly closed behind him. They watched him leave.

When he had disappeared from view, Patsy sighed and turned to Reynolds. "Well, that wasn't pleasant."

"No, indeed not. I'm glad you're on my side, though." Reynolds forced a smile. "Are they crooks, the people behind New Beginnings? Do you think his threats have any substance?"

"I've no idea. Nothing came up, but I was looking at what he was up to, not at them. Would you like me to look?"

"No, let's leave it for now. Thank you, Patsy, I'll call if I need anything." He looked at the staircase. "Would you like me to accompany you to your car?"

"No, I'll be fine. But thank you."

Patsy smiled and left Reynolds in reception. She waved through the smoked glass as she turned to the final flight of stairs. Once outside she hurried to her car. Locking the doors, she pulled her phone from her bag and read Linda's email. Glancing at the clock she noted she had an over hour before her first appointment, enough time to buy some groceries. As she pulled out of the car park she didn't notice Alex Walters sitting in his BMW and jotting down her number plate on the back of a business card.

~ ~ ~

Nancy smiled as Meredith came into the interview room.

"You look better," she observed, and Meredith returned her smile.

Once he had switched on the recorder and gone through the formalities, he studied her for a moment. "Where were we?" he asked when her brow creased. "Where would you like to start?"

"That's up to you. I've been up hill and down dale with this. You're the expert, where would you normally start?"

Meredith bit back his irritation. She delivered the line in a pleasant unchallenging tone, but he sensed she was testing him, or worse playing him.

"I'd normally start by asking you how long you had been planning it." He inclined his head, "How long after she died did you decide what to do?"

Nancy shook her head. "No. I told you it wasn't planned. Nothing was planned. I simply wanted the truth." Her brow was furrowed and her mouth drooped.

"But no one suspected a thing. Are you sure that you didn't kill them, one after the other, believing you would be caught and the case highlighted?"

"No. NO!" Nancy huffed and leaned forward. Her hands rested on the desk and she twisted the small signet ring on her little finger. She studied its progress for a while before looking back up at Meredith. "The only thing I planned was to take Jo. I planned that in about six hours. I have no intention of letting her die."

Meredith blew silently through barely parted lips as he held her gaze. "You see, Nancy, I have difficulty with that. Shall I tell you why?"

"Yes, please do." Nancy was becoming irritated, and her shoulders rocked as she replied.

"Okay, and bear with me on this. Let me tell you how the outside world sees this."

Nancy nodded, leaned back in the chair, her arms across her bosom.

"Your sister is found hanged and you believe it to be murder. There is no evidence of foul play, so you try and convince people that you believe can help to prove that she was murdered. But nothing happens, nothing new is discovered, and slowly they start to lose interest. You can't believe that they might give up on it, so you formulate a plan. Wendy Turnball has changed tack and has told you she won't help you any more. When you think about the implications of this, and with the knowledge Phillip Cowell isn't getting very far, you plan her murder."

Nancy opened her mouth to speak but Meredith held his finger up.

"You are kind, in as much as you fill her with drugs and alcohol so she won't know what's happening, but that backfires. That now also looks like suicide, only no one cared about her, not like you cared about Debbie, so an accidental death is recorded. So now what will you do? You tell Gary about your worry that the truth will never be revealed, and he tells you to forget it as well. So you plan his death too. You lure him to some building site or similar, and somehow you kill him. You bury him in a spot where you believe his body will be discovered. But it's not. The workmen simply throw concrete on top of him and another plan is foiled. All you have left is Phillip. He's safe as long as he keeps helping you. But he doesn't."

Meredith sighed and shook his head. "He too is dispatched. Unbeknownst to you he had been having trouble with his girlfriend and colleague, so rather than focus on you, his colleague, a policeman, is arrested. You are not the centre of attention any more so what can you do? You take another police officer and you lock her up. You don't kill her, not because of any sense of pity or conscience, but because that way you can keep this running for weeks, months even. All the while you and your sister's case are high profile, centre of attention. What if Jo Adler does die? What difference would that make to you? None. Objective has been achieved. You're going to get life for the first three anyway, so what difference would another one make?"

Meredith stretched his legs out straight and crossed them at the ankle. Leaning back, he supported his head with his hands. "How did I do?"

"Oh, you've finished have you? I thought that this fairy tale would be longer. Is it worth me saying anything, or will you ignore that too?" Looking thoroughly disgusted Nancy looked away and stared at the door.

"So you think that I should just accept that a sweet, caring lady managed to kill three people by mistake? You go undetected, and we would never have got you for Cowell, not unless you'd given us the clue, and none of it was planned. And I should also believe that you kidnap and hold a police officer hostage with no forward planning. All these things simply happened, and you had some angel sitting on your shoulder making it all go as far away from you as possible."

"Yes, because that's what happened." Nancy did not look back at him, and Meredith could tell from her tone that she was almost ready.

"All right," he conceded, "I'll give you the murders, I can sort of see that, but not Jo." He lowered his voice, "No. Not Jo."

Nancy slowly turned her head towards him. "Why not? I don't understand, why not?" She didn't look away.

"When I say I don't believe you, I do believe you didn't plan Jo. She just happened to be the one that got the short straw. It could have been anyone, perhaps even a child."

Meredith had hit the right button, and Nancy blew.

"Don't be ridiculous. Why would I take a child? How would that help?" She had raised her voice, and Meredith could see the whites of her knuckles on hands that now gripped the desk.

"Okay, not a child, but anyone. Anyone kind enough to help you! Who was it you had planned on taking?"

"I didn't have a plan."

"You did."

"NO!"

"So how do you stumble across where to keep them at the drop of a hat? Renting a property had to be planned."

"Because it's mine. I already had it!" Nancy was now red in the face.

"How? How does a cleaner manage to keep two properties? You've been a widow for over ten years."

Nancy looked relieved. "You nearly had me then. Oh boy . . ." Nancy held her cheeks in her hands, causing her lips to pucker. "I thought I'd chosen the wrong one for a moment." She smiled happily at him.

"How have I made you happy, Nancy?" Meredith raised one eyebrow.

"Because you were trying to catch me out, trying to make me give more information because you had made me angry. Nearly did too. Now, how are you doing out there?" Nancy jerked her head towards the door. "You know now that there's nothing at home for you. So is it full steam ahead on Debbie's case now?"

Nancy gave a little shrug and looked quite serene as she smiled at him. Meredith frowned. He wasn't sure if she were mad, clever, or a combination of the two. But he realised the only way she was going to give information on Jo was if he gave her something on Debbie. He stood abruptly and ended the interview.

"It is indeed, so I must go and sort out the troops. You'll have to go back to the cell again. I'll get them to make sure you have a regular supply of tea."

"And a book please. I know asking for a telly is too much,"

Nancy giggled, and Meredith decided that the answer to his previous thought was mad. He nodded and hurried back to the incident room.

Trump looked up as he entered. "Anything?" He looked expectantly at Meredith. "We've found Bill Charles and have the last known address for nephew Gary. It's been confirmed. The rest are on their way back from Nancy's. It's spotless, not even a postcard there. I'll make sure someone pops in every day to pick up the post."

"I now know that Nancy owns another property, it's not rented. We need to get onto that." He clicked his fingers and pointed at Trump. "Where did the sister live? Check that out too. When that lot get back, turn two of them round again. Where does Bill Charles live? I could do with some fresh air," he glanced at the clock, "and food. Have either of you two eaten? Come on," he instructed as they shook their heads. "I'll pay."

~ ~ ~

Meredith stood with Trump, and they looked up and around the row of neat, newly built identical houses that formed an arc around a small grassed area on which two children were hitting a ball back and forth with cricket bats that were too big for them. Only three of the houses showed any signs of being lived in.

"It must be odd living in an empty street," Trump observed as Meredith walked towards number fourteen.

"I doubt it will take long for them to fill up, not if the deposit is covered by the benefits office." Meredith nodded back towards the board erected by the agent, Stella Young. "This street is reserved for those on benefits. They've made a nice job of it too. Let's hope it stays that way." He pushed the bell.

Bill Charles sighed and muted the television. He hoisted himself out of the armchair and scuffed his way to the door.

"Are you the police?" he asked unnecessarily, since Trump was holding out his identity card.

"We are. DCI Meredith and DS Trump."

Charles stepped back so that the two men could enter.

"First on the right." He gave another sigh, and followed them into the small sitting room using the wall to assist his balance, his right foot not able to take his full weight. "Take a seat."

"Thank you for seeing us at such short notice," Meredith gave a brief smile. "I'm sure you know why we're here."

Bill Charles looked from one to the other. "I'm guessing it's about Debbie." He shook his head. "I don't know why this has come up again. I told you everything I knew the first time. Go on, ask away."

His shoulders twitched in a half shrug as he settled back into the armchair.

"Why don't you tell me what you know and what you think, that way it will save us going around in circles." Meredith also leaned back, and crossed his legs at the ankles. He watched as Bill Charles closed his eyes before holding out his hands, palms up in resignation.

"This will be short then. Debbie kicked me out about seven years ago. I'd had an affair. She didn't take it well." He rolled his eyes. "I moved in with my lady friend." His nose wrinkled at the thought and he tutted. "The hearts and flowers bit didn't last, but it was only supposed to be a bit of fun. Not a commitment. Debbie couldn't see that, and she hung me out to dry. I didn't realise that at the time though, guilt you know, but I signed the house over to her. It was all I had."

He drummed his fingers on the arm of the chair. "I tried to get back with her. I genuinely wanted to at the time. But she had changed. She was all glamorous, and had this new life. The boy fell out with her for a while, I understand. She was having blokes back to the house. I saw them. I gave up trying when I saw one of them leave, I didn't want her then." He snorted. "Double standards I know, but my pride got in the way. So I walked away."

131

Gazing out the window, behind the couch on which Meredith and Trump sat, Charles got lost in thought.

"When was the last time you saw her?" Meredith prompted him back into the conversation.

"About three months before she topped herself."

"Do you think it was suicide?"

Bill Charles' laugh was mirthless. "It's her bloody sister again, isn't it?" He shook his head in disbelief. "When is she going to give up on this? What's she said to get you so interested? DCI, did you say? That's jumped a rank or two since what's his name came around. DC Peter Cowell."

"Phillip Cowell." Trump corrected him. "When did you meet *Phillip* Cowell?"

"I don't know, maybe a couple of years back the first time. Then about . . ." he whistled as he thought back, "maybe a year ago, if that. He asked the same bloody questions, and got the same bloody answers. I showed him the door when I realised he was working with her."

"Who, Nancy? Why would you do that?" Trump inclined his head.

Meredith noted the set of Charles' jaw. He was clearly getting angry.

"Is this official?" Charles demanded.

"What do you mean?"

"You know what I bloody mean. Have you reopened the case, or has that lunatic convinced more of you that Debbie was murdered?"

Trump ignored the question. "You clearly thought she was suicidal? Why did you think that?"

"I never said that."

"You think she may have been murdered, or that it was a possibility?" Meredith joined the conversation.

Bill Charles banged his hands on the arms of the chair and pushed himself to his feet. He took two long awkward strides to the door and flung it open.

"Piss off. Go on, get out." He jerked his thumb into the hall. "This is done, I'm not sitting here letting you two put words in my mouth. I don't know what that stupid cow tells you lot to get you on side, but I've wasted enough of my time. You go and you tell her from me she needs to get a life. Her own life, and leave the rest of us in peace."

Meredith and Trump hadn't moved. They sat watching him, which wound him up still further.

"I don't know if she did it or not. Why would you care about my opinion after all this time? What's it been, three years? You go and ask the boy, you ask Gary." He nodded rapidly. "The one thing we agreed on after I'd left, was that this should be left . . ." Charles paused and pointed at Trump. "What was that look for? Has he said something different? Has Gary been turned by her too?"

Meredith chewed his lip and looked at the carpet for a second. Bill let go of the door and walked back towards his chair.

"What?"

Meredith looked up and tried to assess his expression. He couldn't work out whether it was concern or fear.

"I think you should sit down, Mr Charles."

Bill Charles dropped heavily into the armchair, he didn't need to be told twice. "This is official, isn't it? What's happened? Has Gary said something or found something?"

"Yes, it's official. When did you last see your son?" Meredith's tone was soft and he watched the changing expression on Charles' face as he attempted to work out the reason for the question. Charles swallowed and clasped the arms of the chair.

"He's done it too, hasn't he? Has he killed himself?" His face was set and devoid of emotion, but the tremor in his hands gripping the chair revealed his concern.

Meredith shook his head.

"No, no he hasn't. I'm afraid to inform you that we believe he is dead, murdered." Meredith paused to let the information sink in. "When did you last see Gary?"

"What do you mean, you believe? You either know or you don't."

"We have information that leads us to believe that your son was murdered. We're trying to verify that information and that's why we need to know when you last saw him." Meredith leaned forward. "We're not trying to put words into your mouth. But we believe his death may be connected with his mother's, albeit loosely." Meredith nodded slightly, his smile brief but encouraging.

Bill Charles' shoulders slumped and he returned Meredith's nod.

"I'm sorry about all that," he glanced towards the door, "I thought you'd come to speak about Debbie." His head drooped and he stared into his lap for a while. He looked up and his pain was evident. "I haven't seen

Gary since his mother's funeral . . . no, no that's not true. I haven't seen him since they read the will. I was . . . let's just say, I didn't do myself any favours." He blinked rapidly. "She left the house to the boy, and a bloody lawnmower to me. I'd done this," he lifted his right leg, allowing his foot to fall awkwardly back to the floor, "and I thought I was due my share." He looked directly at Meredith. "We used to be close, you know."

"What happened?"

"When, at the reading of the will?"

"Yes, is that what broke the bond?" Meredith could see how painful the memories were, and spoke in a low steady tone, not looking away for fear Charles would clam up.

"It was before that. He was almost fifteen when she kicked me out. He blanked me at first, but after a few months he agreed to see me. I'd watch him play football, was even allowed the honour of watching him and his mates rehearse. He formed a band, you know; it was atrocious, well to my ear anyway. But I lied and told him I thought it was great. He started suggesting I come round to the house. He wanted me to try and get his mother back. I already had been." He stared out the window, again. "I reckon it's going to pee down in a minute."

Meredith left him with his thoughts for a while, and gave Trump a slight nudge with his elbow when he wanted to press on.

"What happened, Bill? I can see this is painful, but the more information we have, the sooner we'll be able to discover what happened to him."

"He didn't say, but the reason he wanted me back was because his mother had started seeing other men. She doted on him, and he didn't want anyone getting in the way of that. But like I said, he didn't tell me that. So I tried to convince her, and she said it was too late. Ginny, the woman I was with, found out I'd been round there, and she came close to throwing me out. I wouldn't have cared if I knew Debbie would have me back, but I had to pretend I still wanted her until I had somewhere to go. Until I had Debbie back."

Guilt flashed across his face and he looked at the floor with a slight shake of his head.

"What happened?" Trump prompted, and Charles pulled his shoulders back and looked up and stared out of the window over Trump's shoulder.

"Gary went away one week to some festival, Glastonbury I think, and

I thought I'll go early and take Debbie out for the day. Remind her how it used to be." He looked at Trump who nodded his understanding. "I was coming around the end of the street and there she was. Flimsy little nothing of a slip on, and kissing this bloke. I watched him leave. It was nine-thirty in the morning, and he'd obviously been there all night . . . ahh shit!" He ran his hands over his face. "Do either of you want a cup of tea? I don't keep anything stronger in the house."

Bill pushed himself up out of the chair, and started towards the kitchen.

Meredith followed him and noticed his use of the wall for balance. "How did you damage yourself?"

Lifting the kettle, Bill limped to the sink.

"Had an accident at work, severed my ankle, almost cut my foot off. They saved it, but it's not right. That's how I got this place. I was homeless, unless you can call a shitty little bedsit a home, and I was drinking. I went to work still half cut and hey presto!" Bill opened a cupboard and lifted out three mugs. "Tea or coffee?"

"Coffee for both, white with none for Trump, black with two for me. You didn't get any compensation?"

"It's still ongoing. They say it wasn't their lack of health and safety, it was me being drunk." He turned to face Meredith. "The truth lies somewhere in the middle." He ran his fingers through his hair. "I've made a lot of bad choices in my time. What do you think happened to my boy?"

Once more Meredith ignored the question. "You see that she's been with another bloke and decide to call it a day. What happened with Gary?"

"Nothing at first. I didn't tell him I'd given up at that point. I arranged to meet him one Saturday morning to buy a new guitar, but Ginny got wind of it and told me she'd arranged a day out with her kids." He rolled his eyes at Meredith. "She had two boys, nine and eleven. I called the house and left a message telling him I'd meet him the next morning instead. He didn't get the message as he was staying with a mate. When we got back from our trip I was messing about with her lads as we walked up the street, and there he was, sitting on the wall." He handed Meredith two mugs. "Shall we go through? I can't stand for very long."

Meredith led the way back to the sitting room, and once they were settled he prompted Bill to continue.

"I take it he wasn't best pleased."

"He went ape shit. Told me I was a no-good lying bastard and so on, he said he didn't want to see me again, and hoped I'd be happy with my new family. It was all very embarrassing at the time. When we got indoors, after he'd left, Ginny looked all smug, like she'd won, do you know what I mean?"

Trump and Meredith nodded in unison, and watched as Bill's expression changed.

"Look, can we get to the point? I fell out with Gary, I didn't want his mother now that she'd been . . ." He shook his head. "I messed up with Ginny, and I ended living up in some shit bedsit. None of this is relevant to what happened to Debbie, and I'm bloody sure it has nothing to do with Gary being murdered. If he has been, because you've still not told me about that. Tell me now!"

Meredith could see that they were losing his co-operation, as talking about his past was causing him so much pain. He leaned forward. "Do you think Nancy Bailey is capable of murder?"

"What, you think she killed Debbie?" Charles laughed, but his laughter was cut short as he considered the implications of the question. "Are you telling me she killed Gary?" He seemed unable to believe either possibility and simply said, "Why would she?"

"Nancy believes Debbie was murdered. She's confessed to three murders and one kidnapping." As Meredith spoke Bill Charles' eyes grew wide and his mouth fell open. "One of those she says she's murdered is Gary. She says it was an accident, but it was related to her belief."

"What, Nancy?"

Meredith nodded as Bill shook his head.

"Yep, and she won't tell us where she is holding one of our police officers until we find out what happened to Debbie."

"I . . . she . . . Bloody hell! She accused me once. It sounds like you're telling me I'm lucky to be alive. What did she do to Gary?"

"We don't know. We know what she told us, which makes it an accident, so manslaughter rather than murder. We need to find him. Do you know his last address?"

"Yes, but has she not told you where he is? Why would she admit to it, and then not tell you where?" His frown lifted momentarily. "Perhaps she's lying."

Trump and Meredith exchanged a glance.

"I hope so. His last address . . ." Meredith said quietly.

"No, no come on, you can't take me this far and not tell me."

Meredith pinched the bridge of his nose. "She says she buried him under the floor of the house where she's holding my officer, Jo Adler. Jo has a limited food supply, and I have to find out where she is, or find Debbie's murderer. As I don't know if Debbie was murdered, I need to check all possible properties." He struggled to keep the edge out of his voice, "So if you don't mind, the address please?"

Bill nodded at the coffee table, and the long slim drawer beneath the top shelf.

"There's an address book in there. You'll find two addresses: the first is the house he shared when he first left home, and the second is where he was when his mother . . . Oh God, this is bad, isn't it?" He covered his face with his hands for a second. "Right, ask away, I'll tell you anything you want to know.

An hour later Meredith and Trump had a detailed account of Bill Charles' knowledge of Debbie's last few months, and all he knew about his son's movements. He told them how he had caused a scene when the will was read. As they were not divorced, he had thought the house would come to him, but she'd left it to their son on the understanding he lived there. If he sold it, he had to buy somewhere smaller, and the remainder of the money was to be put into a trust which would be controlled by his aunt, Nancy Bailey. She would release the money to him in five equal amounts over the next five years.

"What did he do?" Meredith asked.

"He sold it. When Debbie wrote that will, I'm sure she didn't think she would be found hanging . . ." He swallowed. "I wasn't party to the arrangements, but I saw the board go up and knew when the new owners had moved in. He bought a three-bed flat, which he shared with some of his musical friends I've been told. Those were the two addresses." Bill nodded at Meredith's notebook.

"Have you got the name of the solicitor who dealt with the will? He could be dealing with the trust too?"

Trump smiled as Bill opened the address book and passed it to him. He noted down the solicitor's details.

Meredith stood and arched his back. He held out his hand to Bill. "Thank you for that. We need to get on now, but if there's anything else you remember, please call." He shook Bill's hand and passed him a business card. "I'll let you know as soon as we find anything definite."

Bill Charles licked away a tear that had reached his lip as he watched them walk away, and he wondered what he had done that was so wrong that he should be cursed with such a life.

"Well, we're off and running. Let's go to this flat Gary bought, and see what we can find out." Meredith hurried towards the car as the first raindrops fell.

~ ~ ~

Patsy sat in her car on a small piece of wasteland and looked at the pub opposite. The British Pride was clearly a football supporters' drinking hole. The local team's posters and scarves adorned the filthy windows. Odd strands of broken bunting, attached to the guttering under the roof, fluttered in the wind, and three men dressed only in tee-shirts and jeans were huddled in the alley to the side of the building, smoking their cigarettes.

The first large raindrops hit the windscreen and she looked up at the dark brooding sky and sighed. If she were going in, now was as good a time as any. Picking up the umbrella lying in the passenger footwell, she grabbed her bag. The three men watched her lock her car and hurry towards the entrance. One grinned a greeting as he rushed forward and opened the door for her.

"There you go, my love, nice to have a lady come visit."

Patsy nodded her thanks and tried not to screw her nose up, as the smell of stale beer and body odour assaulted her nostrils. Peering into the bar her heart sank; the interior was worse than she expected. Stepping over the threshold, she walked towards the smiling barmaid and glanced around. There was a small stage at the far end of the narrow room, the backdrop was a huge union flag, and there were a dozen or so men in the bar, sitting in small groups. They turned to look at her. She raised her eyebrows as a hush fell. If it were not for Madness blaring out 'Our House' from the speakers, she would have whispered her order of a diet coke. The barmaid smiled and polished a glass with a grey towel before filling it with fizzy brown liquid from a hand-held dispenser.

"Are you lost?" the barmaid asked as she placed the glass on the bar, and held out her hand. "One pound twenty."

She smiled and Patsy noticed that one of her front teeth was missing. The lip above was a little swollen.

The barmaid grimaced. "Lovely, ain't it? Had a punch up in here a couple of weeks back. I'm waiting for the dentist to sort it out."

Patsy attempted to look sympathetic. "Here you go." Plucking some coins from her purse, Patsy dropped them into the barmaid's hand. The door was flung open and she turned to look. A short, fat man with a bald head, wearing a large gold chain around his neck, struggled through the opening carrying a huge speaker. He was shortly followed by a larger version of himself carrying a double bass.

"All right, Shirl?" the larger of the two called. "Five pints of lager, and a couple of cheese rolls each. We'll get it in and have that before we set up. You got many coming?"

"'Bout seventy, Alfie. It'll be a good 'un." The gap in Shirley's teeth highlighted her smile.

"My God! What you been up to?"

Leaning forward, Alfie squinted at her mouth. Her response was interrupted by a well built and handsome man entering the bar. He was carrying an over-large black suitcase in one hand and several microphone stands under the opposite arm. One of them poked Alfie in the back.

"Come on, come on," the latest arrival ordered. "It's pissing down out there and . . ." Catching sight of Patsy, Ben Jacobs smiled broadly. "Well, I can only guess that you're Patsy Hodge. A pleasure, and I mean that." He placed the suitcase on the sticky floor and held out his hand. "Take a seat over there. I'll be with you in less than five minutes." He grimaced at Shirley who was still grinning. "Nice look, Shirl, look after the lady for me."

Patsy assured Shirley that she didn't want anything to eat, and taking a seat near the window, she watched the five men rush back and forward with various pieces of equipment, until finally Alfie slammed the doors of the white van and parked it across the road next to Patsy's car.

Ben Jacobs dropped his last load on the edge of the small stage, picked up the pint and plate of rolls from the bar, and sauntered over to Patsy. He sat on the stool opposite and took a swig of his pint.

Smacking his lips together, he winked at her. "I needed that, Patsy. While I eat this," he pointed to the plate containing two cheese rolls, "you tell me again how I can help you. Because I'd like to." He held her gaze.

Momentarily Patsy was reminded of Meredith. She shook the thought away. Jacobs was wearing narrow jeans with Doc Marten boots, and a checked shirt with a buttoned-down collar. She could perhaps see Meredith wearing the shirt, but not the jeans, and certainly not the boots. Jacobs was also prettier than Meredith, and she guessed that he was a huge success with the ladies. Keeping her voice low, she explained that she was trying to find Darren Wilkinson, but not why, and that his daughter had suggested he may be able to help. He licked the remaining crumbs from his bottom lip and nodded.

"Angel said that? I didn't think she'd remember me. She was only this big when I last saw her. Nice kid." He held out his hand to indicate the height, took another swig of his drink, and wiped his mouth with the back of his hand. "I haven't seen Darren for at least a year, and then only briefly. I thought he'd moved away." It was more of a question than a statement and he inclined his head waiting for the answer.

"Where was he living the last time you saw him?" Patsy ignored his prompt.

Jacobs ran the back of his forefinger up and down the stubble under his chin as he considered this. He didn't take his eyes off Patsy who returned the stare.

"Can I ask why you're asking?"

"Does that make a difference to the answer?"

"Not the real answer no, but it may to the one I give you."

His eyes twinkled a challenge, and Patsy marvelled at the length of his dark eyelashes. They would be the envy of most women she knew.

She gave a soft smile before leaning forward. "What would be the reason that would get the true answer?" Her eyebrows twitched.

Jacobs' wide grin revealed perfect teeth, to complement the designer stubble and long dark lashes. Patsy frowned as she realised she found him attractive. Except for the odd actor, she hadn't thought any man was attractive since she'd met Meredith. She pondered on this as she waited for his answer.

Jacobs was used to seducing women, he'd seen the first crack appear in Patsy's defence, and smiled inwardly. It was a long time since he'd pulled a good-looking girl who also had a brain. He glanced up at the clock. He could stretch this out for another hour and still have time for a quick rehearsal before the evening session kicked off. He doubted she would go for a quickie in the back of the van, so he'd need to orchestrate another meeting.

"Was that a difficult question?" Patsy returned his grin. "You seem to have trouble answering me for some reason."

"Because, Patsy, it's not every day that a beautiful woman walks into my life, and only wants to talk about another man." He pouted and put his hand on his chest. "And I have to tell you that hurts. I was thinking about how I could get you interested in me, and not some loser who appears to be lost. You've no ring so you're single, you are clearly intelligent and, did I mention, beautiful? I think I must have." The grin was back, "I'll tell you what I know, which isn't much, and then we'll talk about you. Deal?"

Taking his hand from his chest, he held it towards Patsy. She nodded agreement as she lifted her hand. Once she had the information, she would have a very short story to tell. Jacobs took her hand and static electricity sparked between them. Pulling her hand away, she shook it, and gave a wary smile. Jacobs gave a hearty laugh.

"I'm electric me. I . . ."

He was interrupted by one of the other band members coughing behind him. He turned to answer him, and a relieved Patsy sat blinking at her hand, recovering from the déjà vu she had just experienced. Meredith had used the same line on her. Perhaps that was what happened when she was attracted to a man. A static electricity builds up, and then they use a crap chat up line. She glanced over at Jacobs who was nodding at Alfie, he turned around to catch her watching and smiled.

"You're going to have to hold on for five minutes, Patsy. I need to do something. It's a new backing track we're trying. Our bass guitarist has broken his fingers." He rolled his eyes and stood.

Patsy appraised him as he walked away. Odd clothes for a man of his age, but he was certainly had the physique to match the looks. As he tapped away at the keyboard of a laptop she blinked. Was she getting over Meredith? Or was she attracted to this man because of their similarities. She smiled at how ridiculous that sounded.

Competing music filled the pub, and the barmaid turned a dial on the wall beneath the optics and Madness faded away. Ben Jacobs and the band belted out some foot-tapping, head-nodding music that was familiar and yet unknown to Patsy. They went wrong once or twice but it sounded good. She noticed the other men in the bar nodding and tapping their feet to the beat. When they had finished, Jacobs took the microphone from the stand and called to her as he walked to the laptop.

"Need to do that once more darling, all right?"

Pushing some buttons, he held up his finger, and counted the band in. They repeated the song, and Patsy noted the slight changes to his delivery, and Alfie had changed the volume of his backing vocals. It sounded better. Satisfied, Jacobs turned off the microphone and said something quietly to the shorter version of Alfie. The man's eyes shot to Patsy, and he grinned and nodded. Patsy bristled, but her attention was drawn to two women who teetered into the bar on ridiculously high platform shoes.

"I'm bleeding soaked now. He's such a prick." The woman changed her voice to a high-pitched whine and mimicked the taxi driver. "I can't stop in the middle of the road, I'll hold up the traffic." She leaned across the bar to peer into the mirror behind the optics. "All right, Shirl?" she asked, and ran an expert finger under heavily made-up eyes, before puffing up her hair with her fingertips.

Her companion mirrored the actions.

Patsy hoped her eyebrows had not disappeared into her hair line as she watched them. The woman who had been complaining was wearing very shiny red leggings, above which was a cropped red laced top that covered little and revealed most. Her companion was shorter and a little more sedate, inasmuch as she had opted for black and not red. The taller woman ordered a vodka and Red Bull as Jacobs returned from the stage. Her face lit up when she saw him, and Patsy could tell by the look exchanged that they had been, or possibly were, lovers.

"All right, Ben? You gonna give a good show tonight or what?" she pouted.

"Have I ever let you down, Tina? Have I?" Jacobs slapped her backside as he walked by. The shorter woman smiled nervously at him, and he winked at her. "Hello again, I thought you'd be back." The woman turned scarlet and her friend scowled. Jacobs laughed. "Catch you later girls. I have business to attend to."

He continued his journey to Patsy who smiled at the two women. They ignored her and turned their attention to Shirley who was placing their drinks on the bar.

"Right, where did we get to?" Ben smiled at her.

"You were about to tell me what you know about the whereabouts of Darren Wilkinson, and where he was living the last time you saw him. You also agreed to give me the truthful answer."

"Ah yes, and after we were going to talk about you." Jacobs did neither, and wandered into a conversation about music.

Patsy smiled and hoped that her exasperation was not apparent. "That sounded good, you are a very talented man. But Darren Wilkinson . . ." Patsy attempted to bring him back on course.

Jacobs thought she was miffed because of the two women so he told her what he knew.

"It must have been a year back I saw him. He was living in Somerset somewhere but had come up to see his brother." He clicked his fingers. "That's it, I remember now, we were doing a gig over in Longwell Green and he was in the pub. Told me he didn't use any of his old haunts in case he bumped into his missus. She'd lost it, apparently, the last time he got caught with his trousers down, and he didn't want a repeat performance."

"When did you say this was?"

Jacobs frowned as he tried to remember. He scratched his head. "Not sure, we play there about once every two or three months. It was before Halloween because they had boxes of decorations delivered when we were rehearsing. I'd say late September or early October, is that any good?" He smiled and leaned towards Patsy. "Did I say you also smell fantastic?"

"Yes, thank you," she lied. "Where in Somerset did he say he was liv - "

"That's it!" Jacobs clapped his hands. "His missus had recently been picked up for torching the house, and the police were looking for him. He had nothing to do with it, but was keeping his head down." Jacobs slapped his forehead. "Come back down here tonight. His brother will be in, Ed, I'd bet on it. He only lives round the corner."

"I may just do that, thanks." Patsy looked around the bar. The two women stared at her and she raised her eyebrows. Jacobs followed her gaze. "Look, I must get going. Maybe I'll see you later, thanks for your help."

Patsy stood and held out her hand. Jacobs jumped to his feet and grasped her hand.

He pulled her towards him. "Don't go, you haven't told me about you yet," he pouted, and Patsy smiled over his shoulder at the two women.

"I don't think you'll miss me. Good luck with tonight."

She stepped around the table. Jacobs kept hold of her hand.

"Don't worry about them. They're nothing to do with me, they just sort of hang around. Come on, Patsy, we'll have fun, I promise." He was now standing very close to her and she looked up at him.

"I don't think so, but thanks for the offer."

Jacobs still thought she was concerned about the two women, and he dashed across to the bar. "Shirl, ticket please." He took the ticket and placed it in Patsy's hand, which he then lifted and kissed. "You'll need that to get in. Bring a friend, it admits two. No strings, come and have a laugh."

"I'll think about it. Promise."

Reluctantly Jacobs released her, and watched her walk towards the door. Patsy grinned as she heard Tina ask him who the slapper was. Ed Wilkinson had been mentioned in the paperwork that Angel had given her, and it would be useful to speak to a family member. Climbing back into her car she called Angel.

"Hi, Angel, it's Patsy, I have a lead of sorts." She held up the ticket that Jacobs had given her. "Do you fancy listening to a ska band tonight, whatever that is, and introducing me to Ed Wilkinson?"

"Oh, you've made progress. I haven't seen Uncle Ed for years. It's also ages since I heard any ska, my dad and his mates loved it. Where and when?"

Patsy arranged to pick Angel up later that evening. She had time to go home, grab something to eat and change. She would also check in with Meredith and see if there was any news on Jo.

9

Meredith sat on the edge of the table as his team settled themselves.

"Right, I'll make this quick as Jane Roscoe is waiting for me. We have a couple of locations being covered by uniform. They're the right type of properties in the areas where either Jo or Nancy Bailey's phones were used. They're reporting in to Trump as each street is checked. Fingers crossed we'll get lucky."

Meredith smiled as several of the team crossed their fingers. Standing, he pointed across the room. "In the meantime, we are going to investigate the death of Debbie Charles as though we believe it to be murder. The search of Nancy's house was of no help. This means that, despite the simple, homely exterior, she's a clever and calculating woman. Nothing from her banks yet. Trump and I met with Debbie's husband and he led us to two addresses where Gary Charles has resided. The first was the family home, sold a year after Debbie died, so nothing there. But the flat he bought with the proceeds is still in his name. His two flatmates claim they believed he was travelling. He had boasted he was stepping up a gear in his career. It was not unusual for him to disappear for several months a year, and they simply thought he had hit the big time. There was a small stack of post for him, and they kindly gave us permission to remove his personal papers."

Seaton held up his hand. "If they've been paying the bills I can't see that they wouldn't have tried to contact him. They weren't concerned at all?"

Meredith shook his head. "Nope, because the bills are all paid via direct debit from his account, and they continued paying their rent into it. There's no mortgage so the rent covered the bills. As to why they weren't concerned, his aunt turned up about two months after he'd gone, and confirmed he was in America trying for his big break. She told them to contact her should they need anything."

"Nancy went there to tell them that?" Seaton queried.

"Nope, she went to drop off some things of his. She had keys to the flat and to his bedroom, and she mentioned in passing where he was. This can only mean Nancy is lying. She claims she wanted to be caught because that would ensure her sister's case was looked at, but by telling the boys that, she clearly didn't want questions being asked."

"What did you find there?"

"His passport, and half a ton of paperwork. Most of it seems to be for his music but it's being boxed as we speak, and will arrive shortly. Seaton and Travers, you can take that. Find his bank and get onto them. Nancy controlled his trust fund and was supposed to transfer money in each year. I don't know if that was one payment, quarterly, or monthly. But it could turn up her bank details, which in turn may throw up some addresses. Debbie went to dancing lessons, cookery at night school, and joined a gym apparently. Go back to Phillip Cowell's notes and find out if he managed to tie her to any blokes. Nancy says there were two that were special, and her husband gave us a decent description of the bloke she was seeing at the time of her death."

He stopped speaking as Frankie Callaghan appeared.

"Get on with it. I'll go introduce Ms Roscoe to Nancy and then see what Sherlock has to say for himself."

Meredith strode over to Frankie Callaghan and shook his hand. "Nice to see you, Sherlock, go wait in my office, I'll be ten minutes."

Jane Roscoe was leaning against the counter speaking to the custody sergeant. Meredith smiled as he looked at the ladder running up the back of her black tights. Jane Roscoe was a good solicitor. She was no more than five feet tall, and had a small frame. Her suits always looked a little too big, and her wild red hair refused to be tamed. Meredith believed who anyone that didn't know her would guess she was a schoolgirl; a prefect, of course.

"Ms Roscoe, first you're late, and then you choose to flirt with the custody sergeant. Is that professional?"

Jane Roscoe spun towards him, and her face coloured as she met his gaze. "Unfortunately, Meredith, the judge had more call on my time than you, and as for flirting, quite the contrary, I've been taking your sergeant to task for not arranging to have Nancy Bailey moved to more appropriate accommodation."

"You've met Nancy?"

"Not yet, why?"

"Because if you had you would know why she's here, and why she will be until . . .well, until we find Jo Adler. I take it you're up to speed on that?" Meredith inclined his head.

"I am, and I'm sorry, I'm sure you'll find her safe and well." Jane sighed. "Why me? You always have a reason," she gave a smile, "and it's usually a good one."

"I do. Walk this way, I need to make this as quick as possible." Meredith opened the door that led to the corridor off which the interview rooms sat. He opened the first vacant room and pulled out a chair. "Take a seat. Nancy Bailey is refusing legal representation because it's not portrayed in a good light on television." Meredith sat opposite Jane Roscoe, a smile dancing in his eyes.

She forced herself to return his gaze. "In what way?"

"Apparently, solicitors on the television advise their clients to keep quiet, and rather than help the police solve crime, they hinder them, by giving advice that protects criminals, even allowing them to walk free. What's your take on that?"

"I'll not dignify that with an answer, Meredith." Jane Roscoe allowed herself to smile.

"So how can I help? Do you want me to hinder you?"

Meredith laughed and leaned forward. "I want you to help Nancy, but not by telling her to keep quiet. She wants to be here. To help us in any way she can with regard to her sister's death, and only when we've solved that, if indeed there is a crime to solve, will she tell us where Jo is. She's confessed to three murders, or two and one possible manslaughter, and to kidnapping Jo. She needs legal representation, and she needs that person to convince her to give Jo up. Her sister died three years ago. If it was murder, I will prove that somehow, but it could take months. Jo may not have months, however well Nancy thinks she prepared. So I need you to convince her of that." He smiled, "I'm sure you'll agree I'm not asking you to do anything unethical."

Jane Roscoe looked sceptical. "And you chose me because -"

"Because you're good and because you won't be taken in by the sweet little old lady act. If anyone can make her see sense, it's you. The problem we have is getting her to accept you. What do you say?"

Roscoe glanced at her watch. "I have about an hour before I need to leave for my next meeting. Let's give it a go."

Meredith lunged across the desk, took her face in his hands and planted a noisy kiss on her forehead.

"I knew it. Thank you, Jane."

He left the room quickly, leaving Jane to recover from the encounter. She smiled as she pulled a legal pad from her briefcase. Meredith returned a few minutes later with Nancy. She looked at Jane Roscoe and smiled.

"Hello, dear, are you here to help Mr Meredith? I don't think we've met." Nancy took a seat opposite Jane Roscoe, believing her to be a police officer. Meredith left her where she was and leaned against the closed door.

"Nancy this is Jane, Jane Roscoe. She's here to help both of us. She's a solicitor."

Nancy shook her head at Meredith, a look of disappointment on her face.

"I told you I didn't want one." She looked at Jane. "No offence, but I want to tell them everything. They won't help me otherwise. It's nothing personal, I'm sure you're very good at your job, but I don't need you." Nancy shrugged an apology.

Jane was nodding as Nancy spoke. "Yes, so I understand. I can't make you do anything, Mrs Bailey. I can advise you on points of law, and how to protect yourself. I won't allow you to be bullied or intimidated, and I will protect you to the best of my ability. If you want to speak openly and honestly to the police, then that's what you shall do. But you will at least be doing it with the full knowledge of the possible implications. I -"

Nancy laughed and slapped her hands on the desk.

"Mr Meredith a bully? You don't know him very well, do you? He's wonderful." Nancy glanced up at Meredith. "He's handsome, and clever, and kind. I don't need you to protect me from him."

"Now, now, Nancy, you'll have me blushing." Meredith nodded at Jane Roscoe, who took the signal and smiled at Nancy.

"Nancy, may I call you Nancy?"

"Of course. Get on with it, say what you have to say." Nancy couldn't believe this young slip of a girl could possibly think she could sway her. But she had nothing better to do, so she may as well hear her out.

"Thank you. Do you believe your sister was murdered?" Nancy opened her mouth to speak, but Jane kept going. "Yes, you do. Did that knowledge drive you mad with frustration? Yes, it did. Did that frustration drive you to do things, terrible, terrible things, which you would never, prior to the murder of your sister, have considered? I believe it did. Do you want to be punished for your crimes? Yes, you do. You are an honest citizen, and you realise that there is a price to pay for your actions, whatever the reason for them."

Meredith chewed his lip and held back the smile. Nancy was beginning to nod, mirroring Jane Roscoe's own action. Jane Roscoe held her finger up and pointed at Nancy.

"But will you be punished appropriately?" Roscoe shook her head, and Nancy stopped nodding, her mouth opened a little. "No, you won't." Roscoe continued, "They will throw the book at you, and then throw away the key." Roscoe sat a little straighter. "Without legal representation that's what will happen. You will plead guilty to all charges, so there will be no jury. No one will explain why you did what you did on your behalf, and you'll be given the appropriate sentence for each and every crime. I happen to believe that's wrong. That's not the law being utilised as I believe it should be." She slid her legal pad back into her bag. "There, I've said my piece, but I appreciate your viewpoint. Good luck, Nancy." Jane Roscoe stood and looked to Meredith. "I'm sorry, Meredith, I know you wanted to help Nancy, but she is legally entitled to refuse representation."

Meredith shook his head and looked crestfallen. He held out his hand as Roscoe stepped towards the door.

"What do you mean when you say punished appropriately?" Nancy was leaning forward, a frown creased her brow.

Jane Roscoe grinned at Meredith before turning straight-faced back to Nancy.

"I believe your actions were brought on by the grief and anger at losing your sister in such a way. I don't think your mind was properly balanced. Would you like me to help you, Nancy? Not to pervert the course of justice by getting you off crimes you clearly committed, but by trying to ensure you get the appropriate sentence given the circumstances?"

"Yes," Nancy replied quietly.

Meredith clapped his hands together. "Halleluiah! Well done, Nancy. Right, I have a murder to investigate so I'll leave you girls to it."

He smiled all the way back to his office where Frankie Callaghan was waiting. He strode to his chair and dropped into it with a satisfied sigh.

"Right, Sherlock. Give me news."

Frankie waved two large envelopes. "Looked at both, have opinions on both. Who would you like first, Debbie Charles or Wendy Turnball?"

"Debbie Charles. Did she top herself?"

Frankie raised his eyebrows. Meredith tutted and sighed at the implied indecision.

"It's not that simple. I haven't seen the body in the flesh, and I don't know what may have been missed but, for what it's worth, she may have had help."

"Help? Explain."

Frankie leaned forward and emptied the contents on one of the envelopes onto Meredith's desk. He tapped the written post-mortem report.

"This confirms that the cause of death was asphyxiation caused by hanging from . . . this." Frankie pulled a photograph from the pile. It showed the noose. "Ignore the cut on the rope, that was to remove it without compromising the knot. Look at the knot. Whoever tied that was neither a seaman, nor a Boy Scout. It was fashioned by someone who didn't really know what they were doing. However, it worked, so job done. I messed about with a length of rope trying to work out if there was a reason it would be useful, but it was awkward. Sarah had a go and managed it easily, because she's right-handed, and I'm not. I can only surmise that whoever tied this knot was right-handed. I know you have the sister here, and I think if you check you will find that Debbie was left-handed, so it's unlikely she tied this knot."

"And you know this how? Don't get me wrong, I'm sure you're right, but I'm interested as to how you worked that out without seeing the body or visiting the scene."

"The nail varnish." Frankie fished out several more photographs and placed one in front of Meredith. "Right hand and the nail varnish is perfect. Left hand," he slapped another photograph down, "not so much. See the smudging here, and where it's gone on to the skin here? This indicates a left-handed woman applied her own nail varnish."

"I'm with you, so far, Sherlock. Why the interest in the nails? I know there was no material found under them. Even I read that bit in the report."

"I wanted to see how long they were. Pulling that knot, with that coarse rope should, in all probability, and assuming the noose was made reasonably close to the time it was used, leave fibres under the nails. It did with mine and Sarah's. I wanted to see how short her nails were and noticed that she was left-handed." He held his hand up. "That's not concrete though. She may have made the noose days before, and despite its awkwardness for a left-handed person, she may have tied the knot. But in my book, there's room for doubt."

"Splendid news, I think . . ." Meredith sighed. It was starting to look like he did have a murder to investigate. "Anything else?"

"When I looked at the picture of her naked back, there was a red mark just below the shoulder blade. I checked and it was caused by a twisted bra strap to the left of the clasp. It must have been uncomfortable to cause such a mark, but I suppose if you're contemplating suicide a little discomfort wouldn't be a concern . . . what did I say?" Frankie frowned and looked for an explanation as Meredith threw his hands heavenward.

"Nothing, not really, but that's going to give Nancy more fuel for her fire. Debbie was wearing Nancy's shoes, two sizes too big, and for no obvious reason. She was also wearing mismatched underwear, something, according to Nancy, she never did. It was due to the shoes and the undies that Nancy started all this. If you're also telling me that she couldn't do her bra up properly, it begs the question as to whether all three are because she was not of sound mind, or if Nancy was right, and she purposely left clues to be found after the event." Meredith sighed. "Gut instinct, Sherlock?"

"I agree with the coroner's open verdict. There may be foul play, but it needs to be proven."

"Which brings us neatly to Wendy Turnball. I read the post-mortem report, it was concise and seemed to show an accidental death. The way Nancy described her actions, if she did drown her, I can see why it wouldn't necessarily be picked up. Are you happy with the findings?"

"No, absolutely not." Frankie shook his head as he scooped up the papers on Debbie Charles, and placed them on the empty chair next to him. He took the envelope containing the papers on Wendy Turnball and slid them onto the desk. He leafed through and pulled out two photographs. He held one out to Meredith. "This is the right foot of Wendy Turnball. You will see there is a small bruise just below the toes, and it forms a crescent shape here." Frankie followed the outline of the bruise with his finger. "Due to the colour, I think this bruise occurred within twenty-four hours of death. Nobody questioned what it was or how it had occurred. They should have because -"

"Can I hazard a guess here?" Meredith interrupted. "Because it could indicate that the bruise was caused by impact with the tap. Not something you would expect if someone had simply fallen asleep."

"Very good, Meredith, you've been doing your homework. I had a similar wound on a young girl killed by her jealous spouse. The thing with that one, though, was that she wasn't drugged or drunk. She also scratched half his arms off as he held her under."

Meredith shook his head. "Afraid not, Sherlock. When Nancy described drowning Wendy Turnball, she said that her foot shot out of the water and hit the tap. It looks like she did it. I was still hoping that having found so many dead bodies she had guilt by association." He laughed. "Sherlock, that was a joke. You were supposed to laugh, not look shocked. What else did you find?"

"This one is not so cut and dried. But there is also a bruise to the elbow here." He handed Meredith the second photograph. "Unlike on the foot, bruises on elbows are common place, but this one is fairly new. Almost perfectly round in shape, so no clue as to what may have caused it. But if you go like this," Frankie threw his arms out, causing Meredith to jump, "in a restricted area such as a bath, one could expect to see such a bruise. But, alas, the other arm was free of bruising. It doesn't mean that that wasn't the cause, but it is much less likely to be accepted or indeed considered as evidence."

"Tell me why, whoever did this . . ." Meredith pulled the report towards him to find the name of the pathologist: Jasper James. "Oh. So why didn't Jasper James think it was relevant."

"He listed it as an injury, so it's not like he missed it. But all the evidence from her family, friends and respected work colleagues said she had been acting strange. She was on anti-depressants and sleeping pills. Suicide was favourite, but I guess he was . . . well, I have to say it. Lazy."

"Which is exactly the term Nancy used."

Meredith rubbed his hands over his face and weary eyes stared at Frankie. "Thanks, Sherlock, I think you have confirmed what I suspected and Nancy knew. I have a three-year-old murder to solve, and quickly if I want to find Jo. Let's go and tell them the news."

Meredith led the way back into the incident room. The team sat silently as he updated them.

"Unless we do manage find Jo under our own steam, we have to find out who killed Debbie Charles, and fast. Let's get on with it." Meredith nodded to signal the briefing was over and turned to Frankie. "Come on, Sherlock, I'll see you out. I need a cigarette, and don't look at me like that. It's you that's got to look at my lungs when I pop off, not me."

~ ~ ~

Linda pushed open Patsy's bedroom door, and placed a mug of tea on the dresser. She watched as Patsy applied mascara to her lashes.

"I wish I could come with you, I love listening to live music in pubs. Don't know much about ska though."

"Not in this pub you wouldn't. It's a dive. Grubby, shabby and full of blokes that leer at you. Angel is only eighteen, I think it's probably too rough."

"What pub is it?"

"The British Pride, where you arranged the meeting earlier." She paused in the application of lipstick to look at Linda who was staring at her with her mouth open. "What?"

"I've just remembered. That's the pub where the local Independent bloke, you know the one that stood in the last election, was photographed. That racist one that keeps putting his foot in it." Linda clicked her fingers, "Mitchell Edwards. That's his name."

Patsy shook her head. "Never heard of him."

"It would've been before you moved here. Anyway, he's a nasty piece of work, but the British Pride was sort of his campaign headquarters. Luckily, he only got a few votes. You're right, it looked rough on the news."

"Let's hope Mr Edwards isn't around tonight. I don't think I'll have the patience. How did you get on with Trev whatsit by the way?"

"I was only with him an hour. It was useful, but he was more interested in trying to chat me up. I pretended I had a message from the office and had to go. We agreed he could give me online or phone training. But I've now got this app that -"

Patsy held her hand up and smacked her lips together. "Well, that's me done. I haven't got time for you to educate me tonight. I'll let you bore me to death tomorrow at the office," Patsy grinned, and pulled on a denim jacket. "I hope Louie gets here at a reasonable time for you. I've tried Meredith twice and had to leave a message. Let's hope that's because they're on to something."

Picking up the tea, Patsy sipped it before handing it back to Linda. "Thanks for the thought, but I need to make a move. I could be staying at Meredith's tonight, so don't wait up." She rolled her eyes at Linda's exaggerated grin and thumbs-up gesture.

~ ~ ~

Jo lay on the bed, her eyes open, staring into the darkness, and refusing to give in to the urge to cry. Nancy had not been back for over twenty-four hours, and that had to mean she was with Meredith. That thought gave Jo hope. During the day, she'd made use of the notebooks left by Nancy, using one as a diary. She had started with meeting Nancy at John Lewis, and detailed everything that had happened since, including Nancy's confession to the murders. Although, Jo hoped, if Nancy was true to her word, she would have given Meredith all that information by now. She had also drawn up an exercise regime to help fill the hours. Deciding if she was going to be stuck in this cellar for any length of time that she may as well gain some benefit. Her stomach rumbled and she sighed and sat up, wondering which of the delights in the fridge she would use to make her supper.

Switching on the light, she opened the fridge, and stared at the contents. She had little enthusiasm for cooking, but decided she would make an omelette as that would take up a little more time. She lifted out a couple of tomatoes and a small piece of cheese. Placing the items on the table next to a bowl of eggs, she walked to the shelving unit to get a fork and a frying pan. She glanced at the pile of DVDs and decided she would watch a film once she had cooked her supper. As she looked at the titles she smiled. One of the DVDs was a fitness program. That would help her regime. Picking it up, she read the blurb on the back. Realising she was still smiling, she shook her head in surprise that such a small thing could now please her so much. She hadn't been trapped there for a week yet.

"Well, Bobby, I'm already going mad, we're not a week in yet. I wish you could talk."

~ ~ ~

Patsy parked next to the white van and Angel peered across at the pub.

"It doesn't look very inviting, does it? But then I don't think Dad's side of the family are known for their taste. The music isn't bad though." Angel released her seat belt.

"Exactly what is ska?" Patsy asked as she pulled her jacket from the back seat.

"Hmm, I think the best I can do is say it's like a sort of reggae, but noisier and more frantic."

Patsy turned to look at Angel. "I have no idea what you're talking about, but let's go and find out." She placed her hand on Angel's shoulder as they walked towards the pub. "Unless it's necessary to give me a title, in which case don't lie, don't tell your uncle what I do. I'm finding that people are almost as suspicious of private investigators as they are the police."

Patsy and Angel joined the queue at the bar. Patsy looked around the now busy pub. The main lights were dimmed, coloured spotlights lit the stage and cast their light out onto a small area which she assumed had been cleared for a dance floor. That, with the addition of more customers, made the pub a little more welcoming.

Patsy noticed the number of bald-headed men, natural and shaved, wearing polo shirts and jeans. The shirts were buttoned to the neck, and most of them had elaborate tattoos on most visible skin areas. It was almost as though it were some kind of uniform. They outnumbered other customers by four to one. A dozen or so women of various ages were drinking pints. Tina and her friend were propping up an old fireplace which had been boarded over, watching the band make their final preparations. Tina was swaying on her platform heels. Deciding to give them a wide berth, Patsy smiled as Shirley caught her eye and asked for her order.

"Oh, you're back. What'll it be, love?"

"Diet coke and . . ." Patsy looked at Angel, who ordered a bottle of beer.

Drinks in hand, Patsy looked for somewhere to sit, and as she did so Ben Jacobs spotted her and called out, "I knew you'd come back." Grinning he sauntered towards her.

Patsy shook her head at his arrogance. Another trait he shared with

Meredith. "I'm here to meet Ed Wilkinson. Angel is keen on news of her father." Patsy nodded towards Angel, and Jacobs' grin became broader.

"No! Little Angel Wilkinson," he assessed her with an appreciative smirk. Angel was dressed much like Patsy. Skinny jeans with a tee-shirt, but her jacket was leather not denim, and she was wearing heels which enhanced the shape of her legs. "Didn't you scrub up well?"

He placed his arm around her shoulder as though they had only seen each other the previous week. Angel pulled away. Her look was dismissive.

"Sorry, do I know you? Are you a long-lost uncle or something?"

Patsy bit back the smirk, as Jacobs was placed in the old man category. He wasn't offended and smiled amiably.

"Not quite, I'm a little bit younger than your dad, but I used to knock about with him a bit."

"But you don't know where he is now?" Angel asked, and Jacobs stared at her while he considered this.

He shook his head slowly. "No, I think I told Patsy that this afternoon." He glanced at Patsy. "Ed should be in later, perhaps he can help." Rubbing his hands together, he inclined his head towards Patsy. "I'm on now, but I'll see you later." He turned on his heel, and walked back towards the stage, clapping and shouting, "Right, come on you lot, let's party!"

The other customers cheered and turned towards the stage expectantly. Jacobs leapt onto the small stage and walked to the microphone.

"Any requests?" he shouted out to the crowd as the rest of the band tuned up. Various suggestions were called out and he ignored them. "Great, but not yet, because we've already decided to start with this."

The band played the opening bars, and the audience cheered. Jacobs took the microphone from the stand, and started singing 'A Message To You Rudy'.

Patsy turned to Angel. "I've heard this one. So, this is ska." She looked on as some customers made their way onto the dance floor, the others singing and nodding along with the song. Patsy nudged Angel towards an empty table.

"We have a good view of the door from here, you'll see if your uncle comes in."

As they waited, their conversation was fairly light, mainly commenting on the music, and begrudgingly recognising that not only did Ben Jacobs have a good voice but he knew how to play the crowd. Each time the door opened they looked across expectantly. Patsy went to buy more drinks, and as she did so a tall heavy-set man came in. He was bald and dressed much like the others, except he had an expensive navy blazer on. A heavy gold bracelet caught the light as he waved at Shirley.

"Usual please, love."

"Coming up, Mo."

Placing one glass on the bar in front of Patsy, Shirley pulled a pint and measured a large brandy for him. She handed them past Patsy to the man. His hands were huge and bedecked with several large signet rings. He wasn't asked, and he didn't offer to pay. Patsy gave a half smile as he caught her eye.

"Thanks, Shirl." He looked at Patsy and nodded. "Evening, love, you're new." Shirley had begun to prepare Patsy's second drink. Mo nodded at the glass in her hand. "Those are on me, Shirl. Cheers love." He smiled at Patsy, brushed away her protest with a stern look, and she mumbled her thanks.

Mo nodded and walked away. Patsy noticed that everyone either spoke to him or waved in recognition as he made his way through the room. A path cleared to the table to the right of the stage. He looked at the two occupants, who jumped up and disappeared into the crowd with their drinks. Sitting down he saluted the band. They nodded acknowledgement, brought the current song to an abrupt end, and began belting out the opening bars of a new tune.

Ben Jacobs cupped his hands around the microphone and called, "Don't call me Scarface." His words echoed around the bar.

Mo laughed and nodded his approval, and even more people crammed onto the small dance floor.

Patsy made her way back to Angel. "Do you know who that is?" she asked as she handed Angel her drink. Angel shook her head. "The barmaid called him Mo. It seems like he's a big man in more ways than one in these parts." Patsy watched Angel's eyebrows raise. She leaned forward as Angel beckoned her closer.

"I've never met him, but if he is who I think he is, his name's Maurice Ford. Bit of a gangster, I think. I only know him from gossip and by reputation."

As though he knew they were talking about him, Maurice Ford turned to look at them and raised the brandy glass. Patsy picked up her glass, returning the gesture. Angel smiled at him, and content, he looked back to the stage. The band was completing the number, and he slapped his large hands together much as a child would. Ben Jacobs announced they were taking a ten-minute break, and went to sit with him. Maurice raised his hand, seemingly at no one in particular, and within minutes a beer arrived for Jacobs.

"Well, we'd better keep on the right side of him." Patsy looked at her watch and sighed. "It doesn't look as though your uncle is going to show. That's a pity."

"Shall I call him? I haven't spoken to him for a while but . . ." Her face broke into a grin as the door opened. "He's here."

Patsy watched yet another bald man in a polo shirt and jeans enter the bar. He was tall and wiry and looking around as though searching for someone. He spotted Angel and smiled.

"Blimey, he recognised me. I haven't seen him for about four years."

"You have a very memorable face. Did you notice that he knew you would be here? He was looking for you."

"I don't know how. I only have his number because Mum gave it to me," Angel explained. "Who cares, at least we may get some information."

Ed Wilkinson made his way to Maurice Ford. Ben Jacobs stood and shook his hand, and Maurice stood and pulled the much slighter man into a bear hug.

Greeting over, he took the seat that Jacobs had vacated. Jacobs picked up his beer and sauntered towards Patsy and Angel. As he neared them, he pulled a stool from a nearby table and placed it at theirs.

"You don't mind if I join you for five minutes, do you ladies?"

Patsy smiled at him. "Did you tell him we would be here?" She jerked her head towards Ed and Maurice who were now deep in conversation, their foreheads inches apart.

"I mentioned to Big Mo that you would be here. I didn't know about Angel, he probably told him."

Patsy feigned ignorance. "Big Mo?"

"The bloke he's talking to. Maurice Ford, or Big Mo to his friends."

Patsy shook her head innocently. "Who's Big Mo?"

Jacobs leaned forward and patted her hand.

"He's a local who knows Angel's dad. The Fords are a big family on this side of town. Maurice is the family name, all the boys get it. He's Big Mo for obvious reasons." He grinned and his eyes twinkled at the innuendo, and Patsy shook her head.

"Then there's his cousin Little Mo, and his dad Old Mo. It can get a bit complicated if you don't know which Mo it is." He laughed and finished his pint. The rest of the band were getting ready for the next set. "I have to go, duty calls, I'll buy you a drink later. Perhaps we can grab a bite to eat when I'm done. I know a lovely little Greek restaurant that stays open late."

Patsy didn't answer. Ed had finished his conversation with Big Mo and was walking towards them. He slapped Jacobs on the shoulder on arrival, and took a seat on the vacated stool.

Smiling at Patsy, Jacobs made his way back to the stage.

"Hello, Angel, love. I can't believe how grown up you are. How are you?"

He hesitated and tried to stop his nose wrinkling in distaste. "How's your mum doing? I've heard you been in to see her regular like."

Angel reached out and squeezed her uncle's hand. "I'm fine, Uncle Ed. It's nice to see you, sorry it's been so long, but . . ." she struggled to find the words, "you know how it's been."

Her uncle was genuinely touched by the show of affection, and he patted her hand which lay on the table. "You've had a tough time, love, I know that. If there's anything I can do?"

"I want you to tell me where my dad is. Uncle Brian has been good and all that, but with Mum where she is, it would be nice to see him."

Patsy watched as Ed's eyes shot first left and then right to ensure no one was listening. The volume of the music meant it was impossible to speak quietly. He leaned forward and spoke into her ear. Patsy smiled as he frowned at her. He clearly didn't want her to hear what was being said. Angel nodded as he spoke.

Ed looked up as a man hurried in. He spoke to two men leaning on the bar. They put their glasses down and followed him out into the street. Ed nodded towards the closing door.

"I'd stay here a minute if I were you, girls. That'll be trouble." He turned around to look at Big Mo, who jerked his head, indicating that Ed should go and find out what was happening. "I'll be back in a moment."

He left them watching his departure. When the door had closed behind him, Patsy grasped the opportunity to speak to Angel.

"What did he say about your dad?" She saw the hesitation on Angel's face and shook her head. "Don't hold back, Angel. You know the rules – it's everything or nothing. I'm happy to leave you to it. But if you want my services, I need to know everything." She tapped the table with her fingernail. "And I do mean everything."

"He said he doesn't know where Dad is, but he knows how to contact him. He will let him know that I want to see him, and then it's up to Dad." Angel sighed. "I know I haven't seen him for a while, but the inference was he may not want to see me." Her eyes were sad and her mouth drooped as she held her hands up hopelessly. "There, meet the family. My mother's in prison for burning down our home. My uncle is in cahoots with the local bad guy, and my father might not be bothered to see me." She finished her beer. "And on that happy note I think I'll have a real drink." Standing, she picked up Patsy's glass. "Will you join me, or are you sticking to coke?"

Patsy grabbed her hand, and smiled at her. "I'll stick to coke, and you shouldn't get drunk, it doesn't solve anything." She gave Angel's hand a squeeze. "You know, Angel, your father will want to see you. But he is obviously hiding from something. I think your uncle meant whether he was *able* to see you, rather than wanted to."

"We'll see. A phone call wouldn't go amiss though, would it?" Turning away, Angel walked towards the bar. Whilst she queued to be served, a breathless Ed returned and joined Patsy. He was rubbing the palm of one hand across the knuckles of another. His eyes were cold as he stared at Patsy.

"And you are who?" he demanded. The kindly uncle demeanour had vanished.

"Patsy Hodge." Patsy held out her hand, he took it gingerly and winced. "Have you hurt yourself?"

"Nah, it's nothing. Some darkies wanted to come in, and when they were told 'no', they kicked off." He smirked. "They won't be back."

For the second time that night, Patsy feigned ignorance. "Darkies?" she enquired her brow furrowed.

Ed Wilkinson snorted. "Blacks on this occasion as it happens, but darkies covers the lot of them. Pakis, rag heads." He grimaced. "Just darkies."

"Oh, I see, you're racist. Sorry, I didn't understand." Patsy smiled at him, but her eyes had narrowed.

"Nope, I'm pissed off by being told what to do by a load of foreigners in me own country. It's not complicated. They work for bugger all, so wage rates drop, and that's if they work at all, and are not getting hand-outs by the state from my bleeding tax. They refuse to speak the language, most of them, and try and press us into taking up their religions."

He leaned forward. "I've heard that there's a part of London where they're stopping the shops selling booze, or letting anyone that has booze on them into the area." He shook his head and his lips curled up as though he were about to growl. "Let them try that here." He nodded decisively. "We'll sort them. What I can't understand is that if they don't like it how it is, why stay and make our lives a misery?"

"You do know that most *darkies*, as you call them, are second and third generation?" Patsy tried to keep her irritation from her voice. She was so intent on watching Ed's changing expression, she hadn't noticed Big Mo approach. He leaned down to join the conversation.

"Then they should act British, shouldn't they. Mix in properly, have a drink, and stop moaning that no one loves them because of their colour. They could also support England in football and cricket, instead of the other side." He pointed at Patsy. "They have a choice, don't they? They could always fuck off back to where they came from." He rubbed his nose. "We could do worse than to take a leaf out of the Aussies' book. They know how to call a spade a spade." He grunted out a laugh at his unintended pun, and nudged Ed in the back. "Call a spade a spade!" The two men laughed out loud.

Patsy bit her tongue. This was an argument she would not win tonight, and she needed to keep these men on side, at least for a while.

She nodded. "Ah, I see what you mean. May I buy you a drink, Mr Ford?"

"No, I'm off, but it was nice to meet you, Patsy Hodge." He leaned down and his lips brushed her ear. "If you do have sympathies with our foreign cousins, I'd keep them to yourself. Or find somewhere else to drink of course, and don't be turning that young girl's head." He straightened up. "Oh yes, and give my regards to DCI Grainger. It's been a while."

Laughing, he walked away. One of the men leaning on the bar leapt forward and opened the door. A cooling breeze floated into the bar as he waited for Maurice Ford to finish saying his goodbyes. Patsy looked at Ed

Wilkinson and raised her eyebrows. He leaned forward as the door closed on Maurice Ford.

"Look, love, I don't know you, so it makes no difference to me. Don't piss 'im off, and like he said, don't pull Angel down with you."

Patsy glanced across at Angel who was now ordering their drinks. "I have no idea what you're talking about. I'm only here helping Angel find her father. I have no intention of pulling her into anything. What's wrong with you people?" She pulled her head back as Ed waved his finger in her face.

"And there you have it. 'Us people', what does that mean? It's them people you should be worried about." He jerked his head towards the door, indicating the youths they had seen off earlier. "They're the ones that will make this country a shadow of its former self, bringing it to its knees. *We* people are only trying to keep the streets safe and make this a good place to live again."

"Except you don't mind selling drugs to kids?"

"What? I don't sell drugs. I thought you were some hotshot detective, who told you that?"

"I never said you did. But I've seen packages and money change hands since I've been sitting here, and I'm new to this place. I don't know the faces. Some of these girls look too young to drink, let alone buy drugs of dubious origin, so exactly what are you lot keeping them safe from?"

With a quick movement, Ed leaned forward and grabbed her wrist. His eyes narrowed and he yanked her towards him. "Who? You fucking show me, and I'll show you how we deal with them. We don't slap 'em on the wrist because Daddy did a runner, and Mummy's a whore. We show them the consequences of their actions. So you tell me . . ."

He half stood to pull her to her feet, but Angel returned with the drinks. Dropping Patsy's arm, he forced a smile. Angel had seen the aggression and was concerned for Patsy.

"What's going on here?" she demanded, banging the drinks on the table. She looked at Patsy. "Are you all right?"

Patsy resisted the urge to punch Ed Wilkinson and smiled at Angel. "Your uncle wanted me to dance. I've got two left feet but he wouldn't take no for an answer, you coming back saved me."

Angel looked from one to the other. Ed smiled and nodded agreement, but Angel knew Patsy was lying.

Patsy looked at Ed her face devoid of emotion.

"He can go and find someone else now. Go on, Ed, if you like this song so much, it's nearly over."

Ed didn't move. "No, I'm fine. I'll wait until another comes on that I like."

They sat for the next ten minutes in an awkward silence, all three of them pretending to listen to the band. Ed finished his pint and held his glass towards them.

"I need another, what'll it be, ladies?"

They both refused, and Patsy was relieved to see that Ed had fallen into deep conversation with someone at the bar.

She smiled at Angel. "Right, I think we should be off. You've made the necessary contact, I'm sure your father will be in touch soon."

"What was his problem?" Angel jerked her thumb towards the bar. "And don't give me any crap about dancing."

"Let's just say we don't agree," Patsy smiled, "I doubt on anything. Except, of course, the need to keep you safe." Patsy slung the strap of her bag over her shoulder. "Come on, let's go."

"I'm safe here, you needn't worry about that." Angel glared at her uncle's back. "I'll put him right. He doesn't know you, that's all."

Patsy leaned towards her. "He knows me, all right. He knows who I am, and what I do. I know he's family, Angel, but unless you need him, and can trust him. I'd steer well clear. Now please, for me, go and say your goodbyes and let me take you home. If you want to come back that's up to you, but it'll make me feel better."

Angel nodded. "Okay, give me five minutes."

Angel pushed the half empty bottle of beer to the centre of the table and went to say goodbye to her uncle. Patsy walked to the door and waited for her. As Angel walked to join her, Ed Wilkinson held his finger up and pointed at Patsy as though issuing a warning. Patsy smiled in return.

After the heat of the bar, the night air caused them to shiver. Angel linked her arm with Patsy's as they stood waiting for a gap in the traffic.

"Is that you done now?" Angel asked, "Are you going to stop looking now my dad could contact me?"

Patsy pulled her forward as a gap appeared in the traffic and they ran towards the patch of waste ground.

"That's up to you. They've said they'll ask him to contact you, but my job was to find out where he is, not simply establish if he's alive. I'll let it go if that's what you want."

"No, not at all. I'm not convinced . . ." Angel paused, "What are you doing?"

Patsy had bent at the knee and was peering along the ground towards her car and the white van. With Angel's arm still linked in hers, she was pulled down with her.

"Hush. I think someone's there," whispering, Patsy put the finger of her free hand to her mouth. Angel mirrored her action, freeing her arm to drop lower. She nodded in agreement. Patsy stood upright and put her hand on Angel's chest. "Stay here."

Patsy moved quickly to the side of her car and attempted to see what was happening at the back of the van. She wasn't close enough, and there was not enough light to cast shadows. She moved forward a step at a time until she stood at the back of her car. Angel called out a warning, but it was too late. Someone grabbed hold of Patsy's legs, and she fell forward over him, hitting the ground with a thud. She was momentarily winded. Angel rushed forward from behind Patsy's assailant.

"Stop, I got a knife, and I know 'ow to use it," he spat, his anger apparent. He lifted his hand.

Angel stopped dead a few feet away, unsure as to what to do next. Patsy could see the short blade emerging from the hand inches away from her face, and her breath caught in her throat. She spoke quietly and calmly, overruling the pounding in her ribcage.

"I have no idea who you are, or what you're doing. All we want to do is get in the car and drive away."

"Dat's why you tried to creep up on me den, yeah?"

The sarcasm was followed by a snort, and Patsy detected a forced West Indian accent.

"Are you one of the boys those thugs were after earlier? Because if you are, they'll be out soon, so if I were you, I'd make a move now."

"I ain't frightened of dem."

"Well, you should be, they're bloody maniacs." Patsy looked at him. Of mixed-race, he appeared no older than seventeen. As he considered her words, she saw his hand drop to rest on his leg. She knew he had no intention of using the knife. She braced her shoulders against the hard ground. "Are you going to let me get up?"

"I ain't made my mind up yet, bitch."

With one swift movement Patsy flipped the top of her body forward and knocked the boy off balance. She scrambled to her feet, but he too was quick, and he rammed her against the side of the van. The noise echoed around the empty waste ground. The youth was taller than Patsy, and he pressed his hips forward against her.

"You rough in the sack too, bitch?" He placed his free hand under her chin and tilted her face towards him.

Patsy rolled her eyes. "I'm old enough to be your mother. Don't be ridiculous. Is this how . . ." Patsy sniffed. "Can I smell petrol? Oh no, what have you . . . Shh."

Patsy stopped speaking and closed her eyes as she listened.

"Don't fob me off with no shit, lady."

"Shh, listen, there's someone in the van."

They stood still, the length of their bodies touching, and listened to a muffled banging.

Angel stepped forward. "Is that you, Percy?"

This time it was Percy that hushed them. The banging became more frantic.

"I think someone's locked in there, shall we see who, Percy? I think you've been stupid enough for one night. Torching a van is one thing, torching a van with someone in it is murder. Who have you put in there?" Patsy demanded.

"Ain't nothing to do with me. Who are you, anyway?" Percy turned to face Angel.

She stepped up next to him. "It's me. Angel Wilkinson, I was in your history class at school."

Percy released the pressure on Patsy, and he stepped back to look at Angel. "I used to think that you was cool, man, but you're racist scum like the rest."

"Don't you judge me, Percival Howard. Not when you're stood there with a knife in your hand threatening to rape my friend."

"I didn't say dat, did I? I just asked the bitch a question."

Exasperated, Patsy placed her hands on his shoulders and pushed him away. He stepped back with no argument.

"Whilst you two have a little chat and catch up, I'm going to see who's in this van."

Patsy walked to the rear door of the van and tried the handle. She held up her hand to stop the others moving. Jumping back as she released the handle, she flung the door open. Nothing happened. She peered into the rear of the van. The banging began again, and she stepped forward, motioning to the other two to come forward.

"I think we should call the police. It could be an animal in there. I think it's in that sack to . . ."

As she spoke, the sack rolled into the centre of the van and a groan came from it as it made contact with a wooden box.

"That's not no animal." Percy stepped forward and grabbed hold of the sack and pulled it forward.

There was another groan.

"Right, I'm calling the police."

Patsy realised she had dropped her bag when Percy knocked her to the floor. She hurried to the side of her car to retrieve it. With Angel assisting, Percy was untying the knot at the top of the sack.

"Fuck man, what they done to you?" Percy looked at Angel. "It's my bro, Billy."

Patsy hurried back to them, as starting with the gag, they released Billy from his bonds. Billy gagged and pointed at Patsy. He attempted to speak, but his words were stuck in his dry throat. Patsy threw Angel her car keys.

"There's a bottle of water on the back seat."

Angel collected the water and took it back to Billy. He drank noisily.

Wiping his mouth with the back of his hand he pointed at Patsy. "No police. I mean it. No Police."

"But . . ." Patsy put a finger to her lips and they all stilled, listening.

"Patsy, what are you doing?" Ben Jacobs called with a laugh. "You're not taking a pee behind that van, are you? I can't believe you left without saying goodbye."

They heard his feet crunch on the gravel as he reached the waste ground. Patsy waved the two boys around to the side of the van. She noticed Billy's limp as she pulled Angel with her in the other direction.

"No, I was checking the damage."

She heard Jacobs whistle as she stepped to the other side of the van.

"Have they done all four? Bastards, you must have disturbed them before they slashed the van's."

Patsy looked down at the wheels of her car. The tyres were flat and she bit back a groan.

"Don't know. I've only checked this side. I hope there was nothing valuable in your van, I think you've been robbed."

"No idea, its Mo's van. I'd better let him know. He'll not be happy. Come on."

"Come on where?" Patsy asked. "I've got to get going."

"Well, you're not going anywhere in that, are you? Come and have a drink while you wait for a taxi."

"Ah yes. Good point. You go and tell who needs to be told. I need to make a phone call. I'll catch you up."

Ben Jacobs nodded and walked quickly back towards the pub. Once he was waiting for a gap in the traffic, Patsy hurried back to the two boys.

"Give me your telephone number."

"I don't think so." Percy was still belligerent.

"We don't have time for this. You two get going now, as quickly as possible. You owe me four new tyres and I will expect payment. They'll be minutes, go on. Now!"

The two boys needed no further bidding, and they ran off in the opposite direction to the pub. Billy was lurching awkwardly to the left as they did so. Patsy turned to Angel who took hold of her hand.

"Don't say a word, Patsy, leave this to me. Shit, I really need a drink now." She pulled Patsy back towards the pub.

Alfie and Ed Wilkinson were leaving as they hurried across the road.

"Are you all right, Angel?"

"Fine, they were long gone, but Patsy's tyres have been done, and that van was open. I hope there was nothing worth pinching in it. It seems pretty empty now." Large innocent eyes stared up at her uncle.

"But they haven't damaged it. Thank God for that. I've got a gig in Hampshire tomorrow night." Alfie nudged Ed. "It's why I leave it open. If anyone fancies a look they don't have to damage it, and you'd have to be mad to steal it." He glanced back at the pub as he heard the band starting up. "I'd better get back, do me a favour, Ed, shut it up for me."

He smiled at the two girls and hurried back into the pub. Ed looked hesitant.

"Would you like me to come back across with you?" Patsy kept her voice level. She now knew that Alfie had nothing to do with the boy in the back of the van. But she wasn't sure about Ed, not sure at all. Her question was answered when Big Mo screeched to a halt in a large Range Rover.

The passenger window lowered. "Everything sorted?" he demanded, ignoring Patsy and Angel.

"Yes, some vandals have slashed the lady's tyres, and snooped around in the van. Luckily, there was nothing to be found."

Patsy stepped forward. "How did you know something had happened, I've not even called the police yet?"

"Get in," Big Mo demanded. "Angel, go and buy your uncle a drink, I need a quick word."

Angel opened her mouth as if to argue, but her uncle put his arm around her shoulder and led her into the pub. Patsy stepped forward and folded her arms on the open window.

"Did you want me for something, Mr Ford?"

"Big Mo." He produced an insincere smile. "There's no need for police. I'll sort it."

"Now how would you do that? I have to call the police or my insurance won't pay out. I saw the lad running away. I can give them a description."

"What lad?"

"About seventeen, pale blue sweatshirt, black and red trainers and I think ginger hair. Difficult to tell, he had it in a ponytail and the light's not that good over there." Patsy watched Big Mo's brow furrow.

"A ginger? Ah well," he shrugged. "Don't worry about the insurance I'll sort your tyres tomorrow."

"It's not your responsibility to sort it out. Why would you do that?" Patsy smiled sweetly. "I had the impression you didn't like me earlier."

Big Mo laughed. "Good 'cos I don't. But this is my patch. I'll sort it."

"Did you slit my tyres Mr F. . . sorry, Big Mo? I don't think you did. I'll call the police. I don't wish to be rude, but I find I sleep more easily if I don't owe favours."

"Don't be bloody stupid, you have nothing I want. I think you think you're something special." He opened his mouth as though to add something, but shaking his head decided against it. "Please yourself." He revved his engine and Patsy stepped away from the car. "Be careful, Patsy Hodge. It seems to me like you attract trouble." He hit his indicator and glanced at his wing mirror. "Bye, Patsy Hodge."

Patsy watched him pull away into the traffic and pulled her phone from her handbag. She called the station.

"Hello, George, it's Patsy. How are you?" She listened to him complaining about his lumbago. When he had finished, he told her he'd put her through to Meredith.

"No, no. Don't disturb him. I only need you to log this call and give me a crime number. I've had my tyres slashed and I'll need to make a claim." She gave him the details of her location and punched the crime reference into her phone as he read it out. "Thanks, George. See you soon."

Patsy hung up and shivered. It was too cold to be standing outside, and she went to find Angel. Finding her sitting at the table they had vacated earlier, she waved her over. Ed was at the bar being served and the noise levels had risen as the customers sang along with the band. Patsy allowed herself a smile as she watched numerous middle-aged men bounce about on the dance floor to 'Baggy Trousers'.

Sitting opposite Angel, she scrawled through her phone contacts and located the emergency number for her insurance company. She knew she'd have to go back outside to make the call, and decided she would shelter with the smokers at the side. She may even beg a cigarette from one of them.

Ed returned with the drinks. "There you go. It shouldn't be long."

"What shouldn't?"

"The transporter. How are you going to get that car home without it?"

"It's all in hand. I'm not sure what you're talking about, but I've sorted it."

Ed's face hardened. "Big Mo won't like that."

Patsy had had enough. She stood up, knocking the table as she did so, and the drinks slopped onto the scratched surface.

"Do you know, Mr Wilkinson, I really don't give a shit what Big Mo likes. It's my car, and my problem. I don't need help from -"

"Who?" Ed also jumped to his feet. "From people like us? Were you going to say it again?" He glanced down at Angel, who looked startled at the unexpected confrontation. "I don't know how you found this one, but dump her. She thinks she's too good for us." He lifted his finger and pointed at Patsy, "You want to be careful, you do."

From his vantage point on the stage, Ben Jacobs had seen Patsy jump up. He knew trouble was brewing and handed the microphone to Alfie, who didn't miss a beat and continued with the chorus. Jumping down from the stage he rushed over, hoping to avert whatever was brewing. Tina scowled as she realised where he was going. He caught the end of the exchange and tapped Ed on the shoulder.

Ed allowed his hand to drop, and he turned to Jacobs and jerked his thumb at Patsy. "She might be a looker, Ben, but she's bad news. There ain't a shag in the world worth the trouble that one could stir up." Ed stepped away from the table.

"I know, tell me about it. She'd be a mare I know, but you don't want to get caught up, do you? Leave her to me, I'll sort her out."

Patsy was straining to hear what was being said, and she heard enough to catch the gist of the conversation. She was about to give Ben Jacobs a piece of her mind when she saw yellow flashing lights outside, the sort of lights that a breakdown truck would use. She threw her arms up in despair and rushed outside to check.

Ed sat back down, smirking as Jacobs hurried after her. Patsy's fears were confirmed. The breakdown truck was reversing up over the pavement, onto the waste ground and towards her car. If it hadn't been for the traffic she would have stormed across the road. As it was she had to content herself with waving at the driver, who wasn't looking, whilst waiting for a gap in the traffic.

Jacobs caught hold of her arm. "Calm down. What's the problem?"

Patsy shook his arm off. "I run my own life. I don't like narrow-minded racists interfering. I want to know where my car is being taken."

The traffic lessened and Patsy ran across the road. As she approached the breakdown truck, her phone rang. Irritated she pulled it out, it was Meredith. "Hi, I can't speak right at the moment. I'm dealing with my car."

"That's why I called. Are you okay? What happened?"

"Long story, I'm about to find out where they're taking it. Look Meredith, I'll have to call you back."

"Tell them to take it to the Tyre Shop on Gloucester Road. Bob Travers' brother-in-law runs it. He'll sort you out tomorrow. Give me a call when you're free."

Patsy dropped the phone into her bag, and marched towards the driver of the truck who was climbing out of the cab.

"Where do you think you're taking this?"

"Car park in town, I've been told. The boss wants it away from the pub."

"Well, there's been a change of plan, we're dropping it off on Gloucester Road, and you're giving us a lift home. You get it loaded. I'll be back in five minutes."

The driver nodded acceptance, and Patsy hurried back to the pub to collect Angel. Ed Wilkinson had convinced Angel to stay, and assured Patsy he would put her in a taxi. The two women agreed to meet the next day, and Patsy went back to direct the truck driver. She had had enough of macho men for one night and wanted a hot bath, and a comfortable bed. She hoped the driver was not going to give her any more grief.

~ ~ ~

Meredith sighed as he walked back down to the interview room. It was nine-thirty. He'd sent the rest of the team home, and was exhausted, but his mind wouldn't slow down. Thoughts of the day's events bombarded him as he approached the interview room. All the houses that had the appropriate requirements had been checked, and having gone through half of Gary Charles' papers, they still had no new leads. On the bright side, Jane Roscoe had Nancy on side, and had returned to the station half an hour ago to meet with her. It appeared that Nancy had been correct about Debbie Charles being murdered, so perhaps she did have more information than she really knew. He'd give her another half an hour before calling it a night. He tapped on the door and walked in. The two women looked up at him.

"Evening, Nancy. Ms Roscoe. May I?" He pulled out a chair and sat down heavily.

"You look worn out, Mr Meredith," Nancy observed. "Would you like a mint? Jane kindly brought them in for me." She held a tube of mints towards him.

"What I need, Nancy, is a cigarette, a shower, a decent meal and a good night's sleep. Don't care what order, but a mint will do in the interim." He took a mint and popped it in his mouth. Leaning over the table he hit the record button and made the usual announcement with the mint held in his cheek.

"Has something turned up, Mr Meredith?" Nancy glanced up at the clock. "It's very late, I know Jane is doing me a favour, but I wasn't expecting you."

"A couple of things, Nancy." Meredith moved the mint to the other side of his mouth. "I'll start by saying that our pathologist has looked at Wendy

Turnball's post-mortem report, and has suggested that certain marks found on her body could have been as a result of being held down in the bath. So I accept that you murdered her, and that the original team missed the tell-tale signs. Second, one of Gary's flatmates had a drunken conversation with him about his mother just before he disappeared. It would appear that he too thought there was a possibility that his mother could have been murdered, not for any of the reasons you gave, but because of a conversation they'd had a couple of days before her death. We're looking into that. I should have an update tomorrow." Meredith crunched the mint between his teeth and studied Nancy.

"And? You're going to say something important, I know it." Nancy tapped Jane Roscoe on the hand. "You see, this is why I chose him. He's good, Jo and Patsy were right."

She smiled as Jane nodded agreement. Meredith swallowed the mint and his mouth attempted a smile but he was too tired and it failed.

"And, Nancy, I want to ask a few questions about your sister. Was there anything unusual about her? Something you wouldn't know unless you knew her?"

Nancy looked puzzled. "I don't know what you mean by unusual. Give me a clue."

Meredith shook his head. "Not at the moment. I need you to tell me. If we do it the other way around you could agree to my suggestion and then we'll go off on the wrong track. If we are to prove this is murder, I can't be seen to coerce you in anyway."

Nancy's eyes glistened as she clasped her hands to her chest. "You believe me, don't you?"

Meredith held her gaze and watched as a tear escaped. She made no attempt to brush it away.

"I do, Nancy. What I need now is enough evidence to get the powers that be to allow me to reopen the case properly. For that I need your help. It seems you've managed to bump off all the others that could have been of use." He winked at her. "But that's a story for another day. Now talk to me about Debbie. You've half an hour this evening as I must let Ms Roscoe get home at a decent hour. I'm sure she's being missed."

He glanced at Jane Roscoe who rolled her eyes at him.

"Talk about what? Quick, tell me what you need to know."

"Everything. Her favourite colour, pet hates, schoolgirl crushes, hopes, dreams, boyfriends." He leaned forward and tapped the side of her head lightly. "It's all up there, Nancy. We have to release it."

Nancy nodded and closed her eyes. "She was always a happy person, you know, half full. She had a bit of a blip when that bastard cheated on her, but she was very optimistic by nature. I was always the more serious one."

"What was she optimistic about the last time you saw her?" Meredith prompted.

Nancy's brow furrowed and her eyes remained closed as she considered this. After a moment or two her eyes opened wide, and her hand flew to her mouth. "I'd completely forgotten. A tan. She said she had booked to have one of those tanning sessions as she didn't want to look washed out. She wanted a holiday in the sun and didn't want to be lily white on the beach."

"Had she booked a holiday?"

"I don't think so, but she may have, she was determined she was going. Does that help?"

Meredith nodded. "How did she get on at school? Was she bright, was she popular, what were her favourite subjects?"

Nancy looked at Meredith as though he had taken leave of his senses. She had no idea how that information would help, but she decided to go along with him.

"She was bright, did well in her exams, but like the rest of us, she was keen to be released. She didn't consider college or anything like that." Nancy closed her eyes again. "She liked all the creative lessons best, cookery, art, drama." A smile came to Nancy's lips. "Our dad used to tell her that would never earn her a living and it didn't, but she kept up her art. Used to do watercolour paintings, she was good at faces. I still have one she did of me." Nancy opened her eyes and looked into Meredith's. "Will I be able to take it with me, you know, to prison?"

"Of course, I'll make sure. Was she bullied, did she struggle with anything at school?" Meredith pressed on.

Frowning, Nancy shook her head.

"I have no idea what relevance this has, but no she wasn't. She wasn't brilliant at everything, no one is, but she wasn't bullied. Well, unless you call being forced to use her right hand for a year bullying."

Meredith grinned at her. "Explain."

"Debbie was left-handed, and when she first started school the teacher tried to make her use her right hand. She got so cross with her once that she made her stand in the corner. My mother went crackers. She marched into the school and refused to wait until after assembly to see the headteacher. Debbie was moved into a different class and allowed to use her left hand." Nancy could see the smile playing on Meredith's lips. "Why are you smiling?"

"I don't want to raise your hopes, because it's only one man's opinion. But the chap I had look at Debbie's case believes the knot was tied by a right-handed person. He believed Debbie was left-handed and I needed to check that. It will help."

Meredith watched as Nancy worked out to which knot he was referring. The cloud lifted and she smiled.

"Another clue," she half whispered, "you already have another clue, thank you." Nancy stared into her lap, smiling. After all the months of trying, something was happening at last.

"I'm glad to be able to help, Nancy, and I have to admit I'm not sure how far I would have taken it if you'd simply asked me to look into it, but you must know I will see this through now." He waited until she nodded. "Then tell me where Jo is. You have my word I'll carry on."

Nancy blinked rapidly, and chewed her bottom lip.

Jane Roscoe patted her hand. "It will look better for you if you tell DCI Meredith where DC Adler is, Nancy. They will realise that you only did what you thought was necessary. DCI Meredith has admitted he wouldn't have been so focused if you hadn't, I'm sure he'll repeat that in court."

Her eyes challenged Meredith and he nodded agreement.

"What's more, Nancy, Jo is a great copper. She'll not hold this against you, she'll work just as hard as the rest of us in bringing Debbie's killer to justice." Meredith sighed. Nancy would not look at him, and he knew that was not a good sign. "Please, Nancy."

Nancy shook her head and continued to gaze into her lap.

"Not yet. I don't want you to let it peter out. We already have an open verdict, so nothing much has changed except that you believe me. But so did Phillip and Wendy at first." She looked up and shook her head again. "No, not yet, you need to find something else first."

Meredith's shoulders sagged. He was too tired to argue the point further. Jo Roscoe looked down to avoid seeing his disappointment.

Meredith looked at Nancy, his face grim. "I want your word, Nancy. I want your word, that one more clue that leads us closer on Debbie's case, and you tell us where Jo is. And if you renege on that, I'll drop this case and get on with something else. I'll have you transferred to prison to await trial, and I'll forget all about you and your sister, even if we find Jo without you." He stood abruptly. "Interview terminated at nine fifty-eight pm."

He jabbed the button and walked to the door. "I'll be back in the morning, and you had better spend the night thinking about this. You should also remember every word your sister ever said about her lovers." He saw Nancy blanch. "And grow up. You can't go about topping people, and flinch when someone suggests your sister had sex. Don't play me, Nancy, you won't win."

He slammed the door as he left, and had lit his cigarette before he reached the fire escape.

10

Surely you can't possibly want to work with dead people? It gives me a warm tingly feeling thinking of you curing people and making them better. I feel slightly sick thinking of you cutting open cadavers and having a rummage inside. Thanks." Meredith smiled at Amanda as she placed a plate of scrambled egg on toast in front of him. He looked at the dark brown flecks dotted amongst the egg. She'd only just stopped it burning. "I know we've not had a traditional relationship, but surely, as your father, I can encourage you to take what I consider to be the correct path?"

Amanda placed the coffee next to his plate and joined him at the table. She chewed on a piece of toast and gazed at him adoringly.

"Several things we need to establish, Dad." She grinned as Meredith smiled. She had no idea why he was smiling, but it meant they weren't going to have words. She held up a finger, "One, you are my dad irrespective of what's gone before, so yes you can." Another finger shot up. "Two, this is my second year. My *second*," she emphasised the word with a roll of her eyes, "and I have years more to go before I will decide. And three, I'm your child. I believe I have a moral, if not legal, obligation to disagree with you."

She joined Meredith as he laughed, which caused him to choke on his eggs. She patted him on the back as she finished establishing the facts as she saw them. "Frankie said one of the things he was looking at today was a case that you're working on, so you never know, I may actually be of use to you."

Meredith looked up and spoke with his mouthful, "What case?"

"Something to do with a body in the bath. It all sounded very Agatha Christie."

Meredith frowned. "I didn't know he was still looking at it. Never mentioned it to me. Okay you win, but tell Sherlock from me, if he encourages you to take his path he'll have me to answer to." Meredith sipped his tea. "So Patsy didn't pop in or anything last night?"

Meredith had been disappointed that Patsy wasn't waiting for him the night before, but had been too tired to give it much thought. In the cold light of day, he was quietly fuming that she hadn't even texted him.

"For the third time, no. She didn't call, she didn't pop in. Why don't you just man up and call her. If she promised to come and she didn't, there's going to be a good reason."

"You're an expert on the ways of Patsy Hodge now, are you?" Meredith finished the last of his breakfast and swilled it down with the coffee. Standing, he pulled his jacket from the back of the chair. "Because if you are, you'll be wanting to share some tips with me." Leaning down he kissed the top of her head. "Have a good day in the morgue." He shivered dramatically. "I hope you faint, it'll put you off." He laughed as Amanda placed her hands on her hips. "Love you, poppet. Don't wait up."

Amanda followed him into the hall and opened the door as he knotted his tie in the hall mirror.

"I can't believe you said that at eight o'clock in the morning. Try and have an early one, we'll get a pizza in, and chill in front of the TV."

"I'll do my best. I'll call later." Meredith ruffled her hair as he left the house, and wondered whether to call Patsy. He decided against it. The ball was in her court now.

Meredith's team listened intently as he took the morning briefing.

"To summarise, I've been given a couple of uniforms who have a map. They will be covering each street that's not already been looked at, and will check out each property that fits the bill. I'm going back in with Nancy, waiting for her brief to arrive, and you lot finish going through Gary Charles' papers," he waved his hand to those sitting on the left of the incident room, "and you step up the enquiries at the gyms, dancing schools and everything else on her list of interests. I also . . . ." He looked up as Rob Hutchins walked into the room. "Morning, or should I say afternoon," he glanced at the clock which showed nine-thirty, "I thought you were off changing nappies."

"Mother-in-law has turned up for the week. I've escaped." He smiled. "Think my time would be best spent here. Where do you want me?"

Meredith walked over and slapped him on the shoulder. Whatever he had been about to add at the end of the briefing was forgotten. He shook his head.

"Good lad, speak to Trump, he'll sort you out. I'm off to see if I can get anything new out of Nancy this morning. Anything happens, come and get me."

~ ~ ~

Frankie smiled at Amanda Meredith as she arranged her pad and pencil on the opposite side of the desk.

"How's it going so far, or are you partying too hard to know?"

"Chance would be a fine thing. I've moved in with my father and . . . well, let's just say it's interesting."

"Hmm, I think living with Meredith would be. Right, let's discuss exactly what you want to get out of today. I know it's for your end of year paper, but which angle do you want to come from? Medical, forensic, or a bit of both?"

They spent the next thirty minutes discussing what Amanda hoped to achieve. Both jotted down notes, and they ended up with a plan of sorts.

Frankie nodded decisively. "We should look at the case your father is working on. It's three years old. Some of the evidence will have been lost, and without a doubt some of the notes, witness statements, and decisions will be flawed. It happens in most cases but it's not usually anything that leads to a false result."

He smiled as Amanda frowned and shook her head.

"People, including your father, have opinions and pre-set ideas. They follow the facts as best they know them, but where they haven't got a full story so to speak, they fill in the gaps with probables, possibles, and in the case of Meredith, gut instinct." Frankie shrugged, "For the best part it works. They are, after all, trained and experienced in their own field." He rapped the desk lightly with his knuckles, "We, however, test those theories, but unless we can be one hundred per cent sure of our findings, then we either keep them to ourselves, or ensure that we add caveats to our reports."

Frankie stood, walked to a filing cabinet in the corner, and lifted down a wire basket containing two files. He returned, placed it on the edge of the desk, and lifted out the thicker of the two files and placed it in front of Amanda.

"Start with Debbie Charles. This is all the information we have. When you've done that one, go on to Wendy Turnball. I've got to go and tidy up some ends, so you have an hour or so to read that lot and form your own opinion. When I get back I want you to tell me if, based on what you've read, Debbie Charles killed herself, and if Wendy Turnball was suicide, murder or an unfortunate accident."

He smiled as Amanda's eyes widened at the task she had been set. "Go with your instinct, it works for your father. There are tea and coffee facilities in the room opposite if you want anything. The toilet is at the end of the corridor. Good luck."

Amanda watched him leave before opening the first file. She was excited at the prospect of reviewing the two cases, smiling, she realised she was more excited about discussing her findings with Frankie. Perhaps they would have lunch together.

Opening the top file, she read the original coroner's report on Debbie Charles, which was peppered with what she assumed to be Frankie's notes. By the time she got to the first witness statement, she was engrossed. Her notepad was filling up and by the time she read the summary of Nancy Bailey's assertions she'd made up her mind. She checked her watch, and noted she had been working for an hour. She wasn't sure how long Frankie would be, and she wanted to impress him. She lifted the file on Wendy Turnball from the basket, and turned to a fresh page in her notebook.

~ ~ ~

Patsy sat in the grimy office of the Tyre Shop. She looked through the smeared glass of the door as two young men in red overalls worked on her car. Bob Travers' brother-in-law wasn't there, but he had left strict instructions for his staff. The phone behind the small counter rang, and Patsy winced at the volume. She was glad when the acting manager rushed in and answered it. He had a brief discussion with the caller on the supply of tyres and hung up cursing.

"They're useless, couldn't organise a p . . ." He stopped ranting as he remembered she was there. "So, you're a copper. What was that, someone getting their own back?" He pointed to her car as he grinned at Patsy.

She looked in amazement at the size of his front two teeth, and tried to tear her eyes away. Luckily her attention was captured by her phone ringing. "Excuse me." The call was from Angel. "Hi, Angel, did you get home all right last night?" Patsy stared out at her car as she spoke, aware that the man was still watching her, and clearly wanting to pick up on the conversation when she had finished her call. She was relieved when another mechanic left her car and came into the office.

"All done, Bugs. We'll move it out of the shop for the lady."

He looked at Patsy who agreed to meet with Angel and hung up. Walking to the counter, and without looking at Bugs or his teeth, Patsy rummaged in her bag for her purse. Bugs put his hand on hers.

"No need, love, the insurance company are paying for the bulk, and the boss said to waive the excess. He'll put you back on the road. Don't forget we do MOTs too." He grinned.

Patsy thanked him, and quickly followed the other mechanic out into the workshop. He reversed her car expertly, if a little too quickly for Patsy's liking, out onto the road. Ten minutes later she pulled into Angel's road. Angel had tea and toast waiting for her. She talked nineteen to the dozen as Patsy sipped her tea.

"There is something going on. I asked for Dad's number and he said he didn't have it on him and would call me. Why would anyone not keep the number on their mobile? He knew I knew he was lying too, but he wasn't embarrassed. Big Mo came back as we were leaving and asked if *it* was sorted. I have no idea what *it* was, but Uncle Ed got all cagey and said he hoped so. Then he called me a taxi and gave me twenty quid. As it was pulling away, I saw a huge Mercedes pull up and he went off in that."

"Hmm. So it's going to be a waiting game. Did he indicate how soon your father may get in touch?"

Angel shook her head.

"In which case, you have to decide if you want me to carry on as planned or if I should shelve it for a while. Perhaps you should speak to your mum."

"She should call later, but I want you to carry on. I'm telling you, something isn't right. They were all hiding something, I know it."

Patsy waved her finger at Angel. "Don't get involved with them. I'll carry on speaking to people, and I'll keep you updated. Leave it a couple of days before you call your uncle if your dad doesn't make contact. He'll expect that."

"You think there's something sinister too. I knew it."

"No I don't, not sinister at all. To be honest, and I know you're related to Ed, but they're a bunch of small-minded losers who think they are somehow special. What I think, is that you've done all right without them, and you should continue to do so. You're starting to make your way in the world and you don't want to end up like . . . well, like those two young girls that were there last night."

"The slappers you mean?" Angel laughed. "I think the tall one had plans for Ben Jacobs, which you ruined. She followed you both out you know, when you went to see to the car. She was all over him when he came back in, but he pushed her off. She had a row with her mate then, it was so embarrassing it was funny. I think I resent you thinking I have no taste, you know I . . ." Angel stopped mid-sentence and picked up her phone which chimed out. "A message from Percy."

Patsy rested her chin on her hand as she watched Angel tap out a response.

"How did you find him?"

"Facebook of course." Angel rolled her eyes, but her attention was drawn back to her phone as it chimed once more.

Patsy had taken their dishes to the kitchen and had washed them by the time their exchange was complete. Angel walked out to join her.

"He says he's not paying for the tyres. He thought your car was one of theirs. But he's scared and he's agreed to meet us."

Patsy turned to face her. "Why? Why do we need to meet him? Except, of course, to give him a piece of my mind. He should be speaking to the police, not me. God knows what those idiots were going to do to his friend. Is his friend all right? He could have been killed."

"Ah well, I may have told a little white lie, sort of exaggerated actually." Angel looked sheepish. "I told him you were an undercover police officer looking for my dad who had disappeared in strange circumstances."

"Angel! Why on earth would you do that?" Patsy stood arms akimbo as though admonishing a naughty child.

Angel lifted her chin. "Because I think it's true, except the bit about you, of course. Percy says he could tell us a thing or two as long as it's off the record, so I arranged to meet him in half an hour down on the waterfront." She amended her tone. "You will come, won't you?"

"It doesn't look like you've given me much choice. You need to be careful, Angel. Looking for your father is one thing, but these guys are a whole different kettle of fish."

Angel rolled her eyes for the second time. "I thought you'd have realised I can look after myself."

She looked miffed, and Patsy remembered that she was still a teenager and, like most teenagers, she thought she was indestructible.

Patsy looked at her watch. "Well, he'd better be on time. I have other things I need to do."

Turning her back on Angel to show her displeasure, she called the office. Angel smiled. She liked Patsy, and was glad of the opportunity to spend more time with her. Walking out of the room Angel called in sick. It was the first time she had done so, and she ignored the feeling of guilt, as finding her father was more important. Patsy was attempting to eavesdrop, but Linda's enthusiastic greeting drowned out Angel's voice.

"PHPI, what are you doing in . . . Horfield? You are very close to the prison, you're not visiting someone, are you? And while we're on the subject, you never came home last night, why was that?"

Patsy frowned. "Are you following me?" She ignored the question about the night before.

"Yep. I know that you were in that pub last night, and then for some reason you went to Gloucester Road and stayed there the night. Which, by the way, is a question that needs answering. I also know that at nine-fifteen, this morning, you drove to your current location where you have been for twenty-five minutes."

"This one of Trev's trackers, isn't it?"

"Patsy, it's so good. I fixed it to your car the other morning, forgot to mention it because of the whole Meredith thing. Which brings me neatly back to why did you spend the night on Gloucester Road, and more to the point, who with?"

"You will never make a detective, Linda. I came home last night. You weren't there, so I assume you were with Louie. You arrived home after midnight because I was still awake, and you left at seven-thirty this morning." Patsy laughed as Linda groaned. "My car stayed on Gloucester Road, not me. I had my tyres slashed last night. I'm sorting it out now, so I'm not sure what time I'll be in. Is Chris there?"

"Not until about eleven, but you can get him on his mobile. He's meeting with a client . . ." Linda paused, "Oh, Sharon has just arrived if she's any help."

Angel walked back into the kitchen and tapped her watch. Patsy's eyes widened at the cheek of the girl. She returned her attention to Linda.

"Tell him this case is getting interesting, if a little concerning, and that Maurice Ford, aka Big Mo, sent his regards. Tell him I need info on him. Have to go. Bye." Patsy hung up quickly before Sharon could get hold of the phone, and jerked her thumb at Angel. "Let's go, what are you waiting for?"

Parking the car in the multi-storey car park, they strolled across the centre. The sun was shining, the sky was blue, but the light breeze had a bite to it, and Patsy zipped up her jacket. Once on the waterfront, Patsy was surprised to note how many people were sitting at the tables outside the cafés. Angel led them along the river to Millennium Square and took a seat on a table outside a Spanish-themed restaurant. Patsy joined her as a smiling waitress walked towards them.

"Morning, ladies, are we having breakfast or just coffee?" She pulled a cloth from the large pocket in the front of her apron and wiped the table. Patsy ordered two coffees, but Angel interrupted her and increased it to three as Percy ambled across the piazza.

He sat at the table and looked around. "All right, ladies? Nice down here, ain't it?" He sniffed noisily. "That smell makes me 'ungry, I didn't 'ave time for me breakfast."

Patsy inclined her head and studied him for a while. He was tall and gangly with broad shoulders; he clearly still had some growing to do. His hair was cut close to his scalp and had a small design shaved in above his left ear. Large brown eyes stared at her over the sprinkling of freckles on his nose.

"What? What are you looking at?"

"I was just thinking what a good-looking boy you are, but more, I was wondering what had happened to the West Indian accent. That's a lovely Bristolian twang you have there. Was that a hint you would like me to order you some breakfast?"

Smirking, Percy nodded, the motion causing his shoulders to rock backwards and forwards.

"Bacon roll with brown sauce as you're offering. Ta." He smiled at Angel. "She's all right for a copper."

"Well, I'm glad I'm no longer a bitch. I suppose we should start again." Patsy held out her hand. "I'm Patsy."

"Percy, or if you want my full title because my gramps won the argument, Percival, after him, Joseph, after Jesus's dad, Tyrone, after my dead uncle, who by the way I never met, and finally Howard. That's my dad's family name. I was allowed to keep that, and before you go stereotyping me, my dad still lives at home, with my mum." He grinned at her. "Anything else you want to know?"

The waitress had arrived with the coffee, and she placed it on the table as Patsy ordered Percy's bacon roll.

"First, I want to know what happened to your friend and that he's okay."

"He's fine. They caught him when we ran and chucked him in the back of the van. Only I didn't know that. He thinks there was a cop car or something so they were saving his beating for later." Looking at the ground, he kicked a stone away. "If it *was* a hiding he had coming. They're bad, man."

"If you know that why did you try and get into the pub? Were you looking for trouble?"

Percy shook his head. "It was my mate. He's white and he gets all het up on our behalf." Percy gave a short laugh. "He wants to be black. He's not all there. I reckon his West Indian accent is better than mine." He looked at Angel. "Harry Jones."

This was obviously enough of a statement for Angel to understand why they had tried to get into the pub. She tutted and rolled her eyes. Patsy looked to her for an explanation.

"Harry Jones is one of those always on a mission. Always trying to save the world. He went through a stage of checking the labels in everyone's clothes. Well, those who would let him, to make sure they weren't made in some Asian sweat shop. His mates just cut the labels out in the end, because they couldn't afford to be that choosy." She nudged Percy. "Remember when he was on the save the animals thing and organised a protest at the zoo?"

Percy laughed and nodded along with her.

"The managers at the zoo invited him in. They took him to all these places where they're breeding animals in danger of extinction. He got hooked. One day he was sat outside telling visitors not to go in. The next, he's walking round town with a bucket explaining what a good job they were doing."

Patsy smiled. "Okay, so he wants to take on the bad guys. What made you lot think it was a good idea? Surely you knew it would end in trouble?"

"We were walking towards the pub and we could hear the music. We stopped at the top of the road, sat on the wall and were talking about how good it would be if we were in there. We knew it would never happen. But Harry gets all indignant and says he will demand entry. He told us to stay where we were and call the police if there was any trouble. So he marches down to the bar and tells the bloke on the door that he and his black friends are coming in." Percy shook his head at the ridiculousness of that statement. "I don't know if they even answered him, but next thing we know is that he's flying backwards and lands on his arse on the pavement." Percy held his hands up in a helpless gesture. "We had to come help him, didn't we? We couldn't let him take a beating on our account. Didn't last long, a few punches thrown and we were chased away. We know they caught Billy now, though. He won't come out today, but he's planning a petition to close the place down. He was glad to hear about you. Hopes that the police will back his position." Percy held her eye. "He's innocent like that."

Percy took his bacon roll from the waitress and thanked her. He bit into it and sighed contentedly. Patsy finished her coffee while he ate. She wondered whether to let him continue to think that she was still a police officer. When he had almost finished the roll, she drummed her fingers on the table.

"So you weren't looking for trouble, your mate Harry dragged you into that unwillingly?" She shrugged. "But how do you explain my tyres, attempting to torch the van, and, let's not forget threatening me with a knife? Why were you carrying a knife?"

"I wasn't. I'm black, do you think I'm stupid enough to carry a blade?" Percy snorted derisively. "I went home and got one. Only for protection. I went home to get the petrol my dad keeps for the lawnmower. I was going to do the van, because that's theirs." He looked a little sheepish. "Slashing your tyres was to warn you not to drink there again. I didn't know whose car it was. But I knew the van." He screwed up his nose, "Actually, I knew about the van. That's why I'm here really."

"About the van? What did you know?" Holding her finger up to halt his response, Patsy called the waitress over. She ordered three more coffees.

"I have this friend and, a few years back, he was eating a kebab, minding his own business after a night of clubbing, when this van drives by and screeches to a halt. The back doors open and they pull this bloke into it. The door shuts and they drive off. The next day he thought about it, but as the bloke didn't put up a fight, he forgot about it."

Percy paused as the waitress walked past carrying a plate of muffins. He looked at Patsy expectantly and she told him to tell the story first. He made puppy dog eyes, staring at her through his long lashes, and when she ignored him, he continued with his story.

"Okay I'll starve. Anyway, a couple a weeks ago he sees the van and he remembers it. He's driving, and for some reason he can't explain, he follows it. It stopped at the British Pride. Pulled right up onto the pavement and the back doors open. A couple of blokes come out of the pub carrying something heavy. My friend reckons it was a body. So he pulls onto the waste ground, where you were parked, and decides to have a look. He walks over to the pub all casual like, and as he reaches the van they shut the doors so he can't see in. He pretends not to notice, tries to go into the pub, and he's told it's closed. It was half past six in the evening. There were people in there, he could see movement and music was playing. Loud, he says it was. He tells the bloke it doesn't look closed, and he's manhandled away. Private party, they said."

Percy looked up as the waitress brought their coffee.

"Two raspberry muffins would be nice, please." He smiled at Patsy. "Unless you two want something of course?" He grinned as Patsy shook her head, and Angel laughed.

"You haven't changed, Percy." She looked sceptical as she drew a pattern in the froth of her coffee. "This story is all very interesting, but where's it going?"

Percy sipped his coffee and the froth gave him a white moustache which he licked off. "Well my . . . friend," he almost slipped up and Patsy decided she would push him later if necessary, "he's sure that there was something bad going on, and the next day decides to check the pub out. He knew it was a racist pub by reputation, but his curiosity got the better of him."

Patsy shook her head. "I don't get it. I take it your friend's not black or he wouldn't have tried. What was it he thought he would find? A bloodstain on the floor? Sorry, Percy, I don't know where you're going with this either. I think you need to cut to the chase and put us out of our misery." She narrowed her eyes. "I'm sure you didn't drag us all this way just to get a free breakfast."

Percy glanced at his watch. "Okay, I have to get to work anyway so I'll tell you what he thinks." He glanced at Angel and Patsy saw the hesitation.

"Did he think that it was Angel's father they took from the pub and put in the van?" Patsy watched as he shook his head.

"No, he thinks it was him that got dragged into the van the first time he saw it. When he went back to the pub the next night, he sat at the bar and sipped on a pint. He said he knew as soon as he walked in he would only stay for one. He's minding his own business and some big guy at the end of the bar gets a call. He's not best pleased with whatever is being said and is effing and blinding. Then, my dad says, he thumps the bar and says 'take me to where you took Wilkinson'."

"Your dad?" Angel's eyes were open in amazement. "When did your dad tell you all this?"

Percy covered his face with his hands and groaned. When he looked up at Patsy he tried to keep the tremor from his voice.

"You can't involve him. You can't involve my dad in this. They'd have him, and he's a good bloke." He looked at Angel accusingly. "This is your fault, if you hadn't told me, I wouldn't have told him and he wouldn't have been involved."

The muffins arrived and he ignored them.

Patsy placed her hand on his arm. "There's no need to get anyone involved. We don't know that he's right. Am I right in understanding that your . . ."?

Percy interrupted her. "What, that my dad is white? It does happen you know," he shook his head in a disappointed fashion, "Sometimes white men marry black girls."

Patsy slapped him sharply on the leg. "I was going to say, am I right in thinking that your dad only told you this today?"

"Oh right. My mistake." Percy didn't look embarrassed by his error, he simply shrugged it away. "Yes. We were having breakfast . . ." He laughed as Patsy pointed to the muffins. "I'm a growing lad," he joked. "As I was saying, we were sitting having breakfast and Angel kept messaging me. He asked me what was so urgent, and leaving out a few of the more incriminating details, I told him. He went pale and told me to keep away from the pub. I told him I would, we were only passing, blah, blah, blah, and that's when he told me."

"Did he say anything else? Was there any clue to where this was?" Angel was pale and she wrapped her hands around her coffee, as though she were cold.

Percy shook his head. "No. He could tell what type of pub it was, and he didn't want any trouble. So he finished his beer and left. He did say he felt guilty he'd never done anything about it, but like he said, what could he do? It was just instinct." He looked to Patsy for reassurance. "Can you do anything about it? Without involving my dad, I mean?"

"I don't know, I'll try. One thing that puzzles me though, if it was so long between the two sightings of the van, how did he know it was the same one?"

"I asked that. It was the back doors. He says they're from two different vans, one's original and one isn't." He held his hands up, "I know it sounds weird but he's a mechanic, I suppose it's what he knows. But don't you bring him into it. There's no need, right?"

Patsy assured him that her lips were sealed and he snatched one of the muffins as he stood.

"Thanks. Like I said, you're not bad for a copper. I've got to go, my shift starts at eleven." Biting into the muffin he winked at Angel. "Later. Keep in touch."

The two women watched him saunter away. Patsy picked up the remaining muffin and handed it to Angel.

"Come on, let's get you back. I've got work to do."

~ ~ ~

Meredith greeted the two women who were waiting for him in the interview room. He introduced Tom Seaton and went through the necessary information for the tape. Nancy beamed at Seaton.

"Are you helping Mr Meredith find Debbie's killer?"

"I am, Nancy, but we're going to need more help from you." Seaton turned to a page in his notebook that he had marked by turning down the corner. "In Phillip's notes we found three names with little information against them. I'll read them out, and you tell me what you know about them."

Nancy nodded and settled herself in her chair. Meredith watched her. She looked like she was settling down for her favourite television programme. She had not reacted in any way when Phillip's name was mentioned. Previously she had at least looked upset. Meredith had been naturally disgusted at Nancy's actions and the needless waste of life, but he had somewhere, deep inside of him, understood her actions. Watching her now, he realised that irrespective of the way her sister had died, she enjoyed the attention. He now believed that rather than having killed in a fit of temper, believing her sister did not get justice, Nancy had killed because her own motives were being questioned. His top lip curled as these thoughts crossed his mind. He felt, rather than saw, the change in Jane Roscoe's demeanour and glanced across at her. She frowned at him and he caught the slight raise of her shoulders as their eyes met. She pulled her mouth into a quick smile, and Meredith realised that Nancy was now watching him closely. Patsy's warning about being nice came back to him and he smiled at Nancy.

"Are you sure you're up to this, Nancy? It's been pretty gruelling so far for you."

"Yes, of course. I'm made of stern stuff, you know." Nancy's shoulders relaxed.

Tom Seaton wondered if Meredith was going soft and quickly read the first name. "Fred Bendrick."

"Oh, that was the chap she had to do her fencing out the back. He wasn't her type, not at all."

"Gerard Downley or Dowtly. His handwriting was not as neat on that page," Tom smiled.

"It's Downley, I think. Now, I'm not sure about him. They could have had a little fling, but I don't think so because I met him. Twice, as it happens." Nancy looked at her lap. "She didn't let me meet the men she was romantically involved with."

"Okay, so who was he, what did he do?"

"He was an artist." Nancy's brow furrowed, "I don't know if he earned his living from it, but he went to one of her classes. He lived a couple of streets away. Actually, looking back, he could even have been gay?" She held up her hand in warning. "Mind you, I'm not sure about that. He was gentle though, always washed his mug up too." Nancy gazed at the table as the memories tumbled over in her mind. She gave herself a little shake. "I think Phillip spoke to him. Why would he want to kill her? That's the thing."

Meredith straightened up. "But that is the thing, Nancy, isn't it? That's why we're here. Why would anyone want to kill her? It takes a lot of courage to kill someone. Unless you're some kind of psychopath there is always passion. Love, hate, jealousy, betrayal, greed. There is always a reason. We may not think it normal, but it will have mattered to them." He held her gaze, his face stern. "You, especially, know that Nancy. Who would think you would kill the people who to all outward appearances were helping you. Now stop thinking about why, that will come in time. Start thinking about what she said, when she seemed out of sorts, anything at all that you thought was strange, even if only in passing. Odd outings, change of habit, anything."

Nancy nodded solemnly. "I'm sorry, Mr Meredith. But I don't think it was Gerard. If you want to talk to him his address is in her book in my handbag." She looked at Tom, and drawing her packet of mints from her pocket, she offered him one. "Would you like a mint, Tom?"

Tom and the others refused and Nancy popped one in her mouth. Her chin rotated as she sucked on it. Tom Seaton was about to read the third name when there was a knock at the door and a uniformed officer passed Meredith a note.

Meredith stood and smiled. "I have something I need to attend to. You carry on with Tom, Nancy. I'll be back."

Tom announced Meredith had left the room as the door closed and tuned back to Nancy. "Mitchell. I have no idea whether that's a first or surname? Any idea?"

Meredith hurried up to the incident room. Trump beckoned him over.

"We found this," he waved a dull pink folder at Meredith, "which contained these." He gestured to the various papers spread over the desk. "They were in Gary Charles' belongings." He picked up one of the watercolours. It was a portrait of a middle-aged man. The man's eyes twinkled, his front left tooth had a small chip on the corner, and he had small mole under his left eye. It was a good painting.

"Very nice, Trump, the relevance?"

"Look here, sir, where she's signed it." Trump's finger drew Meredith's eye to the corner of the page where he saw an upper-case C entwined the D. It was written in pencil, and to the side of the signature was a heart with initials printed in tiny script. "W D, or D W, depending on which came first."

Trump lifted another painting. It was also good, although the man in the second painting had eyes that appeared a little lopsided. In the corner were Debbie's entwined initials but there was no heart or other indication as to the identity of the subject.

Meredith shrugged. "So, she was talented. What am I missing?"

Trump pulled a third painting from the pink folder. "This," he said simply. He held up an almost perfect likeness of Nancy.

Meredith grinned at him and tilted his head to the side with a little shrug.

"Okay, she's so good they could be photographs. What else? I can tell by the way you're hopping from foot to foot as though you need to pee that you have something else."

"Indeed we do. Although I would confess at this point, it was not I, but the talented PC Hutchins that noticed it, and working with Travers they think they have broken some of the code."

"Code?" Meredith rolled his eyes and shouted across the room. "Hutchins, get your arse over here before I deck Trump for buggering about. What's this about a code?" Meredith looked around. "Where is Travers?"

"That's the third thing. Uniforms called in. They've found a row of houses in St George, turn of the century, all have basements or cellars, or both, and over half of them have shuttering. He's going to do the door to door with them." He grinned as Meredith rubbed his hands together. "Looks like today could be a good one, sir."

"As you would say, Trump, indeed it does old chap." Meredith turned to Hutchins who stood patiently on the other side of the desk. A small hardback book in hand. "Come on then, Pa, your turn to shock and amaze." He reached across and took the book offered by Hutchins.

"It's a diary, sir. Not the pre-printed type as you'll see. Just a lined book which Debbie Charles used to write in, more of a journal I suppose, the entries are made after the event. She used a proper commercial diary for appointments."

"And. . . come on, man, spit it out."

"Yes, sorry, sir. And they didn't make sense, not really, not when you match them with the appointment diary."

Meredith was still frowning and Hutchins walked around the desk and opened the pocket appointment diary.

"Go to the fifth of May in that one."

Meredith leafed through to that date. It was handwritten and a garland of small flowers had been drawn around it. Meredith glanced up.

"You sure this doesn't belong to a teenager." He read aloud. "'I didn't think it was possible, but the sun shone again today. So happy. With a little luck the cat will stay in bed tomorrow.'" Meredith looked at Hutchins, a look of distaste on his face. "What does yours say on the fifth of May?"

"Dance class two," Hutchins replied, as he turned the page.

"So she liked it when the sun shone on dance class day. I'm clearly missing something so you spell it out."

"Read the entry of the seventh, and you'll see it."

There was no entry for the sixth, so the seventh was the next page. Meredith read aloud once more.

"'Hope the sun shines tonight. The cat has been kind even though it was here yesterday. Baby will be dealt with now. Sunshine kiss.'" Meredith assumed the 'x' was a kiss. He sighed. "Go on, reveal all."

Hutchins walked to the white board and in the bottom corner he wrote the dates, fifth through to the eighth of May and filled in the diary entries.

5th May – Dance Class 2
6th May – Nancy lunch
7th May – 8pm Dance Class 2?
8th May – Gary dinner

Meredith flipped the page to the eighth of May, and again he read aloud.

"'Baby didn't turn up again. Such a disappointment, I can only hope the cat gets hold of him.'" Meredith raised his eyebrows. "So Cat is Nancy and Baby is Gary. Dance class two is a euphemism I'm assuming."

Hutchins and Trump were nodding at him. Trump stepped forward.

"Absolutely. Dance class one is only mentioned in the appointments diary; when she writes in her journal she refers to it as one would normally. Hutchins is working on the rest now. We thought you would want to show these to Nancy."

"You thought right. Bag those up after you've taken colour photocopies. I'm going for a quick ciggy and I'll be back to pick them up."

Meredith smoked two cigarettes in a row before returning to pick up the paintings. He returned to the interview room and Tom Seaton announced his arrival. Meredith placed the painting of Nancy in front of her, and her eyes filled with tears.

"Didn't she do me proud? I'm not sure I ever looked that good. It only took her a morning too." She dabbed the corners of her eyes with a tissue.

"You sat for her?" Meredith was out of niceties.

"Yes, of course."

"Did she ever paint without someone sitting for her, do you know?"

Meredith watched Nancy shake her head. "What, never, as far as you know?"

Nancy stared at him. She chose her words carefully. "No, not as far as I know. When Debbie was in artistic mode," her nose wrinkled a little, "she became a little, well, I'll simply say she acquired artistic tendencies. If she were painting a bowl of fruit, it had to be real, not waxed." She nodded confirmation as Seaton raised his eyebrows, and continued, "If she were painting a landscape she had to be there – a photograph wasn't good enough – and if she were doing a portrait you had to sit." She sighed and scratched her forehead. "It wasn't that painful really, as I say she was quite quick, and always laid on a nice tea. Although, that said, this one time we went down to Devon and -"

"Do you know who this is?" Meredith interrupted her musings and pulled out another painting.

Nancy eyed Meredith before looking at the painting he had placed before her. "No. I suppose it could be someone from her art class."

Her face had set and she wiggled her shoulders into a more comfortable position against the back of the chair. Meredith knew he had irritated her. So he smiled. It was not genuine, and Nancy knew it. Meredith ploughed on regardless.

"What about this one?" He pulled out the final painting of the man with the lopsided eyes. "She doesn't seem to have done so well here. The eyes don't look right."

Nancy smirked and gave a negligible shake of her head. "Well, that's where you're wrong. That's Gerard Downley." She nodded her head. "That's probably why he was there." She leaned forward and tapped the painting. "That, Mr Meredith, is Gerard." She folded her arms across her chest. "What next?"

"I think I need to go and have a word with Mr Downley. How did you get on with Tom?" Meredith half turned to face Seaton.

"Nancy did really well. Didn't you?" he smiled at her before turning back to Meredith. "Nancy thinks the third name was Wilkie. She thinks that was the name of the boyfriend Debbie was keen on. She heard her on the telephone a couple of times."

Meredith glanced down at the second painting. Neither Nancy nor Seaton had picked up on the initials in the heart drawn in the corner. He mentally crossed his fingers; if the W stood for Wilkie they were another step closer to a decent lead.

He lifted his eyes and looked at Nancy. "I'm going to go and try and track down Gerard Downley, and hopefully we will also find out who this Wilkie is. We are getting there, Nancy, we are getting there." Meredith pushed his chair back and stood up.

"Good."

Nancy's response was curt. She was still cross with Meredith for interrupting her. How did he know the trip to Devon wasn't significant in some way? She watched him replace the paintings before he leaned over and whispered something to Tom Seaton. She wondered what it was he didn't want her to know. Nancy caught a movement from the corner of her eye, and saw Jane Roscoe was looking at her watch. A smile threatened, which she controlled as she turned to her.

"Do you have to go, Jane? I know you are busy and I can't thank you enough for bothering about me." Nancy glanced up at Meredith. "My solicitor has other clients, Mr Meredith. I think this interview is terminated."

Meredith's shoulders slumped. He bit back his regret at introducing the two women, and he sat back down.

"Quite right too, I'm sure you could do with a break. Before we leave, is there anything else you want to tell us about Jo?"

"No." Nancy's stare was cold. "Not until you bring me something else. That was the deal, Meredith, I'm sure you're a man of your word."

The lack of a title wasn't lost on Meredith. He was going to have to pull something out of the bag to bring Nancy back on side. Right at that moment, though, he wanted to slap her. Instead he nodded and smiled.

"Oh I am, Nancy. Wind it up, Tom." As Meredith walked to the door, he turned to Jane Roscoe. "A word if you have a minute, Ms Roscoe. I'll be in my office."

~ ~ ~

Bending forward, hands on knees, Jo Adler stared at the muddy coloured rug on which she stood. She drew air in through her nose and blew it out of lips that formed a perfect O as she regulated her breathing. Sweat travelled from her hairline, across her face, and dripped from the end of her nose. She released one knee and wiped her nose with the back of her hand.

"Now slowly bring yourself upright, filling your lungs as you go . . . hold it . . . and release. Now using the weight of your head, allow it to roll slowly around your . . ."

Stepping forward, Jo switched off the machine. She had just completed three thirty-minute workouts in succession. She knew the procedure for cooling down, and the celebrity taking her through her paces had a voice which grated. Jo wiggled her shoulders up and down before stripping off the bra and pants she had been wearing to exercise in, and scooping them up she walked to the shower. Her calf muscles pulled with each step. Veronica Vickers may have false boobs, a six-pack, and a grating voice, but she seemed to know what she was doing. Jo snorted out a laugh. Vickers was just following instructions from a professional, Jo knew that, but understood how easily the public was taken in.

Pulling back the shower curtain, Jo checked the setting. The night before she had had the shower quite hot. Steam had filled the little room, and condensation had run down the silver walls of her prison. She realised this could lead to mould growth and had painstakingly wiped it all up, as much to fill the time as to any worry about the condition of her surroundings, or indeed her health. Throwing her underwear into the shower base she switched it on. As the lukewarm water ran over her body and washed away the sweat, she picked up her underwear and washed it. Wringing it out, she pulled back the curtain and tossed it into the basin. Squeezing a small blob of shampoo into her hand, she massaged it into her hair. There was only one bottle of shampoo so she was using it sparingly. As she rinsed the shampoo away her thoughts turned to what she would prepare for her dinner that night. The water mingled with her tears as she realised it was Thursday, and she wondered whether Aaron would be making his usual curry.

11

When Frankie returned to his office, he paused for a moment and observed Amanda Meredith. She had numerous sheets from one of the files spread around her writing pad, and from where he stood, he could see a page full of neat script. Amanda stared out of the window chewing her pencil. Frankie opened the door and startled her. She spun around to face him.

"How are you doing?" He smiled as Amanda leaned forward and tried to appear casual as she covered her notes with her arm. Frankie scanned the table. "Have you not had a drink or anything? You've been here almost three hours. I am sorry, something came up." Shoving his hands into his pockets he nodded towards the door. "Right, pack that lot up and come with me. I'm buying lunch."

Thanking him, Amanda smiled as she returned the notes to the appropriate file. Closing her notebook, she placed her pencil on it. She was going to have lunch with him! Having already checked that he wasn't wearing a wedding ring, she hoped he didn't have a girlfriend tucked away somewhere. She picked up her notepad and pens from the desk but Frankie stopped her.

"Don't worry about that. We'll come back here. I want to know what you remember. It's what's stayed up here I'm interested in." Frankie tapped the side of his head. Smiling as Amanda replaced her notepad, he opened the door for her. He explained the layout of the building as he led her towards the canteen. "You'll be here a lot soon, so you may as well know your way around. It'll save you hours."

Once in the canteen he handed Amanda a tray and told her to choose what she wanted. Amanda had an appetite much like her father, but she controlled herself and opted for a smoked mackerel salad and yoghurt. She experienced a pang of food jealousy when Frankie heaped a huge pile of chips next to the large portion of lasagne, and for sweet he chose apple and blackberry crumble.

They settled themselves at a table in the corner and Amanda nibbled away at her salad.

"Right, tell me what you found out. Let's start with Wendy Turnball, what thoughts did you have?"

Conscious of his undivided attention, which in any other situation she would have relished, Amanda wrinkled her nose, not wanting to make a fool of herself.

"Nothing really. Everything seems to have been covered now that you've got hold of the file." She gazed up at him, "I don't understand why you don't think it will be enough? If the bruise on the foot is consistent with having been hit forcibly against the tap opening, why is that not enough?"

Frankie swallowed the food he had in his mouth and waved his fork at her. "Because it wasn't measured for development or measured against the actual tap. You see? Bruises continue to develop post-mortem for a small amount of time. Wendy wasn't found for a couple of days, and the foot was immersed in cold water. It all has an effect. Of course it would have helped if they had taken a cast from the tap, but they didn't, so all we have is our best guess."

"Why don't you go and get one? You've got the photographs and the measurements of the bruise. I would have thought it unlikely the bath taps have been changed," she grimaced. "Although saying that, who could relax in a bath where someone died?" She shivered and Frankie laughed.

"That'll soon be knocked out of you." He leaned forward and tapped her hand. "You know, I may just look into that." He forked some chips into his mouth, and then gestured to his plate. "Help yourself, I always take too many."

Amanda picked up a chip and bit it into it.

"And your thoughts on Debbie Charles. Anything jump out at you?"

Amanda considered this for a moment, and shook her head. "Not really, no."

"I can't believe you are so coy, young lady. Nice to see you haven't got all of your father's traits. He would have just said whatever it is you are not saying. What is it?"

"It's the knot," Amanda twiddled the chip between her fingers. "I know it was kept as it was found for evidence purposes, but it looks like it's a pretty tight knot. Was that due to the weight of the body?" Before Frankie answered, she added quickly, "And I am only going on photographs, so I could be wrong."

"No, it wasn't the weight of the body; its purpose was to ensure the smooth running of the rope." He smiled apologetically as Amanda grimaced. "Sorry, not a nice thought. The weight was taken by the rope wrapped around the banister above. Why, what's your thinking?"

"I'm not an expert, and I can be cack-handed, but the only time I tried to tie knots, which was a while ago, I got rope burns. My stepfather took us sailing, and tried to show off by demonstrating the different knots he could tie." She shrugged. "My hand," she rubbed the length of her right hand from the crook of her thumb down the length of her finger, "was raw. He didn't do it unscathed either. So, my thinking is there could be DNA on the rope. But," again Amanda grimaced as though apologising for her naivety, "I'm sure it was tested at the time."

Frankie put his elbow on the table, and rested his chin on his hand. His index finger tapped his lip as he studied Amanda. Flushing, she looked away and finished the chip. Frankie frowned as she played with the remains of her lunch, unable to meet his eye. Why had the girl flushed? Perhaps she thought her suggestion was infantile; he'd done nothing to assure her otherwise. Feeling guilty he sat upright and tapped the table.

"Eat up. That's a darned good thought. I'm sure, as you say, they tested it at the time, but once unravelled who knows what may be revealed. Let's go and look."

Amanda's head jerked up. "Now?"

"It's as good a time as any. I haven't that much on this afternoon that can't wait, and Jo Adler's release depends on your father's success. I'd say that takes precedence over anything else I have in my diary."

As he held open the door to the canteen, Frankie realised that all he had had to do was praise her. As it was now, he'd be working well into the evening to clear the things he needed to do, and he was supposed to be taking Sarah for dinner. As he punched in the code to open the lab door, he realised that this need to please people really did get in the way of a simple life

Ten minutes later they were gowned and gloved, and sitting opposite each other. A sheet of white paper covered the narrow desk, and with a pair of pointed tweezers Frankie worked at the first loop of the knot. Amanda watched in silence, more often than not, looking at his face rather than the knot. Frankie had switched on the recording machine, mainly to demonstrate it negating the need to make notes as he went, and occasionally he gave details about what he was doing. When he had two lengths of kinked blue rope lying on the paper, he looked up at Amanda.

"Nothing obvious yet, but let's take a closer look." As he pulled down the magnifying glass, he thought how nice it would be if there was something to find, although he didn't hold out much hope of that. Resting his forehead on the padded section of the machine he examined the first six inches of one length of rope.

"Hmm. The fibres of the rope have been severed around the exterior, a couple of millimetres, no more, indicating friction. This we have to assume was caused by the tying of the knot." He leaned back and looked at Amanda. "Now there's a thing I've never considered. I wonder why we use the expression 'tying the knot' when we marry. I'll have to Google that when we're done." He leaned forward to look at the next six inches of rope.

Amanda pulled her phone from her pocket. "Origin not known, here are some possible reasons." Amanda smiled as Frankie peered around the machine at her. She looked back at her phone, "Some cultures put a sash or tie around the wrists of people being married, or brides used to knot brightly-coloured bows to their dresses which guests would pull off and keep for good luck," Amanda scrolled down the list, "or the wedding party used to knot rope together which, when finished, was strung between four posts to support the, oh . . . the marriage bed. But there is no definitive origin."

"Well, that's us educated, or sort of. Come over here, you can do the next section." Frankie slipped off the stool and stood back to allow Amanda to take his place.

She stilled as he leaned against her and reached his arms on either side of her to adjust the position of the magnifying glass. He lifted one of her hands and placed it on a control. Amanda wished she wasn't wearing gloves, and rolled her eyes at such a ridiculous thought.

"Just turn to adjust the focus. Shout loud if you find anything."

Frankie stepped away and Amanda relaxed. Following Frankie's quiet instructions, she examined the final six inches of the first length of rope. She found no reason to shout out. They swapped places once more, and Frankie pulled the rope tight several times. Several fibres sprinkled onto the paper, together with a small dark fleck. Frankie frowned and leaned forward, appraising it with his own eyes, before carefully lifting it onto a slide with his tweezers. Swivelling on the stool, and remaining seated, he scooted the stool to the table behind him.

"What is it?"

Amanda sounded excited and Frankie smiled.

"I have no idea yet. It could be paint, fabric, blood, just about anything. We'll know more once we get it under this baby."

With his free hand he tapped the microscope before him lovingly. He flipped the power switch and slid the slide into position. Peering down the lens, he clicked his fingers.

"If you switch that screen on, you'll see what I can . . . Ms Meredith, I think we've found something."

Amanda rushed to the small screen and pushed the button. The screen revealed a fierce white background, which had a brown dot in the middle. The sample Frankie had taken now resembled a raisin. She had no idea what she was looking at. She leaned forward and squinted at the shape. She was none the wiser.

"What is it?" she asked impatiently.

Frankie increased the magnification; his tweezers came into view. "This, my very clever little friend, is, I believe, the root of a hair." With the tweezers Frankie pointed to a small line with a bulbous shape on one end, at the edge of the mass. "Whilst this is what is commonly known as a scab. A dried crust of blood." He pulled his eyes away from the microscope. "What we need now is to get it tested for DNA."

"Can you get DNA from that small a sample?" Amanda was rubbing her hands together, clearly delighted at the discovery.

"You can. I'll get it ready to send off." He smiled as Amanda's face fell. "Patience is a virtue where forensic science is concerned. "It will take a while but I'll see if I can get it pushed forward." His smile fell away. "The fact that Jo Adler is still captive will help."

Frankie carefully put the slide into a tube and labelled it. Collecting the stool, he went back to the rope. "I'll finish examining this and see if it has anything else to reveal."

Amanda stood to one side as Frankie completed the examination. He found no other evidence. Amanda made a sad face as he swivelled the stool towards her.

"Don't look like that. You've already found evidence that has sat undiscovered for three years. That's a huge bonus."

"What if it is Debbie Charles? Does that mean she did kill herself, do you think?"

Frankie nodded slowly. "Probably. That sample was caught in the covered part of the knot. Debbie would have had close contact with that knot prior to or during tying. So unless the rope had previously been used by her, and the sample had been collected previously, it would point to that, yes."

"Even though she is left-handed."

Frankie stood and looked down on Amanda. "You seem keen for it to be murder, young lady. What's the reason for that, I wonder?"

"I know what's going on with Nancy Bailey, or bits anyway. I've also read your notes on the twisted bra and the thing about the shoes. If people have died because Nancy believes this is murder, it sort of helps. Crap reasoning I admit, but better than nothing." Amanda dropped her gaze, embarrassed by her passion. "That's what I think anyway."

"I can't fault that logic, so let's keep our fingers crossed that it didn't come from Debbie." He paused for a moment. "I'll get the police to ask the sister if she recognises the rope. That would also help. I didn't read anywhere in the statements that they asked that question. He ran his fingers through his hair pushing it away from his face. "Well, I'm pleased you came today, Amanda, your father will be pleased too. You've uncovered more evidence for him." He clapped his hands lightly before rubbing them together. "That's us done. Not a lot more we can do now. Can I give you a lift home?"

Amanda had hoped to watch Frankie at work for the whole day, and she forced a smile. A lift home was better than nothing. They returned to Frankie's office and she packed away her things while he made a few calls. She returned the wire basket containing the two files to the cabinet and leaned on the door jamb.

"Are you sure this won't put you out?" She didn't particularly mind if it meant a few more minutes with him, but she was running out of conversation. Frankie shook his head as he pulled on his jacket. "How do you know, I haven't told you where I live yet?" She smiled, assuming that meant that he wanted to be in her company too.

"I know where you live, Amanda. I've stayed there before. But that's a long story I won't bore you with."

As they were leaving, another pathologist rushed up to Frankie and explained that he needed some papers signed urgently. Frankie showed Amanda into the common room and promised not to be long. In the event he was forty-five minutes. As she waited, Amanda read through the notes she had taken. Frankie returned full of apologies. As they walked to the car they discussed the two cases and whether Frankie thought the cause of death would be altered on either case.

"That sort of depends on your father. As Nancy Bailey has admitted murdering Wendy Turnball, I'm sure there will be a new inquest, which should be as much a formality as anything else. My evidence will be provided to the coroner, but it's only my best guess for reasons we discussed earlier."

"Why not see if you can get a cast of the tap? You have photographs of the bath, you'll know whether it's been changed or not. Do you need to get a search warrant to check something like that?"

"Only if I'm refused entry and a judge thinks it crucial to the case." Frankie glanced at his watch. "Wait here, I'll be two minutes." He pointed his key fob at his jeep and unlocked it. "Let's pop in on the way. You never know, they might let us do it." He returned her grin before running back into the building.

Amanda climbed into the car and settled back into the seat. A smile played around her lips as she casually poked around the various bits and bobs sitting in the pockets and glove compartment of Frankie's car. She found nothing of interest. Frankie, true to his word, returned quickly. Opening the rear door he placed a small briefcase behind the driver's seat, and climbing in, he dropped a file onto Amanda's lap.

"Right, you punch the postcode into the satnav. Let's see who lives in Wendy's home now."

Fifteen minutes later Frankie pulled up outside a substantial Victorian semi-detached house. They climbed out of the car and looked at the building.

"Fingers crossed someone will be in. Come on." Frankie led the way.

They walked up the neat gravel drive, the stones crunching beneath their feet. The front door was located up several steps to the side of an imposing bay window. Frankie looked over the railing and down into a small stoned courtyard in front of the basement.

"What are you looking for?" Amanda peered down. There was nothing to see. The windows had been bricked up with a matching stone, and a few leaves blew around a brush and a rusting rake leaning against the crumbling steps.

"When I was a student a couple of my friends shared a flat over this way. Similar house, this one obviously hasn't been converted. No outside access." He looked up at the rest of the house before pushing the doorbell. "It must be huge. A lot to look after, and as I understand it, Wendy Turnball lived here alone." Stepping back, he looked at the front door expectantly. After a minute or so he pushed the doorbell again, tapping his hand impatiently on the side of his leg as he waited.

"Perhaps they're out," Amanda suggested as she looked up at the first-floor bay window. As she did so a light came on. She pointed. "Or not. Look, that light has just come on, there must be someone in."

Frankie nodded and pushed the bell again. No one came.

"Perhaps the bell doesn't work." Frowning, Frankie opened the large letter box and turned his ear to the opening as he rang the bell again. The chime echoed around the large stone vestibule. "It works." Frankie put his mouth next to the opening and called out "Hello" at the top of his voice. Still no one came. Frankie put his eye to the letter box and peered in. "Hmm, there are few leaflets on the floor, but can't see any post. Let's go around the back. There may be someone there."

Amanda followed him around the side of the house. It led to a pretty, enclosed garden. The back door was at ground level, as were the windows. Frankie hammered on the back door.

"Steady on," Amanda warned, "you'll give someone a heart attack."

"Yes, never thought of that." Frankie walked to the first window and cupping his hands around his eyes he leaned against the glass. On the inside of the windows, metal barred shutters had been drawn closed. "That's a shame, that looks like a fabulous kitchen. It must be a little like living in a prison with those shutters closed, not to mention a fire hazard."

Amanda joined him. As she did so a light came on in the corner of the room. She saw the large farmhouse table, and the dresser beyond. There was no one there. She frowned at Frankie and he smiled.

"That explains it. The lights are obviously plugged into timers. It's an old trick to make it look like someone is at home. There's clearly no one in. I'll pop my card through the front door."

"Why do you think they put those metal grills inside rather than out? They wouldn't look nice either way, but I think I'd rather have something outside, don't you?"

"Cost. If you want to put something outside, it has to be constructed so that burglars can't simply unscrew it. Those are much cheaper."

"You sound like an expert."

Amanda stopped at the bottom of the steps as Frankie took them two at a time. He scribbled the note on the back of his card and pushed it through the letterbox. Frankie smiled as he walked back down the steps.

"Not really, but the neighbour in the basement flat of the house I live in wanted my advice when she was looking at security measures. Come on, young lady, let's get you home. I'll keep you informed should they call."

Jo hit the power button on the DVD and Tom Jones was silenced. She dropped the knife onto the table and rushed to the grill. She'd heard something, she was sure of it. Peering up the stairs towards the door she listened intently. There it was again, it was the doorbell. She yelled at the top of her voice, praying that she would be heard.

"I'M HERE. HELP ME. I'M HERE." She paused to listen. Nothing. A few seconds passed, and in the distance she heard a dull thudding noise and tried again. "HELP! HELP ME, PLEASE!" The thudding stopped. She stood still, her knuckles white from clasping the bars of the grill, and listened. There were no more chimes, and no more banging. Her shoulders sagged as she walked back to the table. "It's just me and you again tonight, Bobby, and Tom of course."

She hit the button as she picked up the knife and sliced the remaining cheese. Tom Jones sang to them quietly as she prepared her supper.

~ ~ ~

Chris sat on one of the sofas in Patsy's office and used a magazine as a coaster for his cup.

"He's a nasty piece of work, Patsy. I put him away for three years for demanding money with menaces. That's all I could get him on; there were far worse things we couldn't prove. He fancies himself as a bit of a gangster. When we searched his house, he had loads of books on criminal gangs, the Kray twins were a particular favourite. He never became that big, thank goodness, not clever enough, and he surrounds himself with idiots. That was a good twelve years ago. Picked him up for trying to stir up racial hatred just before I left the force, but CPS said it wouldn't stick." Chris sipped his coffee. "Tell me how you think he may be connected with the Wilkinson case."

Patsy took Chris through the events of the previous day, and her meeting with Percy Howard.

"So there are a couple of things really. He is definitely connected to whatever goes on with the white van, although I don't think the singer, Ben Jacobs, is. But the most concerning aspect at the moment, is that they all knew who I was, to the point that I was connected to you. It was only a couple of hours between leaving the pub after my meeting with Jacobs and returning that night, and they knew."

"Did you leave a card?" Chris asked the obvious question, and Patsy rolled her eyes.

"If I had I think I'd have worked it out for myself! I called him on the number Angel gave me, and gave my name of course, but I introduced myself as a friend of the family." Patsy shook her head. "I also asked Angel not to reveal what I did unless it was necessary. It wasn't necessary."

Chris nodded. "Well, perhaps that's a good thing. If they know about me, they'll know about Meredith, so hopefully they'll give you a wide berth. What's the next plan of action?" His eyes narrowed as Patsy looked sheepish. "What? Spit it out."

"I think you'd better come and see what Linda's been up to." Patsy walked to the door and opened it. She called out to Linda. "Fire up your baby, the boss wants to see."

Chris smiled quietly to himself. He wasn't Patsy's boss, he was her partner, but he appreciated the acknowledgement none the less. Linda smiled at Chris and her body swayed as she tapped the keyboard.

"You're going to like this . . . No, not like. You're going to love this, Christopher, so pull up a chair."

Chris gave Patsy a glance that suggested he doubted that he would. He pulled up the chair, and folding his arms across his chest, he stared at the screen of Linda's computer as the program opened.

"Do your worst, Loopy."

Linda demonstrated the tracking program proficiently. She called up the history of Patsy's car journey, showed him the texts she'd received when Patsy had stopped anywhere, and explained how she thought it would save them hours of boring work.

"That's if we only want to know where they are. If you're watching you can also see who they're with and what they're doing."

Chris leaned forward and pointed to a small icon on the corner of the screen. "What's this?"

Linda shot a look at Patsy. It was almost as though Linda were apologising. Patsy frowned and stepped closer.

"Well, as I explained, you can program in expected locations. With Patsy's car they were here and my house. You can also program in warnings. One of them being length of time," Linda passed Chris her phone. "You will see that I received a warning when Patsy's car remained on Gloucester Road overnight." Again she glanced at Patsy. "The other is key locations, and I only programmed in Meredith's address. I didn't get any warnings on that." Linda's eyes remained glued to the screen as Patsy put her hands on her hips and shook her head. "I wasn't spying. I was testing." Still looking at the screen, Linda's lips twitched into a smile.

"Your suggestion is that we bug the white van -" Chris began, but an excited Linda turned to face him and interrupted.

"Oh, if only. Your equipment isn't sophisticated enough to do anything that isn't within shouting distance. We could work on that though." She nudged him with her elbow. "I am capable though, we'll talk later about that. But my suggestion is to track the van. You never know, it could lead us to Wilkinson and the body." Her eyes widened. "This could help us solve a murder."

Chris threw his hands up in exasperation. "She's too excitable for this game," he said to no one in particular. "We don't know that there has been a murder. If there has, it was weeks ago, and there would be no reason for anyone to return to the scene of the crime. Why would they? To lay flowers? How much will this cost me?"

Linda shook her head at Patsy and pulled a sad face. "What price justice, aye Patsy?" She slapped Chris on the knee. "Firstly, it will not cost you a penny. When you agree that we use this equipment as standard, then it will cost you. For the time being I'm borrowing it from Trev. Secondly, the van has already returned to the scene at least once, so why not again? We don't have to follow it. But it could be useful." She clasped her hands together and, like a child wanting something they may not get, she begged. "Please, Chris, I promise you, you won't regret it. Please."

"How do you fix the tracker to the van? And more to the point, who's going to do it? I don't want you two getting caught. Ford is a nasty piece of work. The fact that you are girls won't cut any mustard."

"And that's where you come in. Patsy and I will go to the pub and keep them busy, distracted, whatever." Linda waved her hand in the air. "Meanwhile, you attach this," she slid open her drawer and pulled out what looked like a large watch battery, "to the van. It needs to be hidden, obviously." She ignored the roll of eyes from Chris. "It's a strong magnet but not impossible to knock off, so somewhere protected from accidental knocks. Inside the van would be preferable but not essential."

Chris was looking sceptical, but had already decided to go with the plan. He liked the thought of being better equipped to do the job, and whilst he didn't think the white van would get them anywhere, it was as good a test as any. Linda clasped her hands and blew him a kiss by way of encouragement.

"I think I'm old enough and ugly enough to have worked out where I should put it. Go on, when?"

Patsy winked at Linda. "Early evening will be best. If they're not there we can get some idea of where they are, or when they are likely to be there."

Patsy looked up and smiled as Sharon Grainger walked into the office.

Sharon took in the scene quickly and shook her head. "I see they've convinced you." She shook her head at Chris. "I told them it would take at least three attempts. Much like it does when I want anything. You caved in quicker with them than you ever do with me." She tutted and walked into the kitchen. "What have they got that I haven't?" she called as she filled the kettle. She ignored the laughter with a smile as she popped tea bags into the pot.

"Why don't you call the guy you met yesterday and find out where they're playing tonight, Jacobs wasn't it? Surely that would help. I haven't really got the time to go wandering." Chris replaced the chair he had used, and looked at Patsy expectantly.

"Because I don't want him to think I'm interested in him. He's got a big enough ego already."

"But he'll think that anyway if you just turn up. You could say you want to ask him more questions." Chris countered her argument. "That way we can get it done, and all get home at a decent hour."

Patsy sighed and chewed the end of her pencil as she considered this argument. "You're right. I'll ring him. But if he becomes a pain, Chris, I'll make sure you pay."

Patsy walked to her bag and collected her phone. Ben Jacobs answered on the first ring. Sharon returned from the kitchen and her three colleagues listened to one side of the conversation.

"Hi, Ben. I'm well thank you. Yes, the car is sorted, just vandals. Look, I wondered where you were playing tonight? If I could grab ten minutes of your time that would be great, I'd like to cover a few things you may be able to help me with. No, sorry I can't, I have a previous engagement tonight. I was hoping to catch you before you get started. Okay great, see you later."

Patsy hung up and Sharon gave her a knowing look.

"What's that look for?"

"He obviously likes you. If I heard right he invited you out."

"If he thought it would get him anywhere he'd invite anyone out. He's got that 'I've got a lot to give, so I'll share it freely' attitude."

"Really? Has he been touched by the ugly stick?" Sharon perched on the corner of Linda's desk.

"Not at all. I mean, he's not my type, but no . . . why would you think that?"

"Because you implied he wasn't choosy. What were the arrangements? I think I'll come along."

Patsy sighed dramatically and shook her head. "What? So now I'm taking my mum, dad and sister along to an interview?"

Sharon gasped and stood up shaking her head. "I am not old enough to be your mother . . . not quite! Don't worry, Chris and I will pretend we don't know you and sit in the corner. Linda, will you be joining us or Patsy?"

"No offence, but Patsy of course. I'll be in the thick of it then."

Patsy looked at her watch. "Right, let's call it a day. I will be meeting him at the Crooked Style on the Frenchay Road at quarter to seven. We've all got time to go home and freshen up. Hopefully, it won't take long so I'll even treat you to a curry after."

Patsy left Linda and the Graingers at the door and walked to her car which was in the far corner of the car park. For some reason she wanted a cigarette and wondered why. That usually only happened when something was going on with Meredith. Slamming her door shut she pondered calling Meredith. She had not been in any mood to soothe him the night before, and had half promised to be there waiting for him. He hadn't made contact today, which suggested he was busy with the case, but had no news on Jo. Perhaps she should go tonight. She smiled at the thought and pulled her phone from her bag. He answered on the second ring.

"Two seconds." He asked her to wait as he gave instructions to Trump. "Sorry, what can I do for you?"

His tone was formal and Patsy pulled the phone away from her ear and looked at it. "I was calling to see how you were, but I've obviously caught you at a bad time. I'll call again tomorrow. Perhaps."

As she spoke Patsy leaned across to the glove compartment and pulled out her emergency packet of cigarettes. There were two left. She tapped the pack on the steering wheel as she listened to Meredith sigh. She knew he was choosing his words carefully. She took a cigarette and lit it as he answered.

"Not a bad time, off to see a witness, well, I hope that's what he is. Trump can wait five minutes. I'm well, thank you for asking, Hodge. How are you? Did you sleep well?"

Patsy lowered her window and blew smoke through the gap and smiled. There it was, he was smarting about last night.

"Not really, no. It took ages to sort the car out, I'd been socialising with thugs and idiots, and didn't want to cheese you off by coming over and moaning." She took another drag on the cigarette, "I should have called or texted I suppose . . ." She blew the smoke out.

"I wouldn't have minded you moaning. As long as Amanda wasn't listening, of course."

Patsy visualised his smile, and the deepening of the lines at the corner of his eyes, and although he could not see she returned his smile.

"Are you smoking? That usually spells trouble for me, and as I haven't done anything, not that I know of, what's the problem?"

"Do you know, I don't know." Patsy smiled as she realised Meredith also connected her smoking with his own misdemeanours. "I was having a similar thought myself."

"Listen, I'm going to be free from eight o'clock if nothing happens. Rawlings has the short straw tonight. Let me buy you dinner. Then we'll see if we get to the moaning stage."

Patsy laughed out loud and flicked her cigarette butt out into the car park.

"Deal. I'll pick you up though, I have a meeting later. I should be free by eight." Patsy slapped her forehead, "Oh dear, I told those three I'd treat them to a curry after. I don't suppose you fancy company, do you?"

"Not really, no. But if that's how I get to see you . . ." Meredith let his words trail away.

"No, no. It'll be fine. They'll all be glad I'm with you anyway. I'll call you when I'm on my way."

"They are very sensible people. I always knew they had good taste. I have to go, Hodge, I'll see you later."

Patsy drove home smiling. She would now make an extra effort with her choice of clothes and make-up. Meredith was playing ball, and he deserved to be rewarded.

~ ~ ~

Meredith climbed into the car and slapped the dashboard.

"Come on, Trump. The sooner we get this done, the sooner we'll be free."

"Are you in a rush, sir?" Trump glanced at Meredith as he pulled out of the car park. "Has something happened that I should know about?"

"No, but I do have a life."

Meredith's smile fell away as guilt about Jo's predicament filled his mind. Trump followed his train of thought; the whole team were low. The normal banter was missing, and with no new leads the task of finding Jo fit and well was becoming more remote. Meredith was particularly burdened as Nancy had taken Jo only to get his attention.

Trump believed he needed to let off some steam. "I take it that was Patsy and you're seeing her tonight. Where are you going, anywhere nice?"

"Why do you take it that was Hodge?" Meredith lowered the window and showed Trump his cigarette packet, "Do you mind?" He lit the cigarette knowing that Trump would deny him, if he gave him time.

"I know it was Patsy – and you really must stop calling her Hodge – because you were smiling. She's the only thing that makes you smile." Trump glanced at Meredith again. "Not my business, but any chance you two are going to become a . . . you know . . . a thing again?"

"A thing? What's a thing? And no, it's not your business. But I am seeing her tonight, yes. Baby steps, Trump, baby steps. Why the sudden interest in my love life anyway?"

Trump coughed and ignored the question, preferring to concentrate on the road ahead.

Meredith nudged him with his elbow. "That was a question, Trump."

Trump swallowed. "I haven't known you that long, sir. What's it been, six months? Maybe a little longer. But I know how you were when you were with her, and I know what you're like without her. Even allowing for this case."

"What you're saying is that I'm a nicer bastard with her than I am without. Am I right?"

Trump shot a glance at Meredith, unable to hold back the smile. "Absolutely sir, absolutely."

Meredith laughed and lowered his defences. "I do know that." He sniffed and coughed. "But let's stick to the case, shall we. I don't discuss Loopy with you, so I'm bloody sure I'm not going to discuss Hodge."

"We can discuss Linda if you like, sir. She's like a breath of fresh air when you've -"

"Shut up Trump, and turn left after the lights."

Trump did as he was bid and drove slowly up the street. Number thirty was halfway down on the left-hand side. Trump pulled in opposite the house. Although still spring, the garden was a mass of colour, and numerous gnomes peeped out from behind the foliage. There were some interesting animals dotted about the lawn, which had been fashioned out of copper pipe.

"Very nice. Oh God, Trump, I hate artistic types. They are either drippy or all enthusiastic, either way it winds me up."

Trump smiled as he rang the doorbell.

Gerard Downley opened it as Trump withdrew his hand. It was though he had been standing waiting at the door. Meredith instantly recognised his eyes.

"Come on in, please come on in. Out of the way, Molly." He pushed a very fat ginger cat away from his legs. "She's nosey, just push her away if she gets on your nerves. Go straight through." He held his hand towards an open door.

Meredith followed Trump into the sitting room. It too was a mass of colour, but an organised mass. Cushions with quilted covers lined the back of the long sofa, and books in order of size filled every shelf in the recesses on each side of the open fire. A long marble mantel held various pieces of colourful homemade pottery, and many paintings were hung on the walls, perfectly aligned and arranged in order of size rather than composition. In one corner a winged armchair held a newspaper and glasses. Meredith's tired senses were assaulted. He sat down heavily on one end of the comfortable sofa, and placed the file he carried on his lap.

Gerard smiled. "You look like I feel. Tea, coffee, or something stronger? I have a fabulous single malt."

"Coffee please, we're on duty. Mine's black with two, his is white with none."

Gerard disappeared and Trump sat at the other end of the sofa and scanned the paintings.

"Some of these are rather good, don't you think?"

Meredith cast a cursory glance around the walls. "Yep. Just too many of them." He screwed his eyes shut and raised his eyebrows as he opened them. "How can anyone relax in this lot?"

"I think it's quite homely actually." Trump leaned back against the patchwork cushions.

"Here we go." Gerard handed them a mug each, and picking up the newspaper and glasses he sat in the chair, placing the glasses on top of his head, and the newspaper on the floor. Molly strode in gracefully and plonked herself on the newspaper. "So gentleman, how can I help? I have to confess to being a little confused, Debbie has been dead a few years now."

"Did you ever meet her sister?" Meredith asked, and Trump wondered where he was going with that, as they already knew the answer.

"Oh yes, a couple of times. Odd woman, I found her quite amusing, but I think her constant presence wore a little with Debbie." He clicked his fingers. "Nancy. That was her name." He nodded confirmation.

"Did Nancy speak to you after Debbie died?" Meredith blew gently on the hot coffee before sipping.

"At the funeral, you mean? Yes, only to thank me for coming and to introduce me to Gary, Debbie's son, but I'd met him before. She wasn't quite with it, but I suppose that was to be expected."

"But she didn't suggest that she thought Debbie had been murdered."

Gerard pulled his head back in amazement and frowned. "No. Why? Was she?" He leaned forward. "To be honest with you, the thought crossed my mind when I first heard about it. Suicide was the last thing I expected from Debbie."

"Why?"

"What do you mean 'why'? How many people do you know that you think may be even remotely considering suicide?"

Meredith's mind shot to his ex-wife, Nicola, and to the many victims of Jasper James and Tanya Jennings.

"You'd be surprised," he smiled. "But I suppose that comes with the job. Was it particularly surprising, or surprising because you didn't think you knew anyone considering it?"

"Ah yes, I see what you mean," Gerard nodded. "I'd say it was particularly surprising as only two days before she was telling me she may be going to live abroad."

Meredith and Trump exchanged glances. It was the first time that had been mentioned.

"Did you speak to Phillip Cowell? He's a . . . was a police officer and friend of Nancy who was looking into Debbie's death." Trump leaned forward and placed his coffee on the floor between his feet.

Gerard stared at the ceiling. "I think I possibly did. Some chap called and asked if I knew Debbie. He said he was trying to trace her boyfriend. May have been the chap you mentioned, but it was so long ago."

"Did you help him?" Trump retrieved his coffee as Molly stood and made a beeline for it. "Were you able to give him any information?"

"Not really. Over the few years I knew Debbie she had several men friends. But this one she was going away with was more important than the others. I didn't know any of them. Only what she told me. I probably passed a couple of them in the street though. As you know, she only lived around the corner. She regularly gave me a lift to classes."

Gerard stood and went to point to a small painting in the middle of the top row.

"She did this. It's very good, she was a talented woman. Such a shame." He shook his head and returned to his chair.

Meredith and Trump looked up at the painting. It was a portrait of Gerard but from a different angle than the one Meredith had in the folder.

Meredith opened the folder and took out the one they had found the day before.

"We found this amongst some of her things." He held out the portrait and handed it to Gerard who smiled.

"Ah yes. She wanted to keep that one. She was going to put together a portfolio of male portraits. That wasn't long before . . . well, before she went. I liked it so much that she did that one for me." He looked in the direction of the painting he had previously pointed out. "How many did you find?"

"Three. How many paintings were there?"

"Oh lots, I couldn't put a number on it. Possibly went over the hundred mark. She'd only just started on the male project though. Only three, you say? The family must have dumped the rest. That's criminal."

Meredith slid out the portrait on the unknown man and held it out to Gerard.

"Is this someone from art class?"

"Oh no, that's thingy . . . can't remember his name. He was from the dance class. I think he only went to placate her. I went once too, I don't know who was worse me or . . . or . . . Oh, it's on the tip of my tongue. It will come to me now I've seen him." Gerard wiggled his fingers and closed his eyes for a few moments. "No. Not yet but I will get there. Is it important?"

Meredith shrugged. "I think so, yes. Tell me what you know about him. How did they meet, how long were they seeing each other? I take it he was one of her *friends*?"

"Yes. Actually, more than likely *the* friend that she was going away with. But there were two at the time." Gerard winked at Meredith. "She was quite a girl. I'm glad she had fun before she went."

"Are you married, Mr Downley?"

Gerard roared with laughter.

"The question you actually asked was 'are you gay', wasn't it? Your body language is not subtle, you know. I could see from your expression that you believed you knew the answer. But for the record I'm not married." He clapped his hands together and laughed again. "Did you think I could be part of some love triangle? Oh dear, that does tickle me." He laughed. "I'm flattered, I think, that you think I'm capable of such a thing. I loved Debbie as a friend but not in any romantic way. Hmm." Gerard looked at Trump. "You didn't know though, did you?"

He smiled as Trump shrugged and avoided meeting his eye.

Meredith noted he hadn't actually confirmed his sexuality one way or the other. Meredith finished his coffee, and placed the empty mug on the floor. He ignored the fact that Molly came over and started licking it.

"Back to what you know about Debbie and that man." Meredith held out his hand and Gerard returned the portrait. "Anything you can remember will help."

Gerard told them what he could remember. Trump took notes, and when Gerard appeared to have come to an end, he prompted.

"What about the other man? Did you meet him, do you know anything about him?" He sighed when Gerard shook his head.

"I know only two things about him. He was married and he was good in bed. Debbie was going to end it." He screwed his eyes up, "In fact, I think her words on the subject were, 'he might be good at what he does in the bedroom, but while he's allowed to share himself, I shudder to think what he'd do if he knew I was sharing me.' She laughed, and when I teased her, she told me he was quick tempered and arrogant, but she would have to see him one more time so she would remember what she was missing. For all his faults, he was good in bed."

Meredith smirked.

"I told you she was quite a girl." He clicked his fingers and pointed at Meredith. "That was the morning I first met Nancy. She arrived as Debbie was telling me. As Debbie went to greet her, she warned me to say not a word to Nancy, she wouldn't approve. I think it's healed up." He laughed again, "Nancy was an attractive woman too, but she'd not been interested in anyone since her husband went. I think that's why she bothered Debbie so much, she was lonely." He looked down at the floor and closed his eyes, before looking up and shaking his head. "No, sorry, I thought I had the name, but it's gone again. Can I get you more coffee?"

Meredith declined the offer, and replaced the portrait in the file before standing. He held out his hand. "Thank you for your time. We'll be off now but please call if you remember that name, or anything else you think may be significant."

Gerard shook Meredith's hand and held on to it. "You haven't told me why you're asking all these questions. Has something happened to make you think Debbie was murdered?"

"Yes, her sister, Nancy, has killed three people because she believes that to be the case."

Gerard released Meredith, and his hand flew to his mouth. "Oh my God. I'll go back through my journal and find out if I perhaps wrote the name down." He walked towards the front door. "Debbie kept a journal too, or at least she told me she did. Perhaps that would help."

"We've got it, and it doesn't." Trump shook Gerard's hand.

Gerard was still in shock at Meredith's revelation and stood in the hall staring at the back of door for some time after they had left, desperately trying to remember the man's name.

Meredith drummed the file as Trump started the engine. "We may need to go public with this painting, but first we'll get hold of the other members of the dance club and see if they can put a name to it. Take me home, Trump, I've got a date tonight, and unless something earth-shattering happens, I'm not going to miss it." As he spoke his phone sounded, alerting him to an incoming message. "Perhaps I've just tempted fate." Meredith pulled the phone from his pocket. "It's from Sherlock." He smiled as he read the message aloud to Trump.

Meredith – a quick note to let you know you have a very bright daughter. She has sound logic, reasons well, and discovered some possible evidence on Debbie Charles' noose. I'll let you know the results as soon as I can. I may need your help in speeding up the tests.

"That's my girl. For some reason she thought working with Sherlock would help her studies. Turns out she's helping us." He fell silent for a moment. "Oh, I hope this hasn't given her a taste for working with the departed. That's worse than her wanting to become a copper. It's not funny." He elbowed Trump in the arm as he laughed.

12

Linda hurried down the stairs and grabbed her coat from the hook at the bottom.

"Sorry, Patsy, but I couldn't decide, what do you think?" Holding her coat away from her she gave a twirl.

"You look fabulous. But you did in the last three outfits too. Come on, we've only got twenty minutes to get there."

Linda grinned and blew her a kiss. "Okay, but Louie is meeting us after, so I thought I should make the effort."

Linda opened the door and set the alarm as Patsy hurried to the car.

They arrived at the Crooked Style on the dot of six forty-five.

"You see, there was no problem. Oh, this wind is picking up. My hair!"

Linda rushed towards the entrance. Patsy locked the car and followed her in. Patsy surveyed the bar. It couldn't have been more different to the British Pride. It was clean, the furnishings were tasteful, and a log fire roared in a huge stone hearth. There was no stage. Linda fished her purse from her bag. She ordered a bottle of Rioja and two glasses.

"I'm driving, Linda, so I hope you're thirsty."

"Well, you can have a small one, and I'll see how I do. Louie should be here by seven-thirty, so if there's any left he can help. Here you take the . . . OMG. Don't look now but the most hunky bloke has just walked in."

As always when told not to look, Patsy turned towards the door. Ben Jacobs grinned at her. He looked different. He was wearing black trousers, a well-fitted white shirt, and shiny black dress shoes had replaced the Doc Martens. The eyes were the same, as was the smile.

Ben was aware she was assessing him as he went to join them. "It seems as though we both scrub up well, Patsy. You look fabulous." Taking her by the shoulders, he leaned forward and kissed her cheek. She felt the stubble from his five o'clock shadow. He released her and turned to Linda who stood, open-mouthed, watching the exchange.

He held out his hand. "Hi, I'm Ben, and you are . . ."

Linda had the wine bottle in one hand and her purse in the other. Much to everyone's surprise she stepped forward and pecked him on the lips.

"Linda, sorry no hands." She held up the offending articles. Ben laughed and Linda swooned.

"I like you, Linda, shall I take that?" Relieving Linda of the wine bottle, he walked to a table a little to the left of the fire. "This is the best table. Any closer and you roast."

The two women followed him. Patsy was frowning. There was no evidence of a stage, and Ben was dressed to impress. She hoped she hadn't given him the wrong impression and he thought that this was some sort of date.

"You look very dapper," she commented as she took her seat.

"You can't sing soul, you have to feel it." He moved his hips from side to side before sitting down.

Linda blinked rapidly and Patsy wondered if bringing her was a mistake.

Ben grinned at Linda. "Are you all right, Linda?"

"I am, but I won't be if you keep doing things like that, you naughty man." She slapped him playfully on the arm as Patsy covered her face and groaned. "Where are you singing anyway? Where's the band?"

Ben Jacobs jerked his thumb to a door in the corner; a sign above noted it to be the main bar.

"Through there. The gig starts at eight, but we have a warm up about half-seven. Do you like soul, Linda?"

"I do now. I think I need a drink. Patsy, you never said we were meeting such a charmer."

Patsy shook her head apologetically. "Soul? I thought you were a ska man."

"I'm whatever pays the bills. Right at this moment I have three regular gigs. Ska, soul and, I'm ashamed to say, middle of the road pop at the British Legion every third Sunday." He smiled. "I'm glad you sorted the car out. The Brit is a bit rough, but they don't usually have trouble like that."

"That's hardly surprising with so many thugs and racists around," Patsy snapped, then she held her hands up, "Sorry I didn't mean to snap, but I'm afraid I didn't like some of your friends."

"Not friends, Patsy, associates. There's a whole barrel of difference, although that said, some of them are good guys. You thinking of anyone in particular?"

"I wouldn't know where to start, so I'll take your word for it." Patsy glanced towards the bar door. "Are Alfie and co setting up?" Her forehead creased as Jacob's shook his head.

"Not their scene really. I have a piano and guitarist tonight. Same guitarist as last night. Was it them you wanted to speak to or me?" He pouted as though disappointed.

Linda didn't think he was acting, and she tutted at Patsy. "Would you like a glass of wine, Ben?" She picked up the bottle and pointed it at him.

"No thanks. I'm a beer man, I'll give it another twenty minutes or so before I start." He turned back to Patsy who had noticed Chris and Sharon Grainger enter the bar. She looked back at Ben as he spoke to her. "What do you want to know?"

"I wanted to talk to you without Angel present. I got the impression that her uncle was being controlled by Big Mo, and that he wasn't being honest with her." She looked him in the eye. "This is important to her, and you seemed like an honest man so I wanted to get your take on them." She blinked. "But if they are friends of yours . . . I'll understand the conflict." Her eyes flicked up to the door as it opened, and Alfie and one of the other band members walked in.

Alfie was as loud as ever. "Ron, he's still in here, you're all right, you're not late." Alfie glanced at the barmaid. "Two pints please, gorgeous." Alfie walked across and slapped Jacobs on the back. "We meet again. I can't stop long, I've promised the missus I'd take her out. But Ron's car's broken down again so I helped him out. Ladies." He nodded acknowledgement to the two women. "I'd never have guessed he'd be sat talking to two birds."

Laughing he walked back to the bar for the drinks he'd ordered. Jacobs laughed and turned to greet Ron. Patsy took the opportunity, and catching Linda's eye, she jerked her head towards the exit. Linda nodded solemnly, and in a sudden flurry of activity she jumped up and waved at the Graingers.

"Aunty Sharon. Hello! I didn't see you come in." Excusing herself, and picking up the wine, Linda rushed over to the Graingers' table. A few minutes later Chris left the bar. Alfie and Ron propped themselves at the bar and Jacobs turned back to Patsy.

"She's a live wire and no mistake." He smiled softly as Patsy laughed in agreement. "You have a wonderful smile, Patsy." He glanced over his shoulder at the two men before looking back at her. "Let's clear a couple of things up whilst we're on our own. I'm not a racist. Nor are half the people at the British Pride, believe it or not, ska is just music. That said, there are some nasty blokes in there so you do need to choose your company wisely if you don't want to get out of your depth."

He glanced over his shoulder again.

"Ed Wilkinson is in debt to Big Mo in some way. I don't know how or why and I don't ask, because with that lot what you don't know doesn't kick you up the arse when you're not looking. Big Mo is bad news, but he hires the acts so I'm friendly. That's it. No more, no less, I have to earn a living and I can't afford to be choosy. He doesn't invite me into his world, and I certainly don't knock on the door." He glanced at his watch. "So in answer to your question, I think Ed would help Angel if he was able, unless Big Mo has told him otherwise. Brother or not. If Big Mo has warned him off, I'd seriously suggest that you back off too." He smiled and tilted his head to one side. "Seriously, Patsy, believe me."

He jumped as Alfie slapped him on the shoulder.

"I hope you're making promises you can keep, mate." Alfie laughed his coarse laugh, and looked at Patsy's cleavage. "He's sound, love. You can believe every word. Honest. Right, I'm off before you start crooning. See you next Wednesday at the King's Head."

Jacobs and Patsy watched him leave, and as he opened the door Chris came back in and gave Linda a nod. Patsy relaxed, glad he was back. Ron called to Jacobs as he walked to the main bar door.

"I'll get set up, Ben. What time do you want to do the sound check?"

"Give me five." Jacobs replied and turned back to Patsy. "I'm going to have to go. Will you stick around and listen or are you going to disappear on me?" He leaned over and picked up her hand. "I'd like you to stay."

Patsy smiled at him and pulled her hand away. "I have to be somewhere later but I'll stay for the first song so make it a good one. Now, I'll take this and go and join Linda and her family if you're going to disappear." She stood and moved her face to the side so that his kiss found her cheek.

"Don't forget, at least the first song." Jacobs stepped away, and waved to Linda who was watching them intently. "Nice to meet you, Linda, I'll sing one for you later."

Linda beamed at his back as he walked through to the main bar. She was gesturing to Patsy to hurry and join them. Patsy ignored the look of amusement on Sharon's face.

"Patsy Hodge!" She admonished as Patsy joined them, "You didn't mention he was hot! Blimey, I'm having a flush and it wasn't even me he was fondling."

"There was no fondling, Linda, get a grip, it's just how he is. And talk about pot and kettle. You virtually snogged him and he was only saying hello." Patsy laughed. "You are seriously, seriously, mental. Do you know that?"

"She is, Patsy, you're right. But that wasn't someone being friendly. He has the hots for you." Sharon's eyes laughed at Patsy. "What I don't understand is if you're not with Meredith, why you were being so coy? If I was a couple of years younger, and free of course," she looked at Chris and winked, "I wouldn't have been turning my face away. What's your problem?"

Chris leaned forward and tapped Patsy's knee. "Ignore them, love. Just because you have taste, and some sense of decorum, they're jealous, that's all."

"As it happens, and not that it's anyone else's business, I'm seeing Meredith tonight. I promised Ben I'd listen to the first song though." She glanced at her watch, "Which is fine, I have time as long as they get going on time, and it sounds like they're warming up."

As she spoke, Ben was counting into the microphone in the next room. A customer opened the door to the main bar, and sounds of the guitar and piano filtered into the room.

"What type of music is it?" Sharon asked. "Chris hasn't taken me out for years, I think we should stay and watch." She turned to Linda who was smirking at her. "What's that look for?"

"You said 'watch', when you may have meant listen, but I think you had it right!"

The three women dissolved into laughter and Chris shook his head. This was going to be a painful night, so he was glad that Linda had invited Louie to join them. At least that meant he would have some sensible conversation.

Sharon pulled her coat over her arm, and picked up her drink. "Come on, we can't *listen* from here." Sharon edged her way around the table and the others followed her through to the main bar. The room was almost full and she chose a table near the back, but placed so that there was a good view of the stage. She waved to Ben Jacobs as she took her seat. He blew her a kiss in acknowledgement, and she turned to Chris. "You see, I still have it. You'd better behave yourself."

Chris leaned forward and said quietly, "You'll always have it my love. I'm safe though, these young blokes couldn't cope with it!"

Sharon threw her head back and laughed before grabbing his face and planting a noisy kiss on the end of his nose. He pushed her away and licked his fingers to remove the lipstick she'd left there. He looked up as Ben Jacobs advised everyone to refresh their drinks, as they would be starting in five minutes. Jacobs winked at the barmaid who handed him his first beer of the night.

Chris stood, and having established who wanted what, he made his way to the bar, taking his phone from his pocket as he did so. Having bought the drinks and made his call, he returned to the table as the main lights were lowered.

Ben Jacobs kicked off the night with 'I Heard It Through the Grapevine'. The three women exchanged glances.

"Gorgeous *and* he can sing. Meredith had better watch out," Sharon whispered too loudly. "I'm glad we came."

Both Chris and Patsy chose to ignore her.

As Jacobs brought the song to an end, Patsy retrieved her phone from her handbag. She was going to text Meredith to see if he was ready to be picked up, and was surprised to find that he had texted her.

Running late I will call when I'm free. X

Patsy placed the phone on the table so that she wouldn't miss his call. Picking up the diet coke she looked at Linda.

"Meredith's tied up with something, so Louie may be late too. Fingers crossed they're on to something." She closed her eyes as a wave of guilt swept over her. She had the ability to sit in a pub being entertained while Jo was still missing. Opening her eyes, she stared into her drink and sighed. Linda put her arm around her shoulder and gave her a hug, assuring her that Jo would be found alive and well. She got very excited as Ben Jacobs sang the opening line to 'Sitting on the Dock of the Bay'.

"My dad sings this one every Christmas. Not like this though." She sighed, and Patsy smiled with her as they settled back to listen and, of course, watch.

On a table in the far corner a man leaned forward to make sure he had not been mistaken. He hadn't. Alex Walters leaned back in his chair and wished he wasn't with his wife. She didn't like scenes, and he had a lot he wanted to say to Patsy Hodge. He pulled his phone from his pocket and sent a text.

~ ~ ~

"Arghh!" Jo dropped the book she was reading onto the bed and strode to the table. She ejected the CD. "Great as you are Otis, I don't want to be reminded of how lonely I am."

She took the CD back to the shelves and shuffled through the stack of CDs that Nancy had left her. She had played them all several times. She read the titles as she went through.

"Best of Tom Jones, nope, sorry Tom. Let's have a party. Ha! If only. Tina Turner, Take That . . . no." She settled on a classical compilation album by the BBC Philharmonic Orchestra, which Nancy had clearly collected free with the *Sunday Times*. "Over to you chaps, bring me some culture."

She walked back to the machine and inserted the CD. She nodded in time as the female soprano sang the opening of Haydn's *Scena di Berenice*. She had never listened to classical music before, but it was growing on her.

"Go on, honey, give it some," she conducted the music with her fingers as she made her way back to the bed, "and hold it," she advised the singer as she hit a top note. "Now I know where Morse was coming from. Shit, I'm talking to myself again. Come on, Heathcliff, take me away from all this." She picked up *Wuthering Heights* and flipped through until she found her page. "You won't win, Nancy. I'll see you again, if only to punch you in the face," she murmured as she settled back against the pillows.

~ ~ ~

Trump assured Amanda that he didn't want anything as he waited in the kitchen for Meredith.

"I hear you had a successful time with Frankie Callaghan today." He smiled at her. "Your father was most impressed."

Amanda beamed at him.

"It was good, yes. It was a bit of a blow that we couldn't get into Wendy Turnball's house, but Frankie says he'll speak to Dad and see if it's worth getting a warrant. Frankie thinks . . ."

"Not still Sherlock, please." Meredith shook his head as he walked into the kitchen. "Sorry to keep you Trump, but I had to listen to Sherlock this and Sherlock the other for twenty minutes before I was allowed to shower." He smiled at his daughter. "You did well though. Good girl." He buttoned the cuffs of his shirt, as he slipped his feet into the shoes he had left on the kitchen floor. "Not sure what's happening tonight, so don't wait up." He gave Amanda a hug and kissed the top of her head.

She coughed and patted her chest. "Blimey, how much stuff did you put on?" She leaned forward and sniffed. "Patsy will pass out if you get too close."

Meredith's eyes narrowed. "She likes it." He turned to go and looked over his shoulder, "Too much?"

Amanda and Trump laughed, and she stepped forward and pushed him towards the door.

"I was kidding. Go. The ladies are waiting."

"I don't know what you're laughing at," Meredith grumbled as he opened the door to Trump's car. "At least my shirt doesn't look like it's a relic of the seventies." He turned his nose up. "You have no taste."

Meredith grumbled, mainly about Frankie Callaghan and his daughter's sudden interest in forensic pathology, all the way to the Crooked Style.

"Has Loopy met Sherlock yet?" he asked as they approached the entrance.

"Yes of course, why?"

"No reason, perhaps it's just the women in my life who seem to find him charming." Meredith shook his head, "I can't see it myself."

Trump grinned as he followed Meredith into the pub. They looked around the lounge bar to find it was almost empty, and walked in the direction of the music. When they entered the main bar they quickly spotted Chris, Sharon and Linda sitting a few tables in front of them. Meredith scanned the room for Patsy. He smiled as he saw her standing at the bar. The smile fell away as the singer who had been walking amongst the audience took Patsy's hand, and she returned his smile.

Ben Jacobs sang the lines from Marvin Gaye's 'Let's Get It On' and gazed into Patsy's eyes, before pulling her closer. Tump looked quickly from Meredith to Patsy as Meredith took a step towards her. Trump sighed, and stepped forward placing his hand on Meredith's shoulder, but Meredith shrugged it off.

Jacobs continued to sing to her. He leaned forward so that their foreheads were touching, only the microphone separated their lips as Jacobs sang on. Embarrassed, Patsy stepped back and shook her head at him. Meredith slowed down and Trump let out a sigh of relief. They were almost behind Patsy now, and she had no idea they were there. Ben Jacobs dropped her hand and turned to a middle-aged woman sitting at the nearest table, but not before giving Patsy a lingering look.

"Having fun?"

Patsy had just picked up the drinks, and she jumped violently, causing them to slop over her hands.

"Oh, that's a sign of a guilty conscience, did I miss something?" Meredith caught the barmaid's eye. "Two pints please, love." He turned his attention back to Patsy. Holding the drinks out to the side she stepped forward and pecked him on the cheek.

"Not at all. We're over here."

Meredith paid for the drinks and he and Trump joined the others. Meredith sat facing the others, his frame blocking the stage. Linda and Sharon had to lean to the side for a clear view. In the end, Sharon made him swap places, and he sat between Chris and Patsy. His foot tapped along to the music as he spoke quietly to Chris. Patsy watched him slowly relax, and smiled as he sang the odd line from a song.

Ben Jacobs advised the audience that the band would be taking a twenty-minute break. He stepped down from the low stage, and walked across the small space that had been cleared for a dance floor. He made his way towards the back of the room.

Sharon gasped as she realised Jacobs was making a beeline for their table. She turned around to warn Patsy, but Patsy had already noticed.

Meredith caught the look and leaned to one side. He frowned as he saw Jacobs approach. He glanced at Patsy and back at Jacobs, who also looked at Patsy. Jacobs was smiling. His smile turned into a broad grin and

Meredith stood. The group at the table stilled, and Patsy froze as Jacobs held out his arms, wondering what on earth he was thinking about. Meredith stepped away from the table and blocked Jacob's view, and he lifted his arm. Trump and Chris jumped to their feet, thinking a punch was about to be thrown, and Linda held on to the edge of the table. Meredith stepped forward and, grasping Jacob's hand, he pulled him into his body, and the two men thumped each other on the back. The three women looked on in amazement. Chris and Trump shrugged and sat back down.

"You old sod. I haven't seen you for what, twenty years?" Meredith continued to pat Jacobs' back. "Is this what you do, try and sing them out of their knickers? Bad choice mate, you're still crap." He turned to face the others, his arm still around Jacobs' shoulders. "This poor excuse for a musician is my old mate Benjamin Jacobs. Ben come and let me introduce you, although I think you've met some of the ladies."

Trump stood and shook Jacob's hand. "Nice to meet you, I'm off to the bar, what will it be?" Trump took the orders and Jacobs sat with them.

Meredith pointed around the table, "Loopy Linda, Sharon, Chris, and . . ."

"Patsy, yes we've met." Jacobs smiled as he caught the twitch in Meredith's cheek.

"Met? Have you really?" Meredith looked from one to the other.

Jacobs threw his head back and laughed. "Yes, met. Not *met*." He looked at Patsy, "Don't tell me . . ." he turned to point at Meredith, "Him?"

Patsy nodded, a smile playing around her lips. Jacobs pulled a face and shook his head. Meredith, whose expression had not changed, relaxed within. In their youth, and less sophisticated days, he and Jacobs had bets on who could pull the best-looking girl in whatever club or pub they were in. The success rate had been balanced pretty evenly, but Patsy was not one of those girls.

He smiled his lazy smile at her. "I witnessed him trying to damage your hearing when I arrived. He was never as good as me."

"You?" Sharon leaned forward. "Don't tell me you sing. I've never heard you sing." She grasped her chin and started nodding. "Actually, yes I have, you used to do karaoke at Christmas. Were you any good? I can't remember, I'd always been drinking."

Ben Jacobs laughed and leaned over to Sharon.

"We used to duet sometimes, many moons ago, but let's just say he was more of a backing singer."

He turned to Meredith. "It's so good to see you, mate. Last I knew you were all settled with a kid . . ." He lowered his voice, "Sorry, time and place I know. Still, it's good to see you."

Trump returned with the drinks and the four men fell into easy conversation until Jacobs had to return to the stage. Meredith returned to sit next to Patsy.

"Well, that was a turn up for the books. So how did you *meet*? I take it I don't need to be looking over my shoulder again?"

"He's someone I needed to speak to for the job. What do you mean, 'again'?" Patsy was irritated and she turned to look at him, arms akimbo. "I really don't like you sometimes, do you know that." Ben Jacobs started singing the next number and she had to raise her voice a little. "Come on, explain yourself, I was having a good time up until that point."

Chris stood up. "I'll get the next round in whilst you two sort yourselves out. Are you sure you're sticking to coke, Patsy?"

Patsy nodded without taking her glare from Meredith. Meredith smiled. "I have told you about him." He jerked his head towards Jacobs who was now encouraging people onto the dance floor. Patsy frowned and shook her head. "I did. You will remember I was told that Amanda's father was one of my friends?" Patsy's eyes opened in amazement, and Meredith nodded. "Yes, that was Ben. Clearly, he wasn't her father, but could have been."

Patsy allowed her arms to fall to her side and she leaned forward and kissed him. "Life is never boring when you're around, but you know that."

Sharon slapped the table. "Well, thank goodness for that. We can all relax and enjoy ourselves. All's well with the world, Meredith is smiling."

The three couples stayed for the rest of the show. Patsy was drinking coke as she was driving, and Meredith monitored his alcohol intake. He didn't want to overdo it. Towards the end of the evening, he glanced at his watch. He had to be in work at seven the next morning, and he wanted to go home. He leaned closer to Patsy.

"Would it be rude if we made our excuses now?" His lips brushed her ear.

She shivered and turned to face him. "Not at all." She grinned at him. "What?"

Meredith had turned to face the stage as Ben Jacobs sang some piercingly high notes to the opening bars of the next song. He smiled and turned back to Patsy.

"This was one of the numbers we used to do. Got the girls going back in the day." He nodded along as Ben Jacobs sang the opening notes of 'Treat Her Like a Lady' by the Temptations. "They don't make them like they used to." Then Meredith's face fell, "He's got to be joking."

Linda started clapping excitedly. "Meredith is going to sing."

Meredith turned and shot her a look. "I am not."

He turned back and Jacobs had reached their table. He held out the microphone. Patsy looked from one to the other, unable to believe what was happening. Meredith looked at her and she nodded. Meredith stood to manic applause from the others at the table. He took the microphone from Jacobs, nodded with the beat, and sang the opening line from the song.

Jacobs took him by the elbow and steered him back towards the stage. Meredith sang as he walked forwards. Several of the women on the dance floor trapped him as he approached the stage. He stood in the centre of their circle, and sang to them. Jacobs hurried onto the stage and collected another microphone, and returned to Meredith. Jacobs was certainly the better singer of the two, but Meredith gave a good account of himself.

Sharon had clamped her fingers to her bottom lip, and was whistling long shrill notes. Trump and Linda were dancing, and Chris was having a fit of laughter. Patsy sat watching, her mouth slightly open, shaking her head. She watched Meredith dance in line with Jacobs, two women on either side mirroring their movements, and she wondered where this man had come from. Meredith never failed to surprise her, and she realised yet again how little she knew about him.

He took his final bow, and refused, despite encouragement from Jacobs and the ladies on the dance floor, to sing again.

He was a little breathless when he returned. Greedily, he gulped down the remains of his pint, before he turned to Patsy. "All I wanted was a quiet night in."

Their eyes locked, and Patsy retrieved her handbag from the back of the chair.

"You can't go now," spluttered Chris, who had only just recovered. "It's your round." He held up his empty glass.

Patsy shrugged and replaced her handbag. "I'll help you." She stood and collected some of the empty glasses from the table, which she placed at one end of the bar, before joining Meredith in the queue.

"You never said you had hidden talents," she teased as she joined him, "I would've insisted on you serenading as well as dating me. How old are you anyway? I was still in nappies when that was in the charts."

Meredith pulled her into his arms. "I was not long out myself. I didn't think I'd remember the words. That was about the time I was thinking of joining the force. I want to go home."

"What, and treat me like a lady?" Patsy laughed. "You know I don't think I'll ever get over the shock. I know what I'm buying you for Christmas."

"Let's concentrate on the treating you like a lady. Which by the way I have no . . . bugger, missed my turn in the queue, stand in front of me, you'll get their attention." He turned Patsy around and watched Jacobs belt out the last number.

Patsy was successful and ordered the drinks. She took the first two back as Meredith paid.

Jacobs took a final bow, and handed over to the DJ. He spotted Meredith at the bar. "Mine's a pint, Meredith," he called and Meredith added to the order.

Patsy returned to collect more drinks.

"I'll have a quick word, and I'll be over." Meredith smiled as he watched her walk away. He caught Ben doing the same as he approached. "Eyes front, Jacobs."

"Just looking, there's no harm in that, John. You lucky bastard. If anyone had asked, I'd have put you with three or four kids, a dog, and a mortgage you couldn't afford. What happened to . . ." He clicked his fingers as he tried to remember Amanda's mother's name.

"Karen. She died." Meredith held Jacobs' eye, and Jacobs knew that he knew about their affair. Meredith grinned and slapped him on the shoulder. "But that was a long time ago for me. What I'm more interested in is how you're involved in Patsy's case?"

Jacobs looked over his shoulder and stepped closer.

"I'm not. I was trying to help, and . . . well, *now* I'm just trying to help. You need a word with her, John, she's getting close to some nasty blokes."

"Tell all." Meredith walked a little further along the bar, and the two men fell into deep conversation.

Patsy watched them. She caught the little movements that almost mirrored each other, and realised why Jacobs had reminded her of Meredith. It was clearly the reason that some of his sorry chat-up lines were the same as Meredith's. She could imagine them comparing notes when they were lads. Sharon nudged her.

"That could have been a close call. I thought for one moment we were in trouble. But all's well that ends well. What a great night." She studied the two men for a moment. "They don't look anything alike, but they're very similar, aren't they?"

Patsy nodded. "I was thinking the same myself." She sighed. "I'd love to know what they're talking about. Every time Meredith manages to relax, it seems to fade so quickly. Look at his face now, you wouldn't believe he was up there surrounded by groupies only minutes ago. He looks like he has the weight of the world on his shoulders again."

"No he doesn't. He looks bloody angry. You didn't, did you? You know, with him." Sharon nodded at Jacobs.

"No, I bloody didn't!" Patsy rolled her eyes, "Oh here they come, subject change please."

Meredith smiled as he reached the table. "Right, we're off. Come on, Hodge, take me home." He held out his hand and she took it. He pulled her to her feet and wrapped his arm around her shoulders. "'Night all, it's been an experience." He turned to Jacobs. "I'll give you a shout, mate. Might even come and show you how it's done one night."

Patsy released herself from his arm and collected her coat and bag. She promised to see the others bright and early in the morning for an update, and turned to Jacobs. She held out her hand. "Goodnight, Ben, thank you for showing me what he's capable of. I'll call you if I need to speak to you again, but if you hear anything in the meantime, you have my number."

Jacobs stepped forward and hugged Patsy. "Look after each other," he whispered, and raising his voice, added, "Patsy, if you ever get fed up with him, you know where to find me." Turning he saluted the others. "Nice to meet you, must dash now, the boys get really stroppy if I don't help pack up."

There were more goodbyes but, finally, Meredith led Patsy into the car park.

"Home, Hodge, quick as you can."

Patsy smiled at him as she unlocked the car. "Are you in a rush?"

"Yes, because I want to take my time." Meredith winked and climbed in the car.

When Patsy woke the next morning, Meredith was gone. She reached over to his side of the bed, which was still warm. Squinting, she peered at the clock: it was six-fifteen. She rolled onto her back and smiled. Life really was too short. If Meredith still wanted her to, she decided she would move back in. She heard him curse and realised he was still in the bathroom. Careful not to wake Amanda, she tiptoed in to join him.

Meredith was singing quietly to himself in the shower and he jumped when Patsy pulled back the curtain. His eyes smiled at her as he continued to sing, and he appraised her body.

She stepped into the shower. "You've gone all musical on me," she whispered.

"I pick my moments, that's all. Why are we whispering?" He pressed his body against hers, and she yelped as her back met the cold tiles.

"Shush. Because Amanda is asleep across the hall. I only came in to say goodbye."

"No, Hodge, you came in to say hello, and you know it." Meredith adjusted the angle of the spray so he could see her properly. "I'm glad. Come home, Hodge." He chased a drop of water from her forehead to her chin with his finger.

"Okay," she said simply.

"Okay? That's it? No ifs, buts, maybes, or rules. Just okay?"

"Yes."

He held her gaze and before she knew what was happening, he'd opened the curtain, stepped out and closed it again. She pulled back the curtain and peeped out, he was tying a towel around his waist.

"What just happened?" she whispered harshly.

"I got sensible. You said okay, and then you said yes. Before I do or say anything that I will regret, or wake Amanda," he added as an afterthought, "I'm going while the going's good. I'll see you here tonight. Enjoy your shower." He stepped forward and took her face in his hands. "I love you, Patsy Hodge." He kissed her wet nose, turned away quickly and left the bathroom. By the time Patsy had showered and returned to the bedroom he was gone. His damp towel lay in a heap at the foot of the bed.

She dried her hair and applied her make-up before dressing and going in search of breakfast. As she left the bedroom, Amanda appeared. She smiled shyly at Patsy.

"Hi, Amanda, I'm sorry, did I wake you?"

"Nope, Dad did. Since when did he sing in the mornings?"

Patsy grinned and went down to the kitchen, promising to bring Amanda a cup of tea. When she entered the kitchen, a browning, wilted daffodil sat in a glass on the table. She picked up the note which had been torn from Meredith's pad.

It was all I could find at this time of the morning. See you later. Que sera, sera, Hodge!

Patsy smiled for the next three hours. She smiled on her way to work, while she opened the post, and while Linda updated them on the white van's movements the night before.

"Not much excitement, it left the Crooked Style, stopped briefly at a petrol station, and remained parked up around the corner from the British Pride for the rest of the night. It's on the move now, don't worry I'm tracking it." Linda turned to Patsy. "Are you okay? I know we've found out that amongst his other talents Meredith can sing, but you've not stopped grinning since you arrived. It's unnerving."

"I'm just happy" Patsy pointed at the screen. "If that's not of any use at the moment, and we don't know that it will be, how did you get on with those lonely-hearts ads?"

Linda lifted a pile of papers from a tray to the left of her desk. She leafed through until she found the one she wanted.

"Here you go. They were from the *Post*, and they are over three years old. I think the girl I spoke to was new, I told her it was life and death, and she's agreed to see you. Surprisingly she's not based at the main office but somewhere in Old Market. I've jotted her name and address down. You're seeing her at eleven, but you should know that." Linda clicked open the diary and checked Patsy's appointments. She turned and shook her head, disappointment written all over her face. "I synchronised your phone, Patsy. It works, but not if you don't check it! If I have to text you every time your diary changes, there's not a lot of point in all this technology, is there?"

Chris was already back at his desk. He held his phone in his lap, beneath the desktop and updated his diary. The others didn't notice. Shaking his head, he looked at Patsy. "I don't believe you forgot. Perhaps you should set alarms to remind you a couple of times a day. I'll get that." He left Patsy to explain herself to Linda and answered the incoming call.

"Can I have a quick word?" Clicking the icons on the screen of her phone, Patsy walked towards her office.

Linda followed her, frowning. "Have I done something wrong?" she asked as Patsy closed the door behind her.

"No, not at all. I wanted to tell you I'm moving back in with Meredith."

"WOOHOOO. And not before time."

Patsy looked at Linda and blinked. "And that's why I had to bring you in here and close the door." She smiled at her friend. "I'll pay my share until you replace me, I won't leave you in the lurch."

"Don't be daft. I was on my own before you moved in. I don't want any . . ."

Chris opened the door and put his head around. "Not interrupting, am I? Good. Have you got another tracker?"

"Yes, I have why?"

Chris crooked his finger at her and returned to the main office. Linda followed him, and listened as he closed a deal. He signed off by promising a report by Monday lunchtime.

Hanging up he pointed at Linda. "I've signed a new client up for you." He tore a sheet from his pad. "Here are the details. You need to have it on the car by lunchtime when the owner returns." He glanced up at the clock. "Plenty of time, but get on with it."

"Yes." Linda punched the air. "I knew this would be a great addition. What do you say?"

"What do you mean, what do I say?" Chris looked bemused.

"I know what you really meant to say was, 'Thank you, Linda, great idea, Linda, another income stream, Linda. What would we do without you Linda?'" Linda smiled and turned her back, "I forgive you though, I know it's just the excitement blurring your manners."

Chris rolled his eyes, and pulled a file from his top drawer. "Of course it was. Now shut up, I have some calls to make."

13

Patsy walked across the bridge that spanned the busy A4 as it snaked its way around Broadmead, and out past Templemeads Station towards Bath. The breeze whipped her hair into her face, and she abandoned any attempt at keeping it under control. Hurrying down the steps towards the huge plate glass building, which provided the regional headquarters for one of the major banks, she frowned. There was supposed to be a lane which would lead her towards the older streets beyond, but she couldn't see it. As she put her foot on the first step leading to the grand foyer to ask, a couple of young lads on cycles flew up the side of the building. The plate glass door opened and a thin elderly man in a double-breasted suit called to her.

"May I help you, madam?"

He beckoned her forward, unwilling to leave the warmth of the foyer. Patsy moved one step closer, and shouted her enquiry. The man waved to the side of the building before closing the door. Patsy retraced her steps, guessing that he must have been asked many times. In less than two minutes it was as though Patsy had been transported back in time. She was in a street full of tall narrow houses, the ground floors of which had once been shops and cafés, but for the best part had now been boarded up. The numbers of the houses had been engraved onto the stones above the doors. She walked briskly to number seventeen. It was one of the few in the rank that showed any obvious sign of habitation. Pushing open the half-glazed door, discarded leaflets blew into building past her ankles, and she bent to pick them up.

"It's murder down here. That road is like a wind tunnel. Come on in." A middle-aged woman wearing an ill-fitting trouser suit turned down the volume of the small radio, and stood to greet her. She held out her hand to take the leaflets. "How can I help?" Rolling the leaflets into a ball, she tossed them into the wastepaper basket.

"You were obviously in the netball team." Patsy nodded at the bin. "Patsy Hodge, I'm here to see Emily."

"That'll be me. Take a seat, the kettle's on. Tea or coffee?"

Patsy asked for tea and sat on what appeared to be an old kitchen chair in front of an oversized pedestal desk with a green leather inlay. The leather was worn and snagged, and had overlapping circular reminders of the many cups it had held. Cheap brown carpet covered uneven floorboards, and magnolia coloured emulsion had been plastered over everything fixed to the walls. With the exception of a woodland calendar there were no paintings or posters. The room was clean but barely functional. Patsy wondered how many hours she would be able to work there without going mad. Emily returned through the door in the corner of the room, and saw her look of distaste.

"Lovely, isn't it? I'm not here for long. The main building is being rewired and they are clearing us out floor by floor. I've got this little palace, and what feels like two million boxes to sort through. I'm only allowed to take back anything that is a necessity." She placed a mug of tea in front of Patsy. "I understand you're looking for some information."

Emily placed her own mug on a coaster, and caught Patsy's smile. She shrugged. "You have to have standards." She opened the top drawer of the desk with difficulty and withdrew a brown folder. She unfolded the A3 copy which topped the pile of papers and handed it to Patsy. "Is this the one?"

Patsy pulled the clear plastic wallet from her bag. She quickly scanned the copy, found what she was looking for, and compared it to one of the clippings in the wallet.

"Yes, thank you." Her eyes darted to the top of the page. Twenty-second of January 2009. "I understand you can tell me who placed this."

"No, not really. I could if I were back at the old place, but I haven't got access to that system here."

Patsy's brow furrowed. "So why did you agree to see me? I'm sorry, I'm a tad confused."

"Your friend said it was a matter of life and death. I take it she wasn't exaggerating."

Patsy shook her head quickly. "No, not at all. The man that had these in his possession," she pushed the newspaper clippings forward, "has disappeared. His wife is in danger, and these are the only clue we have as to his whereabouts."

"He has a wife and he had these? Doesn't she mind?" Emily leaned back and looked down. Her eyes moved from side to side as she attempted to work out how that information fitted together. Patsy could see she was becoming suspicious.

"Can I be honest with you, Emily?" Patsy leaned forward, cupping her hands on the desk. Emily gave a nod. "When I said life and death, what I meant was life, and possibly death. The man who had these," she tapped the wallet, "is missing. His wife has been accused of his murder. She didn't do it, because she didn't care about these," again she tapped the wallet. "But he's been missing for quite some time. His daughter gave me the clippings because she knows he met a woman via a lonely-hearts column, and moved in with her. She knows her mother is innocent because she has seen her father since he disappeared."

Patsy raised her hands and drew commas around the last word. She nodded knowingly at Emily until she nodded her own agreement. "The daughter couldn't tell her mother she'd been seeing her father at the time for all sorts of reasons, and now she is telling the truth the police won't believe her." Patsy leaned back, shaking her head sadly. "Now she may lose her mother because she once tried to spare her feelings. All I need to do is prove he's alive. I don't need to speak to him, or involve him in anything other than confirmation of life."

Patsy watched as Emily processed this information.

"But what if she had killed him? What if she didn't kill him then, but she did later. The daughter wouldn't know, would she?" Satisfied she'd made a good argument Emily leaned forward and spread her hands on her desk. "Have you asked yourself that, Ms Hodge?"

Patsy mirrored Emily's movement until her head was inches away from Emily's. She lowered her voice. "I have, and who knows that could be exactly what's happened. But unless I out we will never know." She leaned an inch closer. "The way I see it, Emily, is that we, you and me, have the power to solve a murder, or save an innocent woman from going to prison for the rest of her life." She paused and blinked at Emily, allowing her to consider this option. "What do you say, shall we try, or shall we just let the police do a half-hearted job?"

The two women remained looking at each other for a few more seconds before Emily nodded.

"Let's do it, Ms Hodge. I'd like to be involved in such a worthy cause. I'm sorry now I can't give you more help." Emily sighed and her shoulders drooped in disappointment.

"What help can you give me, Emily?" Patsy held back her own sigh, and wondered how long it was going to take to prise the information out of her. She started as Emily jumped up and rushed through the door behind them, returning a few moments later with another brown file.

"As I say, I have no names but I have this." Emily opened the folder which contained several sheets of paper. She handed the top one to Patsy. It was some form of accounts ledger. "You see the number at the top? That's the PO Box number. For reasons of confidentiality the accounts are numbered, not named." Emily drew her finger down one of the columns. "That's how many times she placed the advert. Five pounds a time. You can see she paid four weekly in advance, until here." Emily pointed to a number in brackets. "Her cheque bounced, and so . . ." she took another sheet from the folder, "we wrote to her returning the cheque and requesting a new payment. The stupid thing is that when they had the cheque, they knew the name, but still addressed the letter to the number."

Patsy smiled at Emily, nodding. "The advertiser lived here, but no names. I get it. May I have a copy of this?" She looked up expectantly. Emily was nodding but her attention was on the third sheet she lifted from the file.

"What's the name of the accused wife?" She held the paper to her chest so that Patsy was unable to read it.

"Why?"

"No, I asked the question, you need to answer it," Emily tutted, "Come on, Patsy, we're in this together, aren't we?"

Patsy had no idea where Emily was going with this, so she nodded.

"Her name is Kate. Why?"

"Surname?" Emily raised her eyebrows.

"Wilkinson."

"Aha!" Emily held out the third sheet. "She phoned about a year ago. Read that. The girl who took the call made good notes. She explained she couldn't give the information out, but promised to go to her supervisor when Mrs Wilkinson said it was a matter of life and death." She beamed at Patsy. "That's why I agreed to see you. I'd flipped through that file only the day before to see if anything needed scanning. It didn't so it was in the bag for secure destruction. Can you imagine my amazement when your colleague phoned about the same thing? I was flabbergasted. What were the chances? If she'd called a day later it would be in an incinerator somewhere now, or I might not have read the details." She leaned forward her face deadly serious. "It goes to show that things happen for a reason."

Patsy folded the sheet and slid it into the wallet with the two clippings. "What about the other ad? Was it placed by the same person?"

Emily shrugged. "I don't know. Possibly but unlikely; she would have used the same box number. I may be able to help once I get back into the main building, but if nothing went wrong, like a bounced cheque, I doubt it."

"Emily, you're a star to have found this much." Patsy patted her hand. "Let's see where this takes me. It may take a while but I'll keep you in touch with the outcome. I promise."

"Let me have your card. I'm due back in the main building sometime next week. My work here is nearly done. I'll check the old system and see if I can't put a name to that number, and I'll check the other one."

Retracing her steps back to the car park, Patsy hurried across the bridge having decided she would check out the address immediately. She was unlikely to find anyone at home during the day, but it wasn't a huge detour even if she were unsuccessful. As she pulled out of the car park she headed in the opposite direction to the office, and was sitting outside the address ten minutes later. The tree-lined street was a picture, and branches, heavy with blossom, swayed in the breeze. As she climbed out of the car, a woman from the neighbouring house pushed her dustbin down the drive. She was parking it on the grass verge outside as Patsy put her hand on the neighbouring gate. The woman smiled politely. Patsy rang the doorbell as the woman walked back up the drive.

"Excuse me. I don't think there's anyone at home," the woman called, and Patsy turned to face her. "Mike leaves early, and Rachel goes to work after she has dropped the kids off at school."

Patsy's brow furrowed. Darren Wilkinson was pushing fifty, but that didn't mean he wouldn't have an affair with a young mother, but one with a husband around didn't fit.

"I was actually looking for Mr Wilkinson, Darren, or his partner. Do they not live here now?"

The woman glanced around and stepped closer to the fence. "Mike and Rachel only moved in about two years ago," she counted silently on her fingers, "No, about two and a half years ago. I moved in a couple of months prior to that. That place was empty." She looked up at the house next door. "Mrs Brady on the other side told me the lady that lived there killed herself." She shivered as she pointed to the house adjoining her own, and lowered her voice. "I'm not sure if Mike and Rachel know so I don't mention it. How long ago did your chap live here?"

"Oh, much longer than that. Thank you for your help. I'll have a word with Mrs Brady, she may be able to help." Patsy had already begun the journey back down the path.

"Good idea, she's in. She's just put her bin out."

The woman nodded at the bin resting against her neighbour's hedge, and Patsy walked towards it, calling out her thanks as she headed up the path and rang the doorbell. It was answered by a woman of about sixty, dressed smartly and holding a small Yorkshire terrier dog.

"Come in, come in, the kettle's on." The woman turned and walked away down the hall. "Shut the door behind you. I thought they were sending a man for some reason."

She disappeared through the door at the end of the hall. Patsy stepped in and closed the door.

"Mrs Brady, I'm not sure who you think I am, but I'm here to ask you . . ."

The woman reappeared carrying a tray. It held a teapot, a plate of biscuits and two delicate bone china tea cups.

"To ask me about Debbie, yes, I know. The chap who phoned said you wanted to ask me about her boyfriends. I don't know much but he insisted someone come round. Push that door open for me." Mrs Brady nodded at the door to Patsy's right and Patsy pushed it open. "It was a while ago now but still shocks me when I think about it." She placed the tray on a coffee table. "Sit down, please."

Patsy took a seat and once again attempted to explain the misunderstanding. "Actually, I didn't call, I came to ask about your neighbours next door but one."

"Yes, Debbie. She hanged herself, you know." Mrs Brady shook her head, "I'd have never thought that of her. It goes to show, you never really know anyone." Mrs Brady gave a little sigh and leaned forward to pour the tea. "What's the name of this chap you're after?"

"Darren Wilkinson. But I . . ." Patsy was frowning, and her brain was racing. This couldn't be what she thought it was. The world was simply not that small. She changed tack to make sure. "Did Debbie have a sister?"

"Yes, Nancy. Nice woman but very . . . I don't know how to put it. I was going to say nosey, but it wasn't that, she was clingy. Kept turning up, unannounced, which drove poor Debbie mad. But she was devastated when Debbie did what she did."

Patsy stared at her for a moment. Someone from the station was obviously on their way to speak to Mrs Brady. She attempted to assess if their cases were overlapping or if there was a more sinister connection.

"Did you know Mr Wilkinson? I understand he was a friend of Debbie's."

Mrs Brady snorted. "Friend. You can say it, you know. I knew she had lovers, I used to see them come and go." Her hand shot to her mouth. "Oh, dear me, that sounded terrible. I didn't mean, you know . . ." She raised her hand. "She went out with a few different men over a period of time, that's all. You mustn't think anything bad."

Patsy assured her that she didn't. "Did you know any of her lovers by name?"

"No, she never introduced them. Nancy was cross about that. I may recognise them. You said you had a picture?"

Patsy hesitated for just a second, before she pulled out a photograph of Darren Wilkinson from an envelope in her handbag. She handed it to Mrs Brady as the doorbell chimed.

"I wonder who that is. Stay there, I won't be long."

Patsy leaned back on the sofa, and looked out into the garden through the bay window. She smiled at Trump who raised one eyebrow. She didn't see Meredith but she heard him.

"Mrs Brady, I'm DCI Meredith, this is DS Trump. Thank you for seeing us." Meredith caught sight of the photograph in Mrs Brady's hands. He recognised it as the man he was trying to identify. "You have a photograph? I wasn't expecting that."

Patsy stood up, and walked towards the door. Mrs Brady pushed it open as she reached it, and for the first time since she had known him, Meredith appeared lost for words.

"It's not mine it's hers. Is she not . . ."

"DCI Meredith, a pleasure to see you. Mrs Brady here was about to confirm if Darren Wilkinson was one of Debbie's friends . . . sorry, lovers.

Apparently, there were a few." She smiled as Meredith pinched the bridge of his nose and Trump craned his neck to look round the door frame.

"Hodge, I didn't know you would be here." He frowned at her as he stepped into the sitting room.

"Shall I get more cups?" Mrs Brady looked at Trump who had made it into the hall.

"No thank you. I don't think we'll take up too much more of your time. Now, Mrs Brady, you bring me up to date on your chat with Hodge."

Meredith, Hodge and Trump sat close together in a line on the sofa opposite Mrs Brady, who with a few prompts told them as much as she knew about Debbie Charles' love life. There wasn't much to tell, although Meredith made a few notes when she told of a fight between two men in the street, one of whom was Wilkinson; she didn't know the other, and her description of him was vague. Middle-aged, tall and greying at the temples. She also added to her original statement given at the time of Debbie's death. She had heard a shout from the house a few hours before Debbie had been discovered. What she hadn't mentioned at the time was that a little while later she had seen Wilkinson in the corner shop buying cigarettes. She'd been behind him in the queue, but when he'd left he walked in the opposite direction from the house. She hadn't thought it relevant at the time as no one had asked, but now he was of interest, she wondered if it was relevant.

"I don't know, Mrs Brady, it could be. We'll leave you in peace now. I'll call if we need to speak again, unless of course you remember anything else, in which case you give DS Trump here a call."

Meredith stood as Trump handed over his card. They all thanked Mrs Brady for her hospitality, and Patsy ignored the fact that Meredith had placed her photograph of Wilkinson into his breast pocket. Patsy led the way up the path and stopped when she reached her car.

"I think I'm in shock. That was a million to one chance." She smiled as Meredith shook his head.

"Trump, you go and see the other neighbours, Hodge here is going to give me a lift back to the station and reveal how she came to be sitting in our witness's house." Meredith walked to the passenger door of Patsy's car.

"It's almost as though he thinks I planned it." Patsy waved to Trump who was already scanning the house numbers for his next interview. "See you later, Louie." She climbed into the car and started the engine. "Back to the station, sir, are you going to interview me again?" she asked as Meredith slammed the door.

"Probably yes, but first you can buy me an early lunch. Not the Dirty Duck, it gets too busy in there on a Friday."

After five minutes' discussion on where and what he wanted to eat, they opted for a small brasserie that had recently opened not far from Meredith's house. They took a table in the window and ordered, before Meredith opened the conversation.

"You didn't know that she was connected to the Nancy Bailey case, that much I know, but exactly how did you come by a photograph of Debbie Charles' lover?"

"He's Angel's father. That's the man I've been hired to find." Patsy tilted her head to one side. "I didn't know that you had any interest in him until Mrs Brady said."

"Because one, I didn't know his name, and two, we're not allowed to talk about work any more. Although, I now have two reasons for raising that forbidden subject."

"Two?" Patsy frowned. "Wilkinson being one, but what's the other?"

"The British Pride. I had a chat with Ben last night. Not in much detail, but he tells me in the interest of, let's call it helping you, he asked around in the pub before you arranged to meet him. He's not sure if the mention of your name or Wilkinson's caused a stir. But cause a stir it did. Maurice Ford was there asking Ben questions within thirty minutes. Ben wasn't concerned until he met you." Meredith's eyes scanned her face looking for any inkling of guilt. He found none. He tapped the table with his forefinger. "Maurice Ford is bad news. He's a mean bugger and you don't want to get involved there, I -"

"I know, Chris told me. As I understand it, although he's done time, it's only a fraction of what he's due."

Meredith waited whilst the waitress placed their drinks on the table. She was a pretty girl in her mid-twenties. She smiled warmly at him as he thanked her. He resisted the urge to watch her walk away. He sipped his drink and looked at Patsy over the brim of the glass.

"You know what I'm going to ask, don't you?"

"Yes, you're going to ask me for all the information I have because I'm just dealing with a missing person and you have multiple murders on your hands. Yours is bigger than mine and all that."

Meredith was going to tell her to back off the case. In fact, he had been intending to tell her to drop it. He realised from her relaxed demeanour that she would clam up if he did. He needed her information and he needed her back in his life, so he smiled and bided his time.

"I do. So you tell me what's what before the food arrives."

"I will but I'm not giving you any names you don't know. Not until you need them, anyway."

"Like who? Why would you withhold information?" Irritation caused additional lines to form at the corners of his eyes.

"I'm not going to withhold information, only who gave me certain parts of it. I want to protect them from the wrath of Big Mo, because that would be a possible outcome if their names get bandied about."

Meredith considered this for a moment.

"Okay, if I think they are needed I'll find a way of getting that out of you."

"Really? We'll see."

Over the course of their lunch Patsy gave Meredith all the information she had collected. His eyes widened at the use of the white van, but he didn't interrupt. Patsy concluded with her visit to Emily's office which led her to Mrs Brady. When she had finished, Meredith gave her a brief outline of the Nancy Bailey case. They didn't notice the slim, scruffy-looking man with greasy hair, scanning the menu displayed on the window remove his phone and take several photographs of them before getting back into the car which had previously been following them.

"So, still nothing on Jo?" Patsy sighed as she pushed her plate into the centre of the table.

"Not a thing, that bloody woman sits there like butter wouldn't melt, and I have to be nice to her or she won't speak to me." He shook his head. "I have to find out who killed her sister, or hope that Jane Roscoe can convince her not to add another charge to the unbelievably long list that she's already racked up."

Patsy took his hand and was about to say something when her phone sounded. She picked up and scanned the message from Angel.

Meredith watched as she deftly tapped out a response. "Urgent?" he queried.

"Angel wanting to know if I've got anywhere. I haven't the heart to tell her that her dad may be involved in murder. She's already worried that something's happened to him, after hearing he was thrown into the back of a van." Patsy clicked her fingers. "That's it. When I first spoke to Ben he told me that he'd seen Darren Wilkinson recently. Well, more recently than the van incident anyway. We need to speak to him."

"We need to speak to him? Patsy, the last thing in the world I want to do is piss you off right now, but I should be telling you to back off now, you know that." Meredith added the 'should' to test the water.

"I'm glad you said 'should' because my case is not necessarily connected to yours, so that would be stupid. Not to mention that I've already been of a great help to you. So, yes, *we* need to speak to him. Of course, we don't have to go together." Patsy smiled into her drink as she watched him struggle with her response.

Meredith took out his phone. "In which case we'd better get on with it."

Meredith breathed a sigh of relief as he called Ben Jacobs. He'd called it right. He'd get her home first, and sort out the finer details later. His call was successful, and Jacobs was not far away, Meredith agreed to meet him a few hours later. He gave the waitress a wink as he paid the bill, before helping Patsy into her coat. Patsy pulled out into the traffic oblivious to the fact that the car that had followed her to, and then from, Mrs Brady's was now three cars behind.

Meredith had been at the office for less than fifteen minutes before the call from a community officer came in. He grabbed Hutchins and headed back to Mrs Brady's house.

The front door was slightly ajar and they let themselves in. The uniformed officer was sitting on the sofa watching a paramedic bandage Mrs Brady's wrist. He jumped up as Meredith came in. Mrs Brady shook her head at Meredith as he came into her line of sight. She leaned to one side, groaning as she did so, to get a better view. Meredith was taken aback. She looked ten years older than she had a few hours before. Her face had drained of any colour, and there was a lump on her left cheekbone.

"I don't know what you've stirred up, Mr Meredith, but you'd only been gone half an hour before they came. Just as well I have that panic button."

The paramedic turned to Meredith. "Mrs Brady needs to come to hospital. I think she's broken a couple of ribs but she's refusing to go, perhaps you could talk some sense into her."

Mrs Brady flicked her good hand at him, so dismissing the suggestion.

"They left the message they wanted him to have. They'll not be back."

Meredith knelt on one knee, next to the paramedic and picked up the hand which appeared to be undamaged, and gave it a gentle squeeze.

"What's happened here, Mrs Brady? What message are we talking about?"

"They said," Mrs Brady raised a shaking hand to her temple, "now let me get this right." She nodded as she considered her words, "They said, 'Tell Meredith to back off or we'll sort his bird.'" Mrs Brady frowned and shook her head, "I'm sure he said 'sort'. I don't know what that means."

"Don't worry about that, Mrs Brady. How many were there, and how did they get in?"

"Two ugly buggers they were. The bell rang and when I answered they looked wrong, if you know what I mean, so I put my hand on the panic button. One of them pushed the door open and stepped into the hall, so I pushed the button, it makes a racket that thing, and it startled them. The second one pushed me to the floor and squeezed my face, and gave me the message for you." She paused and cleared the lump from her throat. "They were gone in a flash. But I couldn't get up you see. It was quite painful. My neighbour came and helped when she heard the alarm." She smiled, "So they do work, I didn't think I'd ever use it. Anyway, she called the police and the ambulance."

"I'm sorry, Mrs Brady. I will catch whoever did this, I promise. Do you think you'll be able to identify them?"

Mrs Brady shrugged and winced at the pain the movement had caused. "I don't know. One of them probably, but they looked much alike. Both were bald and ugly."

Meredith smiled. "Well, we'll get you off to hospital, and once you've been treated I'll get one of my chaps to come and see you with a laptop. You can look at some mug shots for me."

Mrs Brady told him in no uncertain terms that she wasn't going to hospital. He looked to the paramedic for support. They both tried convincing her, but in the end, Mrs Brady wouldn't be moved. Her neighbour confirmed that she would bring a meal in for her and stay the night if necessary. Meredith instructed Hutchins to go back to the station with the uniformed officer, collect Tom Seaton and a laptop, and return quickly to run through likely suspects before her memory faded. He promised to look in the next day.

Meredith attempted to call Patsy on his way to meet Ben Jacobs. Patsy was speaking to Linda about the movements of the white van at the time, and the call went unheard as she had left her phone in her office. Meredith left a message.

"Patsy, call me as soon as you get this. Mrs Brady has . . ."

His phone beeped and the line went silent as his battery ran out of power. He cursed and threw it onto the passenger seat hoping Jacobs would have a suitable charger.

Meredith didn't bother searching for a legal parking space, and he pulled up on a bus stop situated outside Ben Jacobs' house. Grabbing his phone, he strode up the path where, for the second time that day, he found a door ajar. Frowning, he pushed it open as far as it would go and called to Ben.

Stepping slowly over the threshold, when he received no response, he squinted as his eyes became accustomed to the light in the dim hallway. He glanced at the post scattered on the floor. It appeared to have been knocked from the shelf to his left. He also noted that the rug was out of place and sitting halfway up the wall, and he saw that the telephone had been unplugged.

He scanned the hall for some form of weapon, but there was none. Common sense told him to leave and come back with help, and he had half turned to do so when he heard a noise from behind the door to the right. He walked to face it. It too was slightly ajar. With a roar, he jumped and kicked it open, before standing back against the wall in the hall. The door flew open and Meredith braced himself. Nothing happened, but he had found Ben Jacobs.

Jacobs was tied to a chair in the centre of the room. He hadn't responded to the violent movement of the door, and his head hung forward, a large trail of bloody saliva dripped from his mouth. Meredith rushed forward and had placed his hand on Ben's neck to check for a pulse. He heard the crack of wood against his skull as he felt the pain of its impact. Turning to face his attacker a fist met his face and he dropped to the floor, his last vision before he lost consciousness was a booted foot swinging towards him.

Meredith was unsure how long he lay there, but he came around to the sound of Ben Jacobs lisping his name.

He opened his eyes and stared at the light fitting on the ceiling before attempting to sit up. A sharp pain shot from temple to temple, and a searing pain tore across his torso. They had obviously continued to beat him even once unconscious. He groaned and heard Jacobs snort. Remaining sitting on the floor, he pulled his feet in and rested his elbows on his knees and held his throbbing head between his hands. He ran his tongue along his swollen bloodied lip, and something felt different. Tentatively he ran it along his teeth, there was a gap on his bottom left jaw where a tooth had previously been.

Rinsing his mouth with his saliva he spat the blood from his mouth.

"Oi," Jacobs attempted to shout, and groaned at the effort.

Meredith looked up at him, still tied to the chair, and looking pretty much like Meredith felt. He was staring at the mess Meredith had spat onto the carpet.

"What? It'll clean up. Fuck me, I hurt." Meredith ran his hand over the huge lump on the back of his head and winced. "Who was it?"

"Your fault, you bathdard. I think I win on the hurt thcore"

Ben was still lisping and Meredith pushed himself up onto his knees and peered into Ben's face.

He nodded. "Yes, I think you do. I don't reckon you'll be kissing the ladies for quite a while." He attempted a grin but thought better of it.

"You going to untie me or thit on your ath all day?"

"Don't make me laugh," Meredith held his side as he pushed himself up onto his feet using Jacobs' knee for support.

Jacobs let out a low groan that came deep from within, and his head fell forward. He blew out a breath in an attempt to dispel the pain.

"Did they do your knees?"

Lifting his head, Jacobs nodded and winced, a tear escaped from between the thick lashes of his right eye. His left was swollen shut.

"Sorry about that. I'll untie you and get some help."

Meredith untied Jacobs. Telling him to remain where he was, he called first the incident room, and then an ambulance. As he turned back to Jacobs, he cursed, "Shit! I need to get hold of Patsy, they're after her too and my phone's dead. Have you got a charger for an android?"

"Mine."

Jacobs attempted to lift his arm, but the increase in pain was too much.

Allowing his hand to fall back into his lap, he leaned towards the table in the window.

Meredith saw the phone and scrolled through his contacts until he found Patsy. He noticed that ninety per cent of the contacts were females, and he would have smiled if it didn't hurt so much. Patsy's phone rang several times before the answer phone cut in again. He cursed her for never picking up and told her to phone him. Looking out of the window he saw Trump's car screech to a halt behind his own, and Bob Travers jumped out of the passenger seat. A bus was slowing and wanting to pull into the bus stop. The driver held his hand on the horn to show his displeasure. Travers gave him the finger before rushing up the path behind Trump. An ambulance with flashing lights traveling down the opposite side of the road, siren blaring, swung across the road, and took up the last remaining area of bus stop. The disgruntled driver cursed as he opened the doors, telling the passengers wanting to get off to mind their step.

"Well, you look a mess and no mistake," Trump announced as he looked at Jacobs. "Not so pretty now. That looks painful."

Meredith held back the smirk but only to protect himself. Linda had obviously voiced her opinion of Jacobs' attributes.

"Do we know who it was?"

Jacobs nodded and attempted to raise his hand to catch the saliva dribbling down his chin. He gave up.

"One of them, not by name. He . . ." He stopped speaking as the paramedics came into the room.

One of them was the man that had treated Mrs Brady. His eyes widened as he recognised Meredith.

"They found you then," he observed, as he walked to Ben who flinched, groaning.

"You'll need a stretcher, they worked on his knees." Meredith stepped forward and winced at his own pain.

The paramedic put his arms on his hips. "Righty ho, and you're coming too."

Meredith glared at him. "In my own time. Get the stretcher." He waited until they had gone to fetch the trolley and asked Jacobs who it was he had recognised.

"He was in the Brit the other night. Don't know the name, Alfie will though."

"Good man. I'll come in and see you later. Trump, take me to the British Pride." Meredith stepped to one side as the paramedics reappeared. He hushed Travers' protests and followed the others out to the car. Jacobs' groans were silenced somewhat when the mask supplying gas and air was strapped to his face. Meredith pulled open the passenger door and bent to get in the car. A pain, like he had never felt before, seemed to ricochet around his chest. He didn't have the ability to groan, he simply grasped his chest and fell to the ground.

"I bloody told you," Travers shouted as he rushed back into the house calling for a paramedic.

Meredith's fractured rib had pierced his left lung, and his chest cavity was filling with the escaping air. His face contorted as the pressure built. The paramedic didn't mess about and, much to Meredith's horror, he plunged a large needle into his chest with some force. Meredith relaxed as he heard the low hiss and the air find its escape route. He travelled to hospital alongside Jacobs. Before they took him for a chest scan, he explained to Trump the urgency of contacting Patsy.

Trump walked outside and called Linda. He told her what had happened, and that Patsy could be in danger. Linda passed the phone to Sharon whilst she attempted to call Patsy. It was picked up by the answer service after several rings. Linda gave up after leaving two messages. She tried Chris and got the same result.

Sharon Grainger hung up on Trump, who went back into the hospital to get more detail of the attackers from Ben Jacobs. She walked to Linda's desk and tapped the computer screen.

"Right, show me where they were going. How can they both be ignoring their calls?"

Linda clicked into the program and a map of Bristol and surrounding areas appeared. She traced her finger along the yellow line.

"This is where the van has been. The blue dots are the short stops, and the red ones more than an hour. They were going to the red locations."

Sharon pulled her glasses down off her head and peered at the screen.

"Oh give me strength, where's that? It looks miles away."

"Not really, it's just outside Bridgewater, half an hour on the motorway. The van was there for three hours this morning."

"But what were they hoping to achieve? Sounds like a wild goose chase to me; they may have taken the van in for a service."

"Yes, but then at least they would know that. The plan was to find out what was at each location of all the long stops. Because if that location was visited more than once without there being a good reason, it could be of interest and require more investigation. How else would they know? It's the chicken and egg thing, unless they know what they're looking for they need to know what to discount."

"Hmmm." Sharon wasn't convinced. "I don't suppose we have a tracker on Patsy's car, do we?"

"Yep. But it's still in the car park, they took Chris's car."

"Well, for future reference, get one on his too! Where's the bloody van now?"

"Parked up opposite the British Pride; this flashing light shows its current location." Linda looked up at Sharon. "What are we going to do?"

"Wait." Sharon gave a sigh. "There will be a reason their phones are not being answered. I can't see that they could be doing anything that would take them more than thirty minutes. We have to wait. Go and put the kettle on, and get the packet of biscuits too."

~ ~ ~

Patsy looked at Chris. "Pretty swish for visitors in a white van."

They had pulled into a layby opposite the location on the outskirts of Bridgewater, where the white van had spent three hours. An eight-foot-high stone wall flanked two huge wrought iron gates, before working its way around the perimeter in each direction. To the right of the formidable entrance was a small copse, and off to the left an orchard, where the final blossoms were swaying in the slight breeze. There was an entry phone system set into the right wall, and on each of the pillars supporting the gates, signs warned of the guard dogs behind. A long tree-lined drive wound its way into the distance. On the left of the drive there appeared to be a putting course, but from their position they were unable to see the right.

"Perhaps they were working here. It's a big place, perhaps they want live music for some function they're holding." Chris shook his head. "But I doubt it. Come on." Releasing his seatbelt, he opened his car door. He lifted a small pair of binoculars from the pocket in the door. "Fancy a walk in the woods?"

Patsy climbed out of the Range Rover to join him. It was a good hike to the copse, and as they entered, Chris's phone sounded. He cursed and rejected the call.

"Probably Sharon after a pint of milk, we'd better set them to silent. We don't know who's on the other side of that." He nodded at the wall.

They set off along the perimeter of the property. About a quarter of a mile around they found a small wrought iron gate. It was chained and padlocked, but it afforded them a side view of the property they had been unable to see from the road. The house was substantial, with garaging to the left and stabling to the right. A slender blonde woman was dismounting a horse in front of the stables. Chris put his binoculars to his eyes in search of other signs of life. There were none so they kept walking. The wall swept off to the left and the copse thinned. Hedgerow appeared in its place, encasing fields of rape and potatoes. Chris stopped and cursed. Patsy put her fingers to her lips, and smiled as she noticed he had stepped into a large pile of horse manure.

"That's what the gate back there was for. They clearly exercise the horses out here."

He shot a withering glance at Patsy. "I blame you for this. These shoes are only a couple of weeks old." He attempted to clean his shoe by wiping it in the grass which grew along the edge of the wall.

"Oh, stop being such a baby. It'll wipe -" Patsy was silenced by Chris's raised finger.

The sound of voices got louder, and they stood motionless, straining to hear what was being said.

"He'll be sorted this afternoon. It maybe even done by now. I'm not sure about the copper, but he'll get his, don't you worry, Mitch. None of this will come back to you. One thing we do know is that Willkie's not involved; they paid a visit this morning."

"He'd better not be, he's enough of a liability already. This had better not come back to me. I've paid you good money, and I continue to pay you good money to keep this mess away from my door. What I'm most concerned about is what has set this lot off. It's not only the girl looking for her father that's caused this. I don't like it, Maurice, not one little bit. Put it to bed quickly, whatever it takes."

A phone rang. The first voice answered it. He gave a short laugh, said, "Good, good", and laughed again.

"Turns out they got two birds with one stone. The . . ."

The rest of the conversation was lost to Chris and Patsy as the two men walked away from the wall.

Chris gestured Patsy to follow him back to the car.

"Well, that wasn't surprising. Big Mo is clearly connected with the van driver, but I have no idea who the other bloke was. What did he call him, Mitch?" Chris kept his voice low and walked close to Patsy as they spoke. He jerked his head back in the direction they had come.

"I didn't hear anyone mention anyone called Mitch in the pub." She stopped speaking as they reached the road, and waited for a tractor to pass before crossing to Chris's car. "Mind you, if he lives in a house like that, it's highly unlikely he will be frequenting the British Pride," she added as she pulled the car door shut.

Chris fastened his seatbelt, and drummed the wheel as he pulled onto the road.

"We need to speak to Meredith. It sounded to me like some copper was going to take a beating. Who knows who, but if it happens they'll know where to start looking. We need to find out who owns that house. Let's go and have a drink."

Chris indicated left and pulled in at a pub offering homemade food about halfway between the house and the motorway. "We may get lucky. He could drink here."

They sat on stools at the bar in the almost empty pub. Chris ordered their drinks, and Patsy glanced around. It was a typical country pub bar as far as the décor went. Tapestry-style fabric covered the seating, and heavy curtains framed the leaded windows. The furniture was old and solid; it had clearly seen better days. The landlord returned with their drinks.

"This is lovely," Patsy commented. "It's so nice to find a traditional pub that hasn't been themed." She smiled as her drink was placed in front of her. "How long have you been here?"

"I've been landlord twenty years now, took it over from my dad. We're not that old-fashioned you know, we have a decent garden out the back, and a pool table in the games room." He grinned to show he was teasing her. "You haven't been here before, I'd have remembered."

"No, we had business in Taunton, and came back to the motorway via the scenic route. My navigation skills failed me. We needed a break before we get on the motorway."

"Well, enjoy." He looked along the bar to an elderly man with a mop of wispy white hair reading a newspaper. He was finishing his drink.

"Same again, Bert?" Bert grunted agreement, and the landlord picked up a pint glass. Holding at an angle, he pulled on one of the pumps in front of Patsy. "Far to go?"

"Only Bristol," Patsy smiled.

"You don't sound like a Bristolian to me."

"I'm not, Southampton originally. I love it round here though, I won't be going back. I'm thinking of settling in Somerset or perhaps Devon."

The landlord walked down the bar and placed the beer in front of Bert. Walking to the till, which sat in front of an aged mirror depicting the benefits of coke, he clipped the note into place, and removed some coins.

"Good shout. I am of course biased to Somerset." He handed Bert his change.

"There are some flash properties along this road. You got any local celebrities around here?" Chris joined the conversation. The landlord turned up his nose.

"Not in my book." He glanced around the bar, even though no one else had entered since Chris and Patsy's arrival. "Unless you call that idiot Mitchell a celebrity," he pouted, "mind you these days you reach that status by having a boob job."

Chris shook his head and shrugged. "Mitchell?"

The landlord waved his hand, dismissing the conversation. "If you don't know him, be grateful."

"Now you've got me interested. Who is he?" Chris persisted.

"He's a wannabe politician, never gets elected but gets more votes each time. Hopefully, I'll be long gone by the time he gets a seat." The landlord leaned on the bar and lowered his voice. "It's not that I don't actually agree with some of his policies. We need to shut the gates and stop this bloody immigration, but not just blacks and Asians, anyone. We're full, we can't afford it. It's him I can't stand. Nasty, arrogant piece of work, I'm glad we're not good enough for him."

He stood straight as the door to the bar opened and greeted his new customer. Chris emptied his glass in one gulp.

"We'd better make a move." He waved to the landlord. "Thanks, I'll pop in again if I'm passing, that was a decent pint."

Back in the car he turned to Patsy. "Edward Mitchell, I should have guessed that. He ran his campaign out of the British Pride."

"I remember Linda mentioning that. I'd better call Meredith and let him know what's what."

Patsy pulled her phone from her bag and saw the volume of missed calls. The last one was from Amanda. Frowning, she dialled her answer service, and picked up the messages. Her face fell as she listened to Amanda's distraught message.

"Step on it, Chris, and straight to the General. Meredith has been beaten up, and has a collapsed lung."

Chris had reached the motorway slip road. He indicated to join the traffic and, accelerating, he crossed to the fast lane. He picked up his own phone and shook his head. He too had several missed calls. He called his answer service and Sharon's voice filled the car.

"I don't know where you two are, but get your arses back here fast. Meredith is in a bad way and for some reason thinks Patsy is in danger. If I call again and this phone is not answered, there will be hell to pay."

~ ~ ~

Hutchins stood as Patsy walked purposely along the corridor. He apologised for not staying with Meredith as though that may have saved him a beating. Patsy brushed his apology away, telling him Meredith wouldn't have let him if he'd tried, and asked if a guard was necessary.

Hutchins shook his head and shrugged. "We don't know. We are looking for the bastards who did it, and thought better safe than sorry." He placed his hand on her shoulder. "Sorry, I'm keeping you, through there, and first door on the right."

Amanda rushed to Patsy as she entered the small ante ward. There were two beds, one of which held a sleeping Meredith. An oxygen mask covered most of his face.

"You've got to talk some sense into him. He says he's going to discharge himself in the morning if they don't let him go. It was only a small puncture, but if he doesn't rest there is still a risk of infection and that can be fatal. Even if it doesn't get infected, not allowing it to heal properly will make him susceptible to future collapses. If he leaves there's no way he'll take it easy," Amanda whispered urgently. "I can't lose both of them."

She looked away embarrassed by her outburst. Patsy found her hand and gave it a squeeze.

"How long should he stay in?" Patsy was looking at Meredith rather than Amanda as she spoke.

"Twenty-four hours minimum IF he's going home to bed rest. Three days if he's going home to take it easy. A bloody month if it'll stop him working."

Patsy nodded and walked over to Meredith and reaching the bed, she picked up his hand. His eyes opened, his eyebrows raised, and he opened his mouth to talk. He grimaced at the pain but his eyes twinkled.

"It was a bloody big door, Hodge, and you should see the state of the other bloke." He lifted the mask away from his face. "Give us a kiss, but be gentle."

Patsy leaned forward and kissed him. "I love you Johnny, but you have to stop this attention-seeking."

"I will, as soon as I get out of here. I have a reason to be home tonight."

"About that, I've been thinking." She watched Meredith's face stiffen. "I have a plan."

"Go on, spit it out."

"I'm going to take Amanda back to Linda's with me, and pick up as much of my stuff as I need to last me the week. Then I'm going *home* with her."

Meredith allowed himself a twitch of the lips. "So what's the plan?"

"If you discharge yourself before the doctors say you can go, I'm out of there. I reckon you need a week in here."

Meredith made to raise himself from the bed, but winced at the pain and his head fell back heavily on to the pillows.

"That sort of makes my case," Patsy smiled. "At the end of the seven days, or when the doctors discharge you, whichever is sooner, I'll move everything back. I will officially become your padlock once more."

Despite his frustration at her demands, Meredith's lips twitched again.

"You're taking advantage of me while I'm incapacitated." Meredith rolled his eyes as Amanda leaned forward and replaced his oxygen mask, which was resting on his chest. "I'm outnumbered, that's not fair. I have to find Jo."

"That's the deal, Johnny, take it or leave it. Jo has a good team searching for her. I'm sure you'll get regular updates, and be able to direct from this bed." She smiled a gentle smile. "If I'm coming home, I need you to be fit."

"Fuck me, mate. You're going to argue? What'th wrong with you?

When did you change your name to Johnny, and what doeth being a padlock mean? Are you kinky?"

Patsy hadn't given the patient in the next bed even a cursory glance, and she turned to look at him. The bruising on his face was still developing and she leaned closer and gasped.

"Ben? Is that you?"

Ben gave a slight nod. "That good, eh?"

Meredith snorted out a laugh that was cut short due to the pain.

"Ow. You've just broken his heart, fancy letting him know he's no longer pretty. He'll have to get rid of all those mirrors in his house now." Meredith turned his face to look at Jacobs. "How you doing mate, what were the results? How long have I been asleep?"

"Too long. You snore like a pig." Jacobs was still lisping due to the missing teeth. "I have two broken ribs, a chipped cheek bone, and severe bruising all over. Oh yes, and five missing teeth. My legs are twice the size they were this morning, but they didn't manage to break them." He coughed back a laugh, "The very good news is that the only part of my anatomy they didn't damage still works. That nurse that stripped me for the x-rays, and lifted everything into position for a clear shot, was very cute."

The two men attempted not to laugh, and Patsy and Amanda stood shaking their heads at the series of moans and groans that they emitted.

"You were together when this happened?" Patsy queried. "Where were you?"

"If I told you it was two totally different incidents and one big coincidence, would you believe me?" Meredith watched Patsy sigh. "Then don't ask stupid bloody questions."

Patsy gave a shrug and held her hands up, acknowledging she had stated the obvious.

"Why, is the next obvious question?"

"It seems," Jacobs lisp caused him to pronounce it theemth, and Patsy clamped her bottom lip between her teeth since it was, after all, no laughing matter, "that speaking to Meredith in a boozer is not acceptable. Nor is speaking to you." Jacobs narrowed his one good eye.

Meredith held his hand up and pointed at Patsy. "And that brings me neatly to the next thing we will argue about." He shook his head slowly. "You are not to go anywhere alone. You don't answer the door unless you know who it is, and you certainly don't go gallivanting around the countryside with your phone switched off."

"There is clearly going to be a reason for such a demand, and looking at the state of you two, I'm not going to argue unless it's necessary. Who did this?"

"His dodgy mates. Seems like you stirred up quite a hornet's nest for us to walk into." Meredith raised his eyebrows as he tilted his head towards Jacobs. "I know I would have ended up there anyway, but it's crucial we get hold of Darren Wilkinson. Did you get anywhere today?"

Patsy glanced at Jacobs and leaned closer to Meredith, who waved a finger at her.

"Don't worry about him. He's safe."

Patsy apologised to Jacobs, and told them about Maurice Ford visiting Mitchell Edwards, and the snippet of conversation she and Chris had overheard. Ben Jacobs groaned, and she turned to him.

"Oh shit, Patsy, you listen to Meredith. If Mitchell's involved, the damage they did to us is just a scratch on an elephant's arse. Rumour has it that there have been times he's not bothered taking prisoners." He grunted as he attempted to lie on his side. "Meredith, this is worse than we thought."

Meredith nodded and lifted his mask away from his face. "Get me Chris and Trump in here now. I don't know why Mitchell doesn't want Darren Wilkinson found, and I'm not going to guess, but we need to build a case and sharpish." Meredith looked at Amanda who huffed out her disapproval. "Go home with Patsy, get some things and stay at Chris's tonight until we know what's going on." He looked back at Patsy. "I'm serious, the man's a maniac, and I want you both somewhere safe. Make sure you're not followed."

~ ~ ~

On Trump's insistence, and with Chris's agreement, Linda also packed a bag and went to stay with him. Trump was concerned that Maurice Ford and Mitchell Edwards would know where Patsy was living. Having taken instructions from Meredith he drove back to the station and briefed the team.

"Tom and I are going back in to see Nancy. I don't think we have time to continue with this softly, softly. The rest of you let me know if anything comes up."

He looked across to Rawlings. "Is Jane Roscoe here yet, Dave?"

Having received confirmation she was already with Nancy, Trump ended the briefing and followed Tom down to the interview room.

Nancy frowned as they entered the room. "Where's Mr Meredith? I haven't seen anyone today." She looked up at the clock. "I know it's late, but I would like to see him."

The two men ignored her and Tom Seaton set the recorder. He looked at Nancy.

"DCI Meredith won't be coming so you have to deal with us now."

"Why?"

"You don't get to choose, Nancy. Tell me what you know about Mitchell Edwards."

"Why isn't he coming? When will I see him?"

Again Seaton ignored the question. "Mitchell Edwards, do you know him?"

"Not personally. Why won't you answer my questions?"

Seaton saw the hesitation flicker across her eyes.

Nancy frowned and tapped her nail on the table. "I want my questions answered. Mr Meredith didn't speak to me like this." She looked at Jane Roscoe, who whispered she should answer the question. Nancy's nostrils flared as she attempted to control her temper. "I'm saying nothing until he gets here." Like a child, she looked to the door.

She gave a small scream of surprise as Tom Seaton shouted at the top of his voice.

"How do you know Edwards?" His hands flat on the desk, he leaned forward.

Nancy leaned back on the chair and crossed her arms. She continued to face the door, but her eyes moved to watch him, and her bottom lip quivered.

Seaton also crossed his arms and looked at Jane Roscoe. "I understand that DCI Meredith allowed Mrs Bailey to stay here as she was cooperating with this investigation. If that cooperation is withdrawn, I don't see the point. I'll arrange for a transfer to prison, tonight. You can see your client there in future."

Jane Roscoe nodded and whispered to Nancy, who blinked rapidly.

"I want to speak to my solicitor alone." Her voice betrayed her fear.

Trump nodded and terminated the interview. Standing, he opened the door and let Tom Seaton walk into the corridor. He stood there until Nancy looked up at him.

"You have five minutes. I'll make sure transport is ready." He closed the door quietly and hurried back to the incident room behind Seaton.

Nancy turned to Jane Roscoe. "Can they do that? Without Mr Meredith giving permission, I mean. Where do you think he is?"

Jane Roscoe picked up Nancy's hand and patted it. "I don't know where he is, Nancy. He may have been taken off the case, he could be out working on it, but yes, they can do that. It's nothing short of a miracle you're still here."

"But Mr Meredith and I had a deal. He wouldn't renege on that."

"Meredith isn't here. It may be he was given a time limit and the time's now up. Why didn't you answer their questions?"

"Because they wouldn't answer mine. I don't think that's fair, do you?"

Jane Roscoe gave a short laugh and looked at Nancy's hand for a while before responding. "Nancy, I'm going to be blunt if that's okay, and I don't mean any offence, and you must remember that I am here to protect you. Do you understand and believe me?" Nancy nodded and Jane smiled. "What could be considered to be unfair to them," she inclined her head towards the door, "is that they have a self-confessed murderer and kidnapper sitting in their station calling the shots, whilst their colleague is who knows where. Whilst I have no idea where Meredith is, I do know they are continuing to work on your sister's case. I can do nothing to stop them transferring you to a secure unit, to prison."

"But I want to be here. I don't want to go to prison until Mr Meredith has sorted out what happened to Debbie."

"Then you need to cooperate with them. Are you still not prepared to tell them where Jo Adler is being held? Once they know she's safe, I'm sure they won't be so aggressive with you."

Nancy fell silent and tapped her fingertips together as she considered her options. Jane Roscoe glanced at her watch; it was almost seven-thirty and she'd been on the go for twelve hours. She wanted her bed. The gesture wasn't missed by Nancy, who nodded.

"Right, I'll answer their questions, but I won't tell them where Jo is, not until they sort Debbie out."

Jane Roscoe stood to leave. "I'll get them back. Take my advice though, Nancy, no more games."

She hurried along the corridor to the custody sergeant. "Sam, get DS Trump back, tell him Nancy is willing to answer his questions."

"I can't wait to get her out of here." Sam's lips curled in disgust, "She's holding poor old Jo, who could be dead for all we know, and Meredith is hospitalised by the thugs her sister knew." He waved his finger at Jane, "She'll be getting no more favours from me, that's a promise. She's getting the same as the rest of the prisoners here." He put his hand on the telephone to call Trump.

"What do you mean, Meredith is in hospital?"

"He's taken a good hiding, a proper one, punctured lung amongst other things."

Jane Roscoe's brow creased and she allowed him to continue with the call.

Trump arrived a few minutes later carrying a file. He smiled at her as he approached. "We'll just wait for Tom. He's on the phone to Meredith."

"You should have told her about Meredith. If she knows there's a good reason, she'll be much more co-operative." Seaton hurried towards them and they set off down the corridor. Jane put her hand on Trump's arm as he made to open the door. "You would be forgiven for exaggerating." She smiled at Nancy as the door opened.

After recommencing the interview formally, Trump opened the file in front of him. He took the top photograph and placed it in front of Nancy. "Do you know this man?"

"I don't know him, but I know who he is." Nancy frowned, "Someone Edwards, a right-wing politician I think. Did he know Debbie? I don't think he was her type."

Trump ignored the question and placed the second photograph on top of the first. It was the photograph Patsy had shown Mrs Brady. Trump missed it but Nancy stilled before looking up at him.

"That's the chap from Debbie's painting. Where did you get the photograph?"

"Do you know him now you have seen his photograph?" Trump pressed.

"No."

Another photograph joined the pile.

"Do you know this man?" It was a mug shot of one of the doormen at the British Pride.

"No, who is he?"

"What about this one." Trump added a photograph of Maurice Ford to the pile, and took time to straighten it neatly on the top.

"I think I recognise him," Nancy leaned forward and peered closely at the photograph, "I don't know him, but he looks familiar. Who is he?"

"What about this one?" A mug shot chosen by Mrs Brady of a known thug called Oliver Green was placed on top of Maurice Ford's. Trump closed his now empty file.

"I don't know him. Who is he? Perhaps if you tell me, it may jog a memory. Ignoring me isn't going to help now, is it?"

Seaton snorted as Trump picked up the pile of photographs and chose two of them. He placed them side by side.

"These two here attacked first Mrs Brady, your sister's neighbour," Trump straightened the photographs as Nancy gave a gasp, "before attacking and hospitalising DCI Meredith and his friend." Nancy's hand flew to her mouth. "Do you know why asking questions about your sister and her lovers would cause such a reaction?"

He watched as Nancy shook her head. He pointed to the first photograph. "This is Oliver Green, a thug with a record for violence, and this," he tapped the second photograph, "is Ray Ingles, also a thug, and who works as a doorman amongst other things, at some rough venues. We believe they were instructed by either or both of these two." He placed the photographs of Edwards and Ford above the first two. "And apparently, they attacked DCI Meredith and Mrs Brady because of your sister, or him." Trump positioned the photograph of Darren Wilkinson so that it covered the corners of the other four. "What I need you to tell me is why you think such questions would cause such a violent reaction."

Nancy shook her head repeatedly.

"I don't know. How is Mr Meredith? Do you think they killed Debbie? What did they do to Mr Meredith?"

Seaton leaned forward, crossing his arms on the desk. "They took a piece of wood and they beat him repeatedly, and once unconscious they kicked him repeatedly. His lung is punctured and he's in a bad way."

"Will he be all right?" Nancy's eyes darted back and forth between Trump and Seaton.

Trump shook his head. "The truth is I don't know. You will understand, Nancy, that your popularity amongst the troops is at an all-time low. You killed Phillip Cowell, you are holding or have murdered Jo Adler, and now, albeit indirectly, you are responsible for the serious injury of a very popular DCI. If you can't help us I think you will be better off in prison."

Jane Roscoe leaned forward. "Was that a threat, Detective Sergeant Trump? Because that's what it sounded like." She patted Nancy's hand who was nodding in agreement.

Trump turned his head to look at Roscoe.

"I resent that remark, you should know better. No, it was not a threat. Mrs Bailey here has been getting an unusual level of attention and privilege so far. The officers on duty have kept her supplied with basically whatever she wants, stopped by for a chat, left her with a pot of tea, not to mention bringing her in puzzle books. What I meant, Ms Roscoe, is that unless Mrs Bailey gives us something to work with, all that is likely to stop. She will be provided with three meals a day as required. She will be taken to the bathroom to wash when a female officer is available to accompany her, but that's it. We haven't got the facilities here to exercise her safely, you know, to prevent her escape. So if Mrs Bailey insists she would rather be here, she may within a few days change her mind, unless of course she stops playing with the lives of our officers and gives us something."

Tom Seaton stood and looked down at Nancy. "So you don't know anything about any of these people that would help us?"

Nancy shook her head.

"And you're not prepared to reveal the whereabouts of Jo Adler?"

Again, Nancy shook her head.

Tom's finger hovered over the recorder. "Interview terminated at eight-ten pm." He hit the button and looked at Jane Roscoe. "Do you need to see your client again? You should make the most of it. I'm shipping her out in the morning."

Nancy's head fell, and she watched Trump replace the photographs in the file, before he too stood and walked towards the door.

"Five minutes, please." Jane Roscoe waited until the door had shut. "There is nothing I can do to change that, Nancy. Are you sure you can't give them anything?"

Nancy shook her head and Jane Roscoe stood.

"I have to go now. I'll call in the morning and find out when they are transferring you. If you need me before I next see you, let the warders know and they'll contact me."

Nancy was led back to her cell by Sam. He pushed the door open. The room was bare except for the blue plastic mattress on the concrete bed, a pillow and two grey blankets folded neatly to one end. She turned to Sam.

"Where are my books and things?" her voice was quiet.

"Can't let you have anything that you may hurt yourself with." He gave a gentle push on Nancy's shoulder and she stepped into the cell. "Good night, Nancy."

He slammed the door and resisted the urge to look through the small, thick, Perspex window.

Nancy stood staring at the bunk as she listened to his footsteps recede down the corridor.

~ ~ ~

Bobby sat on the back of the chair and tweeted. Jo allowed the book to fall on her chest and looked at him.

"What? You have water, you have food, you have me. What more could a budgie want?" She closed her eyes for a moment. She had been reading for over two hours without a break and they were sore. Yawning, she wondered how long she would sleep if she dozed off now. She had been struggling to keep normal hours for the past few days, to ensure that when she was released she wouldn't be disorientated. Deciding to watch a film she turned down the corner of the page and swung her legs off the bed.

"And breathe," chirped Bobby, "and breathe."

Jo clapped her hands and laughed. Bobby started and flew to perch on the top of his cage.

"Clever, Bobby, you can talk. Say it again, Bobby. And breathe, and breathe." Jo pulled the chair towards the cage and sat watching him. "Do you like Veronica Vickers? What else do you have for me?"

Jo spent the next thirty minutes trying to encourage Bobby to extend his vocabulary. He cocked his head from one side to the other, clearly entertained by the attention, but didn't utter another word. "We'll work on that tomorrow." Jo walked to the stack of DVDs and ran her finger along them. "*101 Dalmatians* or *Lion King*? We're having a cartoon tonight?" She held them up, and he inclined his head to the right. "*Lion King* it is." Jo removed the DVD and slid it into the machine.

14

Tom Seaton was sitting on the edge of Meredith's bed when Patsy and Amanda arrived the next morning. Meredith held up his hand to halt their greeting and allow Seaton to complete his update.

"Two of the boys are on their way to pick up Ingles now and Green is awaiting questioning, I'll do that when I get back. He can stew a little first. Nancy has gone quiet; she thinks we're transferring her to Eastwood Park today, but we can't even if we wanted to. They have some bug there, and aren't admitting new prisoners until Monday when extra cover is brought in. The other options are too far away to make access easy. Unless, of course, you want us to press ahead."

Meredith shook his head. His bruising had developed and various shades of blue covered half his face while the swelling on his top lip was now black. As Patsy studied him she was pleased to note that the tension around his eyes had gone, and she wondered if that was down to painkillers. She turned to Ben Jacobs, who winked with his good eye. He was also listening intently to Seaton's update.

"You also need to decide whether you want us to bring in Big Mo and Edwards. We've got nothing on them except what Chris and Patsy heard, and while we know it's them, we couldn't prove it. Our thinking was to leave it until we've interviewed Ingles and Green."

Meredith nodded. "And Jo? Anything at all on the house?"

"Nothing. Over half of Bristol has been covered now. With one exception, uniforms have managed to speak to the occupiers of all properties that fit the info you got from Nancy."

"What's the exception?"

Seaton shook his head. "Don't get excited; we spoke to the neighbour and they said a dentist and his family live there, but they're away visiting Scotland."

Meredith pinched the bridge of his nose and winced at the pain. Slowly he ran his fingers up and down as he considered the information. "We need to concentrate on Darren Wilkinson. He's the key to all this. Anything yet?"

Patsy stepped forward. "Can I make a suggestion? From what Chris and I overheard, the white van could have been used to see Wilkinson yesterday. Linda has all the locations, and Chris and I were going to check them out. We can let you have them and that will speed things up."

Meredith turned to face her. "I thought you were lying low."

"No, you thought that I wasn't going anywhere on my own. And I wasn't." Her eyes challenged him and he tutted.

He turned back to Seaton. "Get on the phone to Chris and get those addresses, I think the Graingers can be relieved of this case; our needs take priority. Speak to Nancy again, try and get more information on this house. How can she own two properties and not have a bank account? It doesn't add up. Check her maiden name and try that."

"Sorry, Gov, I forgot to mention that. We spoke to the solicitor dealing with Debbie's estate, and found Nancy did have an account with the post office. But he is making the payments to Gary Charles' account from the fund held in their client's account. The post office account has a pension from her husband going in, and a tidy balance in her savings account, but everything she pays out is in cash. There are regular cash withdrawals, sometimes hundreds of pounds, but no standing orders, direct debits or cheques written against the account. So that's not going to take us anywhere. Being a cleaner she was paid in cash too."

"Bollocks. How are you doing . . ." He paused as Patsy pulled her phone from her pocket and walked to the door. "Where are you going?"

Patsy turned back and rolled her eyes. "Angel has texted me. She wants to know what's going on. She spoke to her mother last night."

"What are you going to tell her?"

"What do you mean? The truth, of course. I can't see any point in not telling her, unless you think that would put her in danger?" She looked at Ben Jacobs. "What do you think? You know these thugs, are they likely to hurt her?"

Ben Jacobs shrugged and winced as his ribcage settled back into position. "I have to stop moving," he groaned as he settled his shoulders back against the stack of pillows. "I don't *know* them Patsy, I'm hired by them, regularly. I hear things, but up until now," he shot a look at

Meredith, "I've managed to avoid getting involved with them." He raised his eyebrows, "I suppose it all depends on what Darren Wilkinson has been up to. They are clearly trying to keep him away from everyone. You also have to remember who her uncle on the other side is. Brian Catchpole is also a nasty piece of work."

"Do you think he could be involved? I heard he's a bad lad too." Patsy returned her attention to Meredith.

He pondered the question for a few seconds. "I think Wilkinson is involved in something heavy. I doubt it has anything to do with Catchpole or something would have hit the radar by now. Tell her enough to concern her, and try and convince her to go and stay with her uncle, or if necessary, you."

Patsy turned to leave.

"We'll also need to speak to whoever led you to the white van."

Patsy remembered Percy Howard pleading with her to keep his father out of it, and she didn't want to let him down.

"Let's see how it goes first. I think they're too scared at the moment."

She left the room before he could argue, and took the first exit out of the hospital. Standing to one side of the ambulance bay at the front of the block she dialled Angel.

"Where have you been? I've heard nothing from you. What happened to keeping in touch? I've had Mum on the phone wanting to know what's what, and I had nothing to tell her, because needless to say Dad hasn't called. I tried Uncle Ed earlier and he's ignoring me too."

"Where are you?"

"At home, it's my weekend off."

"How soon can you get to the General Hospital?"

"Why?"

"Because that's where I am, and I want to see you."

"What are you doing at the hospital?"

"Angel, stop asking bloody questions, and answer some."

"Ooh, you got out of the wrong side of the bed this morning."

"Angel!"

"Half an hour. Where do you want to meet? It's a big place."

"Go to the admissions office and meet me there. Text me when you arrive. Oh, and Angel, don't tell anyone where you're going, and if you see anyone, don't tell them you're meeting me."

"Why? What's happened?"

"Angel, please, when I see you, okay."

Patsy returned to Meredith and updated him.

"Bring her up here when she gets here."

"Why?"

"Because I want her to see what can happen if you get in the way of whatever's going on. If she's frightened she'll be careful."

Patsy met Angel and took her to the café. As they drank their coffee she explained why she was at the hospital. Rather than appear worried, Angel bristled with anger.

"Are you saying Uncle Ed could be involved in this? Because that's what it sounds like." She tapped the side of her cup with her spoon as she spoke.

"I'm sorry, Angel, I know it's difficult to believe, and upsetting that -"

"I'm not upset. I'm bloody furious! If he's been stringing me a line, and . . ." She held her hands up in frustration. "Look, Patsy, as I see it, Uncle Ed is in this up to here," she waved her hand above her head, "and I don't know if that's to protect Dad, or to hinder us finding him. Either way he could have just told me to back off. What did he think? That I would sit and wait and wait for Dad to call? I can't believe he thinks I'm that gullible. So what now?"

"We still have to find your dad. But it's the police who will be doing it, not me I'm afraid. The stupid thing is they dragged the police into this by beating up Meredith. Rather than dissuade the search they've stepped it up a notch. They are nasty guys, Angel, they've threatened me, and given that you started all this off, albeit for your mother, you may be in danger too. Is there any chance you can stay with your Mum's brother?"

"Uncle Brian?" Angel shook her head. "I don't want to, it's all right there, although my cousin gets on my nerves, but I'm in the way. Or I feel I am anyway."

"But it would only be until your father is found. Surely your uncle would want you to be safe. Look, come with me, there's someone I want you to meet."

Patsy took Angel up to Meredith's ward, but a nurse stopped them going in as the doctor was examining him. Amanda had stayed in with them, primarily to find out how her father was doing, but she was also interested from an educational point of view. After a few minutes, she came out and Patsy introduced her to Angel, before asking what the doctor had said.

"You're not going to like this. Dad was insisting on being discharged, and if he was going to take bed rest there would be no reason he couldn't go home. He spun the doctor a line about how he had me to look after him and I was in the trade," she rolled her eyes, "and I did my best to let the doctor know that he wouldn't rest, but they need the bed, and if he's going to be awkward they want rid of him."

"Well, between us we'll have to sort him out, won't we?" Patsy gave a frustrated sigh.

"Them." Amanda raised her eyebrows.

"What do you mean, 'them'?"

"Ben Jacobs is coming too."

"What? Why?" Patsy threw her arms up.

"Because apart from the broken ribs, all that's wrong with him is severe bruising. But he can't go back to his place as, and I'm quoting Dad, firstly, no one knows if he is likely to get another visit from those thugs, and secondly, he has no one to look after him. I think Dad feels responsible. He also has other . . ." She stopped speaking as the door opened. "Oh, he's finished."

The doctor left the ante-ward and nodded at them as he took the discharge papers to the nurses' station. Patsy thought he looked smug.

She pushed Angel forward. "Come and meet Meredith. Brace yourself, and remember he can be charming."

Angel looked puzzled as she walked into the room. Meredith and Jacobs stopped speaking and smiled at her.

Angel's eyes widened as she looked at Jacobs and she bit her bottom lip. "Shit. You won't be singing for a while. Have you got any teeth left?" She stepped forward and peered at him and he snapped his mouth shut.

Meredith laughed. "A girl after my own heart. A spade's a shovel to you too then, Angel."

Angel turned to Meredith. His features had been totally distorted by the bruising, although she caught the twinkle in his eye.

"Absolutely, life's too short for bullshit." She turned to Patsy. "And this is the one you gave up the police force for." She glanced back at Meredith. "I hope he scrubs up well, because looking like that, and if he's as miserable and awkward as you say he is, I can't see why."

"What? Angel, I . . ." Patsy grinned despite Angels words.

Angel looked at Meredith. "That blunt enough for you?"

Ben Jacobs laughed but the pain got the better of him, and he wrapped his arms around his torso and groaned. Meredith smirked, but the bruising on his lip made him look a little manic and Angel took a step back.

"Now I've seen that you two have had a hiding, and I am sorry, because I do realise I started this off, but what was it supposed to prove?"

"That you too could look like this, Angel. In all seriousness, until we find out why looking for your father causes this," he waved his hand between himself and Jacobs, "I want you to come and stay with us, unless of course you have anywhere else you can go."

"Patsy suggested my Uncle Brian. I'm not keen, but I'll ask."

"No, you go and get some things, let us talk to your uncle."

"Why?"

"Okay, spade a shovel time, because he could be involved in some way. He had a meeting in the British Pride a few weeks back with Big Mo Ford. It seemed amicable."

Angel shook her head. "He wouldn't hurt me. I don't know about Uncle Ed, we're not close. But Uncle Brian would not hurt me, or allow me to be hurt." Her tone was confident, but her eyes unsure.

"He may not have a choice." Meredith stared into her troubled eyes.

"Okay, so you've got a mansion or something, have you? I thought he was staying with you."

"A three-bed semi actually, and he is, for a few days anyway. We'll sort something out, don't worry."

"What kind of copper are you?" Angel looked suspicious, "Even on telly they don't take victims and peeps in danger into their own homes. Have you been sainted or something?"

Meredith grinned at her. "I like you. No, it's purely selfish. I'm going to have to stay at home for a few days," he looked up as Amanda coughed and he inclined his head, "maybe a week, and if everyone I may need to speak to is close by, it'll save me a lot of bother. If I was healthy I'd say sod you."

Angel knew he didn't mean it, as his eyes smiled at her. She could see the logic, and she had already decided that it would be an interesting set-up to be part of. "I'll go and pack some things, shall I?"

"In a while. One of my sergeants is on his way back. He'll take you all where you want to go, and pick up some things from Ben's too."

By late afternoon everything had been organised. It had been agreed that Meredith would be effectively working from home, and it was probably best that Angel stayed with Chris and Sharon Grainger. Ben Jacobs was allocated the spare room at Meredith's. Patsy left Amanda to settle them in, and went with Seaton to drop Angel off at the Graingers'. She seemed surprisingly calm about the prospect of living with strangers and Patsy commented as such.

Angel simply shrugged. "It's a life lesson. I'm always interested in how other people live. If I don't like it, I'll just go."

Sharon showed Angel to her room. As she opened the door Jack came out of the bathroom. He stared at Angel a little too long and she stared back. He looked away first, a slight colour rising to his cheeks. Angel grinned at Sharon.

"This is Jack, my son, Angel. You'll be glad to hear that you have an en suite so won't have to use that bathroom."

"Mother!" Jack shook his head and stepped forward his hand held out. "I'm Jack, do you need any help?"

"Angel, and no thanks, but thanks for the offer."

Jack smiled. "Well, when you get bored, which you will, I've got the latest Lara Croft, if you fancy a go."

Sharon left them to it and went back down to Patsy and Tom.

"Another pretty girl to keep his blood pumping. She seems nice."

Sharon raised her eyebrows indicating that she required confirmation.

"She is. She can be a little blunt though."

Sharon laughed. "Well, that's good. Having had Amanda tiptoeing around him for weeks, a little dose of reality will go down a treat. Do you two fancy a cuppa?"

"No, we have to make a move. Thanks for this, Sharon, see you tomorrow."

~ ~ ~

Angel hung over the bannister at the top of the stairs. "Bye Patsy, I'll call you later after I've spoken to Mum."

Patsy agreed and told her to behave herself before following Tom back to the car.

"I hate being mollycoddled, you know."

"I know, but needs must, Patsy."

"Now we're on our own, how did you get on with Green?" She watched Seaton shake his head.

"No good, he's not talking. Says he was drinking in the British Pride at the time. Dave Rawlings is going down there with Hutchins later to check out his alibi, which it will I'm sure, but we're going to charge him later and hopefully get him held until trial, given the violent nature of his offence. That bastard Ingles is proving difficult to pin down. Apparently, he's been on holiday this past week. His missus was good, obviously used to lying for him," he snorted out a laugh, "and you should have heard her language when Trump asked with whom, implying it was a girlfriend."

He followed Patsy into the house when they arrived back at Meredith's, and poked his head around the living room door. Meredith was lying on the sofa and Ben Jacobs was in the armchair facing him, his feet up on the large footstool.

"Do you need anything else, Gov?"

"No, get off home and see your family. Tell the team I'm not dead and to call me if anything happens."

Patsy and Amanda left the two men arguing over whether to watch *Pulp Fiction* or *Predator*, and went to the kitchen to prepare dinner. When it was ready, Patsy went to get them.

"We don't need to come to the dining room. We can have it on trays on our laps, surely. You do know we're just out of hospital." Meredith didn't move and lay prone on the sofa.

"Yes, and against my better judgement. If you're well enough to be out of hospital, you're well enough to sit at the table. Amanda and I won't be here to wait on you hand, foot and finger you know. So you may as well remind your bodies how to function."

Patsy turned and walked away.

"She may be gorgeous, Meredith, but she's a ball-breaker that's for sure. OW!"

Ben Jacobs was starving and the smell of dinner wafting down the hall encouraged him to move a little too quickly. He could hardly bend his knees and walked as though his legs were in splints, swinging one then the other forward towards the smell. Meredith put the film on hold and followed him.

"Smells delicious," Meredith grunted as he sat at the table, "But I thought we'd be having a roast to celebrate our return." He looked at the shepherd's pie, and poked it with his fork.

"You've been gone a little over twenty-four hours, and even though I admit to roasting the most mouth-wateringly tender beef, how would he manage that?"

Patsy pointed to Jacobs who resisted a smile. Amanda giggled, but Meredith, despite his amusement, remained deadpan.

"So, we're on baby food. For how long?"

"As long as it . . . excuse me, you carry on. I must take this, it's Angel." Patsy stood and made her way to the kitchen.

"And bring some wine back with you. He can have a bloody straw if he dribbles."

Patsy smiled as she answered the phone. As Angel relayed the conversation she'd had with her mother she took a bottle of wine from the rack, and fished around in the cutlery drawer for the corkscrew. Terminating the call, she took the bottle to Meredith and handed it to him.

"You can have this if you do something for me."

"What?"

"Promise first."

"Patsy, I'm a grown man."

Patsy sat down. "Yes, you are. Sorry." She picked up her knife and fork.

"Amanda, poppet, go and get the corkscrew for your old dad." Meredith gave his daughter a lopsided smile.

"I've hidden it," Patsy winked at Amanda.

Meredith sighed. "You are acting like a child. I'm not impressed. God only knows what Ben must think."

Patsy looked at Ben who smiled a gummy smile, and despite her attempts to smile, her nose wrinkled.

"Top notch this, Patsy. Much appreciated."

Meredith growled. "What am I promising?"

"To get me into Eastwood Park tomorrow to meet with Kate Wilkinson. If I wait for a visiting order it will be Tuesday or Wednesday, or maybe even longer.

Meredith leaned forward, all thoughts of the wine momentarily forgotten.

"I thought she wouldn't speak to you. That's why Jennings was involved."

"Changed her mind, she's worried about Angel. She's managed to spook her quite badly too."

"You're not a police officer any more, they wouldn't go for it."

"I can go in with one of the boys. Who's in tomorrow?"

"Officially, I have no idea, but they'll all be there." Meredith pointed the bottle of wine at her. "Now pour me some wine, and I'll make the phone call when we've finished."

Dinner over, the two men hobbled back to their film, and Meredith called the incident room. Dave Rawlings answered and took Meredith's instructions. He called back about an hour later. Meredith called to Patsy to update her, but lowered his voice as Jacobs' phone rang.

"Alfie, mate, I thought you were ignoring me." Jacobs said nothing else but listened until Alfie hung up and he muttered, "Cheers."

Wincing as he sighed, Jacobs tapped the phone on the arm of the chair and looked at Meredith.

"Not good news I take it."

"Maybe for you lot. But seriously, Meredith, I want this to stay with you for now, until you've sorted this lot out anyway. I'll tell you so you know, but I don't want you running off all guns blazing; other people could get hurt."

"I couldn't walk off all guns blazing at the moment, but you have my word."

"The reason Alfie hadn't returned my calls is because he was too scared. He's bought a pay as you go, so if they check his phone they will only see the missed calls from me."

"'They' being?"

"Big Mo and the boys. Alfie knew nothing about this until late last night." Jacobs threw his arms wide. "He knew something was up, as was given the cold shoulder in the British Pride. Even Shirl, the barmaid, only said what she had to. He was going to leave, but was asked to stay. Big Mo turns up, tells him to stay away from me, and anyone else asking questions. He pointed out that his boy couldn't play football with broken legs. Alfie told the truth. He hadn't spoken to me and didn't know where I was."

Meredith noticed Jacobs had clenched his fists, and was using his phone as an unyielding stress ball.

"Okay, mate, calm down." Meredith nodded to Jacobs' hands and he allowed the phone to fall into his lap. "You haven't told me anything we didn't know." He shrugged. "How can I use that?"

"Because, I haven't finished. To quote Alfie, 'I don't know where the fuck you are, but disappear'. Mitchell Edwards is involved. He picked Big Mo up after the message was delivered. He stood in the entrance to the bar with some suit standing behind him, looked at Alfie like he was shit on his shoe, and asked Big Mo if he needed sorting. Big Mo assured him that he'd been dealt with. Now there is no misunderstanding. Alfie said he'll call again if he hears anything else, but not to hold my breath as he was lying low." Jacobs snorted a laugh. "He didn't even ask how I was."

"Did he know the suit?"

"He didn't say. And I didn't . . ."

Patsy walked into the room. She looked at the faces of the two men.

"What's happened, you look worried?"

"Nothing, we have confirmation that Edwards is involved. I might have to pay him a visit." Meredith grunted as he shunted further up the sofa to allow Patsy to sit down.

"You think so? Well, I've not unpacked yet so that will be easy." Aware that Ben Jacobs was party to the situation Patsy turned to him. "Sorry, Ben, but he can only just manage to pay a visit to the bathroom."

Jacobs nodded solemnly. He could see Meredith was bristling for a fight, and he didn't want to get dragged into it. Patsy was also aware Meredith was reaching boiling point, and knew it wouldn't have helped that she was challenging him. Picking up one of his feet she rubbed her palm up and down it.

"What news from the station? Anything new on Jo?"

"Nope." Meredith chewed his lip.

"What about the prison visit?"

Meredith remained silent.

"Did they not manage to arrange it?" Patsy picked up his other foot to repeat the process, but Meredith pulled it away from her and bent his knees so that his feet were flat and her access to them removed. "Have I upset you? You couldn't possibly be serious about challenging Edwards? You haven't got anything on him except hearsay, and that from people who are connected to you."

Inclining her head she watched him struggle to retain his temper. She patted one of his knees. "Come on, get if off your chest. You will feel so much better J . . ." She had been going to call him Johnny but thought better of it.

Meredith rubbed his temples with his fingers before responding. "I will concede that you are right about meeting with Edwards, I wasn't totally serious about that. But you know full well that there is no way I'm lying on my comfortable sofa, having my feet rubbed, while Jo is still missing. One more day here and I'll go mad anyway, but I will stay home one more day, then I'm back at work." He held up his hand to stop her speaking. "I'll stay office bound. That's the best I can do. If that means you move out, then that's what you should do. You can't change me, Patsy, not where work is concerned, any more than I could change you."

He dropped his hand onto his knee and his eyes held the challenge.

Ben Jacobs picked up his phone and pretended to be otherwise engaged.

"You are a bastard, Johnny, do you know that?"

"I do."

"And you'll stay in the office?"

"I will."

"Can I trust you on that?"

"Not absolutely, no, but I'll do my best."

His eyes twinkled and although his swollen mouth didn't quite make a smile, the familiar lines appeared alongside his eyes.

Patsy studied his damaged face one eyebrow raised. "Then your best will have to do."

Ben Jacobs felt distinctly uncomfortable as they gazed at each other. They were fully clothed and sitting apart, yet he felt as though he was watching them romp naked on the sofa. He cleared his throat to break the silence. Meredith coughed and rubbed his nose, Patsy jumped to her feet.

"On that note, I think I will go and make some coffee."

"You're going to see Kate Wilkinson at nine-thirty in the morning. Either Travers or Rawlings will pick you up."

Patsy dropped to her knees and placed a tender kiss on his forehead.

"Your best is more than good enough. I wish you were well," she whispered, before standing and walking briskly to the kitchen.

Meredith attempted another grin as he hit the play button on the remote control, and John Travolta's character kicked open a door and ran into a room, guns blazing. As he watched the action, he placed his hands behind his head and felt rather proud of himself. He'd made his point, got his way and controlled his temper, and if he had his way, he would find a way of encouraging his battered body to take its just rewards.

The Wrong Shoes

15

Unwilling to sit at the kitchen table due to the discomfort, Patsy, Jacobs and Meredith sat in the living room awaiting Dave Rawlings. Meredith summed up the briefing he had received from Travers who had covered the night shift.

"Ingles still can't be found, and Green has some hotshot lawyer who will only allow him to say 'no comment'. They have to get him in front of the magistrates first thing, so they'll charge him later today. Sherlock has been promised the DNA results Amanda found tomorrow," he allowed himself a nod of pride, "and I've arranged to see Nancy with the rope. He thinks, and rightly so, that we should find out if it was lying around or bought for the purpose. He has no DNA for Debbie, if you can believe that, but if it's Debbie's blood he wants to check Nancy's; apparently, there will be enough similarities for it to be identified if it is. There's no news on the bloody house," he paused and thanked Amanda who had brought coffee in on a tray, "and the Super is pushing for a special edition of *Crimebusters*, or a local news item if we have nothing by tomorrow night. Someone should know the property from the description and hopefully know that there have been no comings or goings this week." He sighed deeply. "Poor Jo, she's been there a week. She must be beside herself if she's still . . . she must be climbing the walls."

He quickly avoided tempting fate by mentioning what they all knew was a possibility, and that Jo may already be dead. He was distracted by Amanda bending to kiss his forehead.

"I'm off to the gym, I'll be a couple of hours and then I'll be back to wait on you." She made to leave the room.

"Just one moment, madam. I don't think so." Meredith raised his voice and she stopped in her tracks, and turned back to face him.

"What? I'll be fine. Two of the boys are coming to pick me up, and I have done a self-defence class, which is not necessary, as they'll protect me." She rolled her eyes at Patsy, hoping for support.

Patsy shook her head. "Sorry, Amanda, I'm with your dad on this one. I don't think you should go."

"Two of the boys?" Meredith spat as he waved his hand back and forth between himself and Jacobs. "We're two of the men and look what they did to us." He shook his head. "I'm sorry, Amanda, but you're grounded. Those anaemic children you've brought here couldn't fight their way out of a paper bag."

Amanda placed her hands on her hips and laughed. "I'm almost twenty-three, and now you choose to ground me? Seriously, Dad I . . ."

The doorbell rang. Patsy jumped to her feet.

"I'll get that. You two sort this out; I'll take them into the kitchen." Patsy closed the door behind her as she went to answer the door. Three, and not two, young men stood on the doorstep. Patsy's eyes widened and she grinned at them. "Come on in, please. Amanda's just having a word with her father." The sound of the harsh exchange could be heard in the hall. "Her father's worried about her, I think I should take you to meet him." She beckoned them forward and opened the door to the living room. "Come on in."

Amanda and her father stopped arguing and Meredith's mouth fell open. Fighting for space in the entrance to the room stood three six-foot plus, seventeen-stone plus, bulky young men. They smiled politely. The one whose short sleeves had been slit to allow room for his biceps, shouldered his way in. He held out his hand.

"Nice to meet you, Mr Meredith, I'm Tim. I'm sorry to hear about your umm, umm, troubles, sir."

Amanda laughed. "You should see your face. You see, they are more than capable of looking after me."

Tim nodded and smiled at Amanda. Meredith noticed the flare of passion as Tim's eyes took in and appreciated his daughter. He looked at the other two.

"Are you auditioning for *The Return of The Hulk*?"

"Ha ha, very good, sir. No, we're from the Varsity first team. We're all studying medicine with Amanda."

"Do they make white coats big enough?" Meredith was at a loss for a moment but gathering his wits, he added, "I'm sorry lads, but threats have been made against me and mine." He repeated the gesture of waving his hand between him and Jacobs. "I can't let her out of the house."

"I promise you we wouldn't let her out of our sight. All three of us will be with her at all times." Tim spoke over Amanda; he could see her getting angry. "She is a tough cookie, you know. She took Tris out the other day, in training of course."

"Tris?" Meredith knew it would be one of the others. He was right. The tallest of the three ducked to get in through the door, and held out his hand.

"Tristan Wellington, sir, pleased to meet you." He glanced across to Amanda, and again Meredith saw the flicker in the eye. He also saw Ben Jacobs' gummy grin. "She did, you know. It's all about balance and the element of surprise."

Meredith closed his eyes and sighed. "You do know I'm a copper?" They nodded in unison and he wagged his finger at them. "Then let me tell you something, I know ways of hurting you that you wouldn't dream possible, and if anything happens to her, once I've hurt you, I'll arrest you each and every time you even fart in this city. Do you still want to take her?"

Again, the three young men nodded in unison. Meredith groaned, Jacobs laughed, and Patsy stood trying to keep a straight face.

Amanda patted him on the head. "Bye, Dad, I'll bring something nice back for lunch. Patsy's doing roast lamb tonight." She pushed the three back to the hall, and picked her kit bag up. "See you later, Ben, good luck, Patsy."

The front door slammed and they were gone. Meredith opened his mouth to speak as the doorbell rang.

"I expect she's forgotten something." Patsy opened the door, and Dave Rawlings stepped into the hall looking back over his shoulder. Patsy pointed him in the direction of the sitting room.

"Have you had the All Blacks round to stay? Which one is her bloke?" he asked as he walked in.

"None of them. They're her protection squad apparently," Meredith grunted, and shifted himself a little further up on the sofa. Rawlings sat on the arm. "Anything new?"

"New lead on Ingles' whereabouts, Hutchins and Trump are looking into it. Patsy gets me for company. Oh, and the addresses from the van stop-offs, we have a possible location for Wilkinson on the outskirts of Whitchurch. Little detached cottage, no neighbours, and we've called twice but no signs of life. Although empty milk bottles have been put out, and post picked up from the mat. I'm calling in once I've dropped Patsy off. Is he still our favourite?".

"I don't know. As I see it these are our current options." He tapped a different finger as he listed off the names. "Darren Wilkinson, Mitchell Edwards, Maurice Ford aka Big Mo, and of course Debbie herself. We have to hope that this DNA Amanda found helps." Meredith explained.

"What about Nancy?"

The other three turned to look at Jacobs.

"Don't look at me like I'm thick," he protested. "She's bumped off others, why not her sister? It seems to me that she's an attention seeker and perhaps this is her swansong, you know, sending you lot off on a wild goose chase so you take notice of her."

"I've thought about that, and I left it on the back burner until I had nothing else. But I don't think so, not now, because if that's the case, why are the big boys playing rough?" Meredith shook his head. "No, I doubt it's her, it's more likely to be one of them. Edwards is my favourite, and we're ruffling feathers. I like your thought process though. You're brighter than you look." Meredith checked the time. "It's about time you two got going. I'm hoping Mrs Wilkinson can shine some more light on this."

* * *

Rawlings held the door open for Patsy as the warder slid the trays containing their belongings into a cubbyhole behind the counter. Another warder stood waiting for them on the other side. Her shoes squeaked on the polished rubber tiles as she led them down a corridor to an interview room. Kate Wilkinson was sitting waiting for their arrival. Patsy glanced at her through the window that ran half the length of the wall. The harshness Patsy had previously seen displayed had been replaced with a frown of concern as she stared at the blank wall in front of her. Her hands fiddled with the toggles on the end of the drawstring threaded through jogging trousers. Patsy sensed her relief as they entered the room.

"What's happened? Is Angel okay?" Kate Wilkinson made to rise, and the warder stepped forward. She slumped back against the chair.

Patsy smiled at her. "Angel is fine, why did you think otherwise?"

"Because I'm hiked out of my cell, with no warning, to see a copper and you. You've been working with Angel and I know there's been trouble. She told me." Her cold eyes appraised Patsy. "You have to keep her safe."

"I'll try, but to do that effectively I need to know why she's in danger. Why would your search for your husband set off this level of violence?"

Kate Wilkinson looked away. "I don't know." She looked back as Patsy huffed and shook her head.

"Liar." Patsy held her gaze as Kate's eyes widened, and she leaned towards her. "Don't mess me about, Kate, people I know are getting hurt. Your daughter may be in trouble, so now is not a time to play games with me."

"I have no reason to lie. I don't know. But I know the people involved, and they don't mess about. My only guess is that Darren has pissed someone off. I don't know. I'm stuck in here and . . . why are you shaking your head." The harsh, defiant Kate had returned, and her lip curled as she spoke.

"Because you're still lying. Don't you think if Darren had pissed someone off then they would also want him found? So why would they *not* want Darren found?"

Kate shook her head. "I don't know."

Rawlings rubbed his palms together before linking his fingers as though in prayer. "I think we need to start again." He smiled at Kate, who looked at him with distaste. "Why did you want to find him?"

"You know that. Your lot think I killed him to get the insurance money. I burned the house down, but much as the bastard deserved it, I didn't kill him."

"No, I don't buy it. I looked into that. I couldn't find any on-going investigation. The team that dealt with the arson looked for him to ensure he wasn't involved, but the records show he'd been gone a while. There's nothing current on him."

"Then why am I being told differently? I've been told the police have been snooping about asking questions, suggesting that his disappearance is linked with me. It isn't, but I'm not doing time for it. I gave enough for that bastard over the years, and I'll not give him one more day." Kate slapped her hand on the desk.

"Who told you that and when?"

Rawlings believed her, but knew there was no official suggestion or investigation into the possible murder of Darren Wilkinson. He placed his elbows on the table and rested his chin on his linked fingers.

"It's been going on for two months now. I get messages from friends and visitors. Two coppers have been asking where he is. As no one knows where he is, they then ask if it's possible I could have killed him. Did anyone think I was capable of that? I have good friends the answer was no." Kate tilted her chin. "And because I didn't. I called her in," she nodded at Patsy, "because they'd spoken to Angel. They didn't suggest it openly to her, but it was implied. I've not been a good mother, not really. I would kill for her, die for her actually, but I've not been a good mother. I didn't want her thinking that of me. She was close to her dad once." Kate flipped the toggles up and down against the edge of the table. "I don't want to lose her, not for something I didn't do."

There was a brief silence as Rawlings considered this information. "And you didn't think it odd that they didn't speak to you directly? Your face is an open book Kate, they would have known just by asking. I know."

"I assumed they thought I would lie. You would, wouldn't you, if you'd bumped someone off?"

Patsy flipped open her notebook. It revealed a list of names. "Okay, Kate, I'm going to give you a list of names. I want to know everything you know about that person, who they are, what they do, who they associate with. Everything. Most of them you'd noted down for me, but I need background stuff now."

Kate nodded her agreement.

"Maurice Ford, Big Mo to his friends."

"Local wannabe," Kate snorted, her dislike evident. "Thinks he's a big man, but he's just a puppet for those with the power."

"You seem to know him well," Rawlings observed.

"He grew up in the same street as Darren's family. They played together as kids, and he was a friend of Darren and his brothers. When I first met Darren, we used to knock about with him and his wife."

"What changed?" Patsy made a note and looked up at Kate.

"His dad died, and he took over as head of the family. Our families didn't see eye to eye, and he tried to get Darren involved in some seriously dodgy shit, even . . . I didn't approve. We drifted apart, okay?"

"What were you going to say then? Even my brother didn't do that, or something similar?"

"This has nothing to do with my brother, but yes, I was. Darren was useless, never had much backbone. Brian didn't trust him, thank God. It means that, other than a bit of driving, Darren stayed out of bother." Kate shook her head and sighed. "I have no idea why I cared so much. I used to have dreams of us in a different life, especially when Angel was born. But other than shagging around, he can't do anything for more than two minutes."

Kate looked down and tied the drawstring in a bow, then pulling her shoulders back she looked at Patsy. "Next name."

Patsy knew instinctively that, for all his failings, Kate still hurt when she talked about Darren's infidelity. She listed off the other names on her list. Kate confirmed that Maurice Ford headed up a bunch of small time villains, and Green and Ingles were part of it. She also knew that Mitchell Edwards pulled his strings.

"You clearly don't like Mitchell Edwards, why is that?"

"He is a nasty, vicious piece of work. He gets off by hurting people, but as far as I know he has never got his own hands dirty. So to sum up, a mean, cowardly shit." Kate looked at Rawlings and shook her head. "Half of what he gets up to is common knowledge, I can't believe you lot can't touch him. Mind you, I would rather someone gave him what was coming."

"That sounded like it was personal rather than an observation." Rawlings stood and walked to the water cooler in the corner, returning with three plastic cups. He slopped some on the table as he set them down. Kate had not responded. "Was it personal?"

"It was. He's hurt people I know, ruined some of them. He'll get his in the fullness of time, and with any luck Big Mo will go down with him."

"Will they give evidence to that effect?" Rawlings tilted his head and raised his eyebrows. He nodded as Kate gave a snort or derision.

"Up until that point, I thought you may actually be of some use. I should have known better."

"What, you think we can bang someone up because we know that they're bent? If it worked like that, love, there'd be ten of you to a cell in here. Justice can only be delivered when there is evidence, and if people won't or can't help us with that, well, there's not a lot we can do, is there?"

"You can try harder." Kate dragged her eyes to Patsy. "Next name."

"Ben Jacobs. He knows Ed, does he know Darren?"

Kate smiled. "Have you met him?"

"I have." Patsy nodded.

"Then you will know that as pretty as he is, and he is hot, he's not involved."

"You seem very sure of that."

"As sure as I can be. Ben spends his time avoiding men – they could be the husband, father or boyfriend of his latest conquest. I don't know him that well, but I know he plays with the ladies rather than party with the lads." Kate's brow furrowed. "Why are you asking about him? Is he involved in some way?" Her face contorted as anger took over, and she leaned forward. "If he is, you keep Angel away from him."

"Did Angel not tell you about him?" Patsy watched Kate struggle for control over her natural response.

"Tell me what?" Kate regained some of her composure and leaned back against the chair.

"She and I met with Ben Jacobs when we were asking questions about Darren. You had listed his name in the book, or had you forgotten?"

"I thought you would be doing your own legwork." Kate gave a slight shake of her head. "What happened?"

"He was badly beaten together with a friend of mine. It has to be assumed it's linked to this case."

"She said your bloke had been bashed, she didn't mention Ben. Is he all right?"

"Not looking so pretty now, but he'll mend. How well did you know Ben?"

"Well enough."

"Did he have anything to do with Darren's departure?"

Kate looked at the ceiling and laughed. "No. I *knew* him for one night years before, and, as I say, he avoided the menfolk where possible."

Patsy smiled. "Hence you don't want him near Angel."

Kate's features hardened. "Next question."

"Why did Darren leave you?"

"He didn't, I kicked him out."

"What were you rowing about on the day he left?"

"What . . . how do you know that?"

"Angel was in."

Kate looked troubled. "What did she say?"

"Nothing, just that you were rowing and she had to turn the television up. She thinks it was about a woman."

"It was. I'd reached the end of the road with him. He had this aftershave that he didn't wear all the time. I worked out that was when he was going to see his lady friends. He came down with it on, and I'd had enough. I don't think he did much kissing that day."

"No, probably not. I've heard you have a violent temper."

Patsy's look told Kate exactly what she thought about her. Kate exploded, "Don't you bloody judge me, sitting there all prim and proper like butter wouldn't melt. Your shit stinks too. You haven't had my life, you don't know."

"I didn't mean to offend, it was an observation. Tanya Jennings had had a nose job when I saw her."

"Yes, well she's a nosy bitch that asks too many questions. She told me about you. She doesn't like you. I reckon you're lucky she's banged up."

Patsy shrugged. "I know I am. So is the rest of the population. What was she asking questions about? What questions could wind you up enough to hit someone you wanted help from?"

"Next name." Kate demanded.

Patsy made a note and went back to the list. "Nancy Bailey."

Kate shook her head, her brow furrowed and she studied the desk trying to place the name. "Never heard of her. Who is she? One of Darren's mistakes?"

"No, but she may be connected. She's been arrested for murder, the police were investigating that, and it seems it could be linked with Darren in some way. Are you sure you don't know her?"

"No." Kate's response was genuine and she shook her head. "Who did she kill? Anyone I know?"

"Phillip Cowell, a policeman, Wendy Turnball, a coroner, and her nephew Gary."

"What a girl. But no, I don't know her"

"Well, if anything springs to mind, let Angel know when she calls."

"Will do, but I'm good with names. I'd know. Who's next?"

"Debbie Charles." It was the last name on the list, and Patsy closed her notebook.

"No." Kate shook her head and crossed her arms across her chest.

"Are you sure? I think it's a certainty that she had an affair with Darren."

"Good for her. I don't know her."

"This could be tied to her too," Patsy persisted.

"I said NO!" Kate closed her eyes and gave an exasperated huff. "He didn't fucking introduce us, you know. Next name."

Patsy watched Kate pull air in through her nose as she reined in her temper. She felt sorry for the woman; she knew how it felt to be betrayed, and although she couldn't understand why some women felt the need to stick around for more, she understood her pain. She gave a shrug.

"That's it for now, unless you can come up with some reason why a search for Darren would set off this string of events."

Kate pondered this for a moment. "Perhaps he is dead. Perhaps they killed him, and they don't want people looking." She raised her hands in surrender. "That's all I've got."

Rawlings shook his head. "I don't think so. You don't warn a copper off in that way, not if you know where the body is buried. Well, you don't if you have any sense." Rawlings stood and tapped on the door. He frowned when it didn't open straight away. He knocked louder and listened. The sound of the squeaking shoes got louder, and a key turned in the lock.

"Sorry, short-staffed, I'm looking after three of you. Have you finished with her?"

"We have, but can we have a word before we leave?"

The warder nodded. "Come on then, Kate, let's get you back."

Kate stood and walked through to the corridor. She grasped Patsy's arm as she walked past. "I don't give a damn about finding him any more. That job's over. I'll still pay your daily rate though, just keep her safe until this lot find out what's going on."

Patsy opened her mouth to respond.

"Promise me." Kate spun round to the prison officer who was pulling on her other arm. "One minute, please!"

"I'll try. That's the best I can do."

Patsy watched as the prison officer handed Kate over to a colleague at the other end of the corridor, before hurrying back to them. She whispered to Rawlings who nodded agreement.

"What did you want to know?" The prison officer leaned against the wall and yawned into her hand. "Excuse me, I'm knackered. I'm on a double shift, I've still got four hours to go."

"Must be hard being short-staffed in here," Patsy commiserated. "I don't want to add to your burden but is there any chance we can have a brief meeting with another inmate?"

"I'd have to check with the Governor. It's no skin off my nose, but he'll want to know who and why." The prison officer smiled, "He's anal like that."

Patsy joined in her laughter.

"Sorry, mind racing. Kate Wilkinson implied that Jennings may be able to help in tracking down the person that can help locate our missing officer. As we're here it seems silly to waste time."

The prison officer pushed herself off the wall. "Well, that's as good a reason as you can get. I'll go and make the call. Take a seat."

While they waited Patsy and Rawlings came up with a plan of action. Patsy refilled the cups with water, and paused as she returned to the table, her head inclined.

"She's coming back, I can hear her shoes." She put the cups down and held up crossed fingers. She allowed her hands to fall as Tanya appeared in the doorway.

Rawlings jumped to his feet and held out his hand. He hoped his shock at her appearance wasn't obvious. "Tanya, how are you. I mean, I know it's shit in here, but are you coping okay?"

Tanya smiled at him and shook his hand. "I'm fine thanks, Dave. I can't believe that idiot Seaton made sergeant, give him my congrats." She looked over Rawlings' shoulder at Patsy. "Hodge, we meet again." She stepped further into the room and the prison officer closed the door. They all listened to the click as it was locked. Tanya turned her head and glanced at the handle. "I'm not convinced that would be okay with the health and safety freaks. What if there's a fire?"

Patsy opened her mouth to respond, but thought better of it. She took a seat next to Rawlings, aware that Tanya was watching her. She didn't look up, but opened her notebook to a blank page.

Tanya pulled out a chair and sat away from the table. "So tell me how you," she pointed at Patsy, "get to come in here with him," she nodded towards Rawlings, "a serving police officer on a Sunday morning?" She coughed and amusement danced around her eyes. "I was going to ask the Governor, but then he might have cancelled, and I would have missed out on my entertainment for the day."

As planned, Patsy didn't respond and Dave Rawlings spoke quickly in her place. "Not to beat about the bush, Tanya, the job you put Patsy up for has overlapped with one of the cases we're working on. It seems like Kate Wilkinson's old man has been very naughty. Wilkinson wanted to speak to Patsy for her own reasons. I joined in because it was easier than arranging a brief and the rest."

"I like you, Dave, I always have, and while my mind is racing with how I can possibly help on either case, what makes you think I would, even if I could?"

"Because someone is holding Jo Adler." Rawlings watched the frown develop on her forehead. "She's been locked up in a cellar for over a week. The person who took her is in custody. Told us up front that they did it, and they are now blackmailing us into working on something else on the promise that they will give her to us when we've solved the crime they believe was committed."

Rawlings leaned forward and rubbed his hands over his face wearily, allowing Tanya time to consider this. "The whole team have been working around the clock. Everything keeps coming back to Darren Wilkinson. I'm guessing you don't want him found, if Kate gets to do more time. But it's becoming more and more obvious that without him we're unlikely to get Jo back alive."

"Why are you here and not Meredith? Didn't he want to be with her?" Tanya nodded towards Patsy but didn't look at her.

Rawlings snorted. "I doubt it, but he's in hospital. We've been asking the wrong questions it seems. Punctured lung. In fact, I would be as bold as to say, if it wasn't for me, he might not be here."

Tanya nodded acceptance as she looked sideways at Patsy. "Okay that brings me up to speed. Jo's a good girl, I'll help if I can, but I'm buggered if I know how."

Rawlings leaned forward as though sharing a secret. "When we met with Kate she implied she'd broken your nose because you were nosey."

Instinctively, Tanya moved her hand towards her nose, but controlled the impulse and scratched her neck instead. "And that helps you how?"

"She wouldn't say what you were asking that wound her up. We pressed but she ignored us until we changed the subject. It seemed odd, very odd in fact. It may have some relevance."

"It was nothing." Tanya had relaxed and held her hands up. "She was playing the big 'I am', and I was giving some back. I thought I was being subtle, but I never did do subtle well."

Rawlings and Tanya laughed at the shared memories, and Patsy smiled her acceptance.

"What were you saying?"

Tanya drew her chair to the table and rested her chin on her hands. She gave a shrug.

"Seriously, Dave, this is a waste of time. I'm glad to be out of the block, and to see you of course, but I don't think it will help."

Rawlings pulled a pen from his breast pocket, and held it poised above his notebook. "Try me."

"Wilkinson is a face of sorts in here. On a scale of one to ten, she hovers around the seven mark." Tanya laughed. "Me, I'm minus six. Anyway, she showed off the first couple of days I was in, with the usual stuff about pigs, coppers, bent coppers, you know the drill. I ignored her, but I asked some of the women who are probably far too innocent to be in here and found out who she was, and what she was in for. Thought it best to know what I was up against. I kept my distance for over a month. Then one day she appears at my cell door and says she wants a word. I invited her in."

Tanya paused and smiled and shook her head.

Rawlings copied her. "What?"

"The thought of Meredith's reaction sprang to mind. The knowing look, the innuendo that would follow, it's so weird what you come to miss." She looked at Patsy. "Do you miss him?"

"Not often, no. Sometimes, maybe." Patsy looked away, pretending to be embarrassed.

Tanya nodded but for once didn't sneer.

Rawlings wanted to get on so he tapped his notebook. "Much as I'd like to join in, Meredith doesn't do it for me, so please can we get back to the matter in hand."

Tanya threw her head back and laughed. "Of course. She came in, sat on the bed and asked who I would recommend to find a missing person. I'll cut a long story short, because at first I thought she was having me on. When I realised she was serious I knew if I played along I would have something on her. So I did.

"She told me the story I told Hodge when she came to see me. The copper in me kicked in, and I started asking questions. You know, when did you last see him, what did you row about, why did he leave you. As I said, not subtle. She answered some of it, of course, but one question bought me my broken nose." This time Tanya allowed herself to rub her finger up and down the lump.

"And that question was?"

"It must have been someone special for him to walk away and not come back, especially if he had been playing away for years. She looked at me and shook her head. I asked what that meant, and she said something like, 'It was me, you silly bitch, not her', and without warning I gained a broken nose." Tanya shrugged, "I managed to avoid her for a few days, and then she cornered me in the television room with two of her friends. It was then I told her I knew someone who would be able to help." Tanya smirked. "But it seems like that was a mistake as you haven't managed to find him."

"That was it?" Patsy addressed her directly for the first time. "You stated the obvious and she punched you?"

"Yep." Tanya looked back to Rawlings who shrugged at her.

"Some people don't like the truth, they prefer to live with their own version of it." He looked at his watch. "Well, seems like we're done here."

He stood and tapped the door. It opened within seconds. Tanya stood and walked towards it, but at the last minute she turned and hugged him. The show of affection took him by surprise and he froze for a moment, before patting her on the back.

"Bye, Jennings. I hope you get a smooth ride."

"Thanks, Dave, don't forget to congratulate Tom for me." She turned to Patsy. "Bye, Hodge, till the next time."

Patsy nodded, and as Tanya was handed over, she turned to Rawlings. "Next time. She's got to be joking." She patted him on the shoulder. "You got her talking, I knew you would. Fat lot of use it was, but it was worth a try. Come on, I need some fresh air."

They collected their things and walked quickly to the car park. Patsy took a packet of cigarettes from her bag and lit one, and leaning against the car she blew a plume of smoke into the air.

"That will kill you, you know." Rawlings shook his head in disapproval.

"I know, it's not many, but they seem to help me deal with traumas like seeing Jennings, or dealing with Meredith on occasion."

"Blimey, if that's the secret I'll start now." Rawlings laughed and climbed into the car.

Patsy flicked her cigarette away unfinished and followed him.

"You made me feel guilty. Better check my phone." She had one missed call from a number she didn't recognise. The caller had left a message. She dialled the message service as Rawlings pulled out of the carpark. Her eyes widened as she listened to it, and she clicked her fingers to get Rawlings' attention even though he had no idea what she was listening to. The message finished and she hung up. She pointed the phone at Rawlings.

"Home, James, and don't spare the horses. I can't wait to see Meredith's face when he hears this."

* * *

Meredith and Jacobs were arguing about the year that Lionel Richie had released 'Hello' as Amanda burst back into the house. She was calling for Meredith as she opened the front door. She left the door ajar and rushed into the sitting room.

"Dad, where are you? You will never guess! Oh my God. It just . . ."

Meredith's heart jumped into his mouth, and he grunted as he heaved himself up off the couch.

"What? What's happened, are you all right?" He looked past her as her three chaperones ambled in behind her looking bemused.

"Tell me you love me, and I'll make your day," Amanda demanded, grinning from ear to ear.

* * *

Jo looked at Bobby who was sitting in his favourite spot on the back of the chair.

"And . . ." she coaxed.

"And breathe, and breathe." Bobby responded to the prompt and Jo clapped her hands.

"Good Bobby." She blew him a kiss as she selected the exercise DVD. "Do you know, Bobby, I've never been in such good shape. Shall we?" The disc slid in and the small television came to life.

"Good Bobby, good Bobby." The bird cocked his head from side to side, as though pleased with his own achievement.

"Ha ha, you are a good Bobby. We'll work on a new phrase for you after this." She fast forwarded to the beginning of the exercise sets. Much as she appreciated Veronica Vickers for removing the excess flesh from her body, her voice still grated.

Exercise complete, Jo followed the usual pattern of washing her underwear as she showered. As she rinsed the suds from her body she wondered if she would be able to keep up the exercising once she was free. It certainly got easier the more she did. She sniffed and admitted that there was no way she could exercise for three hours a day with her normal schedule. The realisation that she may never get back to normal swept through her, and her body admitted a shuddering sob, catching her unawares. Leaning against the cold tiles she took deep breaths, knowing that if she gave in to morose thoughts she may never escape them.

Stepping out of the shower, she wrapped herself in a towel and considered the contents of her larder. She decided to attempt a bolognaise sauce from the tinned mincemeat and chopped tomatoes with herbs. She had taken to eating her largest meal at lunchtime; that way, if the portion was too big she could eat the remains for supper. She still wasn't convinced that the food wouldn't eventually run out. Her nose wrinkled at the thought of the meat, but she shrugged knowing it had to be used at some stage. She peered into the mirror and fluffed up her damp hair.

"Bobby, we must not let ourselves go. Today I will dress for lunch. No tee-shirt over knickers today. Today we'll go mad and it will be shirt over jogging trousers. What do you think?"

Bobby ignored her and continued preening. Having dressed, she lifted the two tins from the shelf and opened them. The mince slid from the tin in one solid mass and stood wobbling in the saucepan. Jo gagged.

"Do people eat this shit? It looks like dog food." Adding the tin of tomatoes, she stirred it quickly, holding the saucepan as far away from her body as possible and trying not to sniff, as she was convinced it would also smell like dog food. She placed it on the ring of the hob and stirred it slowly until it bubbled gently. Cautiously she lifted the spoon to her lips and touched it with her tongue. Her eyebrows rose, and she took a mouthful.

"Mmm, do you know, Bobby, I have a new task now. When I've managed to boil the spaghetti and then reheat this, and then mix the two together, I'm going to start writing a cookbook. I can see it on the shelves in supermarkets now. *Meals for One in Extreme Circumstances*." She waved her hand across the front of her face as she envisioned the display. "Or, what about, *One Saucepan and One Cooking Ring? Don't Panic!*" She smiled as completed preparing her lunch.

Meal over, she placed a plate over the remains in the saucepan ready to reheat later, and rinsed her plate.

"That was damn good, Bobby. Now what's next, do I start my cookery book, finish reading *To Sir With Love*, or entertain Richard Gere for the afternoon?"

* * *

Meredith beckoned Jacobs. "Come on, move it, if she's right, we're off. I can't leave you here."

Jacobs pushed himself out of the chair, and in slippered feet walked stiffly and slowly towards the door.

"Are you serious?" Tristan ducked back under the doorframe into the hall.

Meredith stopped and looked at him. "Yes, I'm fucking serious. Have you got a problem with that?" He shook his head at Amanda, indicating she had filled his house with imbeciles. "What are you driving?"

"I've got a Corsa and Tim has a 106."

"You're kidding, right. Two of the biggest blokes I know have two of the smallest cars known to man." Meredith shook his head at Jacobs who grinned.

"We are students, sir. Needs must and all that."

"Well, my needs must is driving in a real car." Meredith picked up his car keys from the table, and threw them to Tristan. "You can drive me, Amanda and him," he jerked his head at Ben, "and you two can follow in which ever dinky toy you choose. Come on, follow us, close the door behind you."

The instruction had indicated urgency, but it took a good five minutes for Meredith and Jacobs to get to, and then into, the car. Tim sat at the wheel of the 106, drumming his fingers on the steering wheel. He watched enviously as Tristan started the engine of the BMW, and then followed him as he pulled off the drive.

Amanda gave Tristan directions, and a short while later she pointed up at the house.

"Where are the shutters?" Meredith bit back a groan as he levered himself from the car.

"Around the back on the ground floor windows, there's no need of them on the front. Frankie says -"

"Don't start with the 'Frankie this and Frankie that' thing again, let's get in there and get her."

"Don't hold out too much hope, Dad. I'm convinced but still, you know." Amanda was beginning to doubt herself, and worried eyes looked at her father.

Meredith shook the bunch of keys at her. "We'll soon find out."

Jacobs stood wincing at the bottom of the stone steps leading to the front door as Meredith gave instructions to the three strapping lads in front of him.

"If this key opens this door, this is what you do. You," he pointed to Tim, "run in and take the rooms to the right, and you," it was Kevin's turn, "run up the stairs and throw open each door and check they're empty. You," he said to Tristan, "can come with me."

"Should you not have called for back-up, Dad? Are they going to be safe?"

"I know there's no one in here. I'm convinced, otherwise they wouldn't have bothered with the timers you mentioned, and Nancy was detailed about the provisions. It's just a precaution. Unless these three think they're not up to it, if so I'll call it in and we can wait."

"No, no. Of course we are." Tim led the protest.

Meredith looked at them and smiled. The demeanour of the three young men had changed totally. Gone were the amiable smiles, and courteous gestures. Their faces were set, Tristan actually snarled, and they were swaying slightly. Meredith was glad they were on his side. Jacobs laughed as he slowly climbed the steps to join them. Meredith still knew how to throw down a dare that couldn't be refused. Meredith turned to watch his progress, shaking his head.

"And you two can stay here until we get the all clear. Look after her, Jacobs."

Amanda and Jacobs rolled their eyes in unison. Both knew if anything happened it would probably be the other way around.

Meredith closed his eyes and prayed silently as he slid the key into the bottom lock and turned it. A grin appeared and he opened his eyes when he heard the rewarding click as the levers pulled back the bolt. He pulled

Pulling her phone from her bag, she dialled Meredith. She was thrown when a female voice answered. "Amanda? Is that you?"

"No, it's me."

"Me who? Oh my God. It's not. Dave, guess who it is? Jo, is that really you? Where are you? What's happened?"

Rawlings stepped forward and took the phone from her hand. He repeated much the same questions. Jo confirmed that she was fine and she handed the phone back to Meredith. Meredith updated Rawlings and asked him to tell the rest of the team, whilst he called the Superintendent.

"And, Rawlings, you make sure no one, and I mean no one, tells Nancy. If Jane Roscoe is about don't tell her either, she could let it slip."

"Understood, I'd have thought you'd want to rub her nose in it though."

"Jo would like to do that herself. She'll be in during the morning."

"Ha! Good girl. When do you think you'll get back here? I'll wait with Patsy."

"Bring her round to Jo's, I'm sure she'd like to see you for five minutes. I've decided the debriefing can wait until tomorrow. Adler has some catching up to do."

"Grab your bag. We're off to see Jo," Rawlings told Patsy as he reopened the front door.

The pair agreed that it would be a hug, a few good wishes, and away. They wouldn't let Meredith start the debriefing, as they agreed that tomorrow would be soon enough. Patsy stopped speaking mid-sentence and turned to face Rawlings.

"Are we being followed? You've stopped listening and you are more interested in what's behind than in front."

"I think so, yes. Don't look."

Patsy held her head in the same position and strained to see out the rear window. She couldn't so she slumped down in her chair and focused on the wing mirror.

"Which one?"

"Blue hatchback two cars back. Shit, we're nearly at Jo's, but now I don't want to take him there. Let's test him a little, shall we?"

The next set of traffic lights were red. Rawlings sat waiting at the head of the queue and indicated right. He saw the blue car follow suit. The lights changed to green, and the car followed them around the corner. There was now only one car between them. Rawlings watched as it dropped back.

"I'm going to pull over at the newsagent around the corner. Reach your hand under the seat and pull out the baton," Rawlings instructed.

"You're not going to take them on? You don't know who it is. Look what happened to Meredith. Just drive to the station."

"I'm not going to take them on. I want to make sure they also pull over. That's only for protection if they do start any nonsense."

Rawlings pulled up in front of the shop. He took the baton from Patsy, slipped his hand through the loop, and held the shaft against his forearm.

"They're slowing down. I'll be two minutes, watch what they do."

He hurried into the shop and Patsy watched the blue car drive past and pull into the kerb several cars ahead. Rawlings returned moments later.

"I saw them when I came out." He confirmed as he fastened his seatbelt. "Let's see if the final test works." He drove away past the blue car, and as he reached the next turning the car pulled out behind him. "Gotcha. Right let's get some help."

Rawlings called the station and spoke to the duty sergeant and an armed response was agreed. He was directed to a small industrial estate where one car was already waiting. When it was confirmed that the second car was behind, Rawlings turned into a dead end, and parked in front of the furthest unit. Patsy caught sight of a familiar face in a grey saloon car parked in front of the adjacent unit.

"That's them," she confirmed. "I've seen him at the station."

Patsy turned and watched the blue car pull in halfway up the road in front of a printer's unit. Nothing happened for a minute or so and Patsy grunted with frustration.

"Come on, come on," she encouraged.

Rawlings pulled the handle to open the door. He let it go as the grey saloon next to them screeched away, siren blaring and blue lights in its grill flashing. At the same time a marked police car, followed by Trump's car, blocked the top of the street. The grey saloon pulled across the rear of the hatchback to block its means of escape. Two officers in body armour jumped out, and positioned themselves at the far side of the saloon. Elbows resting on the roof, they pointed their weapons at the blue hatchback.

"Armed police. Get out of the car and lie on the floor," yelled the taller of the two officers, and the two occupants didn't have to be asked twice. The front doors opened simultaneously and they lay, spread-eagled, on the ground. Rawlings climbed out of his car and ran towards them. He waved acknowledgment to Trump and two uniformed officers running from the cars at the top of the street.

Patsy walked quickly over to the two men, who were now handcuffed and leaning against their own car whilst being searched.

Rawlings walked to the opposite side. "Mr Ingles, I believe." He smiled as Ingles snarled at him. Patsy had caught up, and Rawlings turned to her. "That's why we couldn't find Ingles. He's been with us all the time. Don't know the other bloke, though."

Patsy instantly recognised Alex Walters and identified him as such. He looked pale and terrified, but it didn't stop him spitting in her direction.

Puzzled, Rawlings turned to her. "Who?"

"Alex Walters. He worked for Reynolds Relocation, and was siphoning off clients for another business, New Beginnings. What I don't know, is what he is doing with Ingles, and why they are following us."

The two men were cautioned but refused to speak. They were handed over to the uniformed officers, and Trump followed them back to the station.

Patsy and Rawlings continued their journey to see Jo. They were surprised to find Amanda and three strapping lads sitting on the wall outside Jo's house. The door opened as they approached it, and Ben Jacobs emerged. He held it for them.

"Call of nature," he said as he went to join the others.

There were hugs and more tears when Patsy and Rawlings entered the room. Patsy commented on how good Jo looked, despite the now red nose from crying, and the ordeal she had suffered.

"Best shape ever I think, and all thanks to Nancy Bailey and Veronica Vickers." Jo laughed at their surprised expressions.

Meredith took this as his cue, and agreed to meet Jo at the station the next day. Aaron wasn't best impressed, but when it was explained it was now or tomorrow, he shrugged his agreement.

Rawlings left Patsy with Meredith and the others, and went back to the station to assist in interviewing those they had arrested. Once home Patsy updated Meredith with her news, and Meredith explained his plan of action to her and Jacobs as Amanda and the lads made sandwiches.

"One thing I didn't get, was how did Amanda know where Jo was being held?" Patsy asked.

"Ah, well, that's where she's clever like her dad." Meredith raised his eyebrows. "She's obviously been listening to what's been going on, and had picked up bits and pieces of the description of the house. On the way back from the gym, one of those monsters out there asked the others to keep an eye out for a flat or house share for next year. Amanda was telling him about Frankie's friends living over in Brislington, when the penny dropped. If the house was unoccupied, which they thought it was, and it had belonged to Wendy Turnball, what if Nancy still had access to it? In the event, Nancy actually owned it because Wendy left it to her, but Amanda didn't know that." Meredith rubbed his nose. "I'd have got there myself, of course, but as I say, clever girl."

* * *

Meredith's phone rang as they climbed into bed. He listened for a while, agreed with what was being said, and hung up. Grunting he pulled Patsy up against him.

"Your mate Alex Walters has just caved in. Mitchell Edwards doesn't like you. New Beginnings is his baby, and you catching Walters out irritated him as he's running in the next by-election. He wanted to be seen as a proper businessman, and didn't want you dragging him into court. Alex was promised he would keep his knee caps if he kept you from causing more trouble. He's been following you since you exposed him."

"Okay, so that's the connection with Ingles and Co., but what has it got to do with Darren Wilkinson?" Patsy arched her back as Meredith blew on her neck.

"He claims not to know. Apparently when you turned up in the pub asking questions Edwards went ballistic. It was Walters that passed on the message to the two thugs to deal with me and Ben." He pulled her closer. "Top brass are now very interested in what's going on. The lads think that spooks are involved. A judge is signing a search warrant for Edwards' property as we speak. They'll serve it and arrest him early tomorrow."

"But -"

"Hodge."

"What?"

"Shut up, I'm knackered. It's been a long week."

16

Patsy was pleased to see Angel Wilkinson sitting next to Linda when she arrived at the office the next day. Sharon had thought she would be safer where they could see her. Linda was giving her a crash course in something technical. They made tea and Patsy indicated she needed a word in private. Chris and Sharon followed her through to her office. She gave them an abridged update on the events of the previous day.

"So nearly all wrapped up." Sharon smiled, "And a happy ending to boot."

"Not quite. They still have to find Wilkinson. They've searched all the addresses thrown up by the tracker, but they were no use."

"I'm sure they'll get him, especially if they now have Edwards in custody. Right, if that's all, I'll pop out and get my nails done." Sharon inspected her nails and shook her head.

"Good idea. Off you go, light of my life, and bring back some naughty cakes. We're allowed them today," smiled Chris.

Sharon blew him a kiss and went in search of her handbag.

"What?" Patsy asked, her eyes narrowing.

"What do you mean, 'what'?" A smile emerged and Chris winked.

"No sarcasm about the cost, or being on company time? Sharon is sent away to spend money with your blessing. Are you feeling all right, or, as I said, *what*?"

Chris pulled a sheet of paper from his back pocket and handed it to Patsy. It was a list of addresses. "The van was very busy last night. It visited the second address down here twice, the second time for some hours. I haven't given this to the police yet."

Patsy grinned at him. "You miss it so much, don't you? Am I to take it we're going to have a look at these before you hand them over? If so, let's get going before anyone calls. That way we don't have to lie."

Chris nodded and the two walked casually out of the office and to the door.

"Hang on a minute, where are you two going?" Linda called. "Is she allowed out without a chaperone?"

"What am I, the invisible man?" Chris sounded wounded. "Apart from anything else all the baddies are locked up now. We're off to see a client."

"Oh okay. But next time put it in the diary!" Linda scolded and turned her attention back to Angel. "It's like having kids," they heard her explain as the door closed behind them. Linda nodded at the screen. "Now you give it a go. We should get this finished by the time Frankie gets here. You'll like Frankie."

Angel nodded, and her smile faded.

"Oh me and my big mouth. I'm sorry, Angel, but at least you're forewarned if it is your dad's DNA. It will be easier to deal with if it turns out to be him."

"I know," Angel said quietly. She cleared her throat.

~ ~ ~

A ripple of applause went up as Jo walked into the incident room. She looked healthy and happy as she thanked them for the 'Welcome Home' balloons tied to the back of her seat. She had also retained her sense of humour, and laughed as Seaton placed a huge pile of files on her desk, and told her she had some catching up to do.

Once everyone was up to speed with the events of the day before, and given what details had emerged on the raid at Mitchell Edwards' house, Meredith took her to his office. Jo gave an identical account on how she ended up in the cellar to the one that Nancy had provided on the night she was arrested. Meredith was pleased to note that she asked as many questions about Debbie Charles as he did about her ordeal.

Seaton interrupted them. "Roscoe's with her now, Gov. Any time you're ready." He turned to Jo. "Are you sure about this?"

"Never been more so, Tom," Jo grinned. "It's called getting back on the horse."

Meredith tapped on the door and opened it a little. He smiled at Nancy whose eyes widened at the state his face was in. He asked Jane Roscoe for a quick word, and she joined him in the corridor.

"Meredith, I heard you'd had some trouble. Should you be here?" Jane Roscoe squinted at the various cuts and bruises on his face.

"Had to be, Jane, I wouldn't have missed this for the world."

"Why, what's happened?"

Meredith nodded behind her and she turned as Jo Adler walked out of the adjacent room.

"Da daaa. Look what I found."

"Oh I see," Roscoe said seriously, and added with a smile, "glad you're back safe DC Adler, it's nice to see you."

"I didn't want to give you as big a shock as I give her. I'd appreciate your discretion for a few minutes."

"We'll see. Are we going back in?"

Meredith nodded, and Jane Roscoe walked back into the room. Meredith followed leaving Jo in the corridor.

"Morning, Nancy, apologies for the appearance but someone out there didn't like me."

"Mr Meredith, I can't believe someone did that to you. I was told you were in hospital with a punctured lung." Nancy leaned forward and examined his face more closely. "That's going to scar," she advised pointing to the cut above his eyebrow. "I reckon they should have stitched that."

"I was, but enough about me, Nancy, we have a lot to get through today, and I've got some people I want you to meet." Meredith put his file on the table and hit the record button. Once the formalities were out of the way he smiled at Nancy. "I hear you missed me, and that you wouldn't cooperate when I wasn't here. I'm back now. So, will you tell me where Jo is?"

He watched Nancy shake her head repeatedly.

"I can't, you know that. If you get Jo back you'll stop looking. I know she's all right, I can feel it."

"Okay, so tell me why asking questions about Darren Wilkinson earned me a good hiding."

Again, Nancy shook her head. "I don't know, did he do it?" she glanced at Roscoe for confirmation. "It seems like he could have, don't you think?"

"What do you think, Nancy? You knew him."

Nancy's head snapped back round to Meredith. "I didn't. I told you I didn't meet Debbie's men friends."

"I think you met this one. Come on, Nancy, you chose me because I was good at my job. You may as well tell me." Meredith held her gaze. Her expression didn't change but he caught the tremor in her chin. "Let's wrap this up now, Nancy."

"I have no idea what you're talking about." Nancy tore her eyes away and shook her head at Jane Roscoe. "I think today may be a waste of time."

Meredith opened the file and Nancy looked down at it. A blank sheet of paper hid the contents.

"You are sure you never met Darren Wilkinson? Maybe you spoke to him on the phone, or wrote to him?" His fingers stroked the blank paper as spoke.

"What have you got there?" Nancy demanded avoiding the questions. A deep line creased her brow.

"I have proof that he knew you."

Nancy's hands jerked and she grasped them together and held them in her lap. "Don't be ridiculous." Her voice had lost its confidence.

"You won't tell me?"

"There's nothing to tell."

"Okay, let's see if someone else can get through to you. Despite your promises, you don't seem too willing to help me."

Nancy shrugged, and Meredith used the table to help him stand. His damaged ribs reminded him of his condition each time he moved. He opened the door and looked around the frame into the corridor.

"There you are. Would you come in please?"

Jo walked into the interview room as though she had never been away. She ignored the gasp from Nancy, and pulled Meredith's file in front of her as she sat. She looked up into Nancy's confused face.

"Nancy, you are aware that we have charged you with the murder of three people, and the kidnapping of one, namely me."

Nancy nodded.

"You will also be aware that now my holding place has been discovered, the floor will be lifted and we will search for, and probably find, the remains of Gary Charles. Thanks for that, by the way."

Again, Nancy nodded.

"Good. Then you will know we have no more reason to find Darren Wilkinson, even though he is a prime suspect in this case. We can lock you up, throw away the key, and leave Debbie's death as an open verdict, but probable suicide.

"How's Bobby, how are you?"

"Answer the question and I'll tell you."

"Why do you think I know him? Mr Meredith wouldn't tell me, but I know it's something in there."

Nancy made to point at the file, but with a sudden movement tried to grab it instead. Jo snatched it away, and replaced it when Nancy settled back in her seat.

"Nancy, stop messing about. DCI Meredith is prepared to continue. Dr Callaghan is waiting to see you, but if you won't cooperate we'll just close the file, and send Dr Callaghan home." Jo closed the file and rested her hands on it.

"How did they find you?"

"You go first, Nancy, this is a give and take relationship, remember? You've been doing all the taking, it's your turn to give."

"Don't bother Jo, I feel like death warmed up, and I can't be bothered with any more of this shit. Come on, you have a husband to get home to."

Meredith winced as he pushed himself up. Jo took his elbow to assist him as she too stood. Meredith nodded at the recorder, and Jo announced that the interview was terminated before following Meredith out of the room without further reference to Nancy. Out in the corridor Meredith grabbed Jo's face and kissed her on the cheek.

"You played a blinder there. You get the coffee, I'll meet you in room three."

"Nothing changes." Jo laughed as Meredith placed his hands on various parts of his body, and pulled faces to indicate the seriousness of his injuries. She hadn't turned away when the door reopened.

"Nancy would like to speak to you both."

Meredith winked at Jane Roscoe and the interview recommenced.

"I did know him. Briefly, but I knew him. As a laugh, Debbie and I placed adverts in the lonely-hearts column. He responded to both."

Jo opened the file and removed the blank sheet. She turned the plastic wallet containing the two newspaper clippings round to face Nancy.

Nancy nodded. "Yes. I found out quite by chance he was seeing both of us when I saw him dropping her off one evening. The thing that really grated was that I was going there to tell her how wonderful he was." Nancy sniffed and rummaged in her pocket for a mangled tissue. She dabbed her nose. "I had only arrived a few seconds before and was on the other side of the road. When he had gone, I went in to see Debbie. She told me she'd been on a date with a very promising man." Nancy looked down at her hands. "I'd been with him the night before."

"When you say *been* . . ." Jo's question was cut dead.

"Yes. Let's not spell it out. I liked him, and I wasn't getting any younger. Why wait? I had arranged to see him a few days later. When we met, I asked him all sorts of questions about himself, and other women. He told me he'd found the right one. I thought he meant me for a fleeting moment. I told him I'd seen him with my sister and that it had to stop. He was shocked and said that the woman he was keen on wasn't either of us, and he wouldn't be seeing us again. He pretended he knew that was wrong. When he went to the loo, I checked his wallet and got his address from his driving licence."

Nancy closed her eyes and covered her face with her hands. When she looked up her voice trembled.

"Despite knowing what I knew, I still slept with him before he went. Can you believe that? I knew he was seeing my sister, and that he had found another woman who was the one, and still I slept with him." She looked at Meredith. "Women are stupid, men are pigs."

Meredith nodded agreement.

"What happened after that?" His voice was gentle and his agreement genuine. He knew that not too long ago, he would have done the same in Wilkinson's position.

"I got up the next morning and felt cheap. I decided not to see him again." She looked at Meredith, checking his reaction. "No, he didn't call, but I had decided anyway. I went and told Debbie, we agreed he was a bastard, and she would give him a flea in his ear if he made contact."

Nancy sighed and looked somewhere in the distance above Jo's head. They left her for a few moments, before Jo coughed. Nancy nodded.

"A few weeks later Debbie started acting strangely. When I questioned her about it, she told me she had two men on the go, but one was going to be history, but not before she'd shown him what he was missing." Nancy frowned and inclined her head. "I did tell you that, didn't I, and that she implied one of them was married?"

"You did yes. Do you think she was going to get rid of Wilkinson?"

"No, I didn't know then that she was still seeing him. But I found this journal thing in her kitchen drawer when I was looking for a clean tea towel. It was confusing at first, obviously written in code. Took me a few visits but I broke her code. Do you know what my code name was?" She looked at Jo, her pain transparent. Jo shook her head.

"Cat," Meredith announced and Nancy smiled and blinked at him.

"You found it. I didn't get to the end of it. Too shocked to bother, I suppose. Did it give any clues, was it him, do you think?

It was Meredith's turn to shrug. "Possibly. You thought it was him, didn't you?" Meredith held his hands up. "Why didn't you tell me that? Why all this nonsense?"

"I thought it was possible, but I believe they were genuinely in love," she snorted, "whatever that means. So it could have been the chap she was getting rid of?"

"And you promise me you don't know who that was?"

Meredith sighed as Nancy shook her head.

"Where was Wilkinson living at the time? It may be we haven't checked it out yet?" Meredith smiled kindly as Nancy struggled to maintain her composure.

"Sandyleaze. I remember because my friend lived there too."

Meredith nodded. That was the address that Kate Wilkinson had torched.

"Thank you, Nancy. Is there anything else you can tell us that may help?" He nodded as Nancy shook her head. "Okay, shall I go and get the doctor now?" Meredith nudged Jo as Nancy nodded and she left to collect Frankie. "This won't take long, Nancy," Meredith assured her as he announced Jo's departure. There was a tap at the door and Frankie's head appeared.

"May I?" Frankie stepped into the room carrying his brief case.

"Come on in, Sherlock."

Meredith announced Frankie's arrival as he shook Nancy's hand and sat in the chair recently vacated by Jo.

"Hello, Nancy, I want you to look at something for me, and let me know if you recognise it. Is that okay?"

Frankie smiled warmly, but Nancy was mentally exhausted and snapped her response.

"I'm not a child. I know you're going to show me the rope that killed my sister. Get on with it please."

"Yes indeed, well, here we go." Frankie opened his briefcase and pulled out a paper sack. From the sack, he took the length of blue rope. "This is the rope used to end your sister's life. Have you ever seen it before?"

Nancy nodded. "I have, yes. Debbie used it for a line, you know like a washing line, when she cleaned her rugs. She'd tie it between the tree and the back gate, and hang the rugs over it to dry. Does that help?"

"Sort of. It means your sister could have made the noose days in advance."

"How many bloody times do I need to tell you people? Debbie – did – not – kill – herself." Nancy folded her hands across her chest and glared at Frankie.

"I don't think she did either, but I need to provide evidence. Did you ever have occasion to use this rope?"

"No, why?"

"Would you mind if I took a tiny little sample from you to test for DNA? Some blood was found on this rope, a minute amount, but enough to get DNA from. If I am to eliminate it as coming from your sister, you can help prove that. Your DNA will be similar although not identical. When we have recovered her son . . ." Frankie stopped the sentence dead and smiled. "Do you understand what I need to prove?"

Meredith watched her closely for her response.

"Like I said, I'm not a child. There is DNA from that rope, and it may be from the murderer or from my sister." Nancy held out her arm believing he was going to take blood.

"Nothing as bad as that." Frankie drew a mouth swab out of its tube. "Open wide." He scraped the inside of Nancy's cheek and dropped the sample back into the tube and tightened the lid. "Thank you, Nancy. Meredith will let you know the results."

Frankie secured the clasps on his briefcase and left the room. As Meredith announced Frankie's departure, he knew it wasn't Nancy's DNA on the rope. He decided to bring the interview to a close, and extended his announcement. Switching off the recorder, he thanked Jane Roscoe for her time, and said his goodbyes. Hands in pockets, he walked slowly back to the incident room, pondering his options. He would normally have made straight for the fire escape for a cigarette, but he willed himself to keep walking in the other direction.

~ ~ ~

Patsy and Chris drove past the last cottage in the lane. Patsy scanned the windows for any sign of life. The bedroom curtains were closed, and the ground floor curtains were open only a few inches. The garden was neat and tidy, and a black bin stood neatly on one corner of the drive.

"Here we go." Chris slowed and turned into a pub car park a little past the cottage. "We can sit here and watch the house for a while, see what happens."

"Better make myself comfortable then. How's Jack doing?" Patsy released her seatbelt and slid down the seat, putting her feet up on the dashboard.

"He's doing really well, certainly enjoying Angel's company," Chris laughed. "Well, she's female. In all seriousness though, she's a nice kid. Surprising, seeing what she's had to put up with. I told her she can go home tomorrow, unless Meredith tells us otherwise."

"I'm sure she's enjoying it too. I need the loo. I'll pop into the pub, I won't be long."

Patsy went into the pub. It was early morning and the bar was empty apart from an elderly couple drinking coffee. A barman was wiping down the optics. She spotted the door to the toilets in the corner. As she walked back through the bar, the barman called out to her.

"You're not stopping. I take it?"

"In the car park, yes," Patsy walked to the barman. "I'll take two packets of crisps and a couple of cokes please."

Patsy realised that you didn't get to pee for free.

The barman flipped the tops of the bottles and dropped straws into them before turning to the stack of boxes behind him.

"What flavour? What are you doing out there?"

"One salted, one cheese and onion please. We're waiting for the owner of the cottage on the end to come back. We'd like to buy down here, and that location is perfect for us, especially with a pub within walking distance." She returned his smile.

"He's gone into town," the barman looked at his watch. "He caught the bus. If he's on the next one back here, he'll be ten to fifteen minutes, if not, about forty. He doesn't own the house, it's rented."

"Oh, that's a shame. I'll hang around anyway. He may be able to give us the landlord's address." Patsy paid for her purchases and picked them up. "Do you know what his name is?"

"Darren. Don't know his surname. You can come and sit in here, you know. He'll come in here first, he's picking up some lemons for me."

"Thanks, but it's a nice day, we'll wait outside."

Patsy smiled all the way back to the car. She updated Chris and they discussed their next move. They knew that what they should do was call the police and hand it over to them. But they hadn't confirmed it was Darren, and if they were wrong it would simply waste police time. They both knew that that was a feeble excuse for remaining involved, but in the event the bus was early, and they didn't have time to do anything.

Two people left the bus, the second being Darren Wilkinson. He hurried into the bar carrying two bags.

"Do you think we should go in after him? I spoke to the barman about him, he might be spooked." Patsy studied the entrance to the pub rather than look at Chris.

"No. If he tries to do a runner we can follow him. If he has transport it must be in the garage at the cottage. I'd rather speak . . . here he comes."

To their surprise, Wilkinson, now carrying only one bag, walked quickly towards their car.

Chris climbed out to meet him, and held out his hand. "Hello, are you the chap that lives in the cottage up there?" Chris looked at the house. "If so, I'd be grateful if you could put me in touch with the owner."

Wilkinson looked Chris up and down then leaned to one side to see who else was in the car. "I'm the tenant. I'm moving out next week."

"That's fortuitous. Are you going somewhere nice?"

"Yeah," Wilkinson started walking away. "Come with me, I'll get you the info. He'll be pleased, he wanted to sell it."

Chris beckoned Patsy and the two followed Wilkinson to the cottage. He took them through the hall and into the kitchen, where he deposited his bag on the table, and opened a drawer. There were two papers in it; he chose one and slid the drawer shut.

"Do you want to write this down?" He glanced at Patsy who stood in the doorway leading back into the hall. Patsy looked at the man. He was underweight for a man of his size, his shoulders were rounded, deep lines etched his forehead, and his skin was pale. He was a shadow of the man whose photograph sat in her bag.

"Not really, Darren, we just want to talk to you."

Wilkinson's eyes darted from one to the other quickly. The paper in his hand flicked back and forth as tremors of fear ran through his body. Chris watched him draw in a breath and pull his shoulders back and, convinced Wilkinson was going to make a run for it, he braced himself. They stared at each other for a few moments, and Chris started as Wilkinson threw his hands to the side.

The paper fluttered to the floor, and arms wide, Wilkinson snarled at him, "Come on then, do it. I'll not fight you, I haven't any fight left. What's it going to be, execution or staged accident. I'm guessing accident as you went into the pub."

Chris shook his head and looked confused.

"COME ON!" Wilkinson screamed. His face contorted, and his body shook with the effort. Finally spent, his arms fell back to his side, and physically and mentally exhausted, he pulled out a chair and slumped down. Folding his arms on the kitchen table, he rested his forehead on them. "Get on with it, please. I'm not going anywhere." His voice was muffled as he spoke into the small void his arms had created.

"We're here to talk about Debbie. I'm not sure who you think we are, but once we've had a chat, we're taking you to the police." Patsy walked forward and took the chair opposite him.

There were only two chairs and Chris took her place in the doorway.

Wilkinson looked up and smiled at Patsy. "The police, really? Good, because if they get me into one of those witness protection things, I'm ready to spill my guts. Where would you like me to start? With Mitchell Edwards, Maurice Ford, or are you after Brian Catchpole?" He looked at the ceiling and laughed. "You can have all three of the bastards, but I want guaranteed protection." He looked back at Patsy. "I'm guessing you can't give me that assurance, so shall we make a move?"

Patsy watched as he stood up. His smile was one of genuine relief, and Patsy saw a glimmer of the man she had expected to find.

"Do you want to get anything?" she asked quietly.

"Like what? I have nothing of value. The way I look at it is if your lot give me the protection I need, I tell you where the bodies are buried and you'll kit me out." He saw the unspoken exchange and grinned. He held up a finger. "It was only one actually, but there is more, I know who, but not where. If you don't, I'll keep my mouth shut, because either Edwards or Catchpole will do for me in the end." He sighed and stepped towards Chris. "Can we go before they get back?"

Once in the car, Wilkinson laid himself flat on the back seat. "They could be on their way. I don't want to be seen. I'm going to get the bastards one way or another."

"Did you know Angel was looking for you?" Patsy asked as Chris pulled out of the car park.

"Yes. But her mother sent her on a wild goose chase. That's why they've been moving me about."

"What do you mean?"

"Her mother doesn't want me found," he laughed. "It's Catchpole who wants me. She was using Angel. You can let her know I wasn't purposely avoiding her, can you? I'd give the world to see her again, but I have to keep her out of danger too."

Patsy and Chris exchanged glances.

"Why would Kate deliberately put her own daughter in danger? She as good as made it my job to look after her," Patsy turned and looked through the gap at Wilkinson.

"Because she's as frightened of her brother as everyone else. Family means nothing to him, not really. You only get one credit with him. We've both spent ours."

They travelled the remainder of the journey in relative silence, Patsy had telephoned ahead to let Meredith know they were on their way.

A few minutes from the station Patsy turned to Wilkinson. "I know you're saving your powder and all that, but can you tell me if all this has anything at all to do with Debbie Charles?"

"Everything. Poor Debbie." Wilkinson blinked. "We were leaving, the day after she died. Tickets bought, villa rented. She'd even found a possible buyer for the house. A new life together."

"Nancy was right, Debbie didn't kill herself. You know she's spent years trying to prove that."

"I know. Stupid bitch, if she'd kept her mouth shut none of this would have happened, none of it. People are dead because of her. Now stop asking questions. I'll say no more until my solicitor tells me I'm safe."

Patsy turned back, her lips pursed, as she watched the road ahead. It was clear that Wilkinson had no idea what Nancy had done since Debbie's death, and she wondered what she had done before it.

~ ~ ~

Trump was waiting for them with a uniformed officer as they pulled into the car park.

"How's Meredith holding up? Is he coping?" Patsy asked quietly as they walked behind the others into the station.

"He's okay. Actually, he's a little cross with you at the moment. He mentioned something about promising not to go gadding about the countryside, but apart from that all is relatively quiet. He wants a word once he's spoken to Wilkinson."

"In which case that will be soon. Wilkinson won't talk before his solicitor gives him assurances that you will put him into protection. Can you buzz me through? I'll wait for him in the canteen."

"Wilkinson has a solicitor?" Trump looked at Patsy as they waited for the doors off the main reception to open.

"I don't know, we didn't get that far before he clammed up."

"Patsy's going to meet Meredith in the canteen, Sam. Give her a badge, there's a good chap," Trump called to the duty sergeant as Wilkinson was led away. "I must dash, Patsy, catch up soon."

Patsy agreed to meet Chris back at the office, and having accepted her visitor's badge she made her way down to the canteen. She glanced at the clock as she entered. It was lunchtime and she wondered if Meredith had eaten yet. She ordered two teas and picked up a chicken salad for herself, then, scanning the menu on the chalk board, she ordered a lasagne for Meredith. The canteen was busy, and by the time she'd reached the head of the queue, paid, and found a table Meredith had arrived.

He shook his head as he walked towards her.

"You've been breaking promises again."

"I know. I would give you a million excuses, but I want an update. You can punish me later."

Meredith eyed her for a moment. "That's your punishment – I won't update you." He pulled the plate of lasagne from the tray. "Is this mine? Where are the chips?" He turned and called to the girl behind the counter. "Chips please." They arrived moments later. Meredith picked up two and put them into his mouth. "You're not going to argue?"

"No, because if you don't tell me what you know, I won't tell you what Wilkinson told me about Nancy. If you want that deal, you go first."

Meredith shovelled a forkful of lasagne into his mouth. "You don't always win, you know."

"I know, but I'll win this one, or you'll wait for hours, and hours, and hours before Wilkinson will talk."

"You're a hard woman."

"No, I'm not. Just cleverer than most." Patsy smiled and looked back at her lunch. She lifted a piece of chicken, and savoured it. "This is good. Would you like some?"

Meredith swallowed. "Tell me, Hodge. This is serious, we have spooks involved." He filled his mouth again.

"Well, you've started, you may as well finish." She watched Meredith finish his meal, occasionally picking at her own.

He placed his knife and fork on the centre of his plate. "In a nutshell, no details, I must get back." Meredith smiled as Patsy nodded agreement. "Once Alex Walters opened his mouth he told us all he knew. To be honest it wasn't that much, not enough to secure convictions, but retold carefully, first Ingles and then Green caved in believing we knew more than we did. We now have Mitchell Edwards in the frame for some very serious stuff."

He flicked his hand to one side indicating that he had said enough. "We don't get to question him, though. He's being questioned by blokes up from London. It's bigger than we thought." He shuffled around on his chair, attempting to find a more comfortable position. He raised his eyebrows as he smiled. "To be honest, that suits me just fine. Dealing with Nancy is enough for me at the moment. With you tracking down Wilkinson, we should also wrap up the Debbie Charles case." He tapped the table. "Your turn, and make it quick. I need to move, it doesn't hurt so much when I'm on the move."

"Okay," she reached across the table and stroked his hand, "but one more thing. The stuff you're picking up on Edwards, does it include murder?"

"Probably, but no direct information, just 'we heard and they said' stuff at the moment."

"Well, when you get Wilkinson talking he says he knows where the body is buried." She smiled as Meredith rubbed his hands together. "I don't have much other than that, but I don't think he killed Debbie. He said they were set up to go abroad and live somewhere. They were supposed to leave the day after she died. He seemed genuine." She shrugged and pushed her plate towards Meredith who picked up his fork and took some chicken. "What he did say, though, was that he knew enough to take down Mitchell Edwards, Maurice Ford and Brian Catchpole."

Meredith stopped chewing. "Catchpole?" he asked with his mouth full.

"Yep. His brother-in-law. I take it he's not come up yet?"

Lips pursed, Meredith shook his head slowly as his fork released more fish. "Didn't say what, I suppose?"

"No. The only other thing he said which may be of use was that Nancy was a stupid bitch and if she'd kept her mouth shut, none of it would have happened, and that people had died because of her. Do you know what that means?"

Meredith leaned back on his chair. The swelling on his lip was receding, but his smile was still lopsided. "I don't but I will. He was shagging them both."

"What, Wilkinson? Nancy and Debbie? Really?"

"Indeed. On that happy note, I have to get back. Can I trust you to behave yourself for the rest of the day?"

"Can I trust you to finish at five like you promised?"

Meredith looked at his watch. "You can if you leave me in peace now, and if the suits at the end of the corridor don't want me." He winced as he pushed himself to his feet, gently flexing his back to one side and then the other.

"I'll pick you up at five."

"I can get one of the lads to give me a lift."

Patsy held the door open for him. "I'll pick you up at five."

"Six?"

"Done."

~ ~ ~

Meredith turned at the sound of hurried heels clicking along the corridor behind him. Jane Roscoe nodded appreciation as he waited for her to catch up.

"Glad I caught you before we go in, DCI Meredith. Jo Adler is safe now, talk of the devil." They looked up as a door opened further down the corridor and Jo appeared. "Gloves off now."

"What does that mean?" Meredith inclined his head and smiled.

Jane Roscoe was grateful for his injuries, as for once he didn't make her feel naked. "You are well aware of what I mean." She walked to the interview room. "Shall we begin?"

Meredith winked at her and nodded.

Nancy smiled as they filed in, and Meredith started the recording.

"Something's happened, hasn't it? I can tell by your faces. What is it?"

Meredith studied her for a moment. The once attractive woman photographed with her sister was long gone. Deep lines made their way from her eyes and down into her cheeks. Jowls had developed on each side of her square, set chin, and her mouth sagged a little at the corners. He leaned forward carefully and placed his hands flat on the table.

"What did you do, Nancy?"

"What? What did I do when? I didn't kill her, Mr Meredith? Please don't tell me you think that, or all of this has been a waste of time."

"I don't think that, Nancy, no, but I think you know what I do mean."

Nancy's arms folded and she turned to Jane Roscoe. "Is he allowed to do this? Not ask proper questions? I don't want to play games." She turned back to Meredith before Jane Roscoe had the opportunity to speak. "Stop playing with me. I won't have it."

"You want short and sharp?" Meredith raised his hands to question that choice.

Nancy caught the edge in his voice and wondered if it was the pain, or something he knew. She nodded once and blinked. Instead of Meredith it was Jo that spoke and Nancy pulled her head back in surprise.

"You knew your sister was still seeing Darren Wilkinson, despite her promises."

"Yes, I told you that yesterday."

"You knew that they were planning to start a new life together abroad."

"I . . . I knew they were planning a holiday, yes."

Meredith pulled Debbie's journal from his jacket pocket and slammed it on the desk. Jane Roscoe's pen shot up the page of her pad and she looked up.

"You read the journal, Nancy. You told us yesterday you had decoded it. If you knew she was still seeing him, you know what they were planning." Meredith tapped the journal with his finger as he spoke. "The only thing we haven't worked out yet is where. In the journal she calls it Splendipidy or something like that. Where were they going? It doesn't matter of course, but it's another end tied up."

"Corfu." Nancy looked down at her lap.

"So you did know," Jo confirmed.

Nancy nodded into her lap.

"Then I will ask again, what did you do, Nancy?"

Slowly Nancy raised her head; the defiance had returned to her eyes. "I have no idea what you are talking about. Do you have any questions I would understand?" Her tone was sarcastic.

"How about this? Why did Darren Wilkinson say that, and I quote, 'None of this would have happened if she had kept her mouth shut. People are dead because of her.' Again, what did you do?"

"You've found Darren? How is he?"

Meredith gave a grunt as pain seared across his chest as he jumped to his feet. "Interview terminated at two-thirty, non-cooperation from witness." He hit the button on the machine. "Bye, Nancy, we'll see you in court. Jo come on, we have work to do."

Striding to the door he pulled it open and waited for Jo to exit.

"I wrote a letter." Nancy's voice was low.

Meredith stepped back into the room. "Do you want me to return? Are you going to stop wasting my time?" Meredith was already walking back to his seat as Nancy nodded. He set the recorder off again.

"What did you do?"

"I wrote a letter. I wrote to his wife."

"What did you tell her?"

"Everything, of course," Nancy raised her eyebrows and shrugged, "Why not, I had nothing to lose."

"You told her about Corfu?"

"Yes. I thought she would stop them going. I'd lost Darren and I wasn't going to lose Debbie too. If she'd gone abroad I wouldn't have even been able to visit. Not with them together, not there." Nancy's face contorted and her lip trembled as she attempted to hold back her tears. "I couldn't believe she was going there with him. It was where we used to go, after Bill left. We were both on our own, and we joked that we should sell up and go and live there. She would paint and I would write. I've always wanted to write a book." Nancy's voice trailed away as the memories flooded back.

"I take it that's how you knew he didn't do it? You knew he loved her."

Jo's voice was harsh and Nancy glanced at her, and slamming her eyes looked away.

"They hurt me. It was worse than losing my husband. Don't you judge me!"

"Why not? Why would I not judge you? You are possibly the most selfish person I know. All I've heard from you since I met you, is me, me, me, ME! People have died because of you, most at your hand. Why? Because life wasn't going the way you wanted to, and -" Jo stopped when Meredith put his hand on her arm.

Jo swallowed. "I'm sorry, Nancy, that was uncalled for. It was pure luck we found Darren Wilkinson, and even now we have him, it seems he didn't do it. I was thinking about what would have happened to me. I am as guilty as you for selfish thoughts."

Jane Roscoe laid her pen on her pad and sighed. "This is all becoming rather personal now. Do you have any relevant questions for my client? It is clear to me that you don't believe she killed Debbie Charles. We wouldn't be sat here if she knew who did, and on that basis, I think there's little more to be gained." She looked at Meredith and he gave a slight nod.

"One more question if I may?" He looked at Nancy. "Did you get any response from your letter? How long before did you send it?"

"None, I didn't give my address. I gave details of Debbie's of course. I sent it four days before she died. First class post."

"Thank you, Nancy. You'll be transferred to prison later today, pending your trial. I've already made arrangements." Meredith terminated the interview and both he and Jo stood up.

Nancy looked up. "Is Darren here? Can I see him?"

"Yes, and no, you can't see him."

"Will you come and see me again, Mr Meredith?"

The fear in Nancy's eyes caused him to pause. But he shook his head. "No, Nancy. I don't think so."

He opened the door and stepped into the corridor as Nancy's head fell on to her chest.

Jo said goodbye to Jane Roscoe and Nancy looked back up. A tear travelled down her cheek and she dabbed it with her tissue.

"I'm sorry, Jo. I would have told them."

Jo didn't believe her, but rather than argue the point she nodded.

"How's Bobby?" Nancy called as Jo pulled the door to close it.

"Dead."

Jo closed the door and grinned as she pictured Bobby sitting on top of his cage in her conservatory. He was now up to four phrases.

The Wrong Shoes

17"

The next morning Meredith was called to a meeting with the men from London. Trump dropped him off at the regional office, and he was shown into a meeting room. The Assistant Chief Constable, Keith Long, was pouring coffee at one end of a long, highly polished table.

"Ah, Meredith, good to see you. Coffee?" He held up the pot, and Meredith nodded and walked to join him.

"What's happening? I take it this has to do with Edwards."

The ACC leaned forward and inspected Meredith's face. "Indeed. I'll let them fill you in. Not sure how much they'll tell you. You know what they're like, need to know and all that. They did a good job on you. When this is over, take a break!"

"Thank you, sir, I'll take you up on that."

Meredith turned as the door opened. Three men walked in. Two were suited and the third looked like a thug they had pulled off the street.

They didn't introduce themselves when they shook hands and collected coffee. Meredith didn't ask, but he was struck by how young they were. He guessed the eldest was no more than thirty. The three men sat in different positions around the table. Meredith and Long sat in the nearest chair.

The tall, dark one loosened his tie and tapped the table. "Thank you for coming. This won't take long. DCI Meredith, I would start by commending you on a job well done. You've solved many crimes in the last week or so, the public will thank you for that."

Meredith sighed as he leaned forward. He was tired, he hurt, and he was in no mood to listen to bullshit. He raised a finger. "Much appreciated. But may I suggest we cut the crap and get straight on. I'm not as young as you lot, and I hurt. I hurt more when I'm sitting. I'm sure you're busy, and so am I. Let's get on with it, shall we?"

"Meredith!" Keith Long slapped the table. "There's absolutely no need for -"

The thug laughed and held up his hand. He was well-spoken, his gentle tone was similar to Trump's, and at total odds with his appearance.

"Don't fret, Keith. Meredith's correct, we should get on with it." He nodded at Meredith, "I like a chap that tells it how it is, saves a lot of bother." He nodded to his colleague who had clearly been amused by the exchange. Meredith caught his eye, and held it.

"So without further ado," he announced seemingly unfazed by Meredith, "you may wrap up your investigation. Proceed as you normally would, make your charges and move on to the next one. I understand that Ingles and Green have admitted their guilt. Therefore, there will be no need of a jury and the judge will sentence appropriately. I don't think they will be placed in a local jail." He nodded slightly and Meredith reciprocated, and he wondered if either of them had blinked. "The one caveat, and you're an intelligent man, I hope at least I may say that?"

He paused. Meredith saw the amusement had returned, and nodded.

"Good, the only caveat being that Mitchell Edwards' name will not arise in any of the evidence. You may throw the book at his sidekick." He clicked his fingers trying to remember the name, and the well-spoken thug did the honours.

"Maurice Ford."

"But not so much as a mention of Mr Edwards needs to be called for evidence. With regards -"

"Thank you for enlightening me on what I may do. How do we prosecute Ford without Edwards being drawn in? Ford's his puppet, he jumps when Edwards clicks his fingers," Meredith turned to the thug, "much like yourself."

He looked back as the thug sniggered.

"Every crime that Mr Ford has committed he will be tried for. He too will plead guilty and as such -"

"A friendly judge will not want to hear evidence of Edwards' involvement. What does Ford get out of this, what reward for playing your game? He can't be allowed to walk. I think we're going to be digging up bodies." Meredith leaned forward again and the ACC put his hand over his closed eyes. "If he's involved, he'll do his time."

"Oh. I totally agree. But his involvement is peripheral in the general sense. He simply made the arrangement for disposal. Mr Edwards has already admitted to the murder that Mr Wilkinson will tell you about, and Mr Ford will not return to Bristol."

Meredith frowned as he considered this. He wasn't sure if he'd just been told Big Mo would be meeting his end, or set up somewhere after a slap-on-the-wrist sentence for cooperating with whatever they had on Edwards. Shifting in his chair he decided not to ask.

"Glad to hear it. So what will Edwards be tried for?"

"Good question, and brings us to the real purpose of this meeting. When and if Mr Edwards is tried, I have no idea what the charges will be, however -"

"What do you mean, 'if'?"

Meredith drummed his fingers on the desk as he considered his words, "You've told me he's admitted to at least one murder, and I'm guessing there are likely to be more? Are you protecting him or something? Do you lot," he waved his hand around the table, "have plans for a right-wing Britain or something, because I'm sure you'll be disappointed not to get my vote."

"Ha, ha! Very good, DCI Meredith," the thug chuckled. "Quite the opposite, this is to avoid a right-wing uprising. That's all we can say." He stood to indicate the meeting was over. His colleagues followed suit. "Keep an eye on the news over the next few months. I hear tell there are going to cabinet resignations, government and shadow."

He strode to the end of the table, hand outstretched. "Keith, thank you again." He walked round to Meredith who stood and flexed his back. "Nice to meet you, Meredith, you never know our paths may cross again."

Meredith shook his hand.

"I doubt it, but if they do, don't bring him, he talks too much." Meredith nodded to the third man who had yet to speak. The man looked at him, nodded and left the room. "I hope I haven't offended him."

"Of course not." The thug put his arm around Meredith's shoulder, "The least we can do is give you a lift. The car's waiting."

Meredith was aware that this was an offer he couldn't refuse. The remaining suit opened the door and followed them out.

"What about poor old Keith, does he not get a lift?" Meredith asked, as they waited for the car. He felt decidedly ill at ease, and even the ACC would provide some comfort.

"He doesn't need one. What I have to say is for your ears only." The thug raised his eyebrows and held out a hand inviting Meredith into the lift as it opened.

They dropped Meredith off at home some thirty minutes later.

Patsy heard the door shut and walked out of the kitchen. "I thought Amanda had forgotten something, she's not long gone."

Meredith looked at her and shook his head. "What are you doing here? Are you not working today?"

"I am. I'm due in court this afternoon, I came home to change. How did it go this morning? You seem very distracted."

"Fine. I am distracted, sorry." Meredith pulled her to him and kissed her. "Did Jacobs get home okay?"

"As far as I know. Tom gave him a lift. Why are you home, anyway? I thought you were going to interview Wilkinson this afternoon?"

"I am. I wanted time to gather my thoughts without that lot buzzing around." Meredith walked to the kitchen and put the kettle on. "Do you want one?"

Patsy put her hands on her hips. "What's going on? You never come home midday, you never offer to make tea, and you certainly don't get away from your team to gather your thoughts. Are you ill? Do we need to get you back to the hospital?"

"I'm fine." Meredith smiled at her, "In fact, I've got a little more movement today." He showed her how far he could flex his back without pain and winked.

"Something happened this morning? What was said? Who were they, MI5 or MI6?"

Meredith shrugged and poured the water into the cups. "They didn't say. Not even names."

"Are you going to tell me what you talked about?"

Patsy gasped as Meredith grabbed her and pulled her to him.

"I'm not, because if I did I'd have to kill you." He kissed her. "Have you got time to see how well recovered I am, and then drop me off at the station?"

The tea began to stew as she led him upstairs.

~ ~ ~

Meredith waited until Trump had closed the door and taken a seat next to Seaton.

"This is quite simple. I'm going to give you some information and the rules on how to use that information, and you're going to accept it, act on it, and not ask any questions."

Trump and Seaton looked at each other.

"Spooks," Trump announced knowingly, and Seaton nodded.

"Don't get all dramatic, Trump, I've had to put up with one of your lot all morning." Meredith leaned forward, his face serious. "We are going to get on as we would normally do. Ask the questions, make the charges, and collect what evidence may be necessary. With anyone that pleads guilty we don't need too much as there won't be a jury."

Trump and Seaton exchanged glances.

"We will not be going after Edwards, as he's been taken care of. If anyone asks why we're not going after him, brush it aside and say Scotland Yard or something vague. Do not discuss it with anyone, and never ever question it yourselves. Clear?"

There was another exchanged glance, and the two men nodded.

"I take it you won't be drawn, sir?"

"No, Trump, I won't be drawn, and you just agreed never to question it."

"Quite. Sorry. So, what now?"

"Has Wilkinson seen his brief?"

"He's with him now, sir."

"Does he know he's going into the witness protection scheme as soon as we're done with him?"

"He does. He seems very keen to get on with it too. I was to let his solicitor know as soon as you got back, so shall I call?"

Meredith nodded and Trump made the necessary call. Replacing the receiver, he looked up at Meredith. "Has Wilkinson got money?"

"I have no idea, why?"

"He's got a top solicitor. It's a chap that was a year ahead of me at university. I hear he charges top dollar, but I thought he worked in London."

"You don't say, now that's a surprise. Which one of you two is coming in with me?"

Wilkinson's solicitor stood and introduced himself as Meredith and

Seaton entered the room.

"I was expecting you earlier. My client has made a statement giving details of everything he wishes you to know. I've had it typed up. It's concise, but I think you'll find the necessary information. I think it best that you have a read, and once you have done so, ask any questions that are relevant to your case."

He nodded at Meredith, conveying his knowledge of what subject wouldn't be broached. Meredith gave a slight nod and Seaton watched him from the corner of his eye. "I thought you'd be accompanied so I've prepared two copies." He handed each of them a three-page document. It was neatly typed, headed, and stapled in one corner. "All being well we should all be out of here shortly."

Meredith chewed his bottom lip and looked at Wilkinson. "Are you happy with this arrangement?"

Wilkinson glanced at his solicitor who nodded. Wilkinson did likewise.

"Are you going to see your daughter before you disappear off to your new life?"

"DCI Meredith, I really don't see that -" The solicitor attempted to interrupt.

"I don't really care what you see. I know the rules, I understand them, but as a previously estranged father myself, I want to be sure he knows what he's doing. I'm assuming he has a choice?"

Wilkinson frowned. "Why wouldn't I have a choice?"

The solicitor linked his fingers and shook his head at Meredith. Seaton thought he may as well have said "Look what you've done now."

Meredith set the document on the table without looking at it.

"Because once you enter this programme there's no real wiggle room for going back. Not without repercussions. Serious and possibly dangerous repercussions. I thought you would want to see Angel and ask her if she wants to go along for the ride. As I see it, neither of you has any real ties." Meredith held up his hands. "I'm not suggesting that you should, and you may already have decided not to mess her life up any more than you already have. I was frankly curious whether you'd actually considered her at all."

"I have. I didn't know I could take her with me, but she wouldn't come and who could blame her. When you read that you'll understand why. I don't know what happened between you and your kid, but I don't deserve her, and she certainly deserves better." Wilkinson dropped his head. "That's why I didn't bother asking."

Meredith considered him for a moment.

"Fair enough." He picked up the statement which Seaton was already reading. "I'd better take a butchers at this then."

Meredith tried to keep his emotions in check as he read through the statement. He knew his eyebrows rose and at one point he sighed – this more due to the fact that he couldn't question it, rather than what had been written. He knew the words weren't Wilkinson's own, and he knew significant chunks had been omitted. He placed the document back on the table, and looked up.

"You have a nice way with words, Mr Wilkinson. I almost had to get the dictionary out."

Seaton looked at the solicitor, who tried not to smirk. Meredith tapped the statement. Seaton noticed that there was no acknowledgement that the interview was not being recorded.

"If this is the truth, the whole truth and . . . I'm sure you know the rest, it would appear that Nancy Bailey's letter set off a chain of events that has left five people dead, one of my officers kidnapped, you in hiding, a home burned to the ground, me and a good friend in hospital and a child about to lose a parent, however bad, forever." His eyes burned into Wilkinson. "And all because you couldn't keep it zipped up."

Wilkinson looked duly remorseful and nodded. "You said five people dead, who? I only know of Debbie and the bloke Catchpole sent for me. The other one wasn't related to Debbie."

"Nancy knew Debbie didn't kill herself. I think she knew it was her fault, albeit indirectly, and she's killed three people in an attempt to prove it."

Wilkinson swallowed and buried his face in his hands. "Shit."

"You say you arrived home intending to pack your bags and leave for Debbie's, as the next day you were flying off to a new life. Tell me exactly what your wife said."

"She wasn't there when I got home, so I whipped upstairs and threw the essentials into a bag. I slid my passport into my back pocket and put the bag in the car. I went back into the house to say goodbye to Angel and she came home."

"'She' being your wife Kate?"

"Yes. She sniffed as I came in and started laughing. I asked her what was funny, and she said something like, 'You'll need more than that to hide the smell if you take her with you'." Wilkinson put his hand on his chest. "My heart stopped. I heard the beep of a car horn and looked out of the window. Brian, that's her brother waved and pulled away. I nearly shit myself. I knew they'd done something bad and I rushed to the door. She chased me, screaming at the top of her voice, saying stuff like, 'Go on, go to your whore. Go and see what you did to her. Go and see what you caused.' As I opened the door she pulled my passport out of my pocket. She waved it in my face. 'You won't be needing this,' she jeered, and gave me a right hander that broke my nose. I jumped in the car and was gone. I wasn't worried about my nose, my passport or anything. I had to get to Debbie."

Wilkinson ran his fingers through his hair. He looked pale and Meredith wasn't convinced that he wasn't about to throw up.

"What happened next?"

"It's all in there." Wilkinson pointed to the statement.

"Tell me, I want the details."

"I drove to Debbie's like a bat out of hell. As I pulled up outside, Nancy came rushing out. I watched her throw up in the plant pot on the doorstep. She looked like hell."

"Did you go in?"

"No, I knew it was bad. I didn't want to see. Debbie had to be dead for Nancy to look like that, and I wanted to remember her how she was."

"You didn't think that Nancy would need some help. Some closure?"

"I didn't care about Nancy. My heart was broken." Wilkinson slapped his chest and Meredith snorted.

"Spare me the dramatics. What then?"

"My phone went off. It was a text from Brian Catchpole and said, 'You're next if you don't keep your mouth shut'. I panicked and drove down to Weston. I spent two days in a hotel. I only had one more text from Catchpole, and he told me he knew where I was and what I'd done. So I got in the car and drove back to Bristol. I went to the British Pride and waited for Big Mo. He told me he would sort it but it would cost. I didn't have any money, but he knew that, and he said I would be paying with information. He told me to stay close and keep in touch, he'd sort something out. I went out and got pissed. Next thing I know I was being chucked into the back of a van. I thought I was dead, but it was Mo's blokes. They told me they'd sorted one of Catchpoles bloke's and intimated he wouldn't be seen again."

"So your little flit abroad was being financed by Debbie?" Meredith didn't attempt to conceal his dislike of the man in front of him. Wilkinson nodded. "And you bought Big Mo's protection by providing information on his lifelong enemy, Brian Catchpole." Meredith watched the now frantic nodding.

"Where did it go wrong?" Seaton leaned forward. "You were being looked after, and Catchpole was off your back, so what changed?"

"I was being moved about from pillar to post. Mitchell Edwards was blackmailing Catchpole with his knowledge about Debbie and other bits I'd mentioned. One night they all turn up at the place I was living, and they've got this chap tied up and they take us all into the garage. Brian Catchpole was there. Edwards pulls out a gun and hands it to Brian and tells him to do it. Brian raised the gun and rested the barrel against this bloke's forehead. The bloke was blindfolded, but he knew what was happening. He dropped to his knees and messed himself as he pleaded for his life. Brian couldn't do it; he's a bad bloke, and done some nasty things, but he couldn't do it. Edwards laughed at him and stepped forward. He took the gun and fired three shots into this bloke's head. I threw up."

"So he had Catchpole's fingerprints on the gun."

"Yeah, he was wearing gloves. He dropped the gun into a paper bag, and laughed. 'My way now,' he said, 'my way now.' Brian turned to me and I knew without a doubt that he would probably kill me one day. That's pretty much what he said as he left. So I'm stood there in this garage. The floor is covered in shit, brains and vomit and there's a dead bloke, but they all walk out. I called to them, and asked what I was supposed to do. Edwards turned to me and said, 'Clear it up.'" Wilkinson blinked back tears, "So I did. I buried him in the back garden, reckon I dug down about eight foot, and I bleached and hosed down the garage. I did it six times in all, just to make sure."

"Ben Jacobs says he saw you about nine months ago, but that doesn't seem sensible to me. Why risk bumping into someone you don't want to see?"

"I was there to meet Catchpole. You have to understand that living like that isn't good for your health." Wilkinson tapped his temple. "He made sure I got the message that he thought I'd stolen some money from his mother's. He said he needed it, and if I gave it back everything that had gone before would be forgotten. I wanted to set him straight. It wasn't me, it must have been Kate. We met in a busy pub, Jacobs was playing there, and I left when Big Mo's men came to collect me and move me on."

"I have to be honest, Mr Wilkinson. I don't like you very much, but that's neither here nor there. Who do you think killed Debbie? Kate or Catchpole?"

"I don't know. Kate can be evil when she's riled. But my money's on Catchpole." He looked down at his hands. "He knew Debbie. He'd been seeing her."

"What, at the same time as you?" Seaton leaned back in his chair as Wilkinson nodded.

"It was me that introduced them, early on, when I first met her. I didn't want him to know I was seeing her, and he made a play. She was mad at me for that and she started seeing him too. Only for a while, but she finished it. He didn't take it well. Nobody says no to him, or so he thought." Wilkinson sighed. "But if he couldn't kill that bloke in the garage, could he have killed Debbie like that?" He looked up at Meredith. "I keep jumping back and forth between them, so it could have been Kate I suppose, who then called her brother to rescue her. When he sees it's Debbie, he realises what I've been up to."

Meredith nodded and doodled on his pad as he considered this.

"So, over two years later, he's ready to forgive and forget if you give him money that you say you haven't taken. What happened then?"

"I reckon he told Kate he believed me and wanted the money. I think it's why she torched the house, trying to get the insurance money to pay him off, or perhaps even to get nicked and out of harm's way. That backfired on her, but he's still after it, which is why she needs him to find me. This crap about wanting to prove I'm alive to get the police off her back is just a story. She wanted me found, so he could have his revenge. When you lot started looking for me, it caused Edwards and his mob all sorts of trouble."

"Why not give you up? You were no use to them, why didn't they just hand you over?"

"I finally got smart. I told them I'd recorded what went on in the garage on my phone. That I'd given it to someone I trust and it would be taken to the police if anything happened to me."

"Did you record it?" Both Meredith and the solicitor leaned in awaiting his response.

"You'll find out once I'm sorted. You think I'm stupid enough to play my trump card this early in the game?"

The solicitor scribbled a note on his pad, and Meredith closed his. He looked at the solicitor.

"I'm done. He's all yours."

"What, that's it? You don't want to know any more than that? There is another body, I wasn't there but I know -"

Meredith held his hand up.

"Not my case. It won't be me investigating whatever other secrets you have from your grubby little world." He saw the look of panic on Wilkinson's face.

"Why not? Who is?"

Meredith shrugged. "I don't know, they didn't give their names." Meredith stood and arched his back. "Seaton." He jerked his head towards the door and Seaton followed him out.

The pair walked back to the incident room in silence. Meredith paused before pushing open the door. "I'm glad he didn't ask to see Angel, she'll be safe now. If that recording exists, and if he ever hands it over, I don't rate his chances of survival." He punched the door frame. "It pisses me off that I don't care. I know it's because he's a lowlife shit, but how many good men have gone that way? I should care based on principle."

Seaton stepped forward. He pushed open the door, and leaned in close to Meredith's ear.

"You do. You're pretending you don't because it helps." He put his hands in his pockets and followed Meredith to his office, "Do you want me to sort a meeting with Kate Wilkinson?"

"Yes, but tomorrow will be soon enough. I think we deserve an early night."

* * *

Patsy smiled as she listened to Linda gabble away about her first court appearance. She had an opinion on everything, from the time it took to get from one witness to the next, to the shoes the usher was wearing. Linda fell silent, stopped walking, and slapped her forehead.

"I completely forgot. I have to go to the jewellers in St Nicholas'

Market. It's my niece's birthday next week and they're doing a personalised necklace for me. Can we pop in as we're down here?"

"Of course, come on." Patsy waited for Linda to reach her and they walked back up the road. "This jeweller is the one that made a ring for Anna Carter, the girl who was shot. It was the last case I worked."

"How could I forget? She's really good. I explained what I wanted and she agreed she could do it. I think my niece will love it. It's different."

Patsy looked at her Linda and shook her head. "How old is your niece, and how different can a necklace be?"

"Fourteen, my brother's a lot older than me, and as to the necklace, it's tasteful don't worry."

Linda was right. The necklace consisted of large silver links, each fourth link had what Linda called a memory attached. There was a silver ballet shoe, a bicycle, and various other charms that would bring back memories.

"A charm necklace. It wasn't that difficult to describe. It's beautiful, and you're right, she'll love it," Patsy commented as Linda held it up.

"I know, but I think I need two more charms to balance it." She turned to the assistant. "Have you got any standard charms? I may be able to find a couple that would suit."

Linda became engrossed as the assistant nodded and pulled a large tray containing numerous charms from a drawer below the counter. The jeweller arrived; she was carrying two packs of sandwiches, and had a brief conversation with Linda about the type of charm she should choose. Then she turned her attention to Patsy, who was looking in a glass cabinet containing various gold pieces.

"Anything we can help you with?"

Patsy turned to her. "I'm not sure. I didn't know you did gold, I thought you only worked in silver."

"Both, but the cost of gold is such that most choose silver. Did you have anything in mind?"

Patsy glanced at Linda who was pushing the assistant to announce which charm she preferred of two she was holding up. Stepping closer to her, Patsy explained what she had been thinking about.

"Of course, that's not a problem, it will be simple enough. We could use one of these." The jeweller lifted a bracelet from the cabin and demonstrated.

"Let's do it. I'll get back to you with the final detail."

Linda looped her arm in Patsy's as they left the shop. "I want one now," she laughed. "What were you doing, did you buy anything?"

"No, I ordered Meredith's birthday present. I wasn't sure what to get him, but I had a moment of inspiration. It's his birthday in a couple of months."

"What did you get him?"

"It's a secret and you're not good with those." Patsy glanced at her watch. "It's not worth going back into the office. I'll drop you off at home."

Meredith was opening the door as Patsy arrived.

"Blimey, that's two days in a row you've finished on time. Are you sure you're not ill?"

"I'm fine, but dealing with those people knocked the wind out of my sails I guess. I'd rather be at home with you. How was court?"

"Boring and predictable. They got a two-year suspended sentence, a fine, and they have to pay back the ten grand they've not yet repaid by the end of the year." She smiled. "Luckily, I gave evidence before Linda, so I got to see her performance. She was brilliant. Their barrister's sarcasm was lost on her, and she thought he was being dim so she spoke to him like a child. Even the judge smiled."

"I can imagine. I'm glad you enjoyed part of it." Meredith forced a smile.

"Do you want to talk about it?" Patsy slipped out of her jacket and hung it on the bannister. "I can see something is troubling you."

Meredith pulled off his tie, dropping it on the hall table. "Absolutely not, but I want it put to bed. Nancy has now moved out of her residence at the station, and is tucked up in Eastwood Park awaiting trial. All the men involved have put their hands up, so it's simply a matter of process now."

He threw his hands up, "Oh, you don't know this bit: it would appear that Kate Wilkinson did it." He put his finger on her lips to stop her speaking. "I'm not going into details now. But Sherlock should have the results on the DNA tomorrow, and Trump and I are interviewing Kate on Thursday."

"Why wait if you want it done?"

"Because she has this bug. She's been really poorly apparently, and in the hospital wing on a drip. It's only dehydration now, and the doctor says she'll be out on Thursday."

"What happened to-"

"Hodge, subject closed. Feed me." He pushed her towards the kitchen. "The ACC said I should take a break when the last bit slots into place. Fancy a holiday?"

Patsy turned back to him smiling. "I certainly do. Are we allowed to fly?"

"Let's not go mad, Hodge, I hear the Eurostar takes minutes."

"But you were okay on the flight back from Paris."

"I'm a good actor."

Patsy clapped her hands together. "Good, because Greece is only three and a half hours, so not long to act."

She jumped out of the way as Meredith attempted to flick her with the tea towel.

18

Meredith was at his desk reading through the reports when Travers knocked on the open door.

"Wilkinson's solicitor is back. He'd like a word."

Meredith glanced up at him. "About?"

"Don't know, but he was followed into the car park by a blacked-out minibus, and if the gossip is correct the suits who are waiting for him are armed."

"Then I'd better go and see him. Where is he?"

"With the custody sergeant."

Meredith dropped his pen on the reports and pulled on his jacket.

Travers nodded at the pen. "You'll want that, I hear he's got a wad of paperwork."

Meredith slid the pen into his breast pocket and left with a shake of his head and a sigh. He knew the four men held downstairs were being transferred. He didn't know where, and he wasn't going to ask. What he did know was that in the mode of transport suggested, it wasn't going to be one of Her Majesty's usual places of incarceration.

~ ~ ~

Frankie Callaghan rushed up the stairs. He almost ran into Trump travelling in the opposite direction.

"Sorry, Louie, in a bit of a rush today. Is Meredith in his office?"

"No, afraid not. Downstairs signing over some prisoners, He'll be a while, can I help?"

Frankie handed him an envelope. "Thanks, DNA results. Definitely not Debbie or Nancy, but absolutely someone related to Angel Wilkinson."

Trump nodded and took the envelope.

"Her mother, it all came out yesterday. DCI Meredith and I are seeing her tomorrow. We'll get a sample for you."

"Splendid news. Well, all's well that ends well. Must dash, thanks Louie"

Frankie turned and galloped back the other way. He cursed as he looked at his watch and climbed into the car. He was going to be late.

~ ~ ~

The murmur of voices got louder as he pushed open the door. He scanned the room quickly: she was leaving. He called out to her and everyone in the room looked at him. Tanya Jenkins smiled and went back to the table she had vacated.

"I didn't think you were coming. Thank you." Tanya took the chocolate and placed it on the edge of the table. "How are you?"

"I'm well. Been a little busy this morning, but I'm here now. More to the point, how are you?"

Tanya shrugged, closing her eyes as she did so. "Coping is as good as it gets. I'm thinking of taking some qualifications, but I can't make my mind up as to what. I also had an extracurricular visit this week. It was nice to see Dave Rawlings," she paused, "and Hodge too. It is odd how things turn out, or a small world or whatever. Who would have thought that the job I gave Patsy would overlap something the old team were working on? I bet that was awkward for her and Meredith."

"You're right there. Life has a habit of doing that. It probably helped a little. Meredith was badly injured so . . ."

"Injured, yes they did say. How is he?"

"Oh he's on the mend now, but two thugs gave him a thorough beating. Having Patsy at home and working on the case probably made it a little easier for him. It's all done bar the red tape now, or so Louie tells me. It was the mother though, not the father apparently." Frankie waved his hand in the air. "You have no idea what I'm talking about, have you?"

He looked at the stunned expression on Tanya's face, and assumed it was because she had no knowledge of the Debbie Charles case. He was wrong. With both Kate Wilkinson and herself being pulled off the wing without warning, gossip had been rife. Particularly so when Kate had been taken ill, and later transferred to the hospital wing. The rumour was that police were investigating the death of one of Darren Wilkinson's girlfriends some years before, and it appeared that for once the rumour was accurate. But that was not the cause of Tanya's expression. She had realised that Hodge had lied to her. Hodge had let her believe that she had split up with Meredith, and not corrected her when she had made reference to their separation.

Blinking, she focused on Frankie again. "Yes, she said they were back together. How's Sarah?"

They continued to have a stilted conversation until the bell rang to signal the end of visiting time. Frankie hoped he didn't look as relieved as he felt. As he walked back to his car, he wondered whether he would come again. He knew he would if she asked.

Tanya went back to the wing and lay on her bed, staring at the ceiling. Her anger at Meredith and Hodge grew. She was an intelligent woman, and she knew there was nothing she could do about it, in or out of prison, but vicious scenarios of their demise formed in her mind. She was brought back to reality as the bell sounded. Swinging her legs off the bed, she picked up a sweatshirt, and went to join the queue of women waiting to be allowed out for thirty minutes of exercise.

Tanya walked to the far end of the yard and leaned against the fence. She closed her eyes and drew in the fresh air, the sun was warm on her face. Opening her eyes, she watched a group of the younger women gossip and laugh, as though they were at a social function. Tanya was jealous; she missed her friends and having someone to talk to about anything and nothing. The group's demeanour changed, their voices dropped, and they stood closer together. Curiosity got the better of her, and she walked towards them to find out what had caught their attention. They appeared to be looking at an older woman she'd not noticed before. The woman was talking to a prison officer. Tanya raised her eyebrows. The woman was clearly new, and didn't realise it wasn't wise to look too familiar with the prison staff. Reaching the group of women, she slowed her pace.

"Who's that?" she asked.

"You should know. I've heard it's the one that killed three people and took one of your lot." The girl spat on the ground.

Tanya resisted the urge to smile at the banality of the act. "Three people, she doesn't look capable. It goes to show you shouldn't judge on appearances," she murmured in response.

"Too right, her sister was shagging Kate Wilkinson's husband. She was either much younger than her, or he was into grab a granny."

The group dissolved into laughter, and Tanya continued to pace.

"What a small world indeed," she said quietly.

When the bell rang, Tanya stood in line behind Nancy.

~ ~ ~

Meredith took the call at five-thirty the next morning. Patsy pulled the duvet over her head as he switched on the light. She understood from the odd grunted word that he was shocked, exasperated, and not wanting to deal with whatever it was. He rubbed his hands over his face and groaned as he hung up.

"Not good news, I take it. They do know you should be on sick leave, don't they?"

"Kate Wilkinson is dead."

Patsy sat upright and squinted against the light. "What! How?"

"Two guesses. You won't need both."

"No! Not Nancy? How could they be so stupid? What happened?"

Meredith stood and flexed his back. "You know that Kate was in the hospital wing?" He raised his eyebrows as Patsy nodded. "At three-thirty this morning Nancy was taken poorly. They found her calling for help and unable to breathe properly. The night duty staff took her straight to the hospital wing; they knew she was diabetic and thought she was going into a hypo. The doctor got her sorted and left her sleeping. An hour and a half later Kate Wilkinson was found strangled with the tube of the IV drip. Nancy was back in her bed waiting for them. She asked for me."

"Have you got to go?"

"Yes. Trump's on the way."

Meredith stood and walked to the door as Patsy climbed out of bed, and pulled on a track suit.

"Why are you getting up?"

"Because someone has to tell Angel."

Meredith stopped and looked at her. "It doesn't have to be you."

"Who then? She has no one, Meredith, not anyone worth having anyway."

~ ~ ~

Angel blinked rapidly as Patsy broke the news. She didn't cry, but screwed her eyes shut and lowered her head.

"So I'm an orphan. I'm free."

"I don't think your father is dead, Angel."

Patsy went to take one of her hands but Angel shoved them in her pockets.

"He is to me. What should I do with the money? You don't know, but Uncle Brian has gone AWOL now too, Aunt B called yesterday. Apparently, he told her he had to do an errand and never came home."

"Keep it. Or perhaps give it to your Aunt B, if he doesn't come back."

Angel shot a quizzical glance. "Do you know where he is?"

"No, but it doesn't sound good. You don't have to decide what to do with it now." Patsy smiled and picked up her tea and sipped it. "Do you want to get some things together and come back and stay with us for a while?"

"I'm used to being on my own." Angel put her hands on her hips and looked defiant. "I've decided I'll keep the money. They owe me that, I reckon."

~ ~ ~

Meredith sat with Trump in the interview room.

"Poetic justice, Trump, or a mad old woman continuing her reign of terror?" His eyes wide he waved his hands at the side of his face.

Trump considered this for a moment. "Bit of both I think, sir. She is running out of excuses now though. Let's hope this is the last one."

The door opened and Nancy walked in. She was handcuffed, and she lifted her hands to show Meredith, shaking her head to demonstrate her disappointment. Meredith waited until she was seated. The prison officer didn't leave, and stood with her hands behind her back at the side of the room. Meredith jerked his head towards the door.

"You don't need to stop. I don't think she's going to leap over the table and take us both out. She might give it a try though, eh Nancy?"

Nancy giggled. The prison officer didn't move.

"So, Nancy, you decided that despite getting me hospitalised only a couple of days ago, you'd also stop me getting a decent night's sleep. What have you got to say for yourself?"

Nancy gave a shrug and smiled at him. "Someone told me she was in the hospital wing, so I paid her a visit. I made her tell me what happened. She'd been following Darren that morning, and waited outside while he was in with Debbie. When he left, she knocked on the door, and Debbie let her in to have a chat; she probably felt sorry for her. Debbie told her about their plan to go and live abroad. Kate said she saw red and got really mad. She also said Debbie was a whore and had answered the door half naked. I got mad then and pulled tighter,"

Nancy cocked her head to one side. "Did I tell you I wrapped her tube around her neck to wake her?" She shrugged, "Anyway, she told Debbie she had to pay for what she'd done. Apparently, Debbie argued, but Kate told her in no uncertain terms what would happen to Darren if she didn't do what she was told. She told her to get dressed. Debbie obviously knew something awful was going to happen, that's what explains the mismatched underwear and the wrong shoes." Nancy swallowed and looked down. "Kate made her do it. She must have loved him very much, don't you think? How did she know Kate wouldn't hurt him afterwards? Perhaps she thought she would, and she didn't know how she would live without him."

Nancy paused and blinked rapidly as she considered this. When she looked back up, she smiled. "Kate seemed quite pleased with herself. So I ended it. Case closed, Mr Meredith. I'm done."

~ ~ ~

Meredith's birthday party was in full swing in the Dirty Duck. Ben Jacobs, complete with new whiter than white teeth, was attempting to coax Meredith to join him. He waved the microphone at him.

"Come on, Meredith, let's see what you're made of."

"Go on, Dad. Patsy said you were brilliant last time."

Meredith relented, and went to join Jacobs in the bay window which had become an impromptu stage. He turned to face the audience, but his smile faded and a frown appeared. He asked his guests for silence as he peered up at the television screen. He called to the barmaid asking her to turn up the volume. The clipped tone of the newsreader's voice filled the bar.

". . . The Prime Minister is denying that the resignation of both the junior secretary for health, and a top government adviser had anything to do with the suicide of right-wing extremist Mitchell Edwards. Mr Edwards was found dead in his London apartment having taken a cocktail of drugs and alcohol. It is rumoured that a damning dossier, naming and shaming. . ."

Trump and Seaton exchanged glances, and Meredith shrugged.

"Okay, turn it off," he called. "Right you lot, I'll give you one song. What do you want?"

Various requests were shouted out, and he ended up singing four songs in a row, much to the delight of his guests and his daughter. He ended with Rod Stewart's, 'Tonight's the Night', which he dedicated to an embarrassed Patsy. Mopping his brow with a bar towel he announced that the buffet was officially open.

Patsy handed him a pint of water.

"I've got a bone to pick with you," he told her after emptying the glass. "Where's my present?"

"It's not your birthday until tomorrow. Be patient."

"But it's my party today, therefore the law on receiving presents has changed." Meredith's phone rang. He pulled it out and looked at the screen. "Rawlings. I wonder what excuse he's got for not showing up."

Meredith walked away, and Patsy went to the ladies. She sat on the toilet and pulled the box from her pocket. Opening it for the umpteenth time that day, she pulled the ring from box. Shaped like a signet ring, the slim gold band supported a gold padlock. Initially, Patsy had chosen it simply as a present. She was now toying with the idea of asking Meredith to marry her, and using the ring much as a man would when proposing to a woman. She nodded and smiled; she had dithered about for too long, she would do it. Tonight.

Having washed her hands and applied some lipstick, she went back to the party, the box clasped tightly in her hand. As she re-entered the bar she noticed that half the guests had disappeared. Amanda was talking to Jacobs, and seeing Patsy she beckoned her over.

"Dad's gone to work."

Patsy looked around at the remaining guests. Whatever had called Meredith away was serious.

"What's happened?"

"Two young girls have gone missing. One of them is Ellen Rawlings, Dave's daughter."

Patsy slid the box into her pocket. Tonight, was not the night.

ABOUT THE AUTHOR

Having worked in the property industry for most of my adult life, latterly at a senior level, I finally escaped in 2010. I now dedicate the bulk of my time to writing and, of course, reading, although there are still not enough hours in the day.

I began writing quite by chance when a friend commented, "They wouldn't believe it if you wrote it down!" So I did. I enjoyed the plotting and scheming, creating the characters, and watching them develop with the story. I kept on writing, and Meredith and Hodge arrived. In 2017 the Bearing women took hold of my imagination, and the Bearing Witness series was created. I should confess at this point that although I have the basic outline when I start a new story, it never develops the way I expect, and I rarely know 'who did it' myself until I've nearly finished.

I am married with two children, two grandchildren, two German Shepherds and a Bichon Frise. We live in Bristol, UK.
I can be contacted here, and would love to hear from you:
Website: http://mkturnerbooks.co.uk/

Made in the USA
Las Vegas, NV
01 August 2023